'Ann Cleeves is on top form in this atmospheric mystery that gradually expands to include more shifty characters on the mainland, and, on her tenth outing, you feel the pain beneath Vera's blowsy bravado. *The Rising Tide* is exactly the sort of novel she likes – it provides escape and "the joy of loose ends tied up"'

The Times

'Well-paced and plotted, with its evocative Northumberland village setting and excellent characterization, this is a great winter read'

Choice

'A thrilling tale with an ending that catches you by surprise, it's a story both newbies to Vera and diehard fans will enjoy'

The Independent

'This instalment oozes atmosphere and tension'   *Woman & Home*

'Superb . . . This page-turner is must reading for fans as well as newcomers'   *Publishers Weekly* (starred review)

'A character-   ent'
                                                      Reviews

Praise for Ann Cleeves

'As a huge fan of both the Shetland and Vera series of books, I had high expectations for Cleeves' latest. She easily exceeded those expectations with *The Long Call*. Matthew Venn is a keeper. A stunning debut for Cleeves' latest crimefighter'

David Baldacci

'Had me hooked – a promising beginning to another fine chapter in the Ann Cleeves story'   *The Times*

'Clever, compassionate and atmospheric'   Elly Griffiths

'A triumph that cements Cleeves' status as one of Britain's best crime writers'   *Daily Express*

'Evocative and gripping – an absolute triumph'   *Daily Mirror*

'A traditional mystery of the best sort'   *The Guardian*

'Brilliant – a page-turning and sensitively told tale, with a vividly evoked North Devon setting, a powerful emotional heft and a new detective hero in Matthew Venn who you will want to follow for book after book. Wonderful!'

Chris Ewan, bestselling author of *Safe House*

'Cleeves combines a flair for evoking sense of place with a thoughtful, complex plot'   *The Mail on Sunday*

'Unputdownable series debut! With an evocative setting, a gripping plot, and beautifully drawn characters, *The Long Call* is a terrific read – and Matthew Venn is my new favourite detective'

Deborah Crombie, *New York Times*
bestselling author of *Garden of Lamentations*

THE RISING TIDE

Ann Cleeves is the author of more than thirty-five critically acclaimed novels, and in 2017 was awarded the highest accolade in crime writing, the CWA Diamond Dagger. She is the creator of popular detectives Vera Stanhope, Jimmy Perez and Matthew Venn, who can be found on television in ITV's *Vera*, BBC One's *Shetland* and ITV's *The Long Call* respectively. The TV series and the books they are based on have become international sensations, capturing the minds of millions worldwide.

Ann worked as a probation officer, bird observatory cook and auxiliary coastguard before she started writing. She is a member of 'Murder Squad', working with other British northern writers to promote crime fiction. Ann also spends her time advocating for reading to improve health and wellbeing and supporting access to books. In 2021 her Reading for Wellbeing project launched with local authorities across the North East. She lives in North Tyneside where the Vera books are set.

You can find Ann on Twitter and Facebook @AnnCleeves.

Ann Cleeves

THE RISING TIDE

PAN BOOKS

First published 2022 by Macmillan

This paperback edition first published 2023 by Pan Books
an imprint of Pan Macmillan
The Smithson, 6 Briset Street, London EC1M 5NR
EU representative: Macmillan Publishers Ireland Ltd, 1st Floor,
The Liffey Trust Centre, 117–126 Sheriff Street Upper,
Dublin 1, D01 YC43
Associated companies throughout the world
www.panmacmillan.com

ISBN 978-1-5098-8965-5

1 3 5 7 9 8 6 4 2

A CIP catalogue record for this book is available from the British Library.

Typeset by Palimpsest Book Production Ltd, Falkirk, Stirlingshire
Printed and bound by CPI Group (UK) Ltd, Croydon, CR0 4YY

Visit **www.panmacmillan.com** to read more about all our books
and to buy them. You will also find features, author interviews and
news of any author events, and you can sign up for e-newsletters
so that you're always first to hear about our new releases.

To Orla Wren. And her father.
New members of the clan.

Acknowledgements

This is my thirtieth year of being published by Pan Macmillan and I'm so lucky to still be working with this team. There are too many people to mention individually, and everyone has played an important part in supporting me throughout my career, so this is a big shout-out to them all. I couldn't have been with a more enthusiastic and skilful bunch.

My agent and friend, Sara Menguc, has been with me almost from the beginning of this terrific journey. Huge thanks to her and to all her wonderful co-agents.

Minotaur in the US has become a big part of my life in recent years and they now feel like part of the extended family too. I can't wait to get back to the US to meet them all in person again.

Emma Harrow is a fabulous publicist: wise and full of the best advice.

My assistant, Jill Heslop, besides keeping me on track and taking on much of the admin load, has headed up the Reading for Wellbeing project – while allowing me to take much of the credit.

Thanks to Helen Pepper, friend and advisor, for all her help with forensic details in *The Rising Tide*. Of course, any errors are mine. Sue Beardshall is the kindest person I know. Thanks to her for my base in North Devon, for fun and the Cava Sundays.

Charlotte Thomas donated to the Tarset Village Hall Fund, and so became a character in the book. As did Skip the dog.

For more than twenty years I've had the support of Murder Squad, my writing friends in the North. Writing can be a lonely business and we need the company of people who understand us.

Finally, and most importantly, thanks to readers. Readers who buy and borrow our books and keep us in business, readers who are writers too and who have provided an escape and a challenge with their work, and readers who are booksellers that share their passion and spread the joy.

Author's Note

Whilst the Holy Island background for this latest Vera novel is real, any specific settings, on the island or the coast nearby, are the product of my imagination and in no way are intended to resemble or reference any that already exist.

Chapter One

PHILIP WAS FIRST OF THE GROUP to the island. He'd had to drive overnight but it was worth the effort to get here before the morning high water, before the day trippers crossed from the mainland in their cars and coaches to buy ice cream and chips. He tried not to resent the squabbling children and the wealthy elderly, but he was always pleased when the island was quiet. As he did at every reunion, he wanted to sit in the chapel and reflect for some time in peace. This year would mark fifty years of friendship and he needed to offer a prayer of thanks and to remember.

The most vivid memory was of the weekend when they'd first come together on the island. Only Connect, the teacher had called it. Part outward bound course, part encounter group, part team-building session. And there *had* been a connection, so strong and fierce that after fifty years the tie was still there, unbroken and still worth celebrating. This was where it had all started.

The next memory was of death and a life cut short.

Philip had no fear of dying. Sometimes, he thought he would

welcome death, as an insomniac longs for sleep. It was as inevitable as the water, which twice a day slid across the sand and mud of the shore until the causeway was covered. Eventually, he would drown. His faith provided no extra comfort, only a vague curiosity. Almost, he hoped that there would be no afterlife; surely that would take energy and there were days now when he felt that he had no energy left. It had seeped away in his service to his parish and the people who needed him.

He did regret the deaths of others. His working life moved to the beat of funeral services, the tolling of the church bell, the march of pall-bearers. He remembered the babies, who'd had no experience of life at all, the young who'd had no opportunity to change and grow. He'd been allowed that chance and he offered up another prayer of gratitude.

An image of Isobel, so young, so bonny, so reckless in her desires and her thoughtlessness, intruded into his meditation and he allowed his mind to wander.

Was it Isobel who kept the group returning to the Holy Island of Lindisfarne every five years? Had her death at the first reunion bonded them together so tightly that, despite their differences, they were as close as family? Perhaps that deserved gratitude too, because these people were the only family he had left.

In the tiny chapel, with its smell of damp and wood polish, he closed his eyes and he pictured her. Blonde and shapely and sparking with life. A wide smile and energy enough for them all.

From the first floor of the Pilgrims' House, he'd seen her driving away to her death. He'd watched the argument that had led to her sudden departure. Forty-five years ago, Isobel had drowned literally. No metaphor had been needed for her. Her body had been pulled out of her car, once the waters had retreated. Her vehicle had been swept from the causeway in the high tide of the equinox, tossed from the road like a toy by the wind and the waves. Once she'd set out on her way to the mainland, there had been no chance to save her.

Had that been the moment when he'd changed from a selfish, self-opinionated, edgy young man to a person of faith? Perhaps the conversion had begun a little later, the evening of the same day, when he'd sat in this chapel in the candlelight with his friends and they'd cried together, trying to make sense of Isobel's passing. Annie and Daniel, Lou and Ken, Rick and Philip. The mourning had been complicated because none of them had liked Isobel very much. The men had all fancied her. Oh yes, certainly that. She'd featured in Philip's erotic dreams throughout his undergraduate years. But she'd been too demanding and too entitled for them to *like* her.

Philip opened his eyes for a moment. The low sunlight of autumn was flooding through the plain glass windows into the building, but he knew he had time for more reflection – more guilt? – before the others arrived. He closed his eyes again to remember Isobel and that argument which must surely have led to her death. He hadn't heard the words. He'd been in his first-floor room in the Pilgrims' House looking down, an observer, not a participant. Isobel and Rick had been fighting in the lane below him. There'd been no physical contact – it hadn't come to that – but Philip had sensed the tension, which was so different from the weekend's general mood of easy companionship.

The fight had seemed important. Almost intimate. Not a row between casual friends or strangers. Even if Philip had been closer, he might not have made out what was being said, because there was a storm blowing and the wind would have carried the words away. He'd relished the drama of the scene, looking on with a voyeur's excitement, as he'd watched the row play out beneath him.

Then, from where he'd stood, he'd seen Annie rounding the bend in the lane, a woven shopping bag in one hand. She must have been into the village for provisions. No longer a mother, she'd mothered them all that weekend, and now, all these years later, she was still the person who shopped and cooked.

Rick and Isobel hadn't noticed her, because they were so focused on each other, spitting out insults. Rick had hurled one more comment and suddenly Isobel had been flouncing away, her long hair blown over her face, feeling in the pockets of her flowery Laura Ashley dress for her car keys. At that point Philip could have changed history. If he'd rushed down-stairs and outside, he might have stood in front of the car and stopped her driving away. He'd known after all that the tide was rushing in and it would be foolhardy to attempt the crossing.

But Philip hadn't moved. He'd stayed where he was, staring out of the window like a nebby old woman, waiting to see what would happen next. And Isobel had started her car and driven to her death.

So, here Philip was, a priest on the verge of retirement, an old believer, yet with no great desire to meet his maker. Here he sat, hands clasped and eyes shut, waiting for his friends, longing again for the connection and the ease that only they could give, pondering the moment of Isobel's death. It seemed to him now that he'd spent the rest of his life trying to find relationships that were as intense and fulfilling as those developed here. Nothing had lived up to expectation. Not even, if he was honest, his trust in Christ.

Perhaps that was why he'd never married. Later, there'd been women he'd fancied himself in love with, but there'd never been the same depth of understanding, and in the end, he'd refused to compromise. If one of the women who'd shared that first weekend of connection had been free, perhaps that would have worked. Now, it crossed his mind again that Judith, the teacher who'd brought them together, might make a suitable partner, that he might find company and intimacy in old age. They were both alone after all. But Philip knew that he was probably too cowardly and too lazy to make a move. He smiled to himself; he wasn't sure he wanted to share his life after all this time. He was too comfortable, and too set in his ways.

He got to his feet, walked down the narrow aisle and out into the sunshine. He could smell seaweed and salt. He felt at home.

Chapter Two

ANNIE LAIDLER SHUT THE DELI DOOR and locked it. A regular customer turned up two minutes late and looked through the window. Usually, Annie would have let her in, all smiles and welcome – but today she pretended not to see. Jax had already left and this was October, a reunion year. Annie had been planning the moment for weeks.

She began to pack the two wicker hampers with jars and dried goods. They'd already been pulled from the shelves and were standing in a line on the counter. Then she turned her attention to the fresh items. There were green and black olives, all scooped into separate tubs. Slices of charcuterie glistening with fat. Cheese: Doddington, with its black rind and hard, sharp taste, Northumberland nettle, oozing brie and crumbling Wensleydale. Squat loaves of ciabatta and sourdough baked by Jax early that morning. Local butter, wrapped in greaseproof paper. A taste of home for her friends who'd moved away. A reminder to them that she and the region had moved on.

Still, at the last moment she added stotties – the flat-bread cakes that they'd filled with chips when they'd all been kids – then home-baked ham and pease pudding. Traditional Geordie fare. A kind of irony, a joke that they'd all appreciate. Through this food, memories would be triggered, and anecdotes would follow. Images clicked into her head like slides dropping into an old-fashioned projector carousel. A school play dress rehearsal. Rick in full costume as Claudius, collapsing suddenly in giggles and the rest of them losing it. Except Philip, who was Hamlet, furious that his long speech had been interrupted. And Miss Marshall, their English teacher, almost in tears because she thought the performance itself would be a disaster.

More slides. More images of Only Connect – the event originally organized by the school, or at least by Miss Marshall, as an attempt to bring together some of the new lower sixth. She wanted to challenge their preconceptions, she'd said; to open their minds to possibilities beyond Kimmerston Grammar. That initial weekend gathering – a kind of secular retreat – had turned them into this tight group. Still friends fifty years on; still meeting in the same place every five years. This time the recollection was of teenagers, talking endlessly, sitting at the long tables in the kitchen at the Pilgrims' House, dipping stotties into the veggie soup, hardly pausing the conversation long enough to eat.

After the first reunion, and Isobel's death, Annie had wondered if the reunions would continue, but they had. Rick had said to meet up would be an act of remembrance, but after all this time, the mentions of Isobel had become a ritual, no more meaningful than the Friday night drinking, or the Saturday afternoon walk.

The hampers were almost too heavy for Annie to carry to the car. Five years ago, she must have been fitter, stronger.

She'd get someone to help her at the other end. One of the men. Rick was always keen to prove how macho he was, with his tales of marathons run, and trips to the gym.

Outside the sun was low. They'd stuck with October for the reunions, and there was always this sense of the year coming to an end. That first meeting of Only Connect had been a time of transition. They all agreed on that. So the date seemed appropriate.

Later kids had come along. Annie had swallowed her envy and her hurt and pretended to enjoy them. The reunion weekends had grown then; sometimes the place had the vibe of a chaotic playgroup, and later of a youth club for moody teens. They'd only come together for evening chapel at dusk. Now, the adults were alone again, and oddly it was as if they'd gone full circle. They had the same freedom and lack of responsibility as they'd had when they'd first come together as sixteen-year-olds. Tonight, she felt suddenly wild, ready for an adventure.

Some of their children had become friends and they met up too, independently in smart London wine bars. Not in an austere former convent on Holy Island, which had been refurbished now, but still smelled a little of mould and elderly women. As if the ghosts of the original occupants still lingered.

It was early evening when she arrived at the Pilgrims' House. She'd crossed the Lindisfarne causeway over the sand and the mud from the mainland just before the evening tide, and the road was empty. There'd be no day trippers to the island now. The setting sun behind her threw long shadows from the rescue towers and set the shore on fire. Although she lived closest, Annie was always the last to arrive. She drove through the village and on towards the house, isolated in the centre of the island, surrounded by scrubby, windblown trees. From here, it felt like a real island. There was no view of the causeway, only of the castle, towering above them. The others' cars were parked in the lane. She sat in the van for a minute, with a sudden moment of shyness, even foreboding. The usual sense of awkwardness, as if she didn't quite belong.

It had been different when she and Dan had still been married. He'd been at the original conference and she'd fallen in love with him then, deeply, dangerously, self-destructively, as only a teenager can. It hadn't been his scene, and she'd sensed his discomfort throughout, but he'd come back with her to the first reunion. Then there'd been the tragedy of Isobel's death. She couldn't blame him for staying away after that. She couldn't blame him for anything. Not the guilt nor the divorce. Nor her loneliness.

It was almost dark and she could see a soft light of candles in the clear glass windows of the tiny chapel. There was no fancy stained-glass here. She supposed the others were already inside and realized she must be even later than she'd anticipated. Perhaps they were waiting for her before they started their time of silence and meditation. She left the hampers in the van and hurried into the building. The candles had been lit on the table that served as an altar. There was that smell of old stone and incense. The roof was hardly bigger than one of the upturned cobles, the small boats pulled onto the beach during bad weather, and she thought she could smell the wood it was made from too.

Her friends were sitting on the wooden benches, taking the same seats as they always did. Habit now. They turned and smiled at her but nobody spoke. That was the deal for evening chapel. Twenty minutes of silence and private meditation. Prayer for those who believed in it. It had seemed alien to them as teenagers, but now, Annie thought, they welcomed the peace, the ritual.

Annie took a seat near the back, and Phil stood up and gave the welcome, and started them off. 'Take this time to be grateful.' But left to her own thoughts, here in the chapel, Annie found gratitude hard to conjure. She sat with her eyes closed and remembered a baby lying in a cot with blue covers – because Annie had decided she never wanted pink for her little girl – and saw the white cold skin. When Philip brought them all back to the present, Annie found that her cheeks were wet with tears. She was pleased she was sitting at the back and that the light was so poor, because she would have hated the others to see and to ask what the matter was.

Chapter Three

RICK KELSALL SAT IN THE CHAPEL and let his mind wander. He'd never been very good at sitting still, and he struggled to stop his foot tapping on the stone floor. Also, it was bloody cold. His head was full of plans and ideas, all jostling for priority. It had been an interesting day, and he still wasn't quite sure what he'd do with the information he'd gained. Then there was the book, which might redeem him, or at least bring him back into the public eye. He'd complained about the attention when he'd been on the telly every week, but now he missed his public: the smiles, the waves, the recognition. He'd only been gone for a few months, but it was as if he'd disappeared into a black hole. When people did know who he was, there was more likely to be abuse than admiration. He shifted in his seat and wished he'd worn a scarf.

The door opened and he turned to see Annie hurry into the building. She still looked good for her age. She'd never been a beauty like Charlotte, but she was interesting without trying, without realizing. He'd never fancied her, not really. Not like he'd fancied Louisa. He'd always felt close to Annie though. Friendship was too bland a word to describe it. He wriggled again and tried to find a better way to express how he felt about her.

Philip stood up to call them to order. When they'd first come here as teenagers, nobody would have bet on Philip becoming a priest. Not in a million years. He'd been Rick's most exciting friend, full of anger and rebellion and wild, impossible plans. Now he seemed to live his life in a state of complacency and contentment. Philip had achieved, Rick supposed, a kind of wisdom. He no longer battled the inevitable. He knew he was getting old but didn't seem to care. Soon, he'd retire from his parish and his life would become even more boring. He might well move north again – so predictable – and he'd live out his smug, boring life until he died.

Perhaps Philip didn't even miss the adventures of their youth. Rick missed them all the time. He longed for them with a desperation that sometimes overwhelmed him. He would give anything to be seventeen again and sitting in this chapel for the first time. He would sell his soul for it. He wouldn't even mind being twenty-two and fighting with Isobel, then watching her drive away to her death. Then, at least he'd felt alive.

He realized that Philip had sat down once more. Rick hadn't heard anything he'd said, hadn't made the effort to listen; it would, no doubt, be much the same as at every reunion. Every introduction. These days, Philip provided comfort not originality.

The chapel was quieter than any other place Rick knew. He'd lived in the city since he'd left home for university and there was always that background hum. Traffic. The rumble of a train. People shouting in the street, even in the early hours. Rick disliked silence. He wondered why they had to go through this ritual every time they came back to the island, though part of him knew that he'd be the first to complain if one of the others suggested ditching it. Partly to be awkward, but also, he supposed, because this quiet time in the chapel was part of the whole experience. It reminded him again of his youth. For one weekend, he felt as if he was starting out again, at the beginning. Not approaching the end.

Almost before he'd settled into it, the twenty minutes was over. Philip was on his feet again, and they were making their way out. Rick waited for a moment, letting the others go ahead of him, gearing up for the evening ahead. He felt like an actor preparing for another performance, and wondered briefly what it would be like for once in his life to go on stage unscripted and unrehearsed.

Chapter Four

OUTSIDE THE CHAPEL THEY STOOD, CHATTING awkwardly. It was always a little awkward for the first few minutes. But it was cold and quite dark so they quickly moved into the house. Annie asked Rick and Phil to help her carry the food from her van into the kitchen. Afterwards she stood there, unpacking the hampers, stocking the fridge, glimpsing her friends at a distance through the open door in the hall, which led into the common room. The fire was already lit. She couldn't see them all, but did catch Rick parading in, with a bottle of wine in each hand. He set them on the table, then pulled a corkscrew from his jacket pocket, like a conjuror performing some amazing trick, playing as always as if to an audience. The light in the room was dim, and Annie thought his silhouette was strange, almost demonic, with the flames dancing behind him.

The others started on the booze then, but that was traditional too. They'd always drunk far too much on Friday nights, even when they'd had kids with them. There'd been times, she thought, when social services could legitimately have expressed concern about the children's safety, though they'd had two teachers in their number, and really, they should have known better. Annie had stumbled to bed on a couple of occasions in the early hours, aware of children running through the corridors, whooping and laughing in some game of their own.

As they'd all grown older, she'd come across pale-faced teenagers sitting on the floor in corners, with tears rolling down their cheeks. It had only occurred to her later that they'd probably been drinking too, or taken some form of drug. Her child had never been old enough to be troublesome and she'd been naive about such things. She knew Rick and Philip had smoked cannabis when they'd been younger, but in spite of her hippy clothes, the flowers in her hair and the bare feet, she'd always been wary. Not worried about any potential danger to her health, but about making a fool of herself.

She went back outside to the van to fetch a last tray of baking, and the air smelled not of weed, but of woodsmoke and ice. She hadn't bothered putting on a coat and the sudden cold chilled her bones. There was a frost forecast, the first of the year. There would be a dark sky full of stars, when the light eventually seeped away, a sliver of moon. She shut the van again and stepped back into the house.

The door to the common room was still propped open and Annie could look in without being seen. They'd switched on the lights and she had a better view of them. Her first full view after the candlelight in the chapel and the clumsy greeting in the dusk. They'd offered to help when they'd all come inside, but that had been routine politeness. Annie always prepared the Friday night meal and they knew she'd catch up with them once supper was under way. She stood for a moment observing them.

Her first response was shock that they'd aged so much in

the past five years. Perhaps it was Ken, sitting with Lou, attentive by his side, and Skip his dog at his feet, that prompted the thought. Ken looked misty-eyed, seemingly struggling to appear aware of what was going on, and horribly frail. Lou had phoned them all in advance to warn them.

I've been worried about him for a while, but we only got a diagnosis a few months ago. Alzheimer's.

'But he's so young!' Annie had said. Meaning: *He's the same age as me.*

'He's sixty-six,' Lou had said. 'Not so young.' Had there been an edge of smugness in her voice? Because Lou was three years younger than the rest of them. She'd been a fourth year when the rest of them had been in the lower sixth, that year they'd first come here, and stayed up all night, intense, talking until the first rays of the sun had caught the room's mess of discarded crisp packets and overflowing ashtrays. Lou hadn't been here. Perhaps that had always made her something of an outsider. Not quite part of the group.

Ken had very much been seen as a baby-snatcher then, and Annie had resented the arrival of Lou into the mix, her presence at parties, the shows of affection, even in school. Annie had rather fancied the solid, reliable Ken herself. They'd kissed a few times. After lock-ins in the Stanhope Arms, the pub they'd adopted in Kimmerston Front Street. Drunken fumbles when they were walking home. Because they'd lived in the same village a couple of miles out of town. Their dads had both worked in the pit.

Then Ken had shyly announced that Lou had agreed to go out with him. Annie remembered the moment. The start of double French one spring morning. Daffodils in the school garden on the edge of the tennis courts. And of course, she shouldn't have been surprised. She'd had no claim on Ken, and, after all, *she'd* snogged most of the lads in the group at one time or another. Certainly Rick. Nothing Rick liked more than a commitment-free grope. And more, given the chance.

When #MeToo had been all over the news Annie had felt a moment of guilt. Sometimes Rick's approaches had been so bloody forceful that it had felt almost like assault. Not that he'd raped her, nothing like that, but he'd come pretty close. Made her uncomfortable. And she'd gone along with it, hadn't she? Now, she thought she should have been more confident, told him to stop. Then he would have got the message earlier that he couldn't behave like that. He wouldn't have tried it on with his young colleagues. He might still have his show on the BBC.

Now, in the fading light of the Pilgrims' House common room, Louisa was still attractive, but even she was showing her age. The hair was beautifully cut and dyed, but there were lines around her eyes, and horizontal wrinkles between her nose and her mouth.

We're all old! Of course we are. What was I expecting? That by meeting up with my old school friends, I'd magically become the girl that I was when we first came together? We're lucky that we've all survived. All, except Isobel.

Annie switched on the oven and put the pie she'd made inside. She put plates to warm and laid the big kitchen table, with the mismatched cutlery from the dresser drawer. Then she went back to the hall, watching again from the shadows, plucking up courage to interrupt Rick, who was in full flow, when Philip stood up.

'Annie Laidler, what are you waiting for?' The voice loud and rich, and honed in the pulpits of large draughty churches. 'You need some wine, of course you do. You're the one who's been slaving over a hot stove, while we indulge ourselves.' He laughed as he poured a giant glass of red and wrapped his arms around her in a hug. Suddenly all the nervousness disappeared. She was here with her best friends in the world and it would be a fabulous weekend.

And so, the evening rolled on, much as the reunions always did. Friday night supper supplied by Annie, salad brought by the others. Philip always made and brought the puddings. The others made a fuss of his creations, though in Annie's opinion, they never tasted quite as good as they looked. Jax would very definitely have turned up her nose. Later though, when Philip was at the sink in the kitchen, an apron tied round his ample waist, doing the washing-up, Annie felt a moment of overwhelming affection for him. How kind he was! And how much he'd changed since she'd first got to know him.

That first weekend, Philip had been angry, argumentative, arrogant. He'd mellowed a little as Only Connect had progressed, but to the end he'd chafed at the restrictions, the silence of evening chapel. He'd been a swearer in the group sessions and he'd led a break-away group to the pub on one of the evenings. Annie still couldn't quite understand how Philip, the rule-breaker, the non-conformist, the awkward sod, had become an Anglican priest.

Perhaps he was still all those things. Certainly, he stood out in this company of liberal, lefty, angst-ridden individuals. As the rest of them aged and raged against the good night to come, he faced it with equanimity, even with amusement. Death, he said, was the last big adventure. He didn't know with any certainty what lay beyond the grave, but he was curious to find out.

Inevitably, after the meal, they carried on drinking, even

Louisa, who was usually the most sober of them all. Annie had to survive the photos of a new grandchild, the stories of hip and kitchen replacements, of holiday plans and care home choices for very elderly relatives. Things changed in five years. So, Annie brought out the photo she'd found while she'd been sorting through a few boxes at home. The photo of them on that first weekend, standing in front of the Pilgrims' House. All flared jeans and cheesecloth. Her and Dan, Isobel and Philip, Rick and Charlotte. It must have been taken on the first evening because Charlotte was still there. Ken was standing to one side, looking in at them. Judy Marshall standing in the middle, a bit aloof. A bit uncomfortable. Trying to pretend that, as the teacher, she was entirely in control.

As the evening wore on, they regressed back to the age they'd been in that photograph. Back in the common room, when the meal was over, and the plates washed and cleared away, they played sixties music. They danced. How embarrassing it would be if someone walked past and saw them through the uncurtained window! The old anecdotes were dragged out and, as always, there were new revelations, memories that only one of them held deep in their unconscious, and which had never previously been shared. The pile of logs in the basket on the grate shrank and the bottles emptied, and they became less rowdy and more reflective. A silence fell and even a set of footsteps in the lane – probably some islander on his way home from the Seahorse – startled them.

This year, the previously untold story came from Rick. He was sitting on the floor close to the fire, still wearing the leather jacket he always turned up in. Annie thought he must be sweating. But then he'd moved south straight after school, so perhaps he'd become soft.

He turned away from the fire and grinned a wolfish smile. 'Did I ever tell you that I had sex with Miss Marshall?'

The first few words held no surprise. Many of his stories began with: *Did I ever tell you I had sex with . . .*

But Miss Marshall had been a teacher. Young, just out of college. Short skirts and tight, wet-look boots. Straight black hair and a fringe almost into her heavily made-up eyes. She'd taught them English and drama and had been passionate about Dylan Thomas. And Dylan. Serious, intense and rather unworldly. Only Connect had been her idea and she'd been here with them on that first occasion.

Annie still saw Judith around in Kimmerston. Her name wasn't Marshall anymore – she'd married. Annie couldn't remember what she was called these days. Her husband had died. Jax knew her because she did charitable work for the church and the deli donated any stuff approaching its best before date to the food bank there. So, she was someone else who'd changed dramatically if Rick's story was to be believed.

Annie remembered Judy Marshall greeting them at the door of the Pilgrims' House that first time. The pupils had arrived together in one of the school minibuses, but Miss Marshall had driven up herself. She had a little Citroën. Bright yellow. She must have heard the bus on the lane, because she'd been there in the doorway as they'd climbed out of the vehicle. They'd been stretching and groaning because it hadn't been the most comfortable ride.

Back in the present, Rick was telling the story of how he'd screwed Judy Marshall at the post-school play party, but Annie was lost in a different past. She remembered the teacher's words as she'd welcomed them inside.

'Come along,' she'd said. 'You're in for a great adventure.'

Which were almost exactly the same words Philip used now when he was speaking of death.

Annie thought it a little strange that she found this coincidence more interesting than yet another of Rick's tales about his conquests.

Chapter Five

EVEN AS HE WAS TELLING THE story about Judy Marshall, Rick was wondering how much of it was true. It was quite possible that he'd elaborated details in his head over the years. He'd had fantasies about the encounter in the empty periods between wives and girlfriends, before the wonders of Internet dating had filled those times of boredom and misery. It had happened after the school play. His parents had been away – his dad had been a GP and his mother an anaesthetist and there'd been a medical conference some-where – so of course he'd decided he'd have the post-performance party at his house. He might not have been chosen to be the star of the show – and that still rankled – but he could throw a party that people would remember long after some dreary school play. His folks wouldn't be happy when they found out, but he was an only child, spoiled rotten, and they'd get over it.

He'd snogged the teacher. No doubt about that. He remem-bered an intense conversation about Russian literature, just the two of them in the kitchen after most of his friends had left. She'd fixed him with those stary, intense eyes, and his attention had wandered when she started talking about authors he'd never heard of, never mind read. He'd reached out and kissed her. And she'd responded, hadn't she? Of course she had. He'd been pissed, naturally, but then so had she.

'After you lot all buggered off,' he said now, 'I took her upstairs. We had sex in my parents' bed, if you really want to know.'

Of course they wanted to know. Even Phil, who pretended to disapprove, was hanging on his every word. This was what he'd missed since the BBC had axed his show. The audience. Rick needed immediate feedback, a live response. A pre-record was never the same. He always said that he was a serious journalist and he *was*. But he was a serious journalist who needed to interact with his readers and viewers.

Trouble was, he couldn't remember being with the teacher in his parents' room. He knew he'd woken up there, alone the next morning, the sheets crumpled and the room smelling of fags and stale beer, but the rest was just a blur, a blank.

'So,' Lou asked, 'what was she like?'

He was tempted to continue the tale. The words were already in his head: Judy Marshall saying how brilliant it was. He was. That she'd had the best time in her life. But in the end, he looked at Annie, who seemed miles away, hardly interested. And he remembered that he was supposed to be careful now about what he said. These were all close friends, but even close friends leaked to the press. He couldn't afford any more lurid stories.

'Honestly, Lou?' Rick smiled. 'I really can't remember.' A pause. 'You'll have to read all about it when my book comes out. It's fiction naturally, but very definitely based on fact.

You'll find our pasts very much brought back to life. *All* our secrets, actually, finally seeing the light of day.'

Of course, they all demanded more details. He could tell they were intrigued. Some of them a little anxious, which they deserved to be. *Just you wait*, he thought. *Just you wait*.

They drifted off to bed soon after that. The rest of them had become elderly, not just in their bodies, but in their minds. Phil asked if anyone wanted a herbal tea before they turned in. Rick thought that summed him up. Phil might live in London, but he was hardly cosmopolitan.

Although his parish was officially Central London, in reality it felt suburban, a bit left-behind. Rick had been to the red-brick rectory for supper a few times. Philip had invited him after both his divorces, offering sympathy and Christian comfort. He'd gone because anything was better than staying in his flat. He hated being on his own. They'd been best friends at school, even before Only Connect, and Rick had seen more of him than anyone else over the years. He still couldn't quite get used to Philip at work though, dressed up in a black dress with the clergyman's collar. As if he was still performing in a weird school play. Or a pantomime.

Rick's room felt chilly after the warmth of the common room. He supposed the heating was on a timer and had been switched off. The place had stopped being a convent even before Only Connect, but there was still an air of the frugal. Hardship was something to be embraced, not avoided. Before the convent, it had been two farmworkers' cottages, and Rick supposed that they must have been pretty primitive too.

A religious order had taken the place over after the war. Three nuns had lived in one of the cottages. He'd researched their history and they'd been attached to the island's priory, spreading the word about St Cuthbert, following in the foot-steps of the monks who'd lived in the monastery in the Middle Ages. They hadn't been part of an enclosed order – there were no cells or cloisters – and only the little chapel, which the islanders had built for them in the field next door, had any sense of the religious. Rick thought the place must almost have been like a student house-share. Three women, working during the day and coming back to the cottage to eat and sleep together. And, he supposed, to pray.

Then the adjoining cottage had come up for sale and the sisters obtained funding to knock through and extend, to form a place of retreat. Not just for religious groups who came from all over the country to experience the island and its history, but for educational and cultural purposes. The only stipulation had been the dusk time of silence in the tiny chapel. That had been written into the contract signed by everyone who came to stay.

The nuns had moved on. The accommodation had been upgraded a little since the group's first visit as teenagers. He always bagged the downstairs bedroom, the only single large enough to swing a cat. It was part of the more modern exten-sion, created from an attached outbuilding. It had a long window with a view out to the fairy tale castle on its hill, a vaulted ceiling crossed by sturdy beams. He looked out of the window now and looked up at a sky full of stars, the space dizzying, terrifying.

He hadn't slept here on that first weekend. It must have been used by Judy Marshall or the fierce older woman who'd run the place. His room had contained two sets of bunks, metal-framed with stained mattresses thin as cardboard, which had since been replaced. He'd shared with Philip and two boys whose names he'd forgotten and who'd not really participated in any of the sessions. All he could remember was their acne and the gruesome snoring. Yet he'd been able to go straight to sleep and hadn't woken until Philip had shouted that breakfast was ready the next morning.

These days, it seemed, he hardly slept at all. He'd been obsessed with dying when he was a small boy. He'd banged his head against the pillow in an attempt to drive away the thoughts. How was it possible not to exist? How could *he* not exist? As a teenager, the preoccupation was still there, but he'd hidden it more skilfully, turning the obsession into an intellectual pose, a cloak to hide his real terror. Charlotte, his first serious girlfriend and his first wife, had mocked his nightmares.

'Why do you always talk about dying?'

He'd laughed off the question, made more pretentious noises, thrown in a reference to Sartre. She'd ignored the response and returned to painting her toenails with a focus that made that act the most important thing in the universe. More important, certainly, than any abstract notion of life and death.

As an adult he'd always been a bad sleeper. Things had got worse after the last divorce. Now he was getting older and there was the real possibility of death. Rick could cope with the prospect of illness and pain, but a world existing without him terrified and haunted him, especially at night. Even if he dropped off to sleep soon after going to bed, he woke several times, his heart racing, his muscles tense. Astonished, it seemed, to find himself still alive. He thought that was how he would die in the end: a sudden, violent jerk to consciousness would trigger a heart attack. He'd been prescribed blood pressure tablets but had stopped taking them because they had unpleasant side effects – they stopped him making love effectively – and he was as obsessed with sex as he was with death.

Rick supposed there were worse ways to go than a fatal heart attack. Anything, surely, would be better than descending into dementia like Ken. The cloudy eyes and unfocused thoughts, the restless twitching of the hands. That was surely a kind of death. It was as if Ken was disappearing almost before their eyes but becoming at the same time deeper and more nuanced. In health, Ken had been an uncomplicated soul, a husband, a primary school head teacher, a good dad. He'd loved his football and his music, been steady in his happiness. Almost complacent. Now hidden anxieties were emerging and Rick wondered if they'd always been there.

He left the curtains open. He felt close to the landscape outside and even this far from the sea, he fancied he could hear the suck of water on shingle. He undressed. It was a matter of pride that he hadn't worn pyjamas since the age of six and he pulled the duvet round him to keep out the chill. It was still so cold that he worried sleep would be impossible, so he went into the shower room and put on the dressing gown, which had been hanging on a hook behind the door. From his bed, he could see the black, starless shape of the hill and the light-spangled sky behind it. A tawny owl was calling in the woodland at the other side of the house.

His phone rang. He looked at the number, but didn't recognize it. Usually, he didn't bother answering calls like that, but so late at night? It might be an emergency.

'Hello.' He realized that he was quite drunk now and his speech was slurred.

There was a rush of angry words at the other end. A voice he thought he almost recognized.

'I'm sorry,' he said. 'I don't know what you're talking about.'

He switched off his phone and shook his head to clear the memory of the bitterness at the other end of the line. Some mad person. Since the allegations had been made, he'd had a few of those calls. They weren't worth bothering with. It was the price of fame. Soon, the bastards would realize he was more of a victim than his accusers.

As he drifted off, it occurred to him that he could come home now that his show had been pulled. He could work on his book anywhere, and he'd already planned that most of the action would take place in the North-East. Phil might soon retire north. He'd spoken of it. Annie was here so he'd have a friend. Here, in the end, he might sleep.

Chapter Six

ON SATURDAY MORNING, ANNIE WOKE EARLY, so she could get to shower first in one of the communal bathrooms – only Rick had his own – then she made her way to the kitchen. It looked out from the back of the house over the ill-kept garden. There'd been a frost, and each blade of the long grass which made up the lawn was white, separate. It was only just dawn and there was something other-worldly about the scene, the white ground and the pale light.

She checked her phone. There was broadband now at the Pilgrims' House and she messaged Jax about an order for the deli that had slipped her mind before. Jax was her business partner and co-owner of the deli. Jax had founded the place and Annie had started working for her after she and Dan had separated. Later, when Annie's parents had died, leaving her a bit of money, she'd bought into the business.

Jax had become her friend. The woman's parents had come to England with the *Windrush* and arranged for her to be sent from Barbados to join them as a teenager. In the eighties, she'd moved north to Newcastle, following a musician boyfriend, and had stayed in the North-East once the relationship had ended. She'd somehow put up with the confusion and rudeness of locals in a region where there were few people of colour, and racism was as ingrained as support for the Toon, and she'd laughed off the petty aggressions and fought back with humour and style.

Who else would think to open a classy deli in a county where the pits had recently closed, money was scarce and unemployment the highest in the UK? But that had been more than twenty years ago, and here Jax still was. Bread and Olives was an institution. The wealthy would drive miles from the city for the 'artisan' bread or the local cheese.

To be recognized by name by Jax was an accolade. Annie had seen at least one regional celebrity slink out of the shop because Jax had shouted over their head to a customer behind them. She smiled at the thought and turned back to her phone.

When they'd come to Holy Island that first time, there'd been no screens in the house, not even a television. There'd been one pay phone but she couldn't remember anyone using it, except Charlotte summoning her father to take her home. She was sorry for kids now; Annie and her friends had had so much more freedom when they were teenagers. Many nights she'd walked home from Kimmerston after under-age drinking sessions in the Stannie Arms. The roads had been narrow, the street lights few and far between, but nobody had thought it might be dangerous or even unwise. Now, parents seemed to track their kids' every move, and they flew into panic if a text or a phone call was left unanswered.

Annie made coffee. Soon the others would appear. She'd put Jax's freshly baked croissants into the freezer the night before and retrieved them now and put them in the bottom of the oven to warm and crisp. She laid the long table, with the jumble-sale plates, with dishes of jam and honey and her own Seville marmalade. The sun rose slowly, an orange semi-circle on the flat land that ran north-east towards Emmanuel Head, the shape spiked by branches which were already losing their leaves.

Phil popped his head round the door.

'I'm just going out for a wander to clear my head. Start breakfast without me. I won't be long.'

'No worries.'

Almost immediately afterwards, Louisa and Ken came in, the dog at his heels. Ken gave a lovely smile. 'Good morning, Annie!' At least today he remembered her name.

Louisa had said the night before, that sometimes he forgot *her* name. 'Sometimes,' she'd said, 'he thinks I'm his mother.'

Usually, Annie felt a little intimidated by Louisa, who hadn't been one of the core friendship group. She'd only joined them because of her attachment to Ken. Louisa was beautifully groomed, with clear, unchipped varnish on her nails. She'd worked as a head teacher and had been parachuted in to failing schools, to bring them up to scratch. Annie had always felt a failure in comparison, but now, she felt sorry for Louisa and admired her easy care of her husband. There was no sense that she was embarrassed by him. Annie felt a little guilty that she hadn't been a better friend.

'We'll wait, shall we? Philip said not to, but I'm sure he won't be long. He's just gone out for a walk. And Rick will turn up soon.'

'I was talking to Phil last night.' Louisa poured coffee for herself and for Ken. She added sugar and milk to Ken's and set it in front of him. 'He was telling me how special these weekends are for him. At work, it's hard for him to be himself. I suppose it must feel like a kind of performance, being a vicar. So often, you're officiating at ceremonies, and even at a normal service, you're up there at the front with everybody staring.'

'Philip was always an actor,' Annie said. 'I think he rather enjoys it. At school, we knew he'd get the lead role every time. We believed he was destined to be a star. He had the good looks, the attitude.'

'I'd have thought Rick would be the one to take centre stage.'

Annie thought about that. 'Well, Rick wasn't such a good actor and he never had Philip's looks.' This was a stalling tactic while she took herself back all those years. It was true though. Rick had been too short to be traditionally handsome, but he'd made up for that with energy, a charisma that could light up a room. And confidence. He'd had that in abundance. Confidence and charm.

'He hasn't changed, has he?' Louisa broke into Annie's thoughts. 'After all those dreadful rumours and accusations, you'd have thought he'd be quieter, a bit subdued.'

'I can't imagine Rick ever being subdued.'

'Well, that's true.' Louisa turned her attention to her coffee. 'I saw an article by one of his daughters in the *Observer*. Rather cruel, I thought, to go public.'

'I didn't see it.' That was true. They opened Olives and Bread as a cafe as well as a deli at the weekends and she never had time to read the Sunday papers. She'd heard about it though. Rick was a local boy. Some of her older customers had been patients of his father. There'd been gossip over the coffee and the pastries. Annie had wanted to defend Rick, but after all his attitude to younger women was indefensible these days, and she'd remained silent.

'I wasn't even sure that he'd be here this weekend,' Louisa said. 'It showed a certain courage coming to face us all.'

'Rick's always been pretty fearless.' *And we're his friends. He knows we'd accept him. Love him, despite his faults and his ridiculous ego. I can't believe he actually did all the things he's been accused of. Besides, we owe him. He's been there for us through the bad times.*

When Dan had walked away, leaving Annie penniless, Rick had been there, offering a loan, which they'd both realized would be a gift. It had helped pay off a few of her more vocal creditors. It had given her a little dignity, bought her time to think about the future. And before that, when Freya had died, and Dan had been useless, lost in a world of his own, it had been Rick Annie had phoned, sobbing down the line. Rick, who'd jumped on a plane from London to be with her, holding her, sharing her grief. Then when Dan had left the scene entirely, Rick had been back again with the money, helping her to find a place to live.

'Do you really think so?' Louisa set down her empty mug. 'I've always thought he was scared of the world, that all that running after women and stories, the endless travelling, was a kind of distraction.'

Louisa occasionally came out with phrases like that, but Annie remembered what Charlotte, Rick's girlfriend, had said during that first weekend, halfway through Only Connect, just before she'd phoned her rich father and summoned him to take her away. *Rick Kelsall is obsessed with dying.* Perhaps that was a better explanation.

But she just nodded. 'You're probably right.' There was no point, Annie thought, arguing with Louisa. She was one of those women protected by certainty.

There was the sound of a door opening and closing and Philip stood in the doorway. He still had on his outdoor clothes and a strange purple hat with a bobble on a plaited woollen string, knitted, Annie remembered now, by one of his elderly parishioners. He'd mentioned that the night before. Phil leaned against the wall, one foot raised, so he could take off his boots.

'I smell coffee,' he said. 'Wonderful coffee.'

He was still good-looking in a grandfatherly, silver-haired sort of way, though he'd put on a lot of weight. He padded into the kitchen in his thick woolly socks, and Annie wondered, not for the first time, how he'd changed from the edgy, tense boy to this relaxed and generous man. Perhaps that was what faith did for you. He was a walking advertisement for Christianity.

At that point, Annie expected Rick to make an entrance. He'd have been out running, of course, and would put them all to shame. He'd wait until they were all gathered then come in glowing, mud on his trainers. *Only 5K today but I'll go out later, run a bit further.* Though she thought he too had put on a bit of weight round the belly since she'd last seen him. Perhaps he hadn't been getting so much exercise lately.

The others were laying the table and making plans for the day. There was a decision to make. Should they stay on the island or explore a bit further afield? A yomp up Simonsides, or a leisurely day in Berwick.

'Where's Rick?' Louisa asked. 'If we don't get a move on, it'll be lunchtime before we're ready to leave. There's so little light now and we don't have so long because of the tide.'

'I'll give him a shout.' Annie was glad of the excuse to be on her own, even for the few minutes it would take to get to Rick's bedroom. She was so used to living alone that gatherings of people, even people she cared about, freaked her out a bit. It was a sort of claustrophobia and occasionally she felt close to a panic attack. She walked along the corridor to Rick's room and knocked on the door. When there was no answer, she opened it and looked in.

Rick was hanging from a white plaited cord from the beam that crossed the vaulted ceiling. He was wearing a striped woollen dressing gown that had flapped open to reveal a body otherwise naked. Everything about him looked different. It took her a while to believe that this *was* Rick, that it wasn't a stranger who'd taken up residence. There were red pinpricks around his eyes and eyelids. He looked very old, his chest wrinkled and sprouting grey hair. There was nothing attractive about this body. Rick would hate anyone to see him like this.

She reached out and touched his wrist. It was icy, and when she felt for a pulse, there was nothing. Rick had killed himself. There was an overturned chair on the floor beneath him. He'd stood on the chair, strung the dressing-gown cord around the beam, and kicked it away. Charlotte had said all those years ago that he was obsessed with dying and Annie could understand that he might want to choose his own time to let go. This must be suicide. He'd had so much pressure. The accusations of bullying by his young colleagues. The dreadful stories in the press. His former wives selling their tales of his misdeeds. Then the fact that his show had been axed. He'd always liked a dramatic gesture and suicide was certainly that.

What did surprise her was the fact that, under the dressing gown, he was naked. Rick loved clothes and he loved dressing up. He would have prepared his departure from this life with care. He must have been desperate to leave like this, with so little dignity, so little thought for the picture he'd leave behind.

There was something ridiculous, almost clownish, in the figure before her.

The shock hit her then and she opened her mouth. What came out was a scream, but it almost sounded like hysterical laughter. She cupped her hand around her mouth to stop the noise, because, more than anything in the world Rick hated to be laughed at.

Chapter Seven

IT WAS SATURDAY MORNING, AND VERA actually had plans for the weekend that didn't involve work. Joanna, her neighbour, was taking part in a book festival in North Yorkshire. Joanna wrote crime fiction and sometimes she picked Vera's brains, though when the books appeared they had nothing to do with reality. Vera enjoyed reading them for the escape they provided, the joy of loose ends tied up.

Joanna had asked if Vera might like to go along to the festival. For company and reassurance, and at least to get a change of scene because Vera rarely left Northumberland. Though obviously there were worse places to be.

'It's a huge thing for me,' Joanna had said. 'A proper literature festival in a marquee in the grounds of a grand country pile. They'll put us up in the main house. And they've promised that they'll feed us very well.' Joanna had named a few other writers who'd be there: a politician, a TV chef, a forensic pathologist who'd recently written an account of his work investigating the massed graves of the former Yugoslavia.

'I thought you might be interested,' she'd said. 'And of

course, they'll be fascinated to meet you. A real detective, with so many stories to tell.'

Vera had agreed because it had been kind of Joanna to think of her. Kindness had often been in short supply in her life. She was keen to meet the pathologist, who had been a hero for years. Not for his work in the Balkans, but because he'd been involved in one of her cases and he'd had a mind of his own, refusing to be bullied by lawyers or the police. It would be good to meet him again. He'd liked a drink as she remembered, and was especially fond of a good island malt. She was curious too to see Joanna at work, talking about her stories, in front of an audience. Here in the hills, she was very much a farmer. Her life was sleepless nights lambing, struggling to make ends meet.

The phone call came when Vera was packing her overnight bag and was already having second thoughts about the trip. She wasn't good at small talk, unless it was about murder. What if she was put next to the politician at dinner? She'd end up drinking too much and making a tit of herself. The call was from Joe Ashworth, her second in command. Her surrogate son, and her conscience.

'What is it? It's my weekend off.' None of her team thought she had any sort of life away from work and it did no harm to put them right. 'I'm on my way out.'

'We've got an unexplained death.' A pause. 'Well, not so unexplained. Probable suicide. A hanging.'

'They don't need me then. Or you.'

'The boss wants us to take charge.' The boss, Watkins, was Welsh. Vera didn't hold that against him, but she did hate his obsession with rules, forms, emails, Teams talks and webinars. And his youth.

She was going to say that she didn't care what the boss wanted. It was still her weekend off – she wasn't even on call – but Joe had continued talking. 'The dead man is in the news a lot. Local boy made good. Until the rumours and accusations started and he lost his gloss.' A pause. 'It's Rick Kelsall.'

'That irritating little journo?' Despite herself, Vera's interest was piqued. 'The one who's on the telly on a Saturday morning?'

'The one who *used* to be on the telly on a Saturday morning.' Another pause. 'Until he resigned. Or was pushed.'

'That would explain the suicide then.' Her voice was still cheery, dismissive, but she was wavering. Definitely wavering. 'If he'd lost the limelight, he might not have been able to face life. Some people just need the world to revolve around them.'

There was a moment of silence and Vera wondered, just for a second, if there might be an impertinent response: *Not like you then, Vera.* But Joe had worked for her for so long that he knew better than to try a clever remark like that. She never found such banter amusing. She'd been teased at school about her weight and her clothes and her weird father. It had felt a lot like bullying and the jibes still lingered in her brain, even when she was most in charge.

'There are a couple of odd circumstances. There'll be a post-mortem of course. We'll know more then.'

'What kind of odd?'

'It doesn't matter if you're on your way out. I can deal with it.' Joe was calling her bluff.

'Come on, Joe! Don't piss me about.'

'He wasn't wearing any clothes. Only a dressing gown, and as he'd used the cord to string himself up, that didn't cover him up much. The woman who found him thought that was strange. He cared about his appearance. She said he might have wanted to kill himself, but he wouldn't have wanted to look ridiculous while he was doing it.' A pause. 'They didn't find a note. He was a writer. You'd think he'd want to leave a few words for his friends.'

'A bit tenuous, that.' But, thinking about it, Vera could see how it would make you wonder. Especially if you were getting on a bit – and despite his defiantly brown hair, this man was certainly older than her – you wouldn't want the world to see all your bumps and wrinkles. And she'd seen this guy on the television. He'd liked the sound of his own voice. He wasn't the sort to go out quietly, without any sort of explanation. Joe was right about that.

'Anything else to suggest murder?'

'Nothing on the body apparently, but we've only got the evidence of the people he was staying with. They describe marks around the eyes which could be petechial haemorrhaging.' Joe paused. 'But until the tide goes out nobody can get in to check. That's the other complication. The death took place on Holy Island, in somewhere called the Pilgrims' House.'

Holy Island. Known to southerners as Lindisfarne. Vera had been there many times with Hector, her father. She'd acted as lookout while he raided the nests of wading birds, then she'd been forced to wait in the Land Rover while he had a celebratory pint in one of the pubs. Until she'd got older and rebellious and had told him to do his own dirty work.

'When can we get over?' Because Vera had decided she *would* be there. The decision made, she felt lighter. There was a release of tension. She would be happier, and a lot more comfortable, at a potential murder scene than with a handful of famous writers. Very much happier.

'It'll be safe to cross in an hour, apparently, so not worth getting the helicopter in the air.'

'We treat it as unexplained until we know any different. Get Paul Keating there. And have Billy Cartwright on standby. Depending on what the doc says, we'll call in the CSIs.' Her mind was racing now. 'If the death turns out to be suspicious, we might have to stay over. Book us somewhere. Provisionally. You, me and Hol. The doc and Billy can look after themselves and they might even be finished in time to get back before high water. Some of the pubs do rooms.' She'd been working non-stop all summer. Boring, routine shouts. Brawls in bars that had got out of hand. Pathetic little men killing their wives for taunting them about their inadequacies. It felt like years since she'd had a full evening in a pub. She thought wistfully of the smell, the taste of that first, hand-pulled pint. 'It'll save us traipsing back and forth, and we won't be dependent on low water.'

'Okay.' He sounded dubious. Sal would give him bother about an overnight trip. Vera found herself grinning.

She'd just finished the call when there was a tap on the door and Joanna opened it without waiting to be asked. She stood on the doorstep and looked in.

'Just checking everything's okay. I was thinking we should leave about ten. That'll give us plenty of time.' Joanna had kept the voice of her privileged childhood. It was as rich as the family she'd left behind, mellowed by good red wine.

'Eh, sorry, pet. Something's turned up at work. A suspicious death. I won't be able to make it after all. That was Joe Ashworth on the phone.' Vera was already planning the first steps of the investigation. She thought it was just as well she'd already packed an overnight bag. It would come in useful if they *did* have to stay. If this turned out to be murder.

'Oh Vera, that's such a shame.' But something in Joanna's face suggested a fleeting moment of relief. Perhaps she'd been anxious that Vera would make a tit of herself too, in front of her new, influential friends. 'Another time, then.'

'Of course.' As Joanna turned to go, Vera added: 'And thanks for asking me. It was kind. Very kind.'

A brief, almost conspiratorial smile, passed between them. They both knew this was for the best.

It took Vera less than an hour to drive to the coast, and she began to catch glimpses of the sea from the road over the tops soon after leaving home. It gleamed, a line of light on the distant horizon. This was the very north of her patch. She crossed the A1, the main road leading to Scotland, then she drove through farmland, the grass still frosty in the shade, even here, so close to the shore. Through a gap in the hedge and across the wide curve of the bay, she saw Rede's Tower, an ancient pele tower which had been almost derelict when she was a lass and was now the hub of a grand holiday park, with lodges and a spa and a fine-dining restaurant.

Minutes later she'd arrived at the causeway and the wedge shape of Holy Island was ahead of her. She didn't have a spiritual bone in her body, but there was something about this place that moved her. It was history – St Cuthbert, St Bede and the dawn of British Christianity – and it seemed to sum up the importance of Northumberland in the world. Her county. Her home.

Next to the causeway, a line of poles across the sand marked the Pilgrims' Way, where the faithful sometimes crossed by foot, paddling, trousers rolled to their knees, packed lunches in small rucksacks. Ahead of her was the island, the highest point furthest away from her, and perched there on the top of the cliff, the sandstone castle, majestic, looking out towards Scandinavia.

A couple of incomers had pulled their cars into the parking spot to study the crossing times, but she drove on, through the water left by the retreating tide, until she reached the other side. When the water returned, it would be an island proper again, cut off from the mainland, but the boundary between sea and land was shifting, uncertain, made up of sand and mud and dune.

This was a real community, however, once the road rose from the shore, and it attracted the curious tripper as well as the faithful. The car park on the edge of the settlement was already busy. It might be October, but it was half-term, and the morning tide made it possible for families to visit for the day. She drove on slowly through the village, past the guest houses, pubs and gift shops. A stream of walkers flowed towards the slope to the castle. Vera moved slowly, unsure now where she was going, but just beyond the houses, there was a wooden sign marked 'The Pilgrims' House', pointing towards a narrow lane, a lonnen, leading east. The retreat house was halfway along the track, close to the centre of the island. The building was unassuming, not quite what Vera had been expecting. One door had been bricked in, and it was clear these had once been two attached cottages, tied homes probably, belonging to the castle. She'd thought a celebrity like Rick Kelsall would holiday somewhere grander.

She climbed out of the Land Rover and paused for a moment to take note of her surroundings. To one side of the house was a small chapel, stone-built and squat. A skein of geese flew over as she stood there. Their calls made her think again of

Hector and other wild places he'd dragged her to. The far boundary of the house was marked by a hedge, heavy with sloes, and for a moment she was distracted. She wished she had a bag with her. This was just the time to pick them, after the first frost took the edge off the tannin. She was still thinking of sloe gin for Christmas, and that she might make some for Jack and Joanna, save her buying a daft present the couple probably wouldn't need, as she made her way into the building.

As Vera had thought, she was the first of her team to arrive. The residents were waiting for her in the common room. The heating was on, but they'd lit a fire anyway and the room smelled of logs and coffee. There were four of them, all of an age. The fit elderly. Because sixty was the new forty, wasn't it? That, at least, was what Holly, one of her younger colleagues, had told Vera when she'd once complained of aches and pains.

'What are you implying?' Vera had never thought of herself as vain, but Holly's comment had hurt. 'I'm nowhere near sixty!' Which wasn't entirely true. Another few years and she'd be there and HR would be pestering her to discuss the possibilities of retirement.

A black and white springer spaniel was lying on the rug in front of the fire. It looked up and wandered slowly over to Vera. That too was elderly, then. Spaniels didn't usually wander. She stroked its head and neck, looked up at the group and introduced herself.

'Which of you found Mr Kelsall?'

A woman in jeans and a black sweatshirt, with the image of a white dolphin embroidered on the front, stuck up her hand, and triggered a memory of the best bread Vera had ever tasted. Her hair was undyed, pulled back into a clip at the back of her head. Vera thought she'd probably worn it like that since she was a teenager. She still had the build of a young woman, great cheekbones, grey eyes. Still attractive without realizing it. Vera had a moment of envy.

'I know you, don't I? You run that deli in Kimmerston.'

The woman nodded. She'd been crying. 'Annie Laidler.'

'You okay to show me the room, pet? You don't have to go in.'

'Yeah, all right.'

They walked together down the corridor that linked the two former cottages. Annie stopped outside a door. 'He's in there.'

'On the ground floor then?'

'Yes, he liked this room. He said it brought him closer to nature and he needed that because he spent so long in the city.' A pause. 'The real reason was that it's a single, with its own bathroom, the most expensive in the place. Rick wasn't used to slumming it anymore and I suppose he could afford it.'

'You've all been here before?'

'We come every five years. Have done since we were teenagers. There've been a few changes over the years. Wives and girlfriends have come and gone, and the kids have all grown up, but the core group is the same.'

'A school reunion?'

'Yes. Rick, Philip, Ken, Lou and I were at Kimmerston Grammar together.' A pause. 'The reunion is to mark a weekend course the school ran. Only Connect. It brought us together. That was exactly fifty years ago.'

Vera thought about that and had another stab of envy. She hadn't really made many friends at school and she'd left as soon as she could to become a police cadet. That was when she'd found her tribe. In the police service she'd made friends and found a substitute family, still keeping her distance, but at last feeling she belonged.

'I can take it from here, pet.' She pulled on a scene suit with its hood, mask and bootees, making her look like a nurse out of ICU. At the end of the corridor, Annie Laidler turned back and looked at her. She stopped for a moment, shocked by the transformation. Vera gave a little wave. 'Don't mind me! Just a precaution.' She put on the blue gloves and waited until Annie had disappeared from view.

Vera opened the door and stood for a moment, looking in. She could see why Rick Kelsall had liked the room. The ceiling was vaulted – the room as high as it was wide – but a horizontal beam stretched across the empty roof space. The dead man was hanging from this. Vera ignored him for the moment and looked at the rest of the space. It was compact, with a single bed and a small chest of drawers doubling as a bedside cabinet, a narrow white wood wardrobe in one corner. If this was the best room in the place, the others must be pretty basic. The bed had been slept in, the duvet rumpled, still a dent in the pillow where his head had been. There was a long sash window with a view south-east towards the castle.

A bentwood chair had been placed next to the window, and there'd been a bright yellow hand-woven cushion to make it more comfortable. It would be pleasant to sit there and to look out over the island. But now the chair was overturned, lying on one side, and the cushion was on the floor beside it. Perhaps Kelsall had stood on the chair and thrown the rope over the beam to form a noose and then kicked it away so he was hanging unsupported. Perhaps. Vera felt the flutter of excitement that came at the beginning of an interesting case. It was shameful to want this to be murder, but all the same.

Still, she kept her attention away from the body. Gratification delayed. Through an open door she saw the shower room, which was small too, hardly more than a cupboard in one corner. A towel had been folded on a heated rail but seemed not to have been used.

A small cabin bag was open on the floor next to the bed. Inside, a pair of jeans, spare socks and underwear. The clothes Kelsall had been wearing the day before – trousers, shirt, sweater and socks – had been placed on the chest of drawers. Not folded, but then how many people did fold their clothes when they took them off, especially after a few drinks. Because they would have had a few drinks, surely. A bunch of mates getting together for the first time in five years. Vera couldn't imagine that would be a sober affair.

She spent some time searching for a note. Kelsall had made his living through words. She thought again that surely the man wouldn't have killed himself without leaving a message for the people close to him. His friends. His children. This silent slipping away seemed out of character. But there was no note to be found.

At last, she turned her attention to the dead man. Or rather, first to the rope. This was very obviously the cord which would have held his dressing gown together. Kelsall was a small man, but even so, there'd be no guarantee that it would hold his weight. If this was suicide, surely it must have been impulsive, unplanned. If he'd organized this suicide in advance – recognizing the importance of the place to his life, wanting to be among friends at the end – surely Rick Kelsall would have brought rope with him. Vera had a hazy memory of seeing the journalist on television, halfway up some cliff in the Lake District, presenting a feature about the anniversary of the National Parks. Showing off his athletic prowess. He'd seemed at home there, and might well have access to a strong, light rope, which would do the job well. But he hadn't brought it. If this was suicide, it had been an impulsive decision. What had happened during the evening to provoke Kelsall to kill himself?

Now, Vera did look at the body. He was a small man, wizened, almost monkey-like. The hair on his head was quite a different colour from the hair on his chest, and that gave him an odd manufactured appearance, as if he'd been put together using a number of alien body parts. A mini creation of Frankenstein. Another reason, surely, why he would have worn clothes for his final curtain call. Certainly, he looked nothing as he had on the screen. Make-up could do that, she supposed, but as a performer he'd been very alive, always moving, almost manic. It was the energy that had held the viewers' attention; that was why she remembered having seen his programme.

Vera pondered the possibilities. Kelsall might have been small, but a deadweight was tricky to handle. Could one person have strung him up? A fit man could certainly have done it alone. But a woman? Vera went through the motions in her head. You'd make the noose first, then drag Kelsall's body so he'd be almost sitting on the chair. Put the noose over his head and throw the other end of the cord over the beam. Easy enough then to pull him into position. Harder to maintain that tension while you climbed onto the chair to tie the cord in place. Vera thought a strong young woman might do it. But one of these residents, who were in their sixties? It seemed unlikely.

She was still working through the possibilities when there was a tap on the door, and Paul Keating came in. Despite the scene suit she recognized him. He was the forensic pathologist and they'd worked together many times before. He still had the Northern Irish accent of his birth, and he still, despite his work, had his faith.

'Well,' he said. 'What have we got? Murder or suicide?' Asking as a kind of courtesy, not because he needed Vera's opinion. He'd make up his own mind.

She didn't answer directly. 'What do you think?'

He approached the body. 'Everything would indicate suicide,' he said. 'The petechial haemorrhaging certainly. No sign of manual strangulation. And there are faint ligature marks around his neck.'

'I saw those. But that might happen, wouldn't it, if he was strung up soon after death?'

'It would, yes.' He paused and turned to her. She saw serious grey eyes above his mask. 'Do you have any reason to think this was murder?'

'Nothing concrete.'

'But?'

'Ah, Dr Keating, you know me so well.' Vera paused. 'Our victim was a celebrity, a vain man. He was with friends last night and there was nothing to suggest that he was depressed or unstable. He'd been drinking all evening, but he wasn't so drunk that he'd do something completely out of character. I can buy him killing himself. But not like this. Not in a shabby dressing gown, showing an ageing body to the world. And not without leaving a note.'

'I take it you'd like a speedy post-mortem?'

Vera could feel herself grinning and was pleased Keating couldn't see her face behind the mask. He wasn't a man who liked shows of emotion.

'The boss would certainly like it. This man is a celebrity. There'll be a lot of press speculation until we can find out for certain how he died.'

'I could do it today. There's something distasteful, a little humiliating, about the media hovering over a dead body. And you know, Inspector, that I dislike working on a Sunday.'

'I'd like to stay here overnight,' Vera said, 'just in case we have a murder investigation.'

And because I've been dreaming all day about drinking a pint in a real pub.

'But I'll send one of my team to join you at the post-mortem,' she went on. 'Let's get this sorted, shall we? Let's give his friends and relatives some sort of answer as quickly as we can.'

Chapter Eight

PHILIP HAD GONE TO LOOK AT Rick's body before the police arrived. He'd wanted to make sure that the man was dead. Annie had walked into the kitchen, white and trembling, saying what she'd seen, but Philip had struggled to believe it. He hadn't gone right into the room. He'd watched enough cop shows – his way of relaxing after stressful days of parish politics – to know that would be a mistake. Instead, he'd stood at the doorway and looked in. Back in the common room he'd nodded to the others.

'Suicide,' he'd said. 'Poor, poor Rick. Why couldn't he tell us that he was feeling so desperate?'

Annie had stared at him as if she was about to challenge the statement, but she'd just said, 'I've called the police. An inspector is on her way.'

He hadn't known how to answer that, but perhaps a police presence was necessary even for suicide. 'Rick was always obsessed with death,' he said.

Suddenly he was sixteen again, sat in this room, the first morning of Only Connect. It was the first time he'd heard

51

about Rick's fixation with dying. They were sitting in two circles, sprawled on the floor, on cushions or leaning against chairs. A dozen of them split into two groups. Philip had been with Rick, Annie, Daniel Rede, Ken and Charlotte. Two marriages had come out of that weekend. Annie had ended up with Daniel, outsider, rough country lad, not an intellectual bone in his body, and Rick of course had married the beautiful Charlotte. Isobel had been in the room too, but in the other group. Miss Marshall was in charge, though after the first hour they didn't call her that.

The teacher was dressed in purple loons that morning and a skimpy long-sleeved T-shirt. He and Rick would argue later about whether she was wearing a bra. 'I think for this weekend you should call me Judy,' she said, very earnest.

They sniggered a bit, because she was still a teacher, wasn't she? Not one of them. But in the end, they went along with it.

'Introduce yourself to the person sitting next to you,' she went on. 'Tell them something intimate, something you've shared with no other person.'

Philip was sitting next to Charlotte, whom he fancied like hell, but claimed to despise. Charlotte was long-legged and blonde, and going out with Rick. Her father owned a string of nightclubs in Newcastle, and had the reputation of being a gangster, but Charlotte spoke with a cut-glass accent. You'd have thought, from the perfectly formed southern vowels, that her family were aristocrats. She couldn't help it, she said, when they teased her about her voice. She'd had elocution lessons. If she hadn't passed the eleven-plus, she'd have gone to a boarding school. Her parents had wanted that for her anyway, but she preferred to stay at home and go to the local school.

After A levels, which she'd just scraped through, she'd gone to London to be a model and none of them had seen her again until they'd been invited to her wedding. She'd become Mrs Charlotte Kelsall, first wife to Rick, and for a while the couple had been celebrities of a sort, their pictures in the papers. When their daughter had been born there'd been four colour pages in *Hello!* magazine. Rick had sent him a cutting.

Since then, of course, Charlotte had changed career again, reinventing herself, and now she was telling other people the best way to live their lives. She'd never come to the reunions, even when she was still married to Rick, even that first time, when she'd been his fiancée and Isobel had died.

Philip didn't want to think about that now. Another death. Instead, he took himself back to Only Connect and to Charlotte, sitting cross-legged, looking bored. At first, he thought she wouldn't even bother to engage with the bonding exercise, but she spoke in the end.

'I'll tell you something *nobody* knows.' She turned to Philip and gave a languid smile. They'd moved away from the others to share their confidences and now they were sitting together on the floor in a corner. 'Rick Kelsall is terrified of dying.'

'But that's about him. Not you.' Philip thought this was cheating. If you were going to play these ridiculous games, surely you should play by the rules. Charlotte was giving nothing of herself away.

'This is just a game,' Charlotte said, almost echoing his thoughts, 'and I don't want to play.'

She hadn't played. She'd phoned her father halfway through the weekend and he'd come in a very flash car and driven her away. Philip had been on a solitary walk to the Snook, and had seen the giant vehicle travelling very fast, splashing through the water that was already starting to cover the causeway. It had been reckless, too close to high tide, and had the sense of a desperate escape.

Five years later, when Isobel had died in similar circumstances, Philip had thought of Charlotte running away from them all. But her father's car had been solid and grand, and he'd been an experienced driver. Isobel's had been a flimsy tin box and she hadn't stood a chance.

Chapter Nine

HOLLY GOT THE MESSAGE FROM JOE ASHWORTH while she was running. Running had become part of her life. The last thing in the world she wanted was to end up like the boss. Vera was bloated, idle. When the inspector leaned against the desk at the front of the room to address her minions, the fat on her bum spread and made unsightly bulges in those dreadful crimplene trousers she'd taken to wearing now the weather was colder. Though Holly had seen her put on a surprising turn of speed occasionally, not even her biggest admirer – the brown-nose Joe Ashworth – would claim she was fit, and the woman's diet would make any doctor weep.

The trouble was, Holly knew that *she* was as wedded to the job as Vera. She could do with making real friends, having more of a social life, but as running was taking up more and more of her time, becoming, she had to admit, a kind of addiction, that wasn't likely to happen.

She started planning a strategy; there was nothing Holly liked better than a strategy. Perhaps she could sign up for evening classes, maybe even join a running club as a way of meeting people outside the job, but then the phone, which she'd strapped to her arm, buzzed. She glanced at it. Joe Ashworth. She didn't *dislike* Joe, but she saw him as competition. She was single, no kids and no commitments, so it should be easier for her to earn promotion. Yet he was a sergeant and she was still a DC. She blamed Vera for that. Joe had always been the boss's favourite.

Holly slowed to a stop and took the call, stretching her calves, trying to steady her breathing.

'We've got a shout. Unexplained death.'

'Where?'

'A place on Holy Island, called the Pilgrims' House. As far as I can tell it's a kind of retreat. I can send you directions from the causeway.'

'Okay,' she said. 'I'll see you there. You'll probably be there before me.' Joe lived in Kimmerston, which was in the north of the county. He was halfway there. Besides, she needed a shower and to change.

Holly had been to Holy Island before, not for work, but as a tourist. Her parents were history nuts and had wanted to see the priory. She took them to the island now, whenever they came to stay. It made a satisfactory day out: sightseeing and lunch. It helped pass the time until, much to Holly's relief, the couple headed back to Manchester and home. She loved her parents – of course she did – but when they were with her, she had to put on a show. They wanted so much to believe that she was happy here, that she'd made friends and loved her job, and she had to play along with their fantasy. She couldn't disappoint them.

She was just leaving the flat when her phone went again.

This time it was Vera. 'Where are you, Hol?' The voice a little too loud, excitable like a child on a sugar rush.

'Sorry, boss, I wasn't home when Joe called. I'm just leaving now.'

'Change of plan. Dr Keating's prioritizing the PM for us. He's doing it late this afternoon in Kimmerston and I'd like you to attend. I don't want to leave here.'

'Fine.' Holly wasn't squeamish. Not usually, though she still occasionally had nightmares about the body they'd found in the forest at Brockburn, the Christmas before.

'Now listen carefully. This is what I want you to ask him. And give me a shout once it's done. We can decide then whether you need to join us here. Have an overnight bag with you just in case.'

The list of instructions was detailed and as soon as the conversation was over, Holly made notes. Vera usually liked to attend the post-mortem herself. This wasn't a time to screw up. Vera was trusting her, and despite herself, that made the DC ridiculously happy.

Holly arrived at Kimmerston before Dr Keating, and went to Bread and Olives to buy a sandwich for lunch. The place was busy and there was a queue, so she didn't have time to take it back to the station and sat instead, wrapped in her coat, on a bench looking out at the river. Keating and the technician were already in the mortuary when she got there, and that made her flustered. She apologized for being late.

'You're perfectly on time, Constable, but it seems that your inspector has a bee in her bonnet about this one. So, let's get started and prove her wrong, shall we? This seems like a classic case of suicide by hanging to me.' He started his introduction, speaking into a Dictaphone. When he came to a pause, she felt able to speak.

'I have a list of questions from Inspector Stanhope.'

'Have you now? And what does she want to know?'

'I'm sorry to interrupt. This must sound impertinent.' Holly's respectable parents were believers, evangelicals, members of their local church, and a doctor came a very close second to the Lord in their hierarchy of reverence. Despite herself, Holly had picked up the same sense of respect.

'Not impertinent at all. I would never say this to her face, of course, but the inspector is a very intelligent woman. She's very often right.'

'She asks if the hyoid bone is broken?'

'Do you know what the hyoid bone is?' Keating sounded genuinely curious, but Holly felt as if this was some sort of test. She wondered if Joe would be this nervous.

'Isn't it the bone at the front of the throat?'

'Exactly. Shaped like a butterfly. Inspector Stanhope's question is apposite. It usually is broken during hanging and strangulation. But not always. No, that is by no means inevitable.'

'And in this case?'

'In this case, it's not broken.' He frowned. 'But I can see no other probable cause of death. I really don't think we can call this as murder just on the fact of the intact hyoid. Not even for Inspector Stanhope.'

Holly felt as she had as a schoolgirl, asking a question in front of the class. 'The inspector wonders if you'd take a swab of the nose.' A pause. 'She told me specifically to ask you.'

He looked at her sharply. 'Did she, indeed? Is that the way her mind's working? I think then perhaps we should indulge her. Just to put her mind at rest, you know.'

He took a swab and inserted it into one nostril. When he brought it out, he held it, towards her. 'What do you see, Constable?'

'It's yellow,' she said. 'Are they yellow fibres?'

'They are indeed.' He handed the swab to the technician, who slipped it into a bag and labelled it. 'I assume we'll find the same result in the other nostril.' He repeated the process, and again held the swab for her to see. 'What does that tell us?'

Holly scrambled to find an answer. Keating waited.

'It tells us that the victim breathed in fibres just before he died,' she said.

'Exactly that. I don't think you visited the locus, so perhaps it was unfair of me to expect you to be more precise than that. There was a yellow cushion in the room where he was found. This tells us, I think, that Mr Kelsall was smothered. The cushion was placed over his face, and held tightly, so when he struggled for breath some of the loosely woven yellow fibres were inhaled. Smothering, too, causes petechial haemorrhaging, and as your boss pointed out to me at the scene, there would still have been ligature marks on his neck if he was strung from the beam soon after death.'

'So, Rick Kelsall *was* murdered.'

'Just so.' Keating gave a lovely smile. 'Your boss was right, and will be, I'm afraid, insufferable. I think perhaps you should go and tell her, so she can be triumphant, and then start to get the investigation moving. I'll complete the post-mortem uninterrupted and will make sure that she gets my report as soon as I can.'

Chapter Ten

JOE DIDN'T RUSH TO DRIVE NORTH. He thought that by the time he arrived the doctor would have decided that this death was suicide. Vera tended to complicate matters, and often the most obvious explanation was the right one. This part of the county had always been special to him, and the trip felt like a journey back in time. It was the place of caravan holidays with his grandfather, an escape from the routine of home. The blackberry week half-term had been one of his favourite times. He remembered Indian summers, the woodland a riot of colour, scavenging the hedgerows and building dens. He thought *his* kids, with their organized after-school activities, the rigid time-table of sports clubs and music lessons, were missing out.

He'd never gone to Holy Island as a lad. His grandfather had been wary, nervous of the tides and of the islanders, the wildfowlers and the fishermen. They might have been an alien race, a left-behind tribe of Vikings. Joe had visited the island once as an adult with Sal and the kids, but they'd moaned because they were stuck there over a tide and there'd been nothing to do. Of course, there *had* been plenty to do, but nothing easy, exciting. No skate park or fairground or swimming pool with slides. When they'd realized that escape was impossible, the children had actually been quite happy, jumping from the dunes and poking in the rock pools. He'd never brought them back though. Sal liked the *idea* of letting the kids run wild, but wasn't so struck by the reality.

He drove carefully across the causeway, hit the edge of the community with its almost suburban houses, and then he was there in the village, this part of the island dominated by the castle. He followed Vera's instructions down a narrow lane until he saw her Land Rover, pulled into the verge. Here, they were too far from the village to hear trippers' voices or the rumble of the shuttle minibuses carrying the elderly and infirm from the car park to the castle. He stood for a moment, taking in the view, listening to the calls of birds he couldn't identify.

Inside, a uniformed officer, a local lad from Berwick, was waiting in the entrance hall. He logged Joe's arrival, obviously excited. Perhaps the thrill was in being close to celebrity, even though the celebrity in question was dead. Or perhaps nothing this interesting had happened since he'd joined the service.

'Dr Keating's already left. The boss is still at the locus. It's that room at the end of the corridor.'

Through an open door in the opposite direction, he saw a comfortable living room, a group of people sitting in easy chairs, a fire. A couple looked up, but perhaps they'd become accustomed to this invasion of outsiders, because they didn't seem very interested and just went back to their reading.

Vera emerged into the passage, before Joe reached Rick Kelsall's bedroom.

'You took your time!' But she didn't seem upset. The words were automatic. Joe could tell she was as excited as the uniformed constable on the door, twitchy like one of the police dogs they sometimes worked with when it had picked up a scent.

'What have we got then?' Joe never minded feeding lines to the boss, acting as her stooge.

'Paul Keating says suicide.'

'What do *you* say?'

'Murder. Without a doubt.' She shot him a little, complicit smile. 'The doc's agreed on an early post-mortem. He'll come round to my way of thinking. In the meantime, we let the other residents think the poor man killed himself.'

She walked ahead of Joe along the corridor to the entrance hall and then up a tight, wooden staircase. 'I've taken this place over for our use. It's one of the unused bedrooms. A bit basic, but it's got a desk and we've brought up a few extra chairs.'

The royal we, Joe thought. It would be the local plod who'd done all the lifting.

Vera was still talking. 'They've even found me a spare coffee machine. A bit ancient, but it seems to work. We should be well fed too. Annie Laidler from Bread and Olives is one of the guests and I'm sure she'll have brought enough to feed an army.'

The room had two single beds, pushed against opposite walls, a desk under a north-facing window, looking out over farmland, towards a pool. There was a radiator, but it gave out little heat.

'It's a bit chilly in here.' Joe shivered to make his point.

Vera sat on one of the beds, her back to the wall, and spread out her legs, the heels of her flat, scuffed shoes on the carpet, toes pointing to the ceiling.

'Aye well, beggars can't be choosers.' She never seemed to

feel the cold. 'Stick on that coffee machine, will you? There's water already in it.'

Joe filled the filter with coffee from a jar and switched on the machine. He knew his place. Besides, he could do with a drink.

'I've had a quick word with the other residents,' Vera said. 'They'd booked the whole place for the weekend. There's one couple – the Hamptons – and three singles, the dead man, Philip Robson, who's a vicar, and Annie Laidler. Ken Hampton has Alzheimer's so he'll need careful handling. They were all at school together. Kimmerston Grammar. It's a kind of reunion. Apparently they meet up October half-term every five years. They were first here for some sort of school field trip fifty years ago. I've had a quick chat to Annie Laidler. According to her, that first weekend was called Only Connect. It must have been important for them still to be *connecting* after all this time.'

Joe thought about that. His best mates were still the people he'd gone to school with. Sal disapproved of some of them, said they were scallies, but she'd never made the mistake of trying to persuade him to keep away. 'I suppose it means they all know each other well. There shouldn't be any problems getting information on the victim.' *Possible victim.*

There was a moment of silence only broken by the coffee dripping into the jug.

'I'm not sure.' Vera was still lying back and she closed her eyes for a moment. 'It's as if they're all kids again. This weekend seems to be more about recreating those early relationships than keeping up with what's going on now. Maybe it seems safer to live in the past. A kind of nostalgia to escape a messy present. And when you're getting on a bit, it's quite nice to pretend that you're young again.'

Joe was surprised. Vera wasn't usually given to profound thought. 'You're thinking that the killer was one of them?'

Vera considered for a moment. 'Could have been an outsider. Rick Kelsall's room was on the ground floor. An old-fashioned sash window, warped a bit so the catch wouldn't fasten properly. It would have been easy enough to push it open from outside, climb in and then close it again afterwards. No sign though. That'll be down to Billy Cartwright and his team, once we've got a response from Doc Keating. His first thought was that it's definitely suicide, so that's how we treat it at the moment. We'll keep everyone away until we hear back from him, preserve the scene as best we can in case there are any finger or footwear prints on the sill. Don't think there'll be much in the garden. There's gravel just underneath the window and besides, the ground was hard with frost.'

Joe thought of the silence that had hit him when he'd first arrived. The only sound the birds, and surely they'd not be calling at night. 'Wouldn't they have heard a car?'

'Maybe, though I've seen all the bottles in the recycling bin. They'd all had a fair bit to drink.'

'How do you think he was killed?'

Vera tapped the side of her nose and looked mysterious. 'Let's wait and see, shall we? Holly is representing me at the post-mortem and she's going to ring as soon as we have an answer.'

Joe felt a brief moment of betrayal. He was Vera's second in command.

The filter machine hissed to a stop. Joe poured out coffee. There was a pile of little cartons of long-life milk in a bowl. It seemed someone had thought of everything. 'I checked Rick Kelsall out online before I set off. There've been rumours recently about his relationships with his female colleagues. Harassment claims. His show was axed.'

'You think one of the women he flirted with killed him for revenge?' Vera rolled her eyes. 'They should have been a woman in the force in the eighties.'

'More than flirting,' Joe said. 'According to an article I read, he was a bit of a bully. All the rumours flying around, his reputation ruined, his show gone, that sounds like a reason for suicide to me.'

'Maybe. Humour me for a while though.' She'd already finished the coffee and passed him her mug for a top-up. 'Let's just suppose it *was* murder. These supposed victims. One of his interns or junior colleagues. Would they really have followed him all the way to Northumberland to kill him? I'd have thought they'd have found themselves a decent lawyer and screwed him for all they could get. Revenge but without the danger of a life sentence.'

Joe didn't have an answer to that. He supposed Vera had a point.

'It's worth following up, though,' Vera conceded. 'That'll be the angle the press will go after, so we need to show we're taking it seriously. Our Superintendent Watkins does get fussed about the media. We'll get Hol onto it when she gets here. They tell me the broadband is good enough here and she's a whizz with her laptop. She'll be able to get us a list of names. Women he treated so badly that they might be tempted to string him up.'

'What do you want from me?' Joe had finished his coffee too and didn't need any more. He was already restless.

'You and I will chat to the Kimmerston Grammar old boys and girls. Let's dig into their secrets. I can't imagine that something which happened fifty years ago would have killed Rick Kelsall now, but as you said before, they know each other well.'

'Are you planning to interview them individually?'

'Not yet. The death is still unexplained at the moment and that gives us a bit of an opportunity. I don't want them clamming up, thinking of themselves as suspects. Though they will be, of course. Much more likely that one of *them* is the killer than that some mysterious stranger turned up in the early hours and climbed in through the window. That's all a bit Enid Blyton and she was out of fashion even when this bunch were growing up. We need to check the tide times first, and see if anyone *could* have made it over in the early hours of the morning. That might clinch it one way or the other. And let's speak to the island guest houses and hotels. It'd be interesting to know if any of Kelsall's harassment victims checked in for a mini-break in the North.' Vera hoisted herself to her feet. Her tone was cheery. 'Come on then, bonny lad. I think there'll be more coffee in the lounge and there was talk of home-made biscuits.'

Chapter Eleven

ANNIE LAIDLER HAD RECOGNIZED THE WOMAN detective as soon as she'd first walked into the Pilgrims' House. She was a regular customer at the deli and you couldn't miss her. It was her size and those awful clothes, as if she didn't give a shit what she looked like, or what people thought of her. That had always made Annie jealous, because after Dan, she still cared too much. Jax knew the woman better; Annie had the idea that there'd been some shared history or that Vera had once done her a favour, because often Jax served her ahead of the queue and slipped something special into the bag, a treat that was never paid for.

Now, the detective stood in the doorway, her bulk blocking the light. The group had been waiting patiently for the first hour or so, but after all this time they were starting to feel cooped up. They'd made plans for a walk and were fidgeting to be allowed out before the light went. It seemed odd to Annie that the others should be worried about something like that when Rick was dead. She could concentrate on nothing else, other than the fact that he was gone, lost to her forever. Like

Freya and Isobel. But they hadn't seen him, hanging, looking so old and so odd. And she'd probably been closer to him than any of the others.

'We were wondering if we could go out.' This was Phil, using his rich, deep vicar's voice, reasonable and conciliatory. 'Of course, it's dreadful that Rick killed himself, but I'm not sure that we can tell you much about it. I hadn't seen him for a couple of months before last night.'

The inspector moved further into the room. A slender, younger, ordinary man was standing behind her. Annie thought he'd always be in Vera's shadow. Literally and figuratively. 'This is Sergeant Ashworth,' Vera said. 'Joe. He's the one who does the real work.'

Although she was a senior detective, Annie thought of the woman as *Vera* because that was what Jax always called her, shouting at her across the crowded shop, her voice joyful as if it had made her morning that the big woman was there.

'The thing is,' Vera went on, 'until we get a final verdict from the pathologist we have to treat the death as unexplained, so I'd like a quick chat with you all. Just going through the motions. I know none of you felt like eating anything earlier, but maybe we could talk now over a late lunch? I don't see why you shouldn't go out after that though.' There was a pause and a wolfish grin. 'As long as you all stick together. We wouldn't want any of you running away.'

Annie supposed that was intended as a joke, but nobody was laughing. They were staring at the woman in silence. This woman was demanding food, but Annie wasn't sure she could eat. Because suicide was bad enough – Rick, who was so alive and confident and full of himself, no longer with them – but now the detective was implying that perhaps there was another explanation for his death. That took her back more than forty years. To another unexplained death, followed by probing questions from insensitive police officers. She wasn't sure she'd be able to bear it all over again.

All the same, the others seemed hungry. Annie had cooked a big pan of soup at home and brought it with her for Saturday lunch, and they ate that with more of Jax's bread. Annie poured a little into her bowl and pretended to eat. They were sitting, with the two police officers, at the long table in the kitchen. It was scrubbed pine, scratched and stained, and had probably been there that first time, when they'd all really got to know each other. A window let in the autumn light, which reflected from the cutlery and lit up their faces, making everyone look flat, a little unreal, actors in an old movie.

Vera ate greedily, but she still managed to ask questions.

'You've known him since he was a bairn, this Rick Kelsall. What was he like?'

Somehow then, magically, the embarrassed silence left the rest of the group and they started to talk. About Rick's energy and his charisma, his ambition to move away from the North to London. About his parents who were a bit posher than theirs. Doctors, living in a big house on the edge of the town. It was all gossip and anecdote, but Vera listened with an intensity that made Annie want to warn her friends. *Take care! She looks like a bag lady, but she's sharp. So sharp.*

'His folk were lefty liberals,' Philip said, almost back to his younger sarky self. 'They could have lived anywhere, one of the smarter parts of the county, but they liked the idea of mixing with the plebs. They liked the fact that Kimmerston Grammar had a good reputation. They could give their son a good education without compromising their principles.'

'That's a bit unkind.' Despite herself, Annie was drawn into the conversation. She'd loved the Kelsall house, with its space. Once it had probably belonged to a pit-owner. It stood on raised ground looking down at the town. After the cramped council house she shared with her parents and siblings, the airiness and the confident clutter took her breath away. There were books in piles in corners and corridors and one room had a grand piano. Rick had been able to play it, without music, just by ear. Tunes she vaguely recognized from the radio. Jazz. Blues. At Christmas, a huge tree had stood in the hallway, reaching right up to the first floor. It had taken a stepladder to decorate it, and they'd all gone to help. His parents had been easy, relaxed and had fed them wine. Her mam and dad had never drunk wine in the house.

'His parents aren't still around though?' Vera had already checked, Annie could tell. This was more about moving the conversation on, filling a slightly awkward gap.

'No, his mum died quite young, when Rick was still at university. Breast cancer, I think. His father was in sheltered housing, still very bright, very independent, until he passed away earlier this year.' Annie looked down the table. 'A couple of us went to his funeral . . .' Her voice tailed off. She was remembering the crowd at the crematorium, friends, colleagues and former patients. There'd been bright sunshine and the people who couldn't fit into the chapel had stood outside, the eulogies broadcast to them by loudspeaker. Rick had spoken of course. It had been before his public fall from grace and the audience had murmured how brave he was, how well he was holding it all together.

'Did Mr Kelsall have any siblings?'

'No,' Philip said. 'Rick was the classic only child.' His voice was sharp, almost bitter. Again, Annie thought the vicar was turning back into the spiky adolescent; thoughts of Christian charity seemed to have left him.

But you were so close. Such very good friends. Why would you bad-mouth him now?

'Meaning?' Vera turned her gaze onto him and waited for an answer.

Annie wanted to warn Philip to choose his words carefully, but just in time he seemed to remember he was a God-botherer. 'Oh, independent, confident, resilient.'

'Spoiled rotten?'

'Well, you know how it is with only kids. That's probably always the way. Inevitable.'

'No.' Vera seemed to be talking to herself and not to them. Her voice was sad. 'It's not inevitable. Not always.'

Soon after, they all headed out. They'd have coffee when they got back, they decided. The weather was too glorious to stay inside. And they wouldn't drive off to the mainland after all. The detective had made it clear that she'd prefer them to stay on the island, and besides the light would soon be fading. They'd walk out to the coast, and then head north past the lough up to Emmanuel Head to watch the long slow rollers break on the beach. They needed fresh air and to stretch their legs. *To remind ourselves that we, at least, are still alive.*

'We'll be searching your rooms.' Vera shouted this after them, when they were already kitted out with coats and boots, setting off down the lane, away from the house. 'You understand, don't you, pets? You don't mind? I can assume you've given permission?'

What could they say at that point? Rick would have stood

up to her and called her out on it, talked about warrants and civil rights, but the rest of them didn't have his courage. They looked at each other and shrugged awkwardly, then set off towards the rocky east coast.

There was a good footpath following the shore, but they saw few other people. Most day trippers stayed to the south of the island. A couple of birders with binoculars strung round their necks were scouring the ditches that ran into the lough, looking for migrants. One elderly woman in shorts and hiking boots overtook them. Their group walked slowly, adjusting their pace to Ken's, and to the pace of the elderly spaniel. Nobody spoke. Rick wouldn't have been so polite. He'd have run on, needing to get rid of his restless energy, and would have stood at the point, watching their approach, mocking them for their slowness.

Annie moved easily. She thought that working in the shop had been good for her – the lifting and reaching had kept her healthy and strong – but she was quite happy to walk in silence too. She wasn't sure what to say to the others, because surely *they* were the most likely suspects if this turned out to be murder. Her friends weren't stupid. They must realize that too.

They came to a stile and a path leading from the main track, across sheep-cropped grass through the dunes to Emmanuel Head. At the marker stone, they stood for a moment, then they climbed a giant hill of sand, and sat at the top, looking north and east. It was very clear and still, the silence broken by the cries of gulls.

'We should come here later,' Philip said. 'Look out for the northern lights. It's clear enough.'

There was no response. Annie knew that after chapel, they'd want to be in by the fire, not trekking all the way out here with the faint hope of a green light in the sky. The lights had only appeared once in the fifty years they'd been coming to the island.

The first time they'd seen Emmanuel Head had been from the sea. Miss Marshall had arranged for them to go kayaking on the Saturday afternoon of Only Connect. A break from all the talking and introspection and something else to push them out of their comfort zone, she'd said. There'd been an activity centre close to the harbour, a single instructor, who lived and operated out of one of the Herring Houses. He'd been very fit, Annie remembered, the subject of much discussion among the other girls. He'd given them a lesson and they'd paddled sedately north round the island. It had been a still day then too, but not so cold, the end of a late Indian summer.

Rick had shown off, of course. He'd paddled ahead of them, then tipped his kayak sideways using the paddle. They'd watched him perform a complete turn underwater, before righting it, dripping wet and grinning. He'd learned water sports with his dad; they were that sort of family. Back at the jetty, the instructor had been furious and had bollocked him in front of the group. Annie could still remember the man's face, as red as the logoed cagoule he was wearing.

If you want to fucking kill yourself, that's down to you, but not while I'm in charge. I've got a business to think about.

Rick hadn't been thrown at all. He hadn't been rude, or stupid, and he'd apologized. Kind of:

'I was taught you had to practise the move, in case you needed to right yourself after an accident. But I'm sorry, I should have let you know what I was planning.'

He'd stood on the jetty. His sopping clothes had made him look even more skinny, more puny, but he hadn't seemed embarrassed or humiliated by the scene. Nothing really, *had* ever got to Rick, which was why Annie now found murder easier to accept than suicide.

'Can the police really be thinking it might not be suicide?' Louisa spoke out loud, but perhaps they'd all been thinking the same thing. Ken hadn't uttered a word since they'd set out and was sitting beside his wife, one hand absently stroking Skip's neck, the other on Lou's leg. It was as if he needed something solid to hang on to, something to stop him sliding down the steep slope of sand. He was staring into the distance. Annie loved the fact that Lou didn't fuss over him, but sometimes she seemed to ignore her husband altogether. He might not have been there.

'I think it's more likely than suicide,' Annie said.

'It seems so melodramatic, so theatrical.' Lou paused. 'But I keep thinking that Rick would have loved the drama. Being absolutely the focus of all this attention.' A pause. 'He always wanted to be the star in the school play, but Philip was so much better and beat him to it.'

Then they all jumped in again, sharing memories, telling the same old stories, because if they were talking about the past, somehow they didn't have to think too much about the present.

Philip was halfway through another old chestnut – Rick and Charlotte, who were already an item then, playing lovers in a Restoration comedy with so much authenticity that the review in the *Kimmerston Gazette* had said it should be X rated – when Annie broke in:

'Oh my God. Charlotte. Someone needs to tell her.' Because Rick's ex-wife Charlotte had come north again, once her modelling career was over, and had reinvented herself as a life coach.

She ran yoga and exercise classes, and her website talked about building confidence and fulfilling one's dreams. She targeted older women, who remembered her as a celebrity, and millennials, who believed that if they wanted something enough they deserved to have it. Charlotte was still glamorous for her age and she was back in Annie's life, to the extent that she shopped at the deli and they met up occasionally for a glass of wine.

'Won't the police have done that?'

'I don't know. He'd had another wife since her, and how would they know?'

'They were in the news all the time when they *were* married.'

Annie couldn't see Vera Stanhope reading the gossip columns or trashy magazines, and the younger detective was too young to have been around when Charlotte and Rick were at their peak of newsworthiness. She got out her phone. She couldn't bear the idea of Charlotte finding out that Rick was dead through the press. When she was drunk – and despite always being in the media talking about well-being and health, Charlotte very often *was* drunk – she told Annie that Rick was the only man she'd really loved. *I'd have him back like a shot, you know. If he asked me.*

Annie looked at her phone. 'No signal. I should have known. It's crap here. We should get back now anyway, shouldn't we? See if there's any news.'

Ken suddenly moved away from Lou. He lay on his side and before his wife could stop him, he was rolling inland down the sandhill, over and over, like a small boy. The movement was completely deliberate. He must have been pondering the possibility while he was clutching on to Lou's leg.

They scrambled to their feet and chased after him, worried about his safety, because previously this weekend the dementia had made him seem clumsy and unbalanced, but really, Annie could see, there was no danger. Ken was having fun. In his head he was young again. He reached the flat sandy grassland before them, sat up and started to laugh, a huge belly laugh that was so contagious they couldn't help joining in. Philip reached down, took his hand and pulled him to his feet.

Once he was upright, Ken seemed to become confused again. He looked around for Louisa, and appeared to have found himself suddenly back in the present. Annie tried to remember if they'd rolled down the dunes like that on their first weekend. She had a vague memory of dizziness, a tangle of bodies, an excuse for illicit, exciting touching as they rolled together. Then landing in a heap, unable to get up because they were laughing so much. But the image was blurred and uncertain. Perhaps Ken's long-term memory was better than hers.

They took another route back: a path across a marshy field, inland of the lough, straight to the house. The light had faded and the sky was shades of pink and grey, and they wanted to be in the chapel just before dusk. There was a strange group superstition about being late for the gathering. Their breath was already clouding in the still air. It would be another cold night.

Chapter Twelve

HOLLY PHONED NOT LONG AFTER THE residents had headed out for their walk. Vera and Joe were in their makeshift office in the bedroom at the top of the stairs. Joe was hunched over a laptop. He wasn't as good as Holly at digging into the mysteries of the Internet, but he was a lot better than Vera.

'Dr Keating says you're right,' Holly said. 'This is definitely murder. Suffocation.'

Vera listened carefully to the details and grinned. Catching her face in the mirror over the dressing table they were now using as a desk, she thought she never looked so happy as at the beginning of a complex case. She could see the years disappearing. But Rick Kelsall had died before his time, and, really, it was no laughing matter. What was wrong with her that she could take so much pleasure in another person's death? Then she thought that the satisfaction she took in a murder investigation wasn't just about her. She was fighting, raging, for the victims who could no longer fight for themselves. This was an excuse, perhaps, but the idea made her feel better about herself.

'You'd best make your way here then,' she said to Holly. 'There's still time before the tide. It's a full murder inquiry now, so we need all hands on deck.'

Still holding the phone, she thought about sending an 'I told you so' text to Paul Keating, but after all there was no need to gloat. It was enough to know she'd been right. It was just as well she *had* been right because she'd already called in the CSIs and she'd just heard from Billy Cartwright that they were on their way. Instead, she clapped Joe on the back and told him to get the coffee machine on again, because it was going to be a long day.

This was now officially a crime scene and Vera should have closed down the whole building and sent everyone else away. She should have done that as soon as she saw the body and suspected murder. But then her witnesses would have scattered all over the country, and she might have lost track of them. Vera was a control freak, and she liked having the suspects close. The last thing she wanted was to involve another police service in a high-profile case, because leaks would be inevitable. She knew she'd keep things tight here. Besides, she'd always thought that rules were there to be stretched – almost to breaking point – and she had the excuse of the tides.

She phoned the superintendent. 'Nothing I can do, sir. I won't be able to get the potential suspects off before high water, and there's no spare accommodation on the island. It's school half-term holiday and the place is heaving.' Watkins, her boss, had grown up in the Welsh Valleys and had little understanding of the sea. He was panicking about the media – the murder of a high-profile journalist was his worst kind of nightmare – and he was more than happy to leave the details to her. Then, he'd be able to blame her if things went wrong.

She and Joe made their plans, their hands wrapped around the mugs of coffee. This was what she loved best. The beginning of an investigation when she could believe that she was the best detective in the world. She'd soon lose that confidence, but now, before the inevitable cock-up, she felt certain, on top of the world.

'Have you checked last night's tide times and the situation with accommodation?'

'Yes.' Joe was sitting in his overcoat. 'No crossing would have been possible between five p.m. and ten-thirty p.m. and then the tide covered the causeway again between six-thirty and eleven this morning.'

Vera thought about that. She'd crossed before eleven, but in the Land Rover, and half an hour earlier, even with the four-wheel drive, it would have been tricky.

'So, if the killer came from outside the island it would have been between ten-thirty in the evening and six-thirty in the morning. Or they'd arrived before high tide during the day, and waited. That doesn't help much with time of death. We already know that Kelsall must have been killed between midnight and early this morning.' Vera paused. 'Any useful information on people staying on the island?'

Joe checked his notes. 'I've only checked the pubs, hotels and B&Bs. It's harder to track down second-home owners and the holiday cottage contacts. Most of the overnight visitors are families. There was one single woman, staying in the Seahorse, but she gave her address as Kimmerston, so I don't think she can be one of Kelsall's victims.'

Vera thought Joe had missed the point. An abuse survivor planning revenge would hardly give her own name and address. 'Is she still here?'

'No. She checked out this morning and left the island very early before the tide.'

'That's a bit odd, don't you think?' Vera said. 'I can't imagine a tourist getting up that early on a Saturday morning to get off the place. Hardly worth coming just for an evening.' She looked out of the window, thoughtful. 'Have you managed to check out the Internet for information about Rick Kelsall and his relationships with his female staff?'

'I've done a bit of digging. He wasn't a very nice man, our victim.'

'In what way?'

'He was forced to resign from his recent post on the weekend politics show, when a young colleague accused him of harassment. That was early this year. More recently all sorts of past incidents have come to light.'

'What sort of incident? Anything that might have led to criminal charges?'

Joe shrugged. 'I'm still trying to get all the details. There's nothing very specific.'

'Maybe he wasn't so different from most men in the media of his generation,' Vera said. 'Entitled. Thinking he was God's gift, even though he was an old git. A bit ridiculous. Suggestive but nothing physical. Let's not judge until we know. Maybe the production company wanted an excuse to get rid, let in a bit of fresh blood. It'd be useful to talk to the woman who made the first complaint, though. If it *was* something serious and it never got to court, that would be more interesting.'

Joe nodded. 'The complainant's identity was never made public but the company will know. I'll track her down.'

'Anything else?'

'He was married twice, and had other live-in lovers. First

wife was called Charlotte, someone he went to school with. She went on to be a model in London, then a small-time actress. A bit of a celebrity at the time apparently. For a year or so they were a golden couple. I found pictures of them and their babies and their beautiful London gaff in *Hello!* magazine. Until Kelsall found himself a younger model and the dream went sour. After they separated, Charlotte moved back north.' Joe paused but Vera could tell there was more to come. Something significant. 'Her maiden name was Thomas, and she took that again when she divorced.'

That brought Vera up sharp. 'One of *the* Thomas clan?'

'Yeah, her dad was Gerald and her uncle was Robbie.'

'One-time heavies, runners of protection rackets and loan scams.' *Who never got caught. Who went on to become respectable businessmen running much of the hospitality industry in Newcastle and on the coast. Apparently reformed. Who reinvented themselves as pillars of society.* Though Vera wasn't sure she'd ever believed in reformation. They'd be very elderly today, though, even if they were still alive. She couldn't imagine them as potential hitmen these days. She looked back to Joe. 'What's the woman, this Charlotte Thomas, up to now?'

He looked up. 'She's got her own business. Calls herself a life coach. Works from a big converted pub in Kimmerston, near the river. You've probably walked past it. I remember the renovation. It's all yoga and meditation, with a bit of confidence-building and business advice thrown in.'

'How's the business doing?'

Joe shrugged. 'Hard to tell. She's got a very flash website. The business is called Only Connect.'

That struck a chord. 'Annie told me that was what that first weekend was called. The weekend that brought them all together? I presume Charlotte was a part of that too.' *And it must have been important to her. Why else would you give your business the same name?*

'I suppose so,' Joe said, but Vera could tell that he couldn't see that the name was significant. How could some school trip of the past be important to a murder in the present?

'We need to inform her of Rick Kelsall's death as soon as possible,' Vera said. 'Have we got a number for her?'

'Yeah, they sent it through from Kimmerston. Want me to do it?'

'Nah, I'll give her a ring. You carry on digging for info on Kelsall.'

Vera went outside to make the call. It was cold, but she needed a blast of fresh air to help her think straight, to clear the fog in her brain. Through one of the upstairs windows, she could see Joe, staring at the computer screen. Her boy. Her favourite. Sometime, she supposed, she'd have to release him and send him out into the world beyond her sphere of influence, but not yet. She'd miss him too much.

She'd dialled and was still thinking of Joe and how she was a selfish cow for keeping him on the team, given that his wife was so ambitious for him, when a woman answered.

'Yes. Charlotte Thomas.'

The voice was classier than Vera had expected. The Thomas family had never been exactly classy, even in their recent, respectable phase.

'This is Inspector Vera Stanhope, Northumbria Police.'

A brief moment of hesitation. The woman would have grown up with unexpected calls from the police, knocks on the door in the middle of the night, but if she'd had any anxiety at all, she covered it well.

'How can I help you, Inspector?' It was really a very lovely voice. Husky, deep.

'I'm afraid I have some bad news about your ex-husband, Richard Kelsall.' Vera stopped for a moment. She hated doing this over the phone. 'He died, either last night or in the early hours of this morning. I wonder if we might talk?'

Now the silence on the other end of the line was deep and dense. Vera waited.

'So, Rick's dead at last?' Her voice was flat.

'You don't sound surprised,' Vera said.

'I suppose I'm not. When I knew him, it was all he thought about. Dying. And living each day to the full, as if it was his last. A strange paradox. He took risks. Almost a game of dare with himself.' A pause. 'I used to joke that he was playing poker with a God he pretended not to believe in.'

Vera didn't know how to answer that or even what it meant, so she said nothing.

'How did he die?' This time, the woman's question was sharp, quite different in tone. 'Some foolish adventure? He could never accept that he'd get old eventually.'

'Where are you?' Vera asked. 'In Kimmerston?'

'No, I've been visiting a friend in the north of the county.'

'I wonder if you could come here then,' Vera said. 'I'm at a place called the Pilgrims' House on Holy Island. I prefer not to talk on the phone. Do you know it? The tide's fine for crossing until this evening and I'll make sure we're finished while it's still safe for you to get home.'

Again, that moment of hesitation. 'Yes,' Charlotte said. 'I know it. I'll come as soon as I can.'

Back in the office, they continued their search on Charlotte Thomas. Vera stood behind Joe, looking over his shoulder.

'Show me that Only Connect website. I've got no idea what a life coach is about.'

He pressed a couple more buttons. 'It says they "help their clients to fulfil their potential emotionally, physically and professionally".'

Vera thought she was none the wiser. She was still pondering the idea of fulfilling her emotional potential, when there was a noise in the road below: the CSIs and Holly arriving almost at the same time. Vera went down to meet them and gave Billy Cartwright a tour of the house.

'Can you get your guys to start in the bedrooms? The residents are out at the moment but they'll be back soon.'

'They're still staying here! Vera, are you mad? This is a murder scene.'

She shrugged. 'Doc Keating called it as suicide until he did the post-mortem and by then it was too late to bring them all back and ship them off the island.'

'You're playing games, Vera.'

But Billy liked playing games himself and he didn't make any more of a fuss. His investigators moved like white-suited bulky ghosts, silently, searching for any minute piece of evidence which might link an individual to the dead man's room. Because, as all rookie cops knew, every contact leaves a trace.

Back in the makeshift office, the conversation about Charlotte Thomas continued, but now there were three of them. 'Life coach!' Vera said. 'What a load of bollocks.'

'Not everyone's as strong as you, boss.'

Vera stared back at Holly. 'Are you saying you'd consult someone like that?'

There was a moment of silence. 'Maybe not, but I wouldn't condemn anyone who found it helpful.'

Vera stood behind Joe, so she could look at the screen, and saw a photo of a woman who'd been Rick Kelsall's first wife. She looked twenty years younger than the friends staying in the Pilgrims' House. In the picture, she was in black leggings and a black T-shirt, and the page was advertising virtual exercise. 'Is that her? It must be an old photo.'

'No,' Holly said. 'It was only taken six months ago.'

'She's worn well.' Vera struggled to keep the envy, the admiration, out of her voice.

'She's probably had work done,' Holly said.

'Ooh, not like you to be bitchy about a sister, Hol.'

They grinned at each other briefly. Sometimes, Vera thought, she could almost believe that Holly had a sense of humour. That they might end up working very well together. That Hol would become an outstanding detective.

The woman arrived in one of those flash cars, usually driven by ageing men during their mid-life crisis. A red convertible, though there wouldn't be many days in Northumberland when it would be comfortable to drive with the roof down. More fashion statement than mode of transport.

She must have left her friend soon after getting the call and looked as if she'd prepared for a photo shoot for *Homes and Gardens* rather than a country stroll with a mate: groomed, and well dressed in an understated, elegant sort of way, in jeans which would never bag at the knee and a tweed jacket. Vera watched from the window in the room they were using as an office, as the woman got out of the car, one gleaming leather boot after the other. Her loose hair could almost have been a natural blonde. The skin on her face was smooth and tight. Holly was standing beside Vera.

'She's definitely had some work done,' Holly said. 'Look at the wrinkles on her neck.'

'Meow.'

They shared another grin.

One of the uniforms showed Charlotte inside. Vera went downstairs and introduced herself. The woman even smelled expensive, of something citrus-fragranced and subtle. They walked upstairs into the makeshift office and Vera offered coffee.

'No,' Charlotte said. 'I never drink the stuff. I can't take caffeine these days. What's going on? I suppose they were all here for one of the reunions.'

'You knew about those?'

'Of course! I was here for the first weekend when we were still at school, but I didn't even stick that out until the end. Not my thing, that forced jollity. I never returned, even when Rick and I were still together. He was always closer to the others than I was. But I knew all about them.' Her back was straight but her age showed in the hands clasped on her lap, freckled with brown spots, white with tension. 'Inspector, what is going on here? There wouldn't be this fuss for a heart attack, or even a car accident.'

'No.' Vera looked at her. 'Nor for suicide, and that was what this was meant to look like.' A pause. 'Your ex-husband was murdered.'

For a moment, there was no response. Not even confusion or surprise. But perhaps the shock was so great that it took the woman a moment to process Vera's words. Then Charlotte began to laugh. It was deep, throaty and very theatrical, and Vera wasn't convinced by it at all.

'So,' Charlotte said. 'He finally provoked someone beyond

reason. I might have killed him myself, but I never had the courage.'

'Why might you have done that, Miss Thomas?'

The woman took a long time to answer. From outside the building came the conversation of the other residents returning from their walk. A snatch of laughter, which seemed to echo Charlotte's. None of them, it seemed, felt the need to put on a show of mourning for the man. Vera wondered if there'd been something about the victim that made his friends reluctant to display a sadness they couldn't quite feel. Would Rick Kelsall have mocked hypocrisy? She felt herself warming to him.

'Because he was the most self-centred bastard in the world and he treated me like shit.' A pause. 'But that didn't stop me adoring him. He made me feel more alive than I've ever been before or since. I can understand why someone would have wanted him dead, but I always had the feeling that one day he'd grow up and come back to me. And now, Inspector, that will never happen.' She stared, dry-eyed, out of the window, seeming not to notice the sound of the front door opening and the chatter of the others as they made their way into the house.

Chapter Thirteen

HOLLY HAD WATCHED THE ENCOUNTER BETWEEN Charlotte and Vera with interest. She'd arrived at this strange house unsure what she'd find. There had only been a short time to catch up with the geography of the building and its surroundings, and get a quick briefing from Joe on the residents, before this woman turned up. It struck Holly that Charlotte Thomas looked like some sort of minor film star, expecting admiration wherever she went.

Charlotte was the older woman but seemed much closer to Holly in age and outlook. Holly thought of herself as a feminist but could see how tempting it would be to have one's skin stretched, and the years erased. It was more about being taken seriously than for reasons of vanity. Holly would never consider plastic surgery to make herself attractive to men, but might if it made her seem stronger, more powerful.

Vera nodded towards the door. The house was small enough for them to hear the conversation of the people in the hall below, the sound of boots being removed and coats being hung up.

'Do you keep in touch with them all?'

'Only Annie,' Charlotte said. 'She lives not far from me. I use her deli.'

'Of course.' Vera got to her feet, suddenly brusque, almost impatient. 'I'd like you to give a statement to my colleague here. I'll see you before you go.' Then she'd left the room. For someone of her build the boss moved remarkably quickly, and Holly didn't really see her disappear.

Holly felt a moment of panic. She was completely ill-prepared. What did Vera expect of her? Here she was, alone with the woman who'd once been married to their victim, unsure whether this should be considered a formal interview or one of Vera's 'chats'. It felt like a kind of test.

To give herself time, she sat at the dressing table turned desk, found the A4 notebook she always carried in her bag, and took up her pen.

'When was the last time you saw Mr Kelsall?' It seemed as good a place as any to start.

Charlotte was sitting on one of the other kitchen chairs in the room and she crossed her legs. There was a moment's silence. She seemed to be weighing up her answer.

'Thursday.'

'This week?' Holly was surprised. She'd thought that estranged couples would keep a distance.

'Yes. Rick was driving up a day early for the reunion and he asked if he could stay.'

'Was that normal?' Holly paused. She didn't want to sound unsophisticated about other people's relationships. It might be perfectly possible for divorced people to maintain a friendship, or even more than that. But in her conversation with Vera, the woman had given no hint that she'd met Kelsall so recently.

'No. Usually his trips north were flying visits. Literally. He'd get off the plane at Newcastle, hire a car and head here to Holy Island and his friends. Always too busy to make a detour to visit me, especially now that our kids have grown up.'

'How old are your children?'

'Oh, positively middle-aged. And ridiculously successful. Sam's a photographer based in Hong Kong and Lily's a lawyer in London. Rick meets her more often. I see pictures on Facebook of drinks outside bars in fashionable parts of London, delicious meals he's obviously paid for.'

'But this time he drove and he came to see you?'

'Yes, I had a phone call from him on Wednesday lunchtime. I'd just finished leading a virtual meditation session. "You around, Lottie?" He always called me that.' Charlotte looked sad and for a moment seemed almost her real age. '"Any chance I could have a bed for the night tomorrow? Before I connect with the others. It'd be good to catch up."'

'And you agreed?' Holly wondered if perhaps, under the gloss and the sophistication, this woman was as lonely as Holly herself. Certainly, she didn't seem to have the same strong friendship group as the people staying at the Pilgrims' House. And what sort of support could her family, with their background of criminality, provide?

'Of course. I always did what he asked. I even agreed to a divorce when he wanted to marry his new delicate flower of a girlfriend, though it was the last thing I wanted.' The woman paused. 'I'd seen the press of course. All the nasty rumours, which I'm sure were at least halfway true. He'd be struggling to see that he'd done anything wrong, and Rick always needed people to love him. I thought he'd be hurting.'

'And was he?'

'He was, a bit, I think. But he was . . . he was putting on a very good show.'

'Could you take me through the evening?'

'He turned up at about six, quite hyper because he'd been sitting in the car for hours. He was always worse than the children about travelling, having to sit still. He stood just inside the door, bouncing on the balls of his feet, fizzing. I could tell he'd be fidgety all evening if he didn't get some exercise, so I suggested we go for a walk. We wandered down to the river at Kimmerston and stopped for a drink on the way home. He seemed a bit calmer by then. It was a lovely evening and we sat outside that new wine bar that opened just before the pandemic, not far from Annie's deli. The whole area has become a bit bougie lately, with little stores and craft workshops. In the summer the place came to life again, even more buzzy than before. People preferring to shop local maybe, aware of food miles, the climate emergency.'

'You didn't call in to see Annie?'

'No.' Charlotte's voice was cool. 'The shop will have been closed, and even after all this time, I wanted him to myself. We had a couple of glasses of wine and we talked. Rick seemed actually quite upbeat, considering the fact that he'd been sacked. He brushed aside the allegations of harassment. He said that the whole scandal had been triggered by an intern he'd tried to be kind to. A dreadful misunderstanding, which had got out of hand. Then, more ambitious little creatures had come out of the woodwork with their twisted stories and their lies, wanting their moment of fame. His colleagues had refused to support him, because they were scared of the management.'

'Is that how you saw it?'

Charlotte shrugged. 'Who knows? Rick could always tell a

good story, put on a brave face. But, yeah, I believed him at the time.'

'He'd been asked to resign,' Holly said. 'He'd lost his income and his reputation. He didn't seem at all upset?' She found that hard to believe. She wouldn't have been able to bear the humiliation.

'It was obviously a shock. He hated the fact that people would see him as a sordid abuser of women, but he seemed confident that he'd be able to restore his reputation in the end. It would never have been about the money. He's always made far more from his lectures and after-dinner speaking than he did from his salary. I'd guess that most of his audience would have been older businessmen who applauded his attitude to women. He validated their own dinosaur views.'

'And did *he* hold those dinosaur views?'

Charlotte took a while to answer. 'He loved women. Not as sexual objects necessarily, though I think the possibility that he might sleep with them was always close to the forefront of his mind. But he saw them as interesting beings to explore; they sparked his curiosity. He had this energy that made him reach out to them physically and emotionally. He wanted their attention. It would have been quite scary for younger women, I think. All the personal questions, the hand on the shoulder, somehow pulling them in, charming them of course, but intimidating them too.' A pause. 'He wasn't just the groper and the lecher the press has made him out to be, but I can see how he could make junior female colleagues uncomfortable, how they might feel he was making demands on them.' She paused. 'Really, Rick should have stuck with me. I understood him, and, actually, I bored him less than the others did. But he had this need for change, for excitement. He always believed that there was something much more interesting just around the corner.'

'Was there one complainant? Someone who prompted the production company to take action at last?'

There was a pause. Charlotte closed her eyes for a moment. Again, Holly thought, she was wondering how much to reveal. This time, it seemed, the woman had decided to keep the information to herself.

'I presume there was, but I can't tell you anything about her, I'm afraid. Rick didn't go into details, and the young woman has a right of privacy, don't you think?'

You know, Holly thought. *Why won't you tell?* She stared at the woman, but Charlotte remained silent. 'What did you do after your drink outside the wine bar?'

'We went back to my house.' Charlotte gave her address in a swanky street close to the river. 'I'd left a casserole in the oven. Veggie, which he turned his nose up at – he was always such a carnivore – but he ate it. We drank too much wine. Rick did that to excess too. Nothing in moderation. That was his motto.'

'Did he give any indication that he was scared, anxious?'

'No. We did what we always did when we got together. We remembered the old times.'

'When you were married?'

'No.' Charlotte smiled. 'There was nothing so good about *those* days. Things were already starting to fall apart. Before that. When we were still at school. He loved talking about those times. His glory days, I suppose, when everyone really did love him.' A pause. 'I'd heard most of the anecdotes before, of course, but he seemed even more fixated on the past than usual. He told me that he was writing a novel. He was very excited about it. The idea had been sparked, he said, by things that had happened when we were all very young. He was looking forward to going back to Holy Island, because that was where it had all started. He was like the old Rick, excited, buzzing, full of ideas. "Just you see, Lottie," he said. "You'll understand everything in a new light."'

'What did he mean?'

Charlotte shrugged. 'I don't know. I was just surprised, I suppose, that he was taking all the bad press so well.'

Holly couldn't see that stories of fifty years ago could have triggered the violent death of an elderly man, but she jotted that down anyway. Just in case. Vera liked the detail of an investigation. It was the boss's strength, but also her weakness. She could dig away at the tiny details, losing sight of the overall picture. The past was her territory. She always said it explained the tensions and stresses of the present. Holly had learned more about Vera's past during the recent Brockburn investigation, and perhaps it had made more sense of the woman.

'He wanted to sleep with me.' Charlotte was talking again. 'At least he said he did. He knew I'd say no. I've got a bit more pride these days. And I'm not sure he'd have asked if he thought I'd say yes.' A pause. 'So, it was just a goodnight kiss in front of the fire. Very chaste. Rather romantic.' She looked up. 'We were in bed by about one. That's quite early for Rick. I suspect he stayed awake for a while checking his phone for the news. He was a news junkie.'

Holly nodded. 'And the next day?'

'I didn't have any work commitments until the afternoon, so we had a late breakfast. Halfway through his phone rang. He seemed pleased to get the call and went into the other room to take it. *Sorry, darling. Confidential.* Turning it into a drama, though it was probably routine.'

Holly wrote that down too. They'd be able to check the identity of the caller.

'Soon after that he said he should head off. There was someone he had to see, before meeting the others here at the Pilgrims' House. Being mysterious all over again, just for show. He asked me if I wanted to join the group for the weekend. I told him I had work to do, and anyway, I'd rather stick pins in my eyes. I'd had quite enough of Rick's reminiscences the night before. So, there was the obligatory farewell kiss and off he went.' Charlotte sat back in the uncomfortable chair.

'You seem very dismissive of Mr Kelsall's nostalgia for your schooldays, yet you named your business after the time you spent here as teenagers, the weekend when you all became close friends.'

Charlotte briefly closed her eyes again. 'Only Connect? There is nothing nostalgic about that, Constable. It is, I suppose, a mission statement for the company. Our whole ethos is about bringing together the mind and the body, connecting our clients with their real ambitions and helping them to realize them in reality.'

A phrase of Vera's came, unbidden, into Holly's head. *What a load of bollocks!* 'You seem very passionate about the business.'

'Oh I am.'

'So, you have no plans to retire?'

Charlotte smiled. 'Absolutely not! I suppose I'm of an age when I should be thinking of retirement, but I can think of nothing worse. I'm terrified of boredom. I need something to get up for every morning. I'm really not a good works and coffee morning sort of woman.' She paused. 'My father was still running his own business into his seventies.'

'You never considered working with your family?'

There was a pause before Charlotte gave a wintry smile. 'I did for a while, when I first came back to the North-East, but it didn't quite work out.'

'Why was that? Perhaps you didn't approve of your father's business practices?'

'I'm not quite sure what you're implying, Constable.' Charlotte's voice was sharp. 'And I can't see how my family's companies can have any relevance at all to my ex-husband's murder.'

'Your father and your uncle had a reputation for violence.' Holly tried to keep her tone even. 'You can understand why I'm exploring the matter. If Mr Kelsall treated you badly, perhaps one of your family members felt he had a score to settle.'

'None of my relatives has ever been convicted of a criminal offence.' The voice was firm. If Charlotte was rattled, she wasn't showing it. 'And while my father might well have wanted to kill Rick when he ditched me for another woman, that was a very long time ago. He considers now that I'm much better off without the man.' She paused. 'Besides, Dad's very elderly, very frail. He moved in with my sister nearly a year ago and he seldom leaves the house.'

'You don't have any idea where Mr Kelsall might have gone yesterday morning?' Because, Holly thought, the woman would have *wanted* to know, even if she couldn't bring herself to ask. Her love for Rick Kelsall was a scab that needed scratching. Though they might have been divorced for years, she still seemed to be jealous, and to want to be a part of his life.

'No.' Charlotte paused. 'It could have had nothing at all to do with the phone call. He might have gone to Kimmerston cemetery. He sometimes did that if he had time when he was home. It had become a morbid kind of sanctuary for him. He said it brought him peace, though I think there was more to it than that. The idea of all those bodies under his feet gave him an odd thrill. I told the inspector. It seemed as if he was obsessed with death.'

Holly didn't know what to say. For an uneasy moment she seemed to have lost her way in the interview. To cover her confusion, she returned to the easy formula.

'What were you doing yesterday night and early this morning?'

Charlotte must have been expecting the question because she gave another little smile. 'You're asking if I have an alibi for the time Rick was killed? I'm afraid I can't help you. I had a number of online meetings in the afternoon and then I went home. I ate the remains of the casserole and I had an early night. I always find Rick's energy exhausting.'

'You didn't make any phone calls or send any emails overnight?'

'To prove that I was at home? Certainly not, Constable. I'm a great believer in proper sleep hygiene. All screens are switched off an hour before bedtime. If you look at the Only Connect website you'll see it's what we tell our clients, and I have to practise what I preach.'

'And early this morning?'

'I went for a run before breakfast. Just as it was getting light. It was rather a beautiful dawn, if a little icy under foot. One of my neighbours might have seen me.'

Now Holly did set down her pen and she got to her feet.

'Thank you, Miss Thomas. We know where to find you if we have more questions.'

Charlotte stood up slowly, making it clear she was in no hurry to leave, that in no sense at all was she running away.

'Was Mr Kelsall visiting any specific grave in the cemetery?' The thought had come into Holly's head very suddenly. Her flat overlooked a big cemetery in Newcastle, but she'd chosen it for the peace and quiet. She couldn't imagine wandering around it to get a thrill from being so close to the dead. 'His mother and father perhaps?'

'No.' Charlotte paused for a moment. 'A friend. Isobel Hall. She died on the island too. At least on her way back from here. I was working in the South, so I only heard about the accident second hand, but the others will be able to give you the details. It happened at the first five-year reunion. She was one of my best friends. It's one of the reasons why I never come back to the Pilgrims' House with the others. It seems in such very poor taste to be celebrating when she's not here.'

Again, Holly was left floundering for something to say. Charlotte walked out through the door and Holly heard her footsteps, firm on the stairs. She wondered if the woman would make some attempt to see the residents, the close friends of her former husband. A gentle buzz of conversation was coming from the common room. But Charlotte left by the front door, and walked straight to her car. Perhaps she was in a hurry, anxious about being stranded on the island as the tide came in. Perhaps, for some reason, she wanted to avoid them.

Chapter Fourteen

IN THE KITCHEN, ANNIE WAS ORGANIZING tea and cakes. She focused on arranging Jax's magnificent baking prettily on the plates, trying to push out of her mind the picture of Rick Kelsall, hanging from a beam in the bedroom at the end of the corridor. The grey, thin hair on his chest, the staring eyes.

The others had come back from their walk with an appetite, and had decided they'd just have time for a late afternoon tea before heading to the chapel. The shock of Rick's death had left them quiet, subdued, but with a need for routine, to do what they'd always done. It provided a reassurance perhaps that life could continue without him.

Annie had once again refused their offers of help. She felt at ease in the kitchen and after the company of the walk, she needed a moment alone. Besides, Philip would take responsibility for supper. Another tradition. She imagined it would be vegetarian, probably shepherd's pie, his usual standby and easy to make in advance. There was a dish, wrapped in foil, in the fridge. Rick would have teased and claimed a desire for steak or a venison stew, though he'd never volunteered to cook. His contribution had always been the cases of wine.

She carried a tray to the common room where the others were waiting. Someone had revived the fire. The curtains were still open, although it would be dark in an hour. This far north, evening descended quickly at this time of year; soon, it would be winter.

Charlotte had gone. She'd done a little wave at Annie through the window before getting into her car, but hadn't joined them. Annie thought of the last time they'd met up. Charlotte had called into the deli just on closing time.

'Come for a drink with me, darling. I'm *so* bored.' The implication was of course that Charlotte would *have* to be bored to want Annie's company.

It had been the summer, and they'd sat in a pub, drinking pints as if they were students again, and ordering, but not eating much of, a dreadful lasagne. As usual, the talk had returned to the past.

Later, after the second pint, Charlotte had moaned about her business, about how difficult it was for people in a parochial place like Kimmerston to open their minds to the changes that a life coach could make. She hadn't asked Annie any questions about her life, but Annie hadn't minded that. It had been quite relaxing to sit there, getting quietly drunk, listening to the murmur of Charlotte's complaints.

Now, in the Pilgrims' House common room, Annie poured tea and handed around mugs and milk. Vera Stanhope and Joe Ashworth appeared at the door. Annie couldn't help smiling. Vera seemed to have an almost spooky ability to tell when food was being served.

'Ooh, is that one of Jax's coffee and walnut slices?' Vera had already taken a piece from the tray and was holding it with a paper napkin, triumphant as if she'd had to fight the others off for it. She stood in front of them, with her bum to the fire, blocking out most of the heat, and set the cake carefully on the mantelpiece.

'We'll need statements from each of you,' she said. 'Best to do it today, while everything's still clear in your mind, and so you can leave in the morning.' She beamed widely and then she had a mouth full of traybake, so the words that followed were only just intelligible. 'So, we'll start as soon as you like in the spare room upstairs. Holly's using it at the moment, but I think she's just finished. Annie, do you want to come first, pet? You can bring your tea.'

'I can't come now,' Annie said. 'It's nearly time for chapel.'

'Chapel?' Vera seemed bewildered and amused at the same time.

'It's a condition of using the Pilgrims' Retreat House. Chapel every evening at dusk. I'm sorry, we can't miss it. It's only twenty minutes.'

'And do you do the whole thing? A service. Prayers and hymns? On your knees and up on your feet? The glorified hokey-cokey?'

'Nothing like that.' Philip broke into the conversation. He too seemed amused. Certainly, he wasn't offended. Perhaps he saw Vera as a possible convert. A challenge at least. 'It's a period of silent meditation. But those of us with faith use it as a chance to pray.'

'Eeh, this case is so complicated, I could do with a period of peaceful contemplation, myself. Is it okay if I join you?'

'Of course, Inspector. You'd be very welcome.'

They got dressed in their outdoor clothes and trooped out

into the chilly evening, walking slowly, two by two, as if they were real pilgrims, or the monks who'd lived on the island centuries before. Philip lit the candles. They sat in silence, but Annie couldn't feel the peace that usually came with the place. She was aware of Vera Stanhope, sitting in the same pew as her, watching them all with her bright, conker-brown eyes.

Later, walking back to the house, in the chill, clear air, which took her breath away, Annie found Vera beside her once again.

'You're all right to give your statement first? We'll go on up, shall we?'

It wasn't really a question and Annie could do nothing but follow in Vera's wake, like a small tug in the shadow of a giant liner.

A woman in her thirties was in the room, tapping on a laptop. She was wearing office clothes and had an expensive haircut, short and a little severe. Practical, Annie supposed, for a police officer.

'This is our Hol,' Vera said. 'She's part of the team.'

The woman looked up, gave Annie a brief nod, then turned her attention to Vera. 'I could do with a word, boss.'

'Why don't you grab yourself a cuppa and some cake if there's any left? I'll just have a chat to Annie here, and then I'm all yours.'

Annie thought the words were tactless, dismissive, and not the way a boss should talk to a younger colleague, but the constable seemed to take it in her stride. She nodded again and left the room. Vera sat heavily on a chair, which had been carried from the kitchen, and gestured for Annie to take the one opposite.

'So,' she said. 'Tell me about all the people here. Why do

you think one of them might have wanted to kill your old friend Rick?'

Annie was lost for words for a moment. Besides the shock generated by the question, she felt this was not the way a police interview should be conducted. Again it seemed that she was being encouraged to respond in a certain way.

'I don't think any one of us would have wanted to kill him! He was a friend.'

'You're telling me that the perpetrator was some random stranger, who drove out to a tidal island in wildest Northumberland in the middle of the night? You don't think that's even more improbable?' Vera gave a little smile and fixed Annie with a stare.

'Rick had enemies,' Annie said at last, 'but that was all to do with his work.'

'Tell me about this bunch, just the same. Your gang from the school. It was a comprehensive by the time I went there, but I believe it was a grammar in your day?'

'Yes.' Annie tried to gather her thoughts, to decide how much should be shared. Vera seemed to squeeze the air from her. She was finding it hard to breathe, as if she was walking into a gale.

'But it's not the usual school reunion. Not everyone's invited. Only some of the people who were here at the Pilgrims' House for that bonding weekend fifty years ago?'

Annie nodded. 'There was this young teacher, straight from college. She taught English and drama and came with all these new ideas about self-expression. How we should all try to understand each other. She was very intense. Charismatic in a vaguely spiritual way. Perhaps everyone was a bit new age then, trying to find themselves, but it was

103

new to us. A kind of revelation. So, she brought a dozen of the new sixth form here, split us up into two groups, asked us to trust each other and to be completely honest. A kind of prolonged encounter session. I think the others thought it was a bit of a joke, but our group took it seriously and became very close.'

Annie looked up at Vera. 'I suppose it was all self-indulgent nonsense, dangerous even, playing with young people's psyches, but it seemed very important to us then. It changed the way we looked at the world and each other.' She paused. It seemed important to explain. 'It was the early seventies. A different time. School was still strict; we were all supposed to conform. And then this teacher came along who encouraged us to be open and honest. Suddenly feelings mattered. That stayed with us.'

'And the name of the teacher?'

'Judy Marshall.'

'Is she still around, do you know?'

Annie nodded. 'Yes, she comes into the deli. She retired a while ago. I'm not sure she'd enjoy the way education has gone now. According to Lou, it's all tests and results.'

'And how many of this gang were there on that first weekend?'

'Rick was there with Charlotte, his girlfriend of the time.'

Vera nodded. 'I've just met her.'

'Philip and Ken.'

'Philip the vicar and Ken is the poor guy with dementia.'

'Yes. Louisa, Ken's wife, was at school with us, but she was younger and wasn't invited to Only Connect.'

'What's the significance of that name?'

'It was Miss Marshall's idea. She taught us A-level English

and it's a quote from a book we were reading for the exams. *Howard's End*. E. M. Forster.'

Vera nodded as if the book were entirely familiar to her. 'Anyone else part of your special gang? Anyone who doesn't come to these reunions?'

'My ex-husband, Daniel. He was there that first time too.' Annie wasn't sure what else to say about Daniel. 'He still lives locally. He joined the family business. He thinks the whole idea of the reunion's daft. He only came back once, to the first reunion, even when we were married.'

'Is he Daniel Laidler?'

'No, I went back to using my maiden name when he left.' Annie paused. 'He's Daniel Rede.'

'And that was it? Just the six of you in your gang?'

Annie was tempted to lie, but Vera's stare seemed to pierce the skin and bone of her skull, enter her brain and read her mind. 'There was another lass, she was in the other group for Only Connect but she hung out with us. Isobel Hall. Issy. She was there for the first reunion. She's dead now though.'

'Oh?' Just a tip of the head, but Vera was demanding an answer.

'A road accident.'

'And when was that?'

'Five years after Only Connect.'

'So, she died at your first reunion?'

This woman was quick, Annie thought. She hoped the others didn't under-estimate her. 'Yes. Well, not quite. Not in the house here. She was on her way home and crashed off the causeway, just before the tide. No other vehicle was involved, according to the police. They think she must have braked suddenly for some reason, and that the road was slippery with seaweed. Her parents were distraught.' Annie paused again and looked at Vera. 'She was Louisa's older sister. Louisa was at that first reunion, because she'd already hooked up to Ken by then, but she wasn't in Isobel's car. Ken had offered to give her a lift home later.'

Annie remembered Isobel's funeral. No dark clothes, her parents had said. It should be a celebration of their beautiful daughter's life. But it had rained and it hadn't properly got light all day, and the bright coats and scarves had been drained of colour. The small church had been full, so the younger mourners had stood outside under the dripping trees to make room for the rest, listening to the service through the open door. Louisa had been inside, of course, the loyal Ken sitting next to her, holding her hand, belting out the hymns with his glorious tenor.

Vera was speaking now, breaking into the memory. 'Nobody would have born a grudge though for Isobel's death, not after all these years. And why would they have blamed Rick Kelsall?'

Again, Annie hesitated. She could shrug and pretend she had no idea what might have led up to Isobel's accident, but again, she thought this woman would find out the truth, and it would be terrible to be caught out in a lie. A sin of omission at least.

'Rick and Isobel had been bickering on and off all weekend. Not all that serious. Kind of jokey remarks, picking at each other. They were very similar really.' Thinking about it now, Annie thought Isobel had been a female version of Rick. No wonder the sparks had flown. She saw that Vera was waiting for her to continue. 'Then that morning there was an enormous row. They were outside the house and I could see there was some sort of confrontation. Suddenly Isobel drove off in a huff. Upset. Too fast, not concentrating and too close to the tide. The rest of us had decided to wait until later in the afternoon once the causeway was clear.' She looked directly at Vera, willing her to understand. 'But we didn't tell anyone about the argument. Not the police or Isobel's parents. It wouldn't have helped. Better for people to think it was just a tragic accident, not that Isobel had flounced off in one of her tempers.'

'Well, it certainly wouldn't have helped your pal Rick.' Vera's words were hard. 'He'd just be starting off on his career. Out of university and with stardom waiting. It might have made things a bit easier for the lass's parents to understand how it happened.'

'Perhaps. We didn't think so at the time. Knowing that she'd died, after a row with a close friend, feeling angry and unloved. That seemed unkind.'

Vera nodded, accepting that the argument might have some validity. 'Maybe. It's always dangerous to play with the truth though. Playing God.'

Annie thought Vera wouldn't mind playing God if she believed she could get away with it.

The detective stared at her. 'Did you know what the row was about?'

Annie shook her head. 'None of us could understand it. Usually, they got on okay. But he could be cruel if he was in one of his moods. They seemed to be getting on okay for most of the weekend. Like I said, there was the occasional sniping, a kind of banter, earlier on, but nothing serious. In a way, it was almost intimate.' Annie paused and then chose her words carefully. 'I wondered if they'd been having some sort of fling, and he ended it on that Sunday morning. He was already engaged to Charlotte by then. Isobel wasn't used to rejection. I can see how she might have kicked off.'

Vera nodded. 'Well, the man seems to have a history of playing with women's affections, though from what I can tell, he's been bullying his most recent victims, harassing rather than rejecting them. You say Louisa was there, that weekend her sister died. Did she know about the row? Her sister storming off in a hurry?'

Again, Annie found her mind tracking back to that first reunion weekend. They'd all graduated and thought themselves so grown-up. On the brink of an adventure. It was the mid-seventies. There'd been a drought all summer and the ground had dried hard as concrete, and even in October they'd been waiting for rain. Rick had already announced his engagement to Charlotte, but she wasn't at the Pilgrims' House. She'd said something urgent had come up. Some audition or casting. Or perhaps that was an excuse and she was at home with her rich scally family. Louisa had been there with Ken. Rick had teased them all weekend. *You two still together. My God, you're positively middle-aged.* And Dan had been resentful and brooding because the weekend hadn't been as much fun as he'd hoped. Or because he was grieving as much as her. She'd only recently come to realize that might have been the case.

'Yes,' Annie said. 'Louisa was there. But she didn't see the argument. She was out for a romantic walk with Ken, and when they came back, they announced that they were engaged. We'd just started celebrating when one of the islanders rushed in to tell us about the accident.' A pause. 'We didn't tell Lou or Ken about the row either. It was bad timing as it was, and we didn't want to make things worse. We kept it as a secret between us. Rick, Philip, Daniel and me.' She hesitated again. 'Daniel wasn't there when they were arguing, but I told him later.'

'And you've kept the secret all this time?'

'Yes!' Again, Annie took time to choose her words carefully. 'We've never talked about it. Not even among ourselves.'

Vera looked at her. 'Well, *you* might not have blabbed, but I don't see how you can vouch for the others.'

'I know them. They wouldn't.' But Annie wasn't really sure about that. There was nothing Rick liked better than telling stories. He'd been doing it the night before he died, entertaining them all with tales of his exploits with Miss Marshall. And Philip might have used Isobel's death in a narrative of his own, to make some sort of point. What was a sermon, after all, if not a story?

'Last night,' the inspector went on, 'Rick wasn't doing the same thing, was he? Teasing, picking on one of you, being cruel as he had been to your friend Isobel all that time ago?'

Annie shook her head. 'No, he didn't treat us like that. Besides, we'd known him too long to be upset by that sort of behaviour. We'd have called him out on it, given as good as we got.'

'But he could still be badly behaved with young lasses, it seems. Apparently, he thought he was a ladies' man. I gather he was a little old-fashioned in his dealings with women. One of those men that think banter is okay even if it's offensive.'

'Not with us.' Annie made sure her voice was firm. 'He's always the perfect gentleman these days. A good friend.'

'And in the past?'

Annie had a memory of Rick at a party, outside in the garden on a summer's night, pushing her against a wall, hands everywhere. But that had been her fault, hadn't it? She'd probably encouraged him to think it was what she'd wanted. And in one sense she *had* wanted it, had been flattered by the attention. Things had seemed very different then.

'Not then either. Not with me.'

Vera shot her a look, sceptical, but then she moved on. 'Let's just speculate for a moment, shall we? Let's say that one of these people staying here killed Rick. Who would be the most likely? Which of them would have the nerve to hold a cushion over his face, squeezing the air from his lungs, listening to him fighting for breath, and then to string him up to make it look like suicide?'

Annie felt sick. She took a deep breath, then, despite herself, she found herself playing along. 'Not Philip,' she said. 'When he was younger, he had a temper and he could be a bit chippy. But not since he was born again and found religion.'

'Now he's all sweetness and light?'

Annie grinned. 'He is rather. It makes you sick.'

'So that leaves Ken and Louisa.' Vera stopped. 'And you!'

'Rick had a thing about Louisa once he and Charlotte split up. This time, it was a bit different from his usual attempts at seduction. He claimed to love her. Ken was always so laid back he was horizontal, but even he got a bit pissed off.' Annie thought this was safe territory, because not even Vera could think that Ken, who could now barely remember his wife's name, would have the ability to have killed Rick.

'Years ago, was that?'

'Well, it started years ago, but I think Rick turned on the routine every time they met. Blatant, not trying to hide it from Ken. It was kind of jokey: *Come on, Lou! Have a bit of excitement for once in your life. Ken's a lovely guy, but a bit boring. A bit safe.*'

'But not really a joke?'

'I don't know. Perhaps a joke in bad taste.'

There was a moment of silence before Vera spoke again. 'It seems to me that you're pointing me in the direction of someone we know was unlikely to be a killer. Who are you protecting, I wonder? One of your friends? Or yourself?'

Chapter Fifteen

PHILIP WAS INTERVIEWED BY THE YOUNG female detective. She seemed tense, not nervous exactly, but focused, determined to get this right. He thought she felt she had something to prove. He found himself trying to put her at her ease – a habit that went with his job – and perhaps because of that, he was less cautious with his answers than he might have been.

They were in a corner of the common room. Louisa and Ken were upstairs, talking with the sergeant.

'A young woman died here during your first reunion,' DC Clarke said. 'Can you tell me what happened?'

'She drove out too close to the tide, and the car was swept from the causeway. A terrible accident. She was just twenty-two.' He paused. 'She was Louisa's older sister.'

'What led up to it?'

Philip couldn't quite understand how this might be relevant, but it was easier to talk about Isobel than to think through the implications of Rick's death.

'There was some sort of argument with Rick. I couldn't

hear what was said. They were out in the lane and I was watching from one of the rooms upstairs.'

'Could you guess what they were fighting about?'

'Isobel was a little spoiled. She was pretty and bright, and her parents doted on her. I sometimes felt sorry for Lou, who seemed always to be in her shadow. Issy had just graduated with a first from university and her dad had bought her a car. She really believed she could have anything she wanted.'

'And what *did* she want?'

'Rick,' Philip said. 'I think she wanted him, that perhaps there had been some sort of fling on the island that weekend. But Rick was engaged to Charlotte, and there were already plans for the very grand wedding. He would have made it clear that anything that had happened between him and Isobel wasn't serious.' He looked up at the detective. 'She just drove off. As if somehow, she could control the tide, as well as the rest of her life.'

'It must have been a terrible shock.'

'It was. In a way I suppose it locked the rest of us together.' For some reason, he wanted this young detective to understand. 'It changed me, certainly. Afterwards, we sat in the chapel and I had a glimpse of something different. Something beyond the everyday. A new way of living. In the tragedy, there was intense joy too.'

'A religious experience?'

'Yes,' he said simply. 'Exactly that. So of course, I regret the tragedy of an early death, but in a strange way I'm grateful for it too.'

'You were all close before that,' the detective said. 'Because of Only Connect, the weekend you spent here?'

Philip nodded. He shut his eyes briefly. 'Very close. Intense, as only the young can be. We thought we were the first generation to be so open, so honest, though of course our parents had lived through the war, and they must have formed intense relationships too. They were close to death every day.' He looked again at the woman. 'We'd become very selfish. For us, it was glorious parties, hours discussing music and books, too much alcohol.' A pause. 'I saw that, in the moment in the chapel after Isobel's death. I realized there was another way.'

'You remained friends with the others, although they didn't share your faith.'

Philip laughed. 'Of course! Rick was still as close as a brother. And I gave up trying to convert him years ago!'

'When did you last see him?'

'A couple of months ago. He'd just been told to resign. He was very low. He didn't think he'd done anything wrong. *I wouldn't have upset those girls for the world, Phil.* This weekend, he seemed much brighter. Optimistic. Happy. He had a new project. He'd decided to write a novel, and he was full of it. That's why his suicide came as such a shock.'

'He didn't kill himself,' the detective said. 'It was murder.' Her voice was cold, flat. She was stating a fact, nothing more. But Philip felt as if his world was falling apart.

Chapter Sixteen

JOE STOOD OUTSIDE THE PILGRIMS' HOUSE for a moment and looked out at the stars. There was no real front garden, only a strip of grass next to the lane and a white bench leaning against the wall of the house. All the land was at the back. He'd been interviewing Louisa and Ken Hampton, and something about the ill man had moved him almost to tears. Ken had held his wife's hand throughout the conversation, had smiled occasionally, but hadn't spoken. He was still physically big, but now he seemed entirely passive and dependent, a giant, compliant child. Joe had let himself out of the building before Vera could start asking questions about the interview – he wasn't ready yet to replay it for her – but now, standing with his back to the house, the cold air seemed to clear his mind of the discomfort, the upset.

There were no street lights here and they'd shut the curtains in the house, so no light seeped out. Joe didn't have Vera's affection for wild spaces, for the great outdoors, but there *was* something spectacular about this: so many stars and a sense of the darkness stretching for ever, that made him dizzy and a little scared. He'd been brought up as a Methodist and they still took the kids to church when they had a free Sunday, but he wasn't sure his faith was strong enough to cope with this emptiness. The size of it all. His insignificance in comparison.

He heard the door open again and saw Holly standing next to the bench. 'The boss wants us in. A final meeting before calling it a night.' She shivered and he only realized just how cold it was then. It would freeze again in the night, and be another clear day when the sun came up in the morning.

'I just needed a moment,' Joe said, 'after talking to the Hamptons. It must be so hard for them both.'

Holly stood behind him. She was looking up at the stars too. 'It happened to my grandmother,' she said. 'Dementia. It's horribly common, but somehow we never think it'll happen to us.'

'Harder for the relatives maybe, than the sufferer.' But Joe thought that couldn't really be true. He'd rather die than be like Ken Hampton, lost and confused, the object of pity.

Holly touched his arm. She seemed to realize that he was deep in thought. 'We'd better get in. Can't keep madam waiting.' They shared a quick grin and made their way into the house.

Vera was in the bedroom they'd made their base. The filter machine was gurgling, dripping coffee, and now three chairs were placed around the desk. They sat very close to each other, with their knees almost touching. The boss had interviewed Annie Laidler, Joe had spoken to Louisa and Ken as a couple and Holly had taken on the vicar. The friends had had their dinner, and now they were all back together, sitting in the common room, talking quietly. Drinking Rick Kelsall's wine. Joe supposed they'd be sharing the experience of the interviews, checking that their stories matched. He thought suddenly that this investigation, involving a group of elderly people, might turn out to be the weirdest he'd ever been involved with.

'Are you letting them all go in the morning?' Holly was doing the honours with the coffee and set three mugs on the low table. Joe put his hands around his mug, letting the warmth defrost his fingers.

'They shouldn't still be here anyway. Even with Rick Kelsall's room sealed they're contaminating a crime scene. Besides, we can't really keep them.' But Vera sounded reluctant. Joe could tell she would *like* to keep them local. She went on: 'I can't see any of them making a run for it, can you?'

Joe shook his head. 'They've all got too many ties at home.'

'Not just that! They're bright. They were grammar school kids. Nothing would point to guilt like doing a runner.' Vera paused. 'Ken and Louisa live just over the border in Cumbria, so it'd be easy enough to go back to see them if we need to. I wonder if we could persuade the vicar to extend his holiday for a few days, stay in the county. Worth a shot, I think.'

'You really think one of this group killed him?' Joe couldn't see it. They were all so respectable. The only chancer among them had been the victim.

'I don't *think* anything this early in an investigation.' A pause. 'Joe, when you spoke to the Hamptons, did Louisa mention anything about a sister?'

'No.' He was puzzled and couldn't see where this was leading.

'Charlotte talked about a sister who died at the first reunion,' Holly said, 'and I followed it up with the vicar.'

'Annie Laidler gave me the details too. The lass's name was Isobel and she was part of the original Only Connect group. Is it odd, do we think, that Louisa didn't mention the accident?

Her only sister dying too, at one of these navel-gazing gath-erings.' Vera paused before answering her own question. 'Maybe not. We shouldn't read too much into it. After all this time, Louisa might not have thought it was relevant. *I'm* interested though, because Annie said the death occurred immediately after Isobel had a row with Rick Kelsall. Let's get more details of the incident, shall we? There must have been an inquest. I can't see Louisa waiting more than forty years to avenge her sister, but we've got bugger all else to go on.'

She stretched her legs and stifled a yawn. 'Anything useful from the vicar, Hol?'

Holly shook her head. 'Not much. Kelsall went to see him soon after he was forced to resign, but claimed there was no truth to the women's allegations.'

'Well, he would,' Vera said. 'It doesn't get us any further forward.' She gave them both a mischievous glance. 'The whole bunch of them could be in it together of course. Like that film. The train stuck in the snow. We'd never find out if they kept to their stories.'

'But why would they? I can't see that any of them has a motive.'

'How would we know? Unless one of them broke ranks and gave us the low-down.'

Holly looked across at her, very serious. 'Do you really think that was how it happened?'

'Nah,' Vera said. 'Not really. But they're close. Mates. They'll be protecting each other. Keeping secrets. Which might or might not be relevant. Anything else from the jolly vicar?'

Holly shook her head. 'A bit more background on the victim. Because they both lived in London, Rick saw him more frequently than the others. Philip was still a good friend and they'd meet for a drink every now and again. And Rick was writing a book. Charlotte mentioned that too.'

Vera nodded. 'That's interesting. Something else to chase up with Rick's former employer.' She looked across at Joe. 'You were researching that earlier. Did you manage to find someone at the production company willing to talk?'

'Sorry,' he said. 'I didn't get anywhere. Most of the staff aren't working this weekend and when I did get a response, nobody was willing to give out personal contact details.'

The women looked at him. Joe thought they were both thinking that Holly would have done better. This was confirmed when Vera spoke again. 'You take that on, will you, Hol? We need the name of the first woman to make the complaint against Rick Kelsall. The one who started the ball rolling, and lost him his job. I know victims of sexual assault have the privilege of anonymity but we really need to speak to her.'

'Sure, boss.' There was a definite edge of triumph in Holly's voice. There were times when Joe felt as he had in the classroom, when all his pals had seemed brighter than he was.

'How did you get on with Louisa and Ken, Joe?'

'Well, it was Louisa who did all the talking. Ken nodded every now and again as if he agreed, but I wasn't sure he understood the questions.'

'Anything useful?'

'Nothing new at all. As you said, the couple live in Cumbria and they drove over, arriving early afternoon on Friday. Rick was already in the house. Louisa said he seemed in very good spirits. She was surprised after all the fuss in the press.'

'When was the last time they'd seen him? Before this weekend.'

Joe thought back to the conversation. The woman, controlled, upright, and the big man with his hand covering hers on the arm of her chair. 'In the summer. They went to London for a few days. Ken had already been diagnosed with dementia, and they wanted to do things like that while they still could. One of their kids lives and works in the City, and they stayed with him. They met Rick for a meal. He was already feeling under pressure at work then, apparently. Louisa said he seemed anxious, but more worried that anything he'd said might have been misinterpreted. *You know I wouldn't want to offend anyone for the world. You understand that, don't you, Lou? Sometimes I get carried away, that's all.*' Joe looked up. 'That almost sounded like an admission to me, though at that point no specific allegations had been made.'

'According to Annie, Rick always had a soft spot for Louisa. He fancied himself in love.' Vera hesitated for a moment. 'Or maybe he just lusted after her. Did that come across?'

Joe shook his head. 'But I don't think she'd have responded. She appears very level-headed.' A pause. 'A bit cold maybe. Former head teacher. Ambitious. She was sent in to run schools in special measures. Now she does some work for Ofsted, assessing other teachers. You could tell she looks after her husband well, but there's not a lot of warmth there.' He paused. 'It all seemed a bit mechanical.'

'Aye well, I suppose the wife knows she's in it for the long haul. You have to keep back a bit in reserve.'

Joe remembered then that Vera's dad had suffered from dementia in the end and she'd moved back home to help care for him until he died. 'Just before they both left,' he said, 'I asked one question to Ken, directed it only to him. Louisa was already halfway out of the room. I asked him what he made of Rick.'

'And?' That was Holly.

Joe could tell Hol was getting impatient now, because he was the one doing most of the talking. He could understand her impatience. He'd been hoping he'd be able to get home tonight. It was the last weekend of half-term and Sal always got a bit scratchy by the end of the school holidays. But they'd missed the tide and they'd have to stay over, and now he wanted to be in his room in the Seahorse before it got any later, so he could say goodnight at least to the older kids. So, he just answered the question, without discussing what he thought about it. 'Ken gave a little chuckle and said Rick was a rascal. Always had been. And he got away with murder because he could charm the teachers. It was as if in his head they were still teenagers.' Joe looked up at them. 'Then Ken said: *But Rick's closer than a brother. I'd do anything for him.*'

Chapter Seventeen

SATURDAY EVENING DURING A REUNION WAS usually a quiet affair. By the last night of the weekend, they were all talked out and starting to be concerned about their livers, so while, of course, they'd still have a drink, it would be more restrained, less of a party. This evening was even quieter than normal. Annie was starting to realize that Rick had been the person who held them together, the lifter of spirits, the joker. He'd been like some sort of happy drug, forcing them to forget their age and leave their inhibitions behind. Without him, they had all become more boring, less entertaining.

With a sudden clarity, she saw that this would be the last time they'd all be together. In five years' time, Ken's illness would have reached a stage where Louisa would prefer not to bring him away. He might even be living in a care home. Although these days people were more reluctant to send their loved ones into care, Annie couldn't imagine Louisa looking after him herself once he became very demanding. Philip would have properly retired. Only Annie would still be working, holding the fort at Bread and Olives while Jax worked her magic in the kitchen. After fifty years, she thought, she might actually lose touch with these people who'd been so close to her. The years, stretching ahead of her, seemed empty, devoid of light or fun.

There was a noise in the hall behind her and she turned to see Vera Stanhope in the doorway.

'That's us off. Done for the night.' The detective sounded cheery, glad to be going, and in that second Annie wished that she could leave too, that she could drive over the causeway to her little terraced house on the edge of Kimmerston. If the prospect of life without her friends had seemed dark and depressing the moment before, that of the evening *with* them felt like an ordeal to be endured rather than enjoyed.

'Don't worry,' Vera went on. 'There'll still be the uniformed officers keeping an eye.'

Outside there was the sound of a car engine starting. 'That's my colleagues. We're staying on the island though. We've missed the tide to get home tonight.' Vera paused. 'What time are you all leaving in the morning?'

'Not early,' Phil said. 'Late morning.'

'I was wondering,' Vera turned to him, 'if it might be possible for you to extend your holiday for a few days. Not here on Holy Island necessarily, but somewhere local. There might be other questions and I can't stand virtual interviews. I'm so crap at the tech. It would stretch the budget to send an officer down to London just for a chat.'

There was a moment of silence and then Philip gave a little laugh. 'No problem, Inspector. That was already part of the plan. It's a long way to come just for the weekend. A friend of mine owns a holiday cottage here on the island and I'll be staying for the rest of the week. I'll let you have the address and you have our phone numbers.'

Annie stared at him, shocked. How odd that Philip hadn't mentioned this before! It seemed as if it had been a deliberate strategy to keep the information to himself. And who was the friend who owned the holiday cottage? Of course, it didn't need to be anybody local. It could be a Londoner who'd bought a place as an escape. Only a southerner would be able to afford island prices these days. But still the secrecy seemed strange. She expected Vera to leave then, but the woman was still standing, looking around the room. She saw the photo that Annie had brought out earlier, and picked it up.

'Is this from the old days?'

'It was taken on that first weekend fifty years ago.'

Vera turned to Annie. 'Eh, pet, I'd know you anywhere. Those cheekbones.' She put the photo on a table and sat down. Annie had hoped the detective was on her way to her car. Vera unnerved her. 'Tell me about the others.'

So, Annie had no choice but to explain. 'That's Isobel, Lou's sister. She's looking lovely here, Louisa.'

'I remember that dress. Laura Ashley. I envied it, but Issy would never let me borrow it.' Louisa looked down and seemed lost in memories.

'The short one's Rick, Charlotte's the glamorous blonde standing next to him. Philip and Ken are the radgies with the flares and the attitude.'

'And who's this good-looking fellow?' Vera pointed to Daniel.

Annie could see that Dan had been very good-looking. She'd been drawn to him by the dark hair, the almost black eyes. Her nana had said, in her most disapproving voice, after meeting him for the first time: 'That lad's got gypsy blood. You want to steer clear of him.' But her nana had been wary of everyone who lived more than twenty miles from

Kimmerston. Annie had been attracted to him just because he looked different, exotic.

'That's my ex,' she said lightly, and then she changed the subject, turning to the others. 'We'll still kick off with our usual walk before we leave, shall we?'

'Another tradition?' Vera smiled.

'One of Rick's ideas,' Annie said. 'A bracing walk to clear the head before the drive home.' She looked round the room. 'We should still do it, shouldn't we? Just to remember him?'

'He used to swim in the lough, so we'd walk there and watch,' Louisa said. 'But I don't think any of us will be doing that tomorrow.'

'He was one of those wild swimmers?' Vera seemed fascinated. 'They get everywhere, these days.'

'Not so fashionable fifty years ago,' Phil said, 'but he swam then too. And on every Sunday morning at a reunion since.'

'Perhaps we *should* swim!' The words were out before Annie had really thought about it: the icy water, the frosty grass on bare feet, while they were getting ready for the plunge. 'A kind of tribute.'

She was half hoping they would all say she was crazy and they couldn't contemplate it, but nobody did. There was a moment of silence. Perhaps nobody wanted to be the first to dismiss the idea.

In the end, Philip spoke, laughing. 'Why not! Rick would love it! All of us, me especially: overweight – monster belly and wrinkled skin – blue with cold, floundering about. He'd be looking at us and mocking.'

'Well, that'll be a sight to be sure,' Vera said. 'I might come and watch. It deserves an audience.'

'For me it'll be a very quick dip,' Annie said, 'and I don't

have my bathers with me, so it'll be knickers and a T-shirt.'
She was pleased with the plan all the same. Despite the cold
and knowing she'd make an absolute fool of herself. And it
was awesome that the others had agreed. Better something like
this than that they all just slide away without acknowledging
Rick's death. She remembered a poem they'd done in English
A level with Judy Marshall. T. S. Eliot. Better a bang than a
whimper, she thought. Rick's philosophy every time.

'Rick would have gone skinny-dipping.' Louisa's eyes were
glinting suddenly with mischief. This was the old Lou. The
person who'd attracted Rick, made him jealous when it was
Ken who got in first. Not respectable head teacher Lou.

'Is that a challenge?'

'Why not?' Lou looked around the group. 'Why not?'

Chapter Eighteen

WHEN VERA GOT BACK TO THE Seahorse, Joe and Holly were sitting in the lounge bar, with drinks and cutlery in front of them. They were chatting as if they were almost friends. Vera wasn't sure what she made of that. It was good that they had a constructive working relationship, but she wouldn't want them forming some sort of alliance against her.

The lounge had been arranged with tables, like a restaurant, but it still felt like a traditional pub. There was no television. No piped music. A coal fire belted out the heat and covered every undusted surface with a fine coating of soot. The dining tables were a new addition in the lounge. The Seahorse had only just started serving food, an attempt to attract tourists as well as the locals. In theory. In the snug, which had its main door from the street, there was lots of noise. It seemed all the islanders had decamped there.

Vera looked across the hall into the smaller room, at the locals standing at the bar, the elderly men playing dominos, the women at the dartboard, and felt a moment of envy. In the over-heated bar, there was a sense of community which she'd never experienced in her personal life, except perhaps when she went to visit Jack and Joanna. They always managed to make her feel welcome.

'Well,' she said. 'They're planning on going skinny-dipping in the lough in the morning. A kind of tribute to Rick Kelsall. I might go and watch.' A pause. 'I might even join them.'

The look of horror on the young officers' faces made her laugh. 'Ah, I'm only kidding. About me, at least. The world's not ready for that. But really, I thought you youngsters weren't into body-shaming. You should have a word with yourselves.'

A young waitress arrived and Vera ordered pie and chips and a pint. She waited until the lass had disappeared behind the bar before speaking again.

'Did you find out any more about the single woman who was staying on the island on Friday night?'

'Yes.' Holly was drinking white wine and soda, which had never seemed like much of a drink to Vera. Neither one thing nor the other. 'She was staying here. Gave her name as Joanne Haswell, but no ID was required and she paid in cash.'

'So, she hadn't booked in advance?' Vera thought that was very strange. Would you just turn up to a place like Holy Island on spec and risk being stranded with nowhere to stay?

'No.'

'Was that usual?'

'The landlady thought it was a bit weird, but there's not much call for single rooms, apparently, not over half-term at least, so there was no problem finding her a place.'

'Have we got a description?' Vera was running through possibilities. 'Was she a young woman?'

Holly shook her head. 'Middle-aged. The landlady checked

her in and had her down as a teacher making the most of the last weekend of half-term. She didn't remember anything else.'

'Not one of Kelsall's victims seeking revenge then,' Vera said. 'Those were all young lasses, weren't they?'

'I still haven't got any details,' Holly said, 'but that's certainly the impression given in the press.'

Vera took out the photograph she'd taken from Annie Laidler. She wiped the table with a napkin and put it so they could all see. 'This is the Pilgrims' House lot, at that first weekend. Still kids.' She pointed with a stubby finger. 'In the middle is Judy Marshall, the teacher. Let's see if we can track her down. She hardly looks older than they are, so she's probably still alive. Can you recognize the others?'

'That's Annie! She's hardly changed.' Joe shook his head. 'The others? That's obviously the glamorous Charlotte and the short, skinny one is Rick Kelsall.' A pause. 'He'd have been bullied at our school, looking like that.' He pointed to the two lads standing together. 'And they'd have been the ones doing the bullying.'

'Ken and Philip,' Vera said. The lads were staring out at the camera, intense, unsmiling. She stuck out her finger again. 'That's Annie's ex, Daniel. I'll talk to him. He was at the first reunion when this woman died, apparently after having a major row with Rick Kelsall. And this is the deceased: Louisa's big sister, Isobel Hall.' Her finger hovered over the image. 'She's bonny too, isn't she?'

Bonny, she thought, was an understatement. The young woman was wearing a high-waisted floral dress, and she had a black cloak around her shoulders. It looked as if she was an actor in a romantic costume drama, but perhaps the girls did dress like that in the seventies, even when they weren't trying to impress. The breeze had caught her hair and her curls were blowing away from her face. Vera spoke to the woman in the picture.

'Eh lass, let's find out why you died.'

It was nearly closing time and though the noise in the public bar was as loud as ever, the lounge was empty. Holly and Joe had finished their meals and headed upstairs. To their separate rooms. Vera had a little giggle at the thought that it might be otherwise. She'd slipped in another beer when the pie had arrived and drunk it so quickly that it had gone to her head. A proper pint! It was impossible to imagine Holly and Joe having a wild night together. Joe was too upright and Holly too uptight. But all the same . . . She giggled again.

She climbed the stairs with its threadbare carpet to her room. It was big and draughty, and over the bar. She propped the photo up against the dressing table mirror, and random thoughts drifted in and out of her head, as the sounds of the late drinkers provided a background.

Only Connect. Let's connect those young things to the people they've become and we might get some sort of answer. She was still listening to the laughter below when she fell asleep.

Chapter Nineteen

THE GROUP DECIDED THAT THEY'D GO to the lough early, before Vera Stanhope made it out to the Pilgrims' House to see them. She might insist on coming too and this escapade was mad enough at their age. The last thing they needed was an onlooker. Besides, the swim was for Rick, not a kind of performance for an outsider to gawp at. They took the direct path to the lough across the frozen fields. Not more than half a mile from the house, so they'd be able to hurry back into the warm for breakfast. Annie had been up before the rest of them and had put together flasks of coffee, found an airing cupboard with extra towels.

The sun was up, but very low in the sky, the beams sliced by the trees in the spinney next to the house. The branches were almost completely bare now, black against the light. They'd gained an hour, because the clocks had gone back, so it seemed somehow that they were beyond time. In a different zone altogether. There was a buzz of excitement as they walked. They were giggly as kids, but well wrapped up in heavy coats and hats and gloves, so by the time they arrived at the water,

Annie was roasting. They stood, an awkward little group on the bank, and for a moment she wondered if they'd back out. If someone would say: *Look guys, this is crazy, we don't have to do it.* If that did happen, she'd probably agree and traipse back to the house for sausage sandwiches.

But Philip was already taking his clothes off. Hard to believe now that he was a vicar, that if he weren't taking the week off, he'd be giving a sermon, standing in the pulpit for the first communion service of the day in front of a small gaggle of elderly women. And he didn't just take off his outdoor clothes, but everything!

He had his back to them and was running to the water, and then everyone was following. Louisa, firm-stomached and gym fit. Even Ken. Following Louisa's lead, he'd taken off his clothes and folded them on top of the waterproof coat she'd put on the bank, like an obedient child getting ready for bed.

Hitting the water was intense. It was like being stabbed with needles, and the cold took Annie's breath away, making her feel panicky and anxious. She gave a strangled scream of pain. Philip had already swum to the other bank, a brisk crawl, insulated perhaps by all that fat. Louisa followed him, leaving Ken behind on the bank. Her husband watched her, seeming bewildered, bereft, so Annie thought she should go back and check on him. But then he plunged in too, and was spluttering and laughing. Not hurt by the cold, but joyous, as if he hardly felt it, like a child splashing in a paddling pool on a glorious summer's day.

Suddenly, Annie felt more alive than she had since she was a girl. It was a hit better than any drug she could imagine. A high. It was the cold and being with friends, the strange adventure of it, so outside her daily routine. And this place. The quiet, the trees sculptural and reflected in the water. The memories of all those other times.

They didn't stay in long. Soon they were out and shy again, wrapping themselves in towels, shivering. But still glowing. Louisa seemed quite a different person. Relaxed. Annie realized how uptight the woman had been for the whole weekend.

'Wasn't that fabulous?' she said. 'Why haven't we done it before? Why did we just come and watch when Rick took the plunge?'

'He never asked us to join him,' Louisa said. 'He just wanted an audience.'

They sat huddled in their coats and jerseys, drinking the coffee from Annie's flasks, teeth still chattering, and it was only then that Vera approached them.

'Well!' she said, when she was close enough to speak. 'I didn't know where to look.'

'You were watching?' Louisa seemed amused rather than cross.

'I got here just as you were all getting into the water. I wasn't expecting you to have such an early start, but when nobody was there at the house, I knew where you'd be. Then I thought you wouldn't want me here while you were getting dressed. All that fumbling with underwear. I never liked it, even when my dad took me to the beach up at Newton for a treat.' She paused for a moment and seemed lost in reflection. 'Not that he did very often. Only when he had other reasons for being there, and then it was the ice cream I liked best, not the water.' Another pause and a wide smile. 'But you don't need to worry. I averted my eyes.'

Annie got to her feet then. The arrival of Vera had spoilt the moment, made her relive finding Rick's body again and made his death seem real. For a moment the exhilaration of the icy water had made her forget. She led the others back to the house. Vera walked beside her. 'What's the plan now?'

'Breakfast and then everyone will head home. Except Philip, I suppose, as he's staying on the island for the rest of the week. I'll hang on for a bit to tidy up. We've got the place until midday.'

'That's always your job, is it? Doing the cooking and clearing up the mess?'

'No!' But Annie thought Vera was right and certainly there'd been times when she'd resented it. Not the chores themselves but the assumption that she'd be the last person here, to do the last sweep of the place and return the keys. 'We share the cooking and the others have much further to go than I do. It just makes sense.'

Vera didn't comment, but Annie thought the woman had read her mind and understood. Assumptions would probably have been made about *her* too, throughout her career.

Breakfast would be sausage and bacon sandwiches eaten in the kitchen, wrapped in paper napkins to save dirtying plates again. The meat bought from a local farm shop, naturally. Annie grilled bacon and sliced the remaining deli sourdough bread, while the others started packing. Another of the weekend rituals. Sometimes she wondered if it would be different if she had a partner with her. It felt occasionally that because she was single, she was seen as a lesser being, or at least as if there was nobody else on her side. That she was taken for granted. *Good old Annie, provider of hot drinks, comfort food, and sympathy.* As if she never felt lonely and that, at her age, she didn't have a right to expect more than this. As if they were doing her a favour simply by letting her tag along.

Vera hovered while she prepared breakfast, offering to help, but actually getting in the way. All the time, she was probing Annie with questions about the others, their relationships with Rick, and any problems they might have had with him.

'I can't see,' Vera said, 'how a vicar could be so relaxed with someone like Rick Kelsall. All his women.'

Annie looked up, then realized she was still holding the bread knife, as if it were some sort of weapon, and set it down on the counter.

'Philip has never been judgemental.'

'Hating the sin but not the sinner,' Vera said. 'I've never found it that easy to separate the two.'

Annie was saved from having to answer, because the others trooped in. It was almost as if they'd been waiting until the food was ready. They ate quickly. Most years they lingered, chatting, until the last minute, not wanting the weekend to be over, but today they were eager to go, wary of every word they exchanged with the inspector listening in. The carefree swim seemed from a different time. Vera left the building with the rest of them. She stood for a moment talking to Louisa. Annie wondered what that could be about, but the conversation was soon over.

Vera waved the Hamptons and Philip off, and stood by her battered Land Rover until their cars had disappeared down the lane. Annie saw that Rick's vehicle had already gone. The police must have taken it for some kind of forensic investigation. She was willing Vera to go too, so she could clear the place and get home to grieve in peace, but the woman stood, solid as the rock in the crags above them holding Lindisfarne Castle.

In the end she opened the door of her Land Rover, fished

in the dash and handed Annie a card. 'My numbers. Home and work, and the mobile will get me anytime. At least when I've got reception. It's not brilliant in my cottage. If you think of anything that might help, just give me a shout.'

Vera had slipped the card into Annie's hand in a way that was almost furtive, though there was nobody watching. Annie nodded, and, at last, Vera did climb into her vehicle, started the engine and it drove off, belching fumes and noise.

Chapter Twenty

JOE THOUGHT IT WAS ODD TO drive off the island. It was as if he were shifting from somewhere dreamlike, made up of water and shimmering light, back to the real world, solid and mundane. It wasn't like him to have such fancies, but he thought he could understand why the friends had returned to the Pilgrims' House every five years. It wasn't just about catching up with people they were close to. The place had a certain magic. They'd all grown up to have responsible jobs, and commitments, and things had become a little routine and predictable. The island transported them back to a time when they were young and free, and life was exciting and full of possibilities.

He'd almost arrived home when there was a call from the boss, her voice as loud on the phone as it was in person.

'I was chatting to Louisa before she left. Her mam's still alive. She's ninety and living in her own home. It's an address in Morpeth. She's sharp as a tack apparently.'

Joe could tell what was coming next and tried to pre-empt her. 'Sal needs me back. She's planning a proper Sunday lunch and I promised I'd be there.'

ANN CLEEVES

'No rush.' Vera's voice was easy, relaxed. She knew she'd get what she wanted from him. She always did. 'You can go later this afternoon. I'd do it myself but you're so good with old people. A lovely manner. That's what everyone says.' A pause. 'Just talk to her about Isobel. Louisa hasn't been very forthcoming and she said she was in a rush to get home when I tried to talk to her just now. You can understand that, with a husband like Ken. He was fretting when they were setting off, but he provides a convenient excuse. I can't help thinking that Isobel's death is in some way connected to her family. According to Louisa, the lass was her mam's favourite. The apple of her eye. Let's see what she says.'

Joe didn't argue. There was no point. 'It'll have to wait until after lunch.'

'Of course. Whenever suits you best. Give me a shout this evening and tell me what you've got.'

Mrs Barbara Hall lived in a detached bungalow on a quiet street on the edge of the town. The garden was immaculate and a handrail led to the front door. She knew that Joe was coming. She was slender, upright, and looked younger than Joe had been expecting. He thought how sad it was that Louisa's mother was so much more independent than her own husband.

'You're absolutely on time.' There was a hint of a faint Scottish accent in her voice. 'I do value punctuality. The kettle has just boiled. I'll make tea.' She looked at him sharply. 'You do take tea?'

'Certainly.'

'Make yourself at home in the sitting room and I'll bring it through.' She returned with a tray, and a plate of small scones, already buttered and covered with jam.

'The jam is shop bought, I'm afraid. I used to make my own.' A pause. 'Would you pour. I have arthritis in my wrists, and sometimes I'm not so steady.' She looked at him. 'I understand that you're here because of the murder on Holy Island. I've been watching it on the news. I watch far too much television these days. I used to despise it, but it passes the time.'

'The victim, Rick Kelsall, was a friend of your daughters.'

'Of Isobel, my elder daughter. Louisa was younger.'

'You knew him?'

'Oh yes! We knew them all.' Her voice was warm. 'People talk about their schooldays being the happiest time of their lives, but that wasn't true in my case, Sergeant. I grew up during the war, and even afterwards it was a drab time of rationing and restriction. Of boredom. My father had been badly affected by his experiences – he'd been in Burma – and he was constantly angry. My mother couldn't stand up to him and her life was a misery. My happiest time came later, when I was a wife and a mother, watching my girls grow up into strong young women. It was a joy to see them have the happiness at school that I'd missed out on: the friendship, the excitement of new ideas. We had rather a large house then. My husband was an engineer and he had his own business. We were doing very well. We encouraged the girls to bring their friends into our home. I tried not to intrude, but I loved their company.'

'Can you remember the names of Isobel's friends?'

'Oh yes, I can. I remember them all, vividly. There was Annie Laidler. She was the quiet one, shy. It was as if she felt she didn't really have the right to be there. Philip seemed the complete opposite, a bit edgy, arrogant even, but underneath, you could tell he was a very nice boy.' She looked up, suddenly amused. 'He went on to become a priest. In my wildest dreams I would never have predicted that for him. Charlotte Thomas was lovely to look at, but a bit shallow, I always thought. Ken was kind, staid, a bit boring. Daniel had dark, romantic good looks. There was a touch of Heathcliff about him. He wasn't as academic as the others, and that made him something of an outsider, but look what he's gone on to become!'

Joe must have looked confused, because she went on to explain. 'He's Daniel Rede. You must have heard of him! He runs that big holiday park on the bay, very close to the island. And also half the holiday homes in rural Northumberland, if my gossiping neighbours are to be believed. He'll be worth more than the rest of them put together. Certainly, more than Rick, for all that he's become so famous.'

'Rick was a special friend of Isobel's?'

'I think he was. Not a boyfriend, though she had plenty of those too, but the two of them were very close. Rick was an only child and his parents were both doctors, always busy. Rick treated Isobel more like a sister. They confided in each other.' She looked up at Joe and smiled. 'And he was like the son I never had.' There was another pause. 'We gave them a room in the basement. The teenagers played music there, listened to records, ate the suppers I made for them. They drank, I suspect, too much. It was all candles, posters on the walls. And they talked. They never stopped talking. I suppose I was living vicariously, but I loved the fact that those conversations were going on just beneath my feet.'

'You said that Isobel had boyfriends. Did she go out with any of the boys in the group?'

'If she did, Sergeant, she never confided in me.' A pause. 'I did have the sense that she had a serious crush on one of them, but that it was never reciprocated.' There was another moment of silence. 'Or perhaps that the boy was already taken, and she was dreaming of the unattainable. That was probably more likely. Isobel usually told me everything, but she knew I'd disapprove if she tried to break up an established romantic relationship.' Barbara didn't sound disapproving. Joe thought she would have forgiven her elder daughter anything.

Joe considered the information. At the time that the group had first gone to Holy Island, hadn't all the lads been taken? They all had girlfriends. Except Philip. Ken had been going out with Louisa, Rick with Charlotte, and Annie with Daniel. Who was most likely to have caught Isobel's fancy? If there'd been sibling rivalry, perhaps Ken had been the object of the young woman's desire. She certainly wouldn't have admitted to her mother that she lusted after her younger sister's boyfriend! But the argument outside the house before Isobel's accident would suggest it had probably been Rick who'd floated through the lass's dreams at night. Joe decided to move on, or rather to go back to the beginning.

'They went to Holy Island, on some sort of team-building course run by the school.'

'Yes,' Barbara said. 'Only Connect. That was the start of it, the trigger for those intense, very close friendships. Isobel came back changed. Lit-up. It seemed almost as if she'd had an evangelical experience. All that mattered, she said, was honesty. You could forgive anything if you had a true understanding of the other person, if there was a real connection. My husband disapproved. He thought it had been wrong for people with no training in the field to mess with the young people's minds. He still believed that emotions should be tightly restrained.'

'And you? What did you think?'

'I thought it was glorious. It felt as if they were properly alive, vivid, in a way that I never was as a young person.' She paused. 'I envied them. I wished that I'd been there.'

'Was Louisa a part of the group? Was she invited to the gatherings in the basement?'

Barbara Hall frowned. 'Not at first, though she very much wanted to be. She was three years younger, and I suppose she felt left out. She was always competitive, always saw Isobel as some sort of rival, though really there was no need. Louisa was stunning in her own right: bright, beautiful. But perhaps a younger sibling can sometimes feel daunted when the older sister is so successful.'

'She must have joined in when she started going out with Ken?'

'Yes.' The old woman paused. 'I did wonder if that was the only reason that she went out with him. To infiltrate the gang.'

Joe thought infiltrate was a strange word to use. It sounded aggressive, almost as if Louisa was a sort of terrorist. 'She and Ken married, though, so there must have been more to the relationship than that!'

'Yes.' Barbara sighed. 'I suppose there must. I never thought that the marriage would last. I'd have found the man far too boring. And yet here they are. Forty years on. Poor Ken. They've been happy enough, I suppose. Until the illness took hold of him, at least.'

It didn't seem to Joe like much of an endorsement, but he wasn't here to talk about Louisa's relationship with her husband. 'It must have been dreadful when Isobel died.'

She stared at him, clear-eyed now. 'Do you have children, Sergeant?'

'I do.'

'Then perhaps you'll understand. It's the guilt that's so hard. We gave Isobel the car to celebrate her graduation. She'd got a first-class degree and we were very proud of her. Otherwise, she'd have taken a lift home with Louisa and Ken, and she'd have been safe. That haunted my husband until he died.'

'Did you ever find out what caused the accident?'

A silence. 'I suspect Isobel caused it, Sergeant. She was always reckless, a little wild. It was what made her so intriguing. Of course, I *could* blame Louisa and Ken for disappearing onto the island, so that Isobel hung around at the Pilgrims' House until just before the tide. I *could* blame her other friends for not persuading her to wait until the causeway was clear again.' A pause. 'But long ago, I decided that way lay madness. It was easier to accept the guilt myself.'

'I think perhaps her friends did try to persuade her,' Joe said.

When Annie Laidler had seen Rick and Isobel arguing just before the accident, Joe thought it was likely that the man had just been telling Isobel to wait on the island for the tide to go out again. There was possibly nothing sinister in the encounter at all.

'Why are you here, Sergeant?' For the first time since he'd arrived the woman sounded tired. 'All that happened so long ago and I can't believe that my daughter's death can be relevant to your present investigation.'

It seemed to Joe that she was right, and that they were clutching at straws. 'My boss is always keen on the detail,' he said. 'On the background. And we thought it might be upsetting. Another Holy Island death. Even though so many years have passed, it must bring back distressing memories.'

Barbara Hall sat so long in silence, that Joe wondered if she was ill, if she'd had some kind of mini-stroke perhaps. 'Mrs Hall?'

'Then it was very kind of you to visit,' she said at last. 'I've enjoyed telling you about Isobel. She comes alive for me when I talk about her. As she was then of course, not as she would be now. She'd be an old woman too now and I suspect she'd have hated that. I have more lovely memories than bad.' There was another pause, and when she spoke again her voice was bitter. 'I wish my younger daughter had been as thoughtful. She didn't phone to tell me about Rick's murder. *She* didn't realize that all those memories would come back. She let me find out about his death on the television news. I find that hard to understand.'

Chapter Twenty-One

VERA GOT OFF THE ISLAND JUST before the tide. She could feel the tug of the current, swirling around the Land Rover's wheels at the deepest point of the causeway. She could see how Isobel might have misjudged it. A young lass, a bit head-strong, after an argument with a lad, wouldn't want to hang on, waiting in a toxic atmosphere with no escape. She'd be prepared to take a risk. She'd been driving a light little car, with no weight to it, and the power of the water had swept it away. There was probably no more to the accident than that.

Vera was at home when Joe phoned. She was restless, not able to settle to anything, the facts of the case rolling round in her head like breakers on a beach, making no sense.

'Well? What have you got for me?'

She listened as Joe described his conversation with Barbara Hall. 'So, Annie's ex is Daniel Rede, who runs that place on the coast!' Until then, Daniel had been a shadowy figure, on the edge of the group. Because he hadn't been at the Pilgrims' House on the night of Rick's murder, Vera had dismissed him as a possible suspect.

'According to Louisa's mother and I'm sure she'd know.' Joe paused. 'She said that Rede's minted. Worth all the rest of them put together.'

'Well, it's a big place he's got there.'

'I used to go camping with my grandad when I was a lad. It was canny rough then, but now it's all glamping and luxury lodges. They say the restaurant at the top of the old tower is up for a Michelin star!'

'Fancy!' Vera wasn't impressed. She thought that meant you'd come out as hungry as when you went in. 'Did you get anything else useful?'

'It's probably not relevant now, but it sounds as if there was a real rivalry between Isobel and Louisa. And you were right. Isobel *was* the apple of her mother's eye. There still seems to be a tension between Barbara and Louisa. I'm not sure there's very much contact.'

'Any idea why?'

Joe took a moment to answer. 'No. Unless Barbara blames her somehow for still being alive. If one of the daughters was going to die, I get the impression Barbara would much rather it had been Louisa.'

'Oh!' Vera couldn't quite restrain a little gasp of pain. She knew what it was like to be an unwanted child, the unloved survivor. Hector, her father, would have saved his wife over his daughter every time.

She switched off her phone and looked again at the yellowing photograph of the young friends. They were all becoming more alive for her now. Apart from Isobel who was dead. And Daniel, who lived as close to Holy Island as it was possible to get and still be on the mainland. Daniel, who was apparently minted. Vera thought of Annie Laidler, working in the deli from dawn to dusk, living in a little terraced house, and wondered what she made of her former husband's extreme wealth. Vera pulled on her coat and set out again.

Rede's Tower was on the coast to the south of Holy Island. It didn't call itself a holiday park. That would have sounded far too vulgar. The classy sign next to the road said Rede's Tower Lodges, and a drive swept down through managed woodland to the old pele tower, a tall stone building which must have been built as a look-out against raiders from the sea. The tower had been renovated, to provide the hub of the site. Tall windows had been built into the top floor and must provide a magnificent view. The restaurant might be worth visiting, Vera thought, even if the food was shite.

She'd been here once with Hector, keeping watch while he was stealing peregrine chicks. That had been long before the place was tarted up and turned into a playground for the wealthy middle classes. The falcons had bred on the tower's parapet and Hector had risked his life scrambling up the crumbling stonework to reach them. The adventure, the adrenaline rush, had been as important to him as the cash he'd made from the Middle Eastern falconer who'd bought them.

The building was close to the water. The tide was out and there were acres of sand stretching across the bay towards the island. At low tide, it might seem as if it would be possible to paddle across, but Vera knew that gave a false impression. The bay was crossed with deep gullies, invisible from the shore, full even at dead low water.

There *were* still caravans on the site, but they were closer to the main road and hidden from the tower by a belt of pines. The lodges spread across landscaped acres and had the best views of the sea. The geography of the site seemed deliberately to mark class distinctions. Social mobility meant moving from the vans to the wooden lodges, with their hot tubs, firepits and the hammocks strung from the veranda roofs.

Vera parked by the restored pele and went into reception. A young woman in a burgundy uniform sat behind a desk. The walls were thick and it was strangely quiet inside. They'd kept and glazed the slit windows on the lower floors, so there was little natural light.

'If you're here about the cleaner's job, it's the room at the top of the stairs, first door on your right.'

'Ah no, pet, I'm not a cleaner. Not in the way you mean, at least, though I've cleared up a few messes in my time. Detective Inspector Vera Stanhope.'

'Oh God, I'm so sorry! There've been women in all day. We wouldn't usually interview on a Sunday, but we've got lots of people off sick and we're a bit desperate. The place has been booked up for months.'

'Nothing to be sorry about. And nothing wrong with being a cleaner.' Vera leaned against the desk. 'I'd like to talk to Mr Rede. Mr Daniel Rede.'

The woman looked up and her tone changed, became a little less open. 'I'm not sure. He's taken the weekend off and that happens so rarely that I wouldn't want to disturb him. Perhaps I could help you?'

'Sorry, pet. It's not to do with the business. I do need to speak to him.' She paused, then made her voice confidential. 'This is personal. An old friend has died.'

'Oh right.' The woman still sounded doubtful, but more sympathetic. 'I suppose it'll be okay in that case. He and Katherine are at home.'

'He's not here then?'

'They built a house on site. If you follow the track through the nature reserve, past the No Vehicles sign, you'll come to it. I'll give them a ring to let them know you'll be on your way.'

'You do that, pet.'

But Vera was wondering about the nature reserve. As a child, she'd pretended to hate Hector's distorted passion for the natural world, but somehow his knowledge of birds and plants had seeped into her consciousness and hatred had turned to affection. She had binoculars in the Land Rover and thought she might go for a wander, afterwards.

She hadn't been expecting much in the way of a reserve. She'd thought it might be a gesture to the eco-minded, affluent families who'd stay here. But driving past, she saw a substantial pond with a reedbed to one side, surrounded by scrubby bushes and trees. A couple of wooden hides looked out over the water, which reflected the coloured, dying leaves. It was tranquil, but with the turning of the year, a little sad.

The track turned sharply and there, on the edge of the woodland, stood a spectacular house. It was all wood and glass, a part of its landscape, the colour of the trunks of the trees. When the leaves were new and green, it would be completely hidden from the public spaces of the site. A Range Rover was parked outside next to a smaller hatchback, and Vera pulled up beside it. She got out and stood for a moment.

Daniel Rede opened the door almost immediately and knew who she was. As she'd promised, the receptionist had phoned to warn him of her approach.

'Come on through.'

He led her down a passage and into a room that was full of light. It faced east, one wall made of glass, and outside there was nothing to cast a shadow. This room looked out over the bay. The incoming tide was sliding over the sand. There was a view to Holy Island, which seemed so close that she felt she could reach out and touch it. With binoculars it might be possible to make out the Pilgrims' House, though the drive north to the causeway would take at least half an hour. And there *were* binoculars, on a table next to the window. Perhaps the nature reserve had been created through passion, not through affectation or a pretence at a green credential.

This outlook was so different from the part of the house built into the woodland, that the view was a shock. For a moment, Vera could do nothing but stare at it. She had a brief moment of envy. She was happy in Hector's little house in the hills, but this was spectacular. It was like living on a great liner, or in a lighthouse, and she'd never before been indoors but felt so close to the sea.

Vera turned her attention to the room itself. The furniture was sleek and smelled of money. The pale stained floorboards were covered in a long and beautiful rug in primary colours. She hoped she didn't have dog shit on her shoes. Somehow though, the space wasn't intimidating or pretentious. There were books on the shelves, piled on top of each other, the Sunday newspapers lay on a coffee table beside a couple of used mugs. Through an open door, Vera could hear a television and she caught a glimpse of a smaller, darker room. Football. A splash of black and white on the screen. Newcastle United. This place was classy but, still, it was definitely a home.

'It is a bit special, isn't it?' Daniel was standing beside her, looking out at the view. 'I never get tired of it. Different every day.' The accent was local. He glanced back towards the room with the television.

'I'm sorry,' she said. 'I'm making you miss the match.'

He smiled. 'It's nearly over and we'll not make up the difference now. It'd take a miracle. Probably best not watching the final agony.'

'You're a Toon supporter.' It wasn't a question.

'Lifelong. For my sins.'

He was wiry, tough. Not an inch of spare flesh. The dark hair of the photograph had gone, but he still had eyes the colour of coal. 'Sorry, Inspector, take a seat. How can I help you?'

She'd been preparing to dislike him, because Annie was, if not a friend, an acquaintance, and after a divorce it seemed it was impossible not to take sides. But there was something tentative and diffident about him, which she found very appealing.

'What a beautiful place!' She needed time after the shock of the light and the sea to prepare her questions.

'When I first started working here for my grandfather, I lived in a rusty caravan, so yes, this is a little bit different from that. We built here two years ago. Katherine wasn't sure about living on the job, but I talked her round.'

'Katherine's your wife?'

'My partner.' He smiled again. 'I keep asking her to marry me, but she says we're fine as we are.'

'I want to take you back a bit further than two years.'

'You're here about the murder on Holy Island. Rick Kelsall.'

'You'd heard?'

'It was on Radio Newcastle this morning.'

'Annie Laidler didn't tell you?'

He shook his head. 'Annie and I don't communicate much these days. I can't blame her.' He paused. 'Of course. It'll

151

have been one of their daft reunions. It's that weekend. She'll have been there.' Another beat. 'How is she?'

'Shocked,' Vera said. 'She found the body.'

Someone must have scored because there was a distant sound of fans cheering, but he wasn't distracted.

'Poor lass.'

'I'm just looking for a bit of background. You were at school with most of them. Did you keep in touch?'

'Not so much after Annie and I split up. I was the one to leave so you can understand why our friends stuck by her. But, yeah, we keep in touch a bit. We used to meet up for a drink occasionally if the lads were back home visiting relatives. Now, it's the odd Zoom call.'

'You were there for that first weekend fifty years ago. What did they call it? Only Connect?'

He nodded. 'They wouldn't get away with it now. Letting kids stay up all night. Drinking. Smoking.'

'Is that how you remember it?'

'That's how it was! The others might have been taken in by all the fancy ideas, but it was just a glorified party, with the teacher so keen on wanting to appear cool that she turned a blind eye.'

'You were there for the first reunion?'

'Yes. Annie's idea. We were a real item by then. Only just married, but we'd been together since school.'

'What was it like?'

He shrugged. 'More of the same. Drinking. Staying up all night.' He paused. 'Drugs.'

'That was the weekend Isobel Hall died.'

'Yes.' He looked at her. 'I never went back after that.'

'Were you close to Isobel? Is that why you didn't go back?'

He shook his head. 'No, nothing like that. It just wasn't my scene.'

'What do you remember about the afternoon before she drove off? I understand she'd had a row with Rick Kelsall.'

'Oh, Rick had been picking at her all day. I'm not sure exactly what triggered it. Probably the fact that she hadn't been taken in by his charms. He was all extremes. If you couldn't love him, he provoked you to hate him. I didn't care about him enough to do either, which is why he left me alone.'

'You were still married, though you never went to another reunion?'

'Yeah, we struggled on for a few more years.' He seemed about to elaborate on the disintegration of the marriage, but thought better of it. 'I didn't mind Annie meeting up with her old mates, and I always had work as an excuse. I'd inherited this place by then.' He nodded vaguely towards the door through which they'd entered, towards the outside world. 'It wasn't plain sailing and I was working every hour in the day. We came close to losing it. The worst time of my life.' He thought and corrected himself. 'One of them, at least.'

'It was a family business?'

'Yeah, my grandfather had it first.' A pause. 'He'd not recognize the place now.' Vera thought the idea made him sad rather than proud.

'You must have made a fortune from it! Did that make it hard to get on with the others?' Vera was still trying to work out why Rede had never made it back to Holy Island to meet up with his friends. Even if he didn't want to stay all weekend, he was close enough just to pop in for a meal. Maybe to gloat a bit, throw the cash around, prove how well he'd done in the end, even if he'd never been as brainy as them. 'Was there a bit of envy creeping in? I can imagine Rick Kelsall not liking someone else being top dog, at least when it came to money.'

He shook his head and gave a little laugh. 'Nah, nothing like that. As I said, it just wasn't my scene. I'd only scraped into the Grammar at the thirteen-plus and I was never going to make it to university. They were all about words. Ideas. Talk about books and plays and feelings. It left me cold. Maybe they were just showing off how clever they were, but it made me feel that I shouldn't be there.'

She nodded. She'd met people like that. Folk so insecure that they needed to put other people down.

'So, you weren't tempted to go over to meet them all this weekend?'

He gave a little laugh. 'I wasn't invited, Inspector!' A pause. 'And even if I had been, I wouldn't have gone.'

'When was the last time you saw Rick Kelsall?'

'Oh goodness, quite a while ago.' He seemed to be choosing his words carefully. 'He was the one of that gang that I had least in common with. He was so confident. It was like he could get away with anything. He charmed the teachers and he could get good grades without putting in much work. I was a plodder. Everything was so much more of an effort. So, I kept in touch with Ken and Philip more. Katherine has got to know Rick a bit through her work. He interviewed her a couple of times for his show.'

Vera was about to ask for more details about that – who was this Katherine that Rick Kelsall had wanted to interview – when there was the sound of the front door opening.

'That'll be her now,' Rede said. 'She's been out for a walk. She's not really into footie. She'll do anything to avoid it.'

A woman came in and Vera had her second shock of the day. She caught herself staring, open-mouthed, like a character in some kids' cartoon. Because this was Katherine Willmore, Police and Crime Commissioner for North Northumberland. A lawyer turned quasi-politician, voted into post by the community, and essentially Vera's boss. It hadn't for a moment occurred to her that Rede's Katherine might be this woman. Vera forced her mouth shut and stood up. An automatic response, though Willmore, in jeans and a long black jumper, in stockinged feet, looked very different from the woman in the smart suit who appeared in conferences and on the media.

Vera had met her several times but didn't expect to be recognized. Willmore looked at her, however, and smiled.

'Inspector Stanhope? I thought I recognized the Land Rover. It has reached mythical status within the service. Are you here for work? To see me?'

'For work, ma'am. But not to see you.' Vera had never liked the idea of political appointments to oversee the police force, but she had time for Willmore, who was efficient, intelligent. She listened to grass roots police officers and backed them when they needed support, even when the management team seemed oblivious. 'I'm investigating the Rick Kelsall murder.'

'Yes, of course.' Katherine sat on one of the sofas, her legs tucked beneath her. 'Do sit down, Inspector. You might be at work, but I'm very definitely not. So, let's drop the formality, shall we?'

'Your partner was at school with Rick Kelsall and knew the people staying with him in the Pilgrims' House on Friday night. I'm here for a bit of background.'

'Are they all potential suspects?'

'They are. And certainly witnesses. I was hoping for an

outsider's view. But Daniel said that you'd seen Mr Kelsall more recently than he had.'

Katherine looked at her partner, but she'd spent too much time in court for her face to give anything away.

'I was telling the inspector that you'd given him a couple of interviews,' Daniel said.

'I had,' Katherine said. 'I've been trying to change the attitude to domestic abuse throughout my career, and I'll continue putting that at the top of the agenda as PCC. I've become the go-to person on the subject for many members of the press, and I'm happy to oblige. Anything that keeps the subject in the public eye. And in the minds of politicians.' She smiled at Vera. 'But you'll know that, Inspector. You've heard me on my soap box often enough.'

Vera nodded. 'Yet Rick Kelsall has been accused of harassment himself recently.'

'So it seems.' Katherine seemed about to add to the comment, but didn't continue.

'The accusations around his behaviour didn't put you off appearing on his show?' Vera was intrigued. It seemed an odd decision.

'Oh, the last time I appeared with him was almost a year ago, long before his reputation was tarnished by the popular press.'

That seemed a strange way to describe what had happened to Kelsall's career, especially from a person who was known for championing the need for victims of abuse to be heard and believed. Vera thought she'd get Holly to dig up some of those old interviews. She'd be interested to see a recording of any conversations between Kelsall and Willmore.

The PCC must have picked up Vera's confusion because she added: 'Of course, I wouldn't do it now.'

Vera nodded again to show that she understood. 'I think that's all I need to know at the moment. Thanks for your help. I'll let you get back to the match, Mr Rede.'

He smiled sadly. 'They'll have lost, most likely. I always start the season with great hopes, but by this time of year, I'm already disappointed.'

Vera smiled back. It was Katherine who led her back through the house to the door into the woods. 'Of course, do get in touch if we can help in any way.'

Vera stood for a moment in the shade. She was hungry now and decided she wouldn't bother with the walk around the pool. That could wait for another time. She was just about to get into the Land Rover and drive away when she looked up at the house. From an upper window, a woman was staring down at her. It wasn't Katherine Willmore. This woman was younger, hardly more than a girl. She saw Vera looking and the face disappeared. It was as if she'd never been there at all.

Chapter Twenty-Two

ON MONDAY MORNING, ANNIE SET OFF for work early even though she knew she'd be there long before Jax turned up. It had taken her hours to get to sleep and she was awake again before dawn. She'd taken a mug of tea back to bed, but once it was finished, she was restless and had to get up, get out. It was milder, a hint of dampness in the air, a blustery wind from the west. The washing from the weekend was still in the machine, but there was no point hanging it on the line. She could smell that rain was on its way.

In the street the dead leaves on the pavement were already soft, without their icy crunch. She unlocked the door of the deli and went inside, and was immediately wrapped up in the smell of the place, savoury and yeasty, with an undertone of spice. She put on the coffee machine, so that the drinks would be ready when Jax got in.

Annie had hoped that the routine of work would help her to relax, to forget the sight of Rick, hanging like a strange misshapen puppet from the rafter in the grandest of the Pilgrims' House's bedrooms. But she'd been in the shop on the day that he'd died and she wasn't sure she'd be able to relax here again. This place and the details of his death were twisted together, like the puppet's tangled strings.

Jax burst in soon after, big and loud and full of sympathy. 'Oh honey, I heard on the news. I know he was a friend.' But she wanted the story, and Annie had always given Jax what she wanted, so she had to relive that moment again.

'You were the person to find him?' Horror and theatre mixed together and she put her arms around Annie and held on to her, squeezed her so tight that Annie almost stopped breathing. She felt like a small mammal squashed by a boa constrictor, and she had to push Jax away.

The morning passed almost in a daze, a dream. She went through the motions, but was hardly present. It was hard to imagine her life continuing without Rick Kelsall. He'd been there for her for every crisis in her adult life and suddenly she felt very alone.

Daniel appeared suddenly. Annie had her back to the door, stretching to pull a bottle of balsamic vinegar from the shelf behind her, and when she turned around there he was, standing just inside the shop. By now it had started to rain. He was wearing an old Barbour jacket, which could well be the same as the one he'd worn when they were still together. He might be rich now, but he'd never liked shopping. There were rain-drops in his hair.

Jax had seen him before she had.

'Why don't you take a break? We won't be busy for the rest of the day. Monday's always quiet.'

It would have taken Annie too much effort to have come up with an excuse, so she fetched her coat from the cupboard in the kitchen and walked with Daniel out into the street. He led her into a coffee shop, which was empty too. There was a hissing coffee machine and condensation was running down the window. It felt as if they were completely alone here, separated from the rest of the world.

'I'm sorry,' Daniel said. 'I know how much he meant to you.'

No. You really don't. You have no idea.

'What do you want, Dan?' Her voice didn't sound angry, though it had upset her, his turning up in the shop. Thrown her and made her confused. It sounded distant and very tired.

He waited before answering because the waitress was heading over to take their order.

'It is still a cappuccino you like?'

She nodded, though these days she usually went for a flat white. Again, she couldn't summon up the effort to explain that she was no longer the person he remembered.

'A woman detective came to the tower yesterday,' he said. 'I couldn't work out why. She didn't really explain. I mean, I knew Rick Kelsall was dead, but why would she want to talk to us?'

'They think he might have been murdered by one of us.' Annie could tell the words were flat, that they showed no emotion. Better that, than that she should break down in front of Dan. She imagined him holding her, stroking her hair, reassuring her that everything would work out. He'd done that when Freya had died, before he'd lost patience with her. 'By one of the group staying at the Pilgrims' House. She seems very thorough. I suppose she was looking for background information from someone who once knew us all well.'

'She believes one of the people at the reunion killed Rick?'

A pause. 'But that's crazy! I never particularly liked them, but they're not killers.'

'Why are you here?'

He shrugged. 'I don't know. An impulse, maybe. I just wanted to check you're okay.' He paused. 'And I suppose out of curiosity, if I'm honest. To know what happened over the weekend.'

'Nothing happened over the weekend. No rows! No dramas!'

'Do the police think they'll be able to sort it out quickly?' He looked up from his coffee. 'The woman who came to the house didn't seem very sharp.'

'Was that Vera Stanhope?'

He nodded. 'Katherine said she's an inspector.'

'I had to tell her about Isobel's accident. She's been digging into all our pasts.'

'What did you tell her?'

'Just that Isobel had a row with Rick and then she drove off the island at high tide and killed herself.'

'She asked me about that too.' Daniel looked up at Annie, and she found herself staring into the dark eyes. 'It was an accident, wasn't it? You're not keeping anything from me?'

'Of course not! What could there possibly be to hide?'

He didn't answer.

Eventually she found the silence intolerable. 'Why are you really here, Dan? What's this all about?'

'I suppose I'm worried that the business might be affected.' He had the grace to sound sheepish. 'The past year has been hard enough, with the weather so unreliable, and the last thing we need is an unsolved murder of a minor celebrity on our doorstep, all over the press, just as we're getting back on our feet . . .' His voice tailed off. 'I'm sorry, that must seem crass.'

Of course, she thought, *the business. That has always been his passion. He cared more about the tower than he did about me.* But somehow, she resented the obsession less than she had in the past. It was good to be with someone who'd known Rick, who had, despite the men's differences, been a good friend.

It had been months since she'd last seen Daniel and that had been at a distance in Kimmerston market. She'd glimpsed him through the crowds. He'd been standing at the cheese stall, laughing with the owner. Easy. Confident. Now, she felt a pull of the old attraction, despite his age, despite the lingering sense of betrayal. His hand was lying on the table next to the folded paper napkin and she was tempted to reach out and touch it.

'Does Katherine know you're here?'

He looked at her and shook his head. 'This is nothing to do with Katherine.' A pause. 'She's always so busy, though of course this will be difficult for her too. If the connection were to get into the press.'

Annie thought there was no connection. Not really. 'Did she send you to talk to me?'

'No!' Daniel sounded genuinely offended. 'No! Of course not.'

The waitress came with the coffees. There was a dusting of chocolate powder on the top of hers. She hated that, the sweet graininess of it, but she sipped it just the same. There was another moment of silence until the woman walked back to the kitchen.

'Vera Stanhope's a clever woman,' Annie said. 'Don't be fooled by her appearance. She'll sort it out quickly. By next season everyone will have forgotten about Rick Kelsall's death, and tourists will be flocking to Rede's Tower, glad of a holiday in your eco paradise.'

He smiled, unoffended by the mocking tone. 'Perhaps. Look, I'm sorry, I probably shouldn't have come.' He'd finished the coffee and stood up, so he was looking down at her. 'Really, I did want to check you're okay.'

'It was kind.' Annie wasn't sure what else to say. She couldn't ask him to sit down again, to be company, to stop her brooding about what had happened at the weekend. 'Keep in touch, yeah?'

'Yeah.' He smiled suddenly, and though his face was older, the smile was just the same as when he'd been a teenager. 'I'd like that.'

Then he disappeared, almost as suddenly as he'd arrived in the shop. Annie could hardly believe that the encounter had taken place. She finished the coffee and walked back to Bread and Olives. Jax was serving a couple of middle-aged tourists. When they left, she put her arm round Annie.

'What did that rat want?'

Jax knew more than anyone else about the background to their marriage and divorce. Once, on the anniversary of Freya's death, Annie had drunk too much and everything had spilled out. The grief and the guilt. Most especially the guilt. They'd been in Jax's home, a flat in a converted warehouse on the edge of the town looking out over the river. It had been late summer, rolling out towards autumn, warm and laid-back. They'd sat on the balcony in the golden light reflected from the water. It should have been a relaxed conversation, funny, entertaining.

'What is it with you and men?' Jax had asked.

For some reason, Annie had ditched her usual answer about loving her own space, not needing a man in her life. She'd started talking and she couldn't stop.

'I was young, still at Newcastle Poly. Not planning to get pregnant. Certainly not, but chaotic, not eating properly, stressing about finals. All that stuff. I always was a bit obsessive. And Dan and I were together, properly together. He was working for his grandfather, but we met up most weekends, and every vacation I went and stayed with him. Then, when I found out I was expecting, there was this excitement, you know, and the sense that everything was right. That being a mother was what I wanted. What I could do. Because I was a *very* mediocre student. Kind of semi-detached, I suppose. I wanted Dan's baby more than anything.' The words had tumbled out. It had been years since she'd talked about it. Perhaps she'd never talked about it. Not properly, except to Rick Kelsall. Her parents had been sorry about Freya of course, but there'd been an element of blame too. Of suspicion. They still hadn't quite been able to accept that Freya's death had been unavoidable. And nor had Annie. Guilt had lingered and tarnished every part of her life.

'Rede's Tower was a very different sort of place then. His parents gave us a caravan on the site to live in. It had a leaky roof when we moved in, but Dan mended the roof and really, I made it very cosy. Not a bad place to bring a baby. It was a little girl. Dan was with me when she was born and he gave her the name. Freya.' Annie had paused. Gulped for breath and gulped the wine, though Jax *never* offered wine that should be swigged.

'And in the delivery room afterwards, he asked me to marry him. There were tears running down his face. He said he wanted us to be a real family. I could see my life stretching ahead of me. I had everything I wanted. A few months later we were in the registry office, with our families and our very close friends.' *Rick, Phil, Charlotte, Ken, Lou, Isobel. Everyone in the*

pub afterwards, getting giggly drunk. Even me, although I was
breast-feeding. Then back to the caravan.

In the apartment with its stylish art and the evening sun
pouring through the window, Jax had poured more wine and
waited for the rest of the story. Annie had known she couldn't
stop there.

'Freya had been with us all day, and seemed happy and well.
But she didn't wake up in the night for a feed, and when I got
up late, panicked and sick with anxiety she was lying still and
cold in her cot. Dead. Cot death. You don't hear so much about
it now, but then it was a thing. I was twenty-one, with a new
husband and a dead baby.'

'Oh, my love.' Jax had been in tears. 'My poor love.'

A couple of months later it had been the Pilgrims' House
reunion. The first time Annie had been away from Rede's
Tower since Freya's death, apart from the funeral. She'd been
reluctant to go but Rick had persuaded her. He could charm
anyone to do what he wanted, but especially Annie. 'Come,'
he'd said. 'It'll be good for you to be with friends.'

And for a while, it had been. Dan had been a bit quiet, but
he'd wanted to be there. He'd enjoyed being somewhere
different, where the atmosphere lifted occasionally and people
felt they could laugh. There hadn't been much laughter in the
caravan. Everyone had understood when Annie had wanted
long walks on her own, or time alone in the chapel. They'd
swept Daniel off to the pub, provided him with company when
he'd needed it. Then Isobel had crashed her car and there'd
been another death. Another funeral.

'Is that why you divorced?' Jax had asked that late summer
evening in the airy apartment, as she'd opened another bottle
of wine. 'Because you lost Freya?'

Annie had thought about that and tried to explain:

'I guess so, though we were very young. Perhaps it wouldn't have lasted anyway.'

I stuck memories of the baby in a big black box at the back of my head. But sometimes they jumped out, like a jack-in-a-box, and nothing between us was the same again. I couldn't love Dan like I loved Freya, because she would always be perfect. Of course, he resented that. I couldn't blame him.

She hadn't spoken those words though. Jax had reached out for her hand and they'd sat in silence, staring over the water, until the sun had set.

Back in the present, in the shop that had become a second home, Annie leaned into Jax's chest, then pulled herself gently away. 'Dan's not a rat,' she said. 'He came to offer support, to see how I was doing.'

'Just take care,' Jax said. 'He'll be after something. I've never yet met a man who only wanted to offer support.'

Chapter Twenty-Three

THERE WAS A BLUSTERY SHOWER JUST as Vera was running from her car into the police station. The place was an anachronism, Victorian red brick, not fit for purpose, and soon, she knew, the authority would decide to flatten it, move the officers to a new concrete building out of town and sell the site for residential development. Kimmerston was going up in the world and it would make someone a fortune. Vera thought that might be the time she'd start considering retirement. Though she was always moaning about this place, she couldn't imagine being based anywhere else.

She called her core team into her cramped office to plan actions for the day. This wasn't the formal briefing she'd organize for the whole team that evening, but a chance for them to gather their thoughts and think of an immediate way forward. She hung her coat over the radiator to dry and throughout the meeting it steamed, smelling like wet dog, causing a stream of moisture to run down the filthy window like tears down a made-up face.

'Joe, you went to see Isobel and Louisa's mum. Fill us in.'

There weren't enough chairs for him to sit, so he was leaning against the door.

'It seems there's no love lost between Louisa and Barbara, her mother. Louisa only lives just across the border in Cumbria, and Barbara's very elderly now, but there doesn't seem to be much contact.' He frowned. 'It wouldn't hurt her to phone or Facetime once in a while.'

'I'm guessing Louisa's got her hands full with her husband,' Vera said. She thought you could only do *so* much caring, and it was easy for Joe to judge. He talked about his kids a lot, but left most of the hands-on childcare to Sal.

'Maybe, but I think the coolness goes back a lot further than that. There was a good bit of sibling rivalry as the girls were growing up, I'd say. And the mother didn't hide the fact that Isobel was the favourite. If Rick was killed because someone blamed him for Isobel's death, I really don't think that person would have been Louisa. I'm not saying Louisa was glad her sister died, but I don't think she was so moved by the loss that she's brooded over it for all these years and taken revenge.'

'I agree,' Vera said. 'That never made sense to me. Why now? This must have been triggered by something much more recent. But you got some useful info on Annie Laidler's ex from Barbara, and we've been able to follow that up.'

'Yes.' Joe directed his answer to Holly and Charlie. 'Daniel, who was in the Pilgrims' House at the original weekend and the first reunion, turns out to be Daniel Rede, the owner of Rede Tower lodges, that flash holiday place not far from the island.'

'I went to see him yesterday afternoon.' Vera paused and took a deep breath before making the dramatic announcement. 'And who should be in his house but our esteemed PCC, Katherine Willmore.'

'What was she doing there?' Holly seemed almost starstruck. She'd always admired Willmore. Vera had guessed that she liked the style and the politics of the woman: sleek, professional, pragmatic. Now, she thought Hol might see Willmore's involvement in the investigation as a chance to get to know the woman better; Holly might even see the contact as a potential step to promotion.

'She's Daniel Rede's partner.' Vera paused again. 'Which they've been very discreet about. Has been for years apparently, though I've never seen anything about the relationship in the press. I haven't told Watkins yet. This is really going to rattle his cage. A high-profile journo is one thing. The big boss on the edge of the case is another altogether.'

'We have to treat her as any other potential witness, don't we?' Charlie always looked half-asleep, as if he were hardly listening, but often, Vera thought, he was the sharpest member of the team.

'She's not even that though, is she?' Holly was standing up for the woman already, battling on her behalf. 'They might live on the same bit of coast as the locus, but there's no evidence that either she or Daniel were on the island that night. All they can do is provide a bit of background information. I still think that Rick Kelsall's treatment of younger colleagues is more relevant as a motive than something that happened years ago.'

'You're probably right, Hol.' Sometimes, Vera thought, managing the team was like dealing with a bunch of squabbling teens. She might never have been a mother, but she certainly understood the concept of sibling rivalry. 'Have we tracked down the complainant in the harassment case yet?'

Holly shook her head. 'Nothing so far. The production

company have really kept a lid on it and I haven't found anyone in the media who's willing to talk.'

'Well, if anyone can track her down, you're the person to do it.' Vera had learned that, while *she'd* find these snippets of praise patronizing – would make her feel like throwing up in fact – they could motivate her DC. 'And can you front up contact with Rick Kelsall's former colleagues and bosses? I assume he had some sort of business manager or agent. Talk to them as well as the executives at the TV company. Persuade them to give you a bit more than the company line. Rick had talked to Charlotte and to his friends about writing this book, about bringing the past back to life. We really need to find out more about that. If he was planning some major reveal about what happened, we might find that Isobel's death is relevant after all.'

'You think someone killed him to stop the book being written?' Charlie was sceptical.

'Well, it's some sort of motive, and we don't have a lot else to go on so far.'

'What about money?' Joe said. 'According to Barbara Hall, Kelsall wasn't as rich as Daniel Rede, but he won't have been on the breadline. Do we know who benefits financially?'

'Not yet. I'll chase it up today.' Vera was juggling priorities in her mind. She'd need to see Watkins to explain about Katherine Willmore's involvement. That would have to come first. 'Joe and Charlie, you take the local angle. See if you can track down Judy Marshall, the teacher who set up that first weekend in the Pilgrims' House. She wasn't much older than the students, and we know she's still local.'

'You really think we need to go back that far, boss?' Holly was sticking her oar in again. The scrap of praise hadn't kept her content for long. Now she was back challenging Vera's judgement. Poking the bear.

'I wouldn't ask if I didn't think it was important.' But Vera's voice was reasonable, conciliatory. The last thing she'd really want was a 'yes-woman', who couldn't think for herself. 'Rick Kelsall hadn't lived here for years. But this is where he was killed. Why? Something about those early relationships had become toxic, destructive. Let's scroll back and find out where that could have started.'

Watkins had a large office at the top of the building. He was much more comfortable with conference calls and Teams than in-person conversations. He'd been fast-tracked through promotion without much real policing experience, but he was great with budget planning and spreadsheets and he could talk a good game. He'd embraced the new technology, the impor-tance of digital investigation, as a drowning man does a lifebelt. When Vera knocked on his door, he seemed shocked to see a live human, though she'd warned his secretary that she was on her way.

'Vera, how can I help?' He always sounded warm, supportive, though in Vera's experience real support was seldom forth-coming.

'It's the Rick Kelsall murder, sir.'

'It definitely *is* murder, is it?'

'Yes, the post-mortem confirmed that on Saturday.' Vera tried to contain her impatience. The man already knew that. His preferring this to be suicide wouldn't change the facts. 'But we have an additional complication.'

'Tell me.'

'I visited one of Rick Kelsall's friends yesterday afternoon.

There's a possibility that an event in the past played a part in his murder, so we're doing a bit of digging into his history.'

Watkins tried to smile. 'I do know how you enjoy a bit of digging, Vera, but don't get distracted. We're investigators not archaeologists.'

And you're neither. You're a glorified pen-pusher, who wouldn't know a killer if he bit you in the arse. 'It does seem relevant in this case.' A pause. 'Sir.'

'Go on.'

'When I went to the home of a potential witness – a man called Daniel Rede – I met his partner. Katherine Willmore.'

She'd been expecting shock, horror, but the man seemed unsurprised. 'Of course, she's moved in with Daniel now, hasn't she? They've been an item for years, of course. They met when she was still a lawyer. At some charity do.' He looked up, aware of the danger despite the easy words. 'Is Daniel a suspect?'

'Not at this point. I was there for background information.' Vera thought she should have realized that Watkins would know the pair socially. When it came to brown-nosing, he'd put the wiliest politician to shame, and he had an instinct for gossip.

'No reason to overreact then, is there?' Watkins's smile was genuine now. 'The last thing the service locally needs is our PCC all over the media. Another distraction in a high-profile case, I'm sure you'll agree.'

Vera had just sat back at her desk when her phone rang. A call-handler taking initial responses from the public. 'There's a guy on the line who says he's Kelsall's solicitor. Shall I put him through?'

'Please. What's his name?'

'Stanwick. Gordon Stanwick.'

'Isn't he local?' Vera had been expecting someone high-powered from London.

'Yeah. He's from Stanwick and Crosby. They're in Market Street.'

'Tell him I'll come and see him in his office then, would you?' Unlike the boss, Vera thought she preferred face-to-face contact every time. You couldn't read body language on a screen. Or smell fear. 'If it's convenient, I'll be there in half an hour. Any problems, give me a shout.'

It seemed there were no problems, so she grabbed the coat, which was almost dry, and went out into the town.

Vera had come across Gordon Stanwick before, not because he was a criminal lawyer, but because he'd handled Hector's affairs. Hector had left everything to her in his will, which had surprised her. She'd always assumed that her father was closer to his small gang of friends than his daughter, and that they might benefit instead of her. Stanwick was a grey, ageless man, who thrived on detail. There'd been very little money left in Hector's accounts, but she'd been glad of the cottage and the Land Rover. Stanwick had offered her a glass of very good single malt, with the gravity of a priest at communion, when he shared the details of the will with her. 'I always feel that these moments deserve to be marked.'

Now, he was waiting for her in the downstairs lobby. He hadn't changed at all in the intervening years. She'd thought him middle-aged then, but he must have been a young man, playing the role. He led her upstairs.

'I saw about Mr Kelsall's death on the news and thought I should get in touch.'

'I was a little surprised that you were handling his affairs.'

'Well, we looked after his parents,' Stanwick said. It sounded as if he were a care worker rather than a family lawyer. 'A lot of people like the sense of continuity, even when they move away.'

'You prepared Mr Kelsall's will?'

'We did, and I updated it earlier in the year after his father died.'

'That will have been before Rick lost his job with the television company?'

'Indeed, it was. But really his salary was only a minor proportion of his total income. He made far more through his freelance work and he still has a considerable sum to pass on.' He looked at her over his rimless spectacles. 'But I'm sure you're a busy woman, Inspector, and you'd like to know who benefits from his will.'

'Indeed I would, Mr Stanwick.'

He raised his eyebrows at her repeating one of his favourite phrases and then he smiled.

'He has two children from his first marriage and they inherit his London flat, which would, at today's valuation, be worth at least a million pounds.'

'For a flat?'

'I understand that it's a well-appointed flat in a sought-after area. They also inherit the greater proportion of his savings. There are modest legacies of twenty thousand pounds each to Philip Robson and Kenneth Hampton, with thanks for their friendship over many years. The remainder of his wealth, including the value of his parents' house in Kimmerston, is to be split equally between two women: Charlotte Thomas and Annie Laidler.'

It took Vera a while to take in all the information. Twenty thousand pounds didn't seem particularly modest to her, and while passing on the bulk of his wealth to his children seemed normal and appropriate, the substantial sums bequeathed to Charlotte and Annie were astonishing. She knew Rick's parents' house. The doctors had been well known in the town for as long as she could remember, and while it wouldn't fetch anything like London properties, it was substantial, in a good part of town, and would make the women a lot of money.

'Did Mr Kelsall explain that last bequest? To the two women?'

'No. I did ask him about it, but he wasn't forthcoming.'

'Was it a part of the original will, or did he add it while he was updating after his father's death?'

'It was a part of the update. Dr Kelsall remained in the family home until not long before his death, so I suppose it would have seemed more relevant after the funeral.'

'Do Charlotte and Annie know of the provisions of the will?'

'I haven't informed them yet. Of course, Mr Kelsall might have done.'

'He saw both women in the days just before he died,' Vera said, 'so perhaps he did tell them.' She thought that would fit in with what she'd learned of the man. He'd love the role of benefactor. Saviour. He'd want their gratitude, their adoration.

Out in the street, she was already planning her next move. She'd talk again to Annie and Charlotte. Of the two, Annie probably had more need of Kelsall's money, but sometimes appearances were deceptive. Jax had told Vera that Annie had invested in the deli, and besides, Vera found it hard to imagine Annie killing for the prospect of a more comfortable retirement. Charlotte, however, seemed to have a lifestyle which would be expensive to maintain. Vera knew that her prejudices were influencing her judgement here. She liked Annie, but had found Charlotte, with her smooth and glossy exterior, hard to fathom.

She was thinking she might call into Bread and Olives to buy something for her lunch, was drooling at the prospect of one of Jax's sandwiches, when her phone went. Holly. A little breathless.

'Ma'am, I've tracked down the identity of the woman who made the complaint against Kelsall, the first one that went public.'

'And?'

'It was a young intern, who was there on work experience after she graduated.'

'Do we have a name for her?'

A pause. 'Yes. She's called Eliza.' Another pause. 'Eliza Bond.'

'Should that mean something to me?' Because Vera could sense Holly's excitement at the end of the line.

'She took her father's surname,' Holly said, 'and kept it after her parents separated. Her mother's name is Willmore.'

Vera remembered the pale face staring down at her from Rede's astonishing house.

'She's the PCC's daughter?'

'Exactly.'

'Bugger!' Because, although Vera felt a moment of glee when she thought of Watkins's discomfort at hearing this news, there was no doubt that it would make the investigation very much more complicated.

Chapter Twenty-Four

IT WAS CHARLIE WHO TRACKED DOWN Judy Marshall, former teacher, former charismatic changer of young people's lives. She was working in a food bank based in a church hall, just off Kimmerston Front Street. It was only half a mile from the police station, so the detectives decided to walk.

'How did you find her?' Joe realized that Charlie had a network of informal contacts but this was quick work, even for him.

'One of my elderly neighbours is a volunteer there. She's chatty. Lonely, I suppose. I've only got to be in the garden five minutes and she's there, offering cups of coffee and home-made cake.'

'You want to be careful. She might have designs on your body . . . A handsome bloke like you . . .'

Charlie was single now, with a daughter who was a final-year student at Newcastle Uni. He'd been through a patch of loneliness and depression himself, after a messy divorce. There'd been times when Joe would have been more careful, and certainly wouldn't have made bad jokes about a new relationship. But these days, his colleague seemed in a much better place.

Charlie grinned. 'I think I could do better than that, even if I *was* in the market for romance. She's eighty if she's a day.' A pause. 'Does good cake though. I remembered her talking about a Judy who works with her. A woman who used to teach at the Grammar. Apparently, it's *our* Judy and she's in charge at the food bank today.'

A gust of wind blew a scrap of litter along the pavement. Joe picked it up and threw it into a bin. He'd been in the food bank before. He'd taken along a young lass who'd been picked up for shoplifting. She'd had no previous convictions and it'd been baby milk she'd been hiding under the quilt in the pram, not luxury items for her own use. Her man had been made redundant when the firm he worked for went bust. Joe had seen desperation in her face, and shame, and in the end, they'd let her go with a caution. Vera's decision. And it had been Vera who'd sent Joe after the lass.

'Take her to the food bank at St Paul's. Go in with her. She'll be too proud or too embarrassed to go there herself. Make out you're a friend. Last thing she needs is to go in with a cop.'

Joe had felt awkward walking into the building, anxious despite himself, that he'd be seen by someone he knew. Knowing it was ridiculous, but feeling second-hand the stigma of someone who couldn't feed their kids.

The church was old and squat. He and Sal had been married there, and had had their photos taken on the steps outside. His family had been a bit wary at first. They were Methodist not C of E, and were worried they might get things wrong, but the elderly vicar had put them at their ease, and they'd recognized all the hymns. The food bank was in the hall next door, a big barn of a place, built at a time when the congregation had been bigger, when the Sunday School had been thriving.

Judy Marshall was quite clearly the person in charge. She was tall and slender, with white hair, cut short, slightly curly. Her skin was clear and her eyes were very large and very blue. She moved like a dancer and Joe could tell she'd have been stunning to look at as a young woman. She was supervising the filling of the shelves and must have said something amusing, because suddenly the people around her began to laugh.

She walked up to them with a smile of welcome. The hall was high-ceilinged, dusty. She was wearing a long sweater over leggings and ballet pumps, which added to the first impression Joe had of her as someone who could dance. The soft shoes made a sliding sound on the wooden floor. 'How can I help you? Is this your first time?'

'You *are* Judith Marshall.'

'That's me!' The voice was still professionally cheery, but she was curious. 'At least that was my maiden name. It's Judith Sinclair these days. Judy to my friends.' She looked at them. 'Did I teach either of you?'

Joe shook his head, smiling. Her good humour was infectious. 'Any chance of a chat?' He introduced himself and Charlie, and held out his warrant card to convince her.

'Of course.' She called out to a colleague. 'Can you take over for a bit?' She led them down the length of the hall, past makeshift wooden shelves piled with tins and jars, and through a door, which led down a short corridor and into the church itself. There was a smell of wood polish, candle wax and incense. At the centre of the church she stopped, so suddenly that

Charlie nearly walked into her. She turned towards the altar and bowed her head, a gesture of reverence, and stood for a moment before continuing. An automatic response, but one that still seemed deeply felt. She was a believer then, a member of this church. They walked through another door and into the vestry. The vicar's robes were hanging on a coat hanger on a hook on the door. There was an electric kettle on a tray, half a dozen mugs and a jar of instant coffee.

'Can I offer you a drink?' She seemed completely at home. 'This is my sanctuary when things get too much at the food bank. The vicar's very good about letting us use it. We hear such heartbreaking stories and sometimes we need a place of escape.'

Joe shook his head.

'What is this about, Sergeant?'

'One of your former pupils died at the weekend. Rick Kelsall.'

'Yes. I saw the news. I remember him, of course. Not just because he went on to become something of a celebrity. He stood out even then. We all knew he was destined for something special.' She paused. 'It wasn't only that he was academically gifted. He had a confidence, an ambition that set him apart from the other students.'

'Is that why you remember him so well? You must have taught thousands of pupils over your career.'

'One of the reasons. But I was in my first year as a qualified teacher. Very young. Very idealistic. I saw teaching as a vocation. I remember most of that cohort. The ones who came later have become rather a blur.' She paused and stared at him with the startling blue eyes. 'Why are you speaking to me after all this time, though? I haven't seen Rick for years.'

Joe didn't answer directly. 'You were never invited to one of their reunions?'

She paused, playing for time, he thought. Something about this conversation was making her uncomfortable. 'I'm not sure I know what you mean.'

'Rick Kelsall and a group of other students became close friends at a weekend you organized called Only Connect. Now, they come together every five years in the Pilgrims' House on Holy Island. You must remember it, because it was where the first weekend took place. That happened in your first year as a teacher too.' Joe waited for a moment, but she didn't respond. 'It seemed to have made a huge mark on them at the time. One of the parents described the kids as coming back different, lit-up, almost evangelical.'

'They were a very sensitive group. It was a privilege to be there with them. Actually, it was probably the highlight of my teaching career. I never managed to achieve the same response from any other group of students.'

'Yet you didn't go to their first reunion? I'd have thought they would have invited you to join them. As you were so influential.'

'They did invite me to the first reunion,' Judith said.

'But you didn't go?'

She shook her head and seemed to be choosing her words carefully. 'I was a bit naive when I first started teaching. I wasn't much older than the sixth-formers and I was in a strange town, a long way from home. Perhaps I didn't keep sufficiently detached from them. That was probably why I found the weekend so moving, why it was such a success. I was a part of it, as much participant as leader.' She looked up and smiled. 'It changed me as much as it changed the kids. Something very special happened in those quiet evenings in the chapel.' Another pause. 'It was the start of a journey into faith. When we got home, I started to come here, to St Paul's. I met Martin, my husband, here.'

'You're married?'

'I'm widowed. My husband worked as an intensive care nurse throughout his career. The week after he retired, he was killed in a road traffic accident.' She looked up at Joe. 'A truck swerved across the carriageway and into his car. The driver was on his phone and lost concentration.'

There was a moment of silence. Joe couldn't think of anything at all to say. It seemed such a tragedy, such a waste. He couldn't understand how the woman could remain so positive. He was still struggling to find an appropriate response, when Judith continued talking, explaining her relationship with her pupils.

'By the time the first reunion came around, five years after the Only Connect weekend, I was a bit more savvy, and I'd developed more appropriate friendships. By that time, I was going out with Martin. I was flattered to be asked, of course, but I knew it would be a mistake to go.'

'Even though by then you were no longer in a position of responsibility where they were concerned?' Joe wasn't sure he bought this explanation. 'I can see you'd want to keep your distance when you were teaching them, but not when they were adults.'

'As I said, by then I'd moved on. The last thing I wanted was to spend a weekend with a bunch of young people in an uncomfortable house on the island.'

'When was the last time you met Rick Kelsall?'

'Oh gosh, years ago. He was on the other side of Kimmerston Front Street and I went up to him and introduced myself. I was a bit starstruck I suppose – not my style at all – but he was at the height of his fame at that point. He had his wife with him. Charlotte. I taught her too.'

'Did they remember you?'

'They did! It was all rather wonderful. Rick said I'd given him a love of the written word. We chatted for a bit and then they went on their way.'

'They didn't talk about Only Connect? It was so important to them they've been meeting every five years ever since.'

Judith shook her head. 'I don't really think it was *so* important, you know. The Only Connect weekend seemed to have taken on a kind of mythical status within the school, but that group would have become close friends anyway. They were into the same things. Music. Drama. They all took part in the school play that I produced.' She seemed to think carefully before speaking. 'I think it was the island that made it so special, the evenings in the chapel, the sense of history and spirituality. Did you know that one member of the group later became ordained?'

'Philip? He was there this weekend when Rick Kelsall died.'

'Yes, Philip. I *have* kept in touch with him. He's spending this week in my holiday cottage on Holy Island and he's invited me to go and see him. I'm looking forward to it.'

'You own a property on the island?'

She nodded. 'My husband and I bought it years ago. It was our escape from work.'

'Did you spend the whole of your career in Kimmerston Grammar?' Charlie asked. 'You never wanted a change?'

'Well, it became a comp soon after of course, but yes. Martin was a local man. We settled down and had children. Any ambition I once had seemed less important than the family. I suppose I got complacent. I was happy enough as a classroom teacher and I never wanted to go into management. Our sons have grown up and moved away.' She paused. 'It was dreadful when Martin died. Such a shock and we had so many plans, so many adventures left to experience. I struggled at first, but I've got good friends, and the church. I've thrown all my energy into the work here.' She gave a little smile. 'When I meet the folk who use the food bank, I realize I'm so much better off than many people of my age.'

Charlie seemed satisfied by the response. Joe wasn't convinced. He didn't think the woman was lying, but there was something missing, something she wasn't telling them.

'Have you kept in touch with any of the others? Any of Rick's friends, I mean, besides Philip Robson.'

'Not really. I see Annie Laidler in Bread and Olives when I go in. I do see more of Charlotte. I treat myself to a weekly class in her new studio. I've always enjoyed yoga and after Martin died, I found her meditation sessions very helpful. She's rather a good instructor. Much more empathetic than you might expect.' She paused to emphasize her confusion. 'But really, Sergeant, I don't understand this fixation with the past.'

'Rick Kelsall was murdered,' Joe said. 'Somebody put a cushion over his head and held it there until he could no longer breathe.' He looked at her, trying to gauge her reaction. 'And he died at the Pilgrims' House, at one of the reunions when he was with his old school friends. They all have to be considered potential suspects. That's why we're fixated with the past.'

There was another silence. 'I'm sorry,' she said. 'I hadn't realized. Of course, then I can understand the focus on the old friendships.'

'I know it's a long shot,' Joe went on, 'but nothing happened all those years ago, which might have come back to haunt them?'

Judith held his gaze for a moment, before shaking her head.

'After fifty years? Really, Sergeant, I don't think that's very likely, do you? They were kids, interesting, lively kids. I didn't meet anyone there who would possibly have gone on to become a killer.'

Back at the station, Holly was at her desk, speaking on the phone, intense, focused as only she could be. She ended the call and looked up at Joe and Charlie as they walked past.

'I've just arranged calls to someone at the TV production company where Rick worked and with his agent. They won't be free until this afternoon.'

'Giving them time to get their story straight.' Charlie could be a cynical bastard, Joe thought, but this time he was probably right.

'Probably.' Holly gave a quick grin. 'But they wanted to foist me off with a secretary and someone from HR, and at least I've persuaded them to speak to me in person.' A pause. Joe sensed an elation, a moment of triumph. 'But that's not the most important call I made today. I've finally tracked down the complainant in the Rick Kelsall sexual assault case. I told the boss earlier. It was Katherine Willmore's daughter Eliza.'

'Well,' Charlie said. 'The PCC didn't pass on that gem of information when she was talking to our Vera yesterday. I'm not sure how she thought she'd be able to keep it secret.'

'Willmore's got powerful friends,' Holly said. 'She worked in London before she moved here. She'll have contacts in the police and the press. And she knows the law well enough to persuade them of the need to keep the victim's identity secret.'

She tipped her head towards the ceiling. 'The boss is talking to Watkins now.'

'How did you get the info?'

'I was at school with a journo on one of the tabloids.'

'Is that who you were talking to when we came in?'

Holly shook her head. 'No, that was Rick's mobile provider. They'll send through the full list of transactions but I wanted to know if there'd been any significant calls in the days before his death.'

'And?'

'Apart from a couple of texts to his kids, there were only two numbers, both phone calls, both incoming. One was the call he took when he was at Charlotte's on the Friday morning before heading to the island. The other he received late on the evening of his death. That's probably the most important because it might give us a more precise time of death. I'm trying to track it down. I'll let you know as soon as I get it.'

Joe nodded. This was all valuable information and would probably be more use to them than a foray into the past, but he was still thinking of Judith, still trying to reconcile the seventy-year-old woman in the food bank with the idealistic young teacher who'd changed the way a group of teenagers had looked at the world. He thought of the faded photograph, the group of kids squinting into the sun, and the teacher in the centre, who'd looked no older than the rest of them.

Chapter Twenty-Five

WHEN VERA LEFT THE SUPERINTENDENT, she was almost sorry for the man. She'd asked him if he'd like to talk to Katherine Willmore about the fact that her daughter had been the victim of Rick Kelsall's harassment. The *apparent* victim, because so far there'd been no criminal charge brought. And with Kelsall dead, there probably wouldn't be. 'It might come better from a more senior officer.'

'Oh, I don't think that would be at all appropriate.' The words had come tumbling from Watkins's mouth, a torrent of panic. 'There'd be a conflict of interest. We meet socially. It would be much better coming from you.'

They'd looked at each other, both of them knowing that he was a coward and that this was an excuse.

In her office, Vera phoned Willmore's secretary, a young man with an impeccable public-school accent.

'I'm afraid Miss Willmore is working from home today. I could probably set up an appointment for tomorrow morning in the office. She's got a free slot at eight-fifty.'

'Nah, you're okay, pet.' Attempting the kind of West End

Newcastle Geordie spoken by the older members of the Thomas clan, and just about making it. 'This is personal. I'll catch her later.' She wasn't entirely sure that he'd understood a word she'd said.

Vera had planned to see Charlotte to talk about Rick's will before the bombshell about Katherine Willmore's daughter had hit, but that would have to wait until she'd spoken to the PCC. Vera wandered out into the main office and perched on Holly's desk.

'What do we know about this life coach business of Charlotte's?'

'I haven't gone into it in any detail. Not since that first day on the island. And that was just checking out her website.'

'I'd be interested to know how solvent she is. Since the Thomas family has gone almost legit in their old age, they'll likely have had less coming in, and she's not the celebrity draw that she once was. Rick's left her all that money in his will, and it might be a motive.'

'She hardly looked on the breadline when she turned up to Holy Island.'

'A few smart clothes and a fancy car,' Vera said. 'That could all be show. She might have had the clothes for years. I understand that the classics never go out of fashion.' She'd read that in a magazine in the dentist's waiting room, but she could tell that Holly was impressed.

'I'll see what I can find out.'

'Then I'd like you to go and see her. I want to know if Rick told her he was leaving half his parents' house to her in his will. You built up a good relationship when you spoke to her on the island. Get her to trust you. Encourage a bit of girly gossip about the rest of the group. See what she made of Isobel

Hall. They sound like two of a kind. Charlotte might not have been on the island when the lass drove her car off the causeway, but maybe she had some idea about the background to the accident.'

Holly nodded, pulled out a notebook, and started writing.

Vera continued talking. 'We know Rick stayed with Charlotte the night before he died. What did they talk about? Does she know Katherine Willmore? It's possible after all. They could even be friends. Charlotte was at school with Daniel, and while Katherine might not have needed a life coach, I can see her doing yoga to relax in her spare time. They could mix in the same circles.'

Holly nodded again. She looked earnest, the swotty school-girl trying to gain her teacher's approval. Vera felt a little moment of affection. Of pride.

'I'm going to chat to Katherine Willmore. That's a big coincidence, her daughter being the person to make those allegations against Kelsall. Let's see what she has to say for herself. We'll catch up this evening at the briefing.'

'Sure.' At last Holly looked up from the notes. 'Cool.'

This time, when she got to Rede's Lodges, Vera didn't stop at reception in the tower. She hadn't phoned to make an appointment with Willmore. She drove on through the nature reserve. The branches seemed stripped of leaves after the wind overnight and a breeze pushed the water in the nature reserve pool into little waves. The place was quieter than it had been at the weekend. She parked outside the house, camouflaged by trees. There were no other vehicles there, but all the same she rang the bell and waited. No reply. She looked up to the window where she'd seen the pale face the afternoon before. It was still there, peering out. Did the lass spend all her time in her room, staring out at the world? A kind of modern Rapunzel, waiting for someone to rescue her. Vera waved just before the face disappeared from sight, then rang the bell again. She heard faint footsteps inside the house and then the door was opened.

The young woman who stood inside was wearing a shapeless brown woollen dress that reminded Vera of a sock. She still managed to look good in it. Vera thought perhaps the young could look good in anything.

'You must be Eliza. I work with your mother. I was here yesterday.'

'Mother's not at home.'

'It's not really your mam I want to speak to.'

Eliza stood aside and let Vera in. They stood in the hall with its sharp, white walls and pale wood floors. A kind of no-man's-land between the woods and the sea.

'You must know why I'm here, pet.'

Eliza might be in her early twenties, but Vera saw her as a girl, delicate, only half-formed. It was hard to believe that she'd had the courage and confidence to take on Rick Kelsall and a TV production company. Vera couldn't imagine her ever being brash or defiant.

'You had a run-in with Rick Kelsall and now he's dead. You can see why I might want a chat. Nothing formal. Do you want to give your mam a shout? We can wait until she gets back.'

Eliza shook her head. 'No, come on through. I wanted to come down and speak to you yesterday, but I didn't quite have the nerve.'

'Were you listening then? While I was speaking to Daniel?'

'I was on the stairs.' She smiled. 'I couldn't hear much

though, and Mum shooed me back upstairs when she came in.' A pause. 'I'm kind of in hiding. Not from the police. From the press. My mother's got a horror of my name coming out.'

'Daniel,' Vera said. 'He's your step-dad?'

'Kind of. They're not married though.'

'What do you make of him?'

'I like him! He's very different from my dad, but they divorced ages ago. Daniel adores my mother. He makes her very happy.' She considered for a moment. 'I love spending time with them.'

Vera nodded towards the door leading to the long, light living room with its view of the water. 'Shall we find somewhere a bit more comfortable to sit?'

'Oh God, of course. Sorry. I'm all over the place. Everything's just been a bit shit.'

Vera thought it had been more than a bit shit for Rick Kelsall, but she didn't say anything. The view was quite different this afternoon. A grey, stormy sea, lit by occasional blasts of sunlight as the clouds parted.

'How long have you been back? I thought you were living in London.' Vera settled on a very comfortable sofa.

'I was, but Mum thought I'd be better here. She didn't trust me not to blab.'

'About the sexual assault complaint against Rick Kelsall?'

The girl nodded and blushed. 'She drove down and got me. And honestly, it was a relief to get home. I don't think I'm actually a city girl.'

'How long have you been here?'

'Just over a month.'

'Did you have any contact with Kelsall when he was here in Northumberland?'

She looked up at Vera and seemed to shrink inside the loose, woollen dress. '*I* didn't.'

'But Katherine and Daniel did?'

She didn't answer and Vera could hear the stormy waves outside, the sound a background rumble, even through the expensive triple glazing of the enormous windows.

'It was Daniel who got me the internship,' Eliza said at last. 'He'd been to school with Rick and I wanted it so much. An experience like that, it's gold dust if you want to work in the industry.'

'So, Daniel pulled a few strings?' He did it for Katherine, even though he and Rick hadn't been close as boys, and Rick would have loved that, acting the benefactor again, handing out favours, knowing how hard it must have been for Daniel to ask.

She nodded.

'Where did they meet, your parents and Kelsall?'

'Here. He was on his way to Holy Island.'

'On Friday lunchtime?'

She nodded again. 'It was a last-minute thing.' The phone call he'd got when he was at Charlotte's.

'What was the meeting about? To give Kelsall a chance to explain his crass behaviour to you, to apologize? Yet you say you didn't see him.'

'No, I left it all to Daniel and my mother. It was a secret that I was here at all. Nobody else knew. I stayed in my room.' A pause. 'Mum said she might be able to sort out the situation, that if she talked to him, she thought she'd be able to make the mess go away.'

'But, as I understand it, pet, he was the person in the shit. Not you. You were the victim. Nothing to blame yourself for.'

A silence. Eliza was thinking through the answer.

We all turn our lives into stories, Vera thought. We all want to make excuses for the stuff we're ashamed of.

'The whole thing was blown out of proportion,' Eliza said. 'And once it had started, I couldn't find a way to stop it.'

'Was there a sexual assault?'

The direct question seemed to take her by surprise. She stared back, but there was no answer.

Vera went on: 'Did Rick Kelsall touch you in an inappropriate way?'

Still no direct answer. 'He made me feel uncomfortable.' The words were mumbled, half-hearted.

Vera nodded slowly. 'Some men can do that to you, and they mean to do it; they like the power. I can think of a few in my time.' A pause. 'But there was no physical contact? No assault?'

Eliza shook her head.

'So, it was the bullying that upset you and started the whole thing off?'

'He behaved in the same way to all the younger staff.'

'But you were the one to make the complaint?' Vera was struggling to understand how this had become such an enormous story. There must be overbearing boors in many offices throughout the country. Of course, not all the complainants were the daughters of Police and Crime Commissioners, but that didn't explain why two people had been killed.

'I was set up,' Eliza said. The words came out in a rush. 'I've been such a bloody fool.'

Vera was aware that time was passing and that Katherine and Daniel could turn up at any moment, but Eliza was in no state to be hurried. 'Who set you up?'

'There was a runner in the office. Stella. Not much older

than me. Bright. Ambitious. I thought she was my friend. Nobody else took much notice of me. I've always been a bit in my mother's shadow. Stella and I were in the pub after work one night and her boyfriend was there. We were talking about Rick, about what a lech he was, about how he treated the younger women.' She looked up at Vera. 'They were listening to me, laughing at my jokes. Nobody much has ever done that. My mother was the centre of attention wherever we went and I was shy. I didn't mind being overlooked. At university I kept to my own small crowd. But it was quite heady that night in the pub and I'd had a few glasses of wine.' She looked up at Vera. This was confession time. 'I exaggerated a bit to get a reaction. And agreed with Stella when she made him out to be a bit of a monster. To make the story more interesting.'

Vera nodded. She'd known police officers who were more keen on a good story, a story that would lead to a conviction, than the truth.

'Stella's boyfriend was a journalist on a tabloid. Also, it seemed, hugely ambitious. Two days later it was plastered all over the front page. *Rick Kelsall is a sex pest. Pretty young intern tells all.* It was a nightmare. They'd exaggerated even the story I'd given them, and I thought everyone who knew the company would be able to work out who'd told the press. There was nothing concrete. It was all innuendo, but the implication was that I'd been raped.'

'Did you explain to your mother what had really happened?' Vera thought that, despite what she'd said, Eliza had been the victim in the case. She'd been abused twice. She'd been bullied by a powerful man in the public eye, and then she'd been exploited by a journalist for his own ends.

'I phoned her. The press had already contacted her for her

views. She said she'd sue if they made my name public, and she called in every favour she was owed. It was a nightmare for her. If it all came out, she couldn't be seen to support Rick Kelsall over her own daughter. Not in a case like this. Not when her reputation rests on her support for women in cases of abuse.'

Not even if Kelsall had done nothing wrong. Vera thought this gave them the strongest possible motive for murder. She wondered why the man hadn't already gone public to clear his name. Some strange notion of chivalry? Because there was at least some foundation in the allegations, if not in Eliza's case, of some of the other women who had since come forward? Because he enjoyed the notoriety? Or because it made him feel good to do a favour for a powerful woman?

'I suppose it all became a bit of a circus.'

Eliza paused for a moment. 'The press had gone to the company for comment. It was like a snowball rolling down a hill, getting bigger and bigger and completely out of control. I got called in to HR at work. I was really anxious, certain I'd been found out, but instead they were dead sympathetic: "We're so sorry, we'll do anything we can to support you." There was even a promise of a job when the internship ended. I did try to explain but, honestly, they weren't interested. They just wouldn't listen.' Eliza stopped talking and looked up at Vera, willing her to understand.

'What happened then?' Vera was sympathetic, but she needed the whole story.

'I took a couple of weeks' sick leave. I thought the whole thing might just blow over. But then more women started posting stuff online about Rick, and as soon as I went back to work, the management were on my case again, wanting me to make a statement and a formal complaint to the police.'

'Maybe they had their own agenda.' Vera thought management often did.

'I think they'd been looking for an excuse to get shot of Rick. He was under contract at a high salary and his ratings were down.' She looked up at Vera. It was confession time again. 'In the end I stopped protesting. I would have felt such a fool to admit that I'd exaggerated for effect.'

'Aye, and perhaps they wanted to prove to the world that they took allegations of bullying and harassment seriously. It was all about appearance. Nobody was really interested in the facts.' Vera smiled at the girl. 'By then, it must have seemed as if you'd lost control of the whole thing.'

'It was horrible!'

'It must have been quite a relief when Mr Kelsall died. The story would have died with him.'

'No!' Eliza's horror seemed genuine. 'All I felt was guilt. I wanted to apologize, and I knew now that I wouldn't have the chance. The false allegations would be linked to him forever. That Friday when he came for lunch, I was all for coming downstairs and explaining to him what had happened, but my mother said not to. She said she and Daniel would sort it. I could hear them talking in the room below my bedroom, but I didn't do anything to put it right.'

'Do you do everything your mother tells you?' Vera was genuinely curious. She didn't have much knowledge of young people, but she'd disagreed with everything Hector, her father, had stood for, just as a matter of principle. Wasn't it the role of children to rebel against their parents?

'I suppose I do,' Eliza said. 'She has a very strong personality and I'm a bit pathetic. I hate confrontation.'

'Did they sort things out? Katherine, Daniel and Kelsall?'

'I think they must have done. My mother seemed more relaxed that afternoon after he'd gone.'

'Do you know what they'd decided?'

Eliza shook her head. 'Mother said it was best that I didn't know, but that they'd come to an agreement.'

Vera thought that would be a very interesting conversation to have with Katherine Willmore. 'Where are your mother and Daniel? Do you know when they'll be home?'

'Not until late this evening, they said.'

'Ah well, I'll leave you in peace then.' *And after all, that interview would be better had formally, in the police station.* 'Can you let me have your mam's mobile number?'

'Sure.'

'You will be okay here on your own until they get back?' Because she still couldn't see Eliza as a fully formed woman. She seemed so innocent, so childlike.

'Of course.' Eliza stood up. 'Thanks,' she said, 'for properly listening.'

'Eh, pet, that's what detectives do. That's what'll help us catch Rick Kelsall's killer.'

Chapter Twenty-Six

HOLLY WENT ONLINE TO RESEARCH THE women she intended speaking to before she made the calls. These were the professionals who'd played a big part in Rick Kelsall's working life. Sally Baker was the executive producer at the television company where Rick Kelsall had been employed for most of his career. There were photographs of her at awards ceremonies, looking glamorous if slightly dishevelled. She was in her late forties. Holly could find no mention of a husband or children, but in the photographs, she was often on the arm of a good-looking man, an actor or another producer. She was a short woman and her head was usually tilted upwards, staring adoringly into her companion's eyes.

The resignation of Rick Kelsall was widely covered, and Sally Baker was quoted in most of the articles. *We will not tolerate this kind of behaviour, even in our most established stars. Rick has recognized that he acted inappropriately and has resigned.*

'Poor Rick,' Baker said, when Holly was put through to her. 'Though really, I think he might have enjoyed all this drama, and being the centre of attention again.'

It seemed an unsympathetic response.

'You don't seem surprised that somebody killed him.' Holly's tone was conversational. She didn't want to sound too disapproving. She needed the woman to talk.

'Honestly? I'm not. He provoked me almost to murder at least once a month.' A pause. 'He was a consummate professional, of course, but he hadn't realized that the business has moved on. We don't have the resources that we had when he started out. He could be rather demanding.'

'So, you weren't sad to let him go?'

'I'm not saying that. I actually liked the man. As a person. To spar with and bounce ideas off. I had the confidence to stand up to him and he knew better than to mess with me, but he was becoming a bit of an embarrassment.' Baker paused. 'A dinosaur.'

'You weren't surprised when Eliza made her allegations?'

'Well, I was rather. She's a timid little thing. I wouldn't have thought she was Rick's type. He was never particularly attracted to the innocent little interns.'

Holly wondered if Sally Baker had been Rick's type. She could imagine the two of them having a fling after a few too many drinks at some wrap party. Then Sally living with the awkwardness of seeing him at work every day, wondering if he was going to make her indiscretion public. Perhaps she'd had her own, very personal, reasons for wanting to get rid of him.

'Yet you believed Eliza?'

There was a moment of silence and Holly wondered if Baker had hung up on her or if the connection had been lost, but after a few seconds the woman responded.

'Of course! We have to, these days. There can be no more

sweeping these things under the carpet and blaming the victim. Really, if there was any sniff of a cover-up, the press would rip us apart.'

So, truth, Holly thought, had nothing to do with it.

The woman was still speaking. 'Then there was Eliza's mother. Of course, we had to take Katherine Willmore into account. She's a very powerful woman, with an axe to grind when it comes to women's issues.' There was another pause. 'Though she was much more concerned about keeping her daughter's name out of the press than pushing for justice. She'd have been perfectly happy, I think, if we'd taken no action at all against Rick.'

'So why *did* you get rid of him?'

Baker took a while to answer. 'We decided that the whole thing was bound to come out in the end and we couldn't be seen to have been complicit.' She paused, then her tone softened, became more confidential, almost conspiratorial. 'And to be honest, Rick didn't present the image that the company needed anymore. He had a loyal following with the oldies, but we're trying to target a younger audience, and Rick Kelsall wasn't the man who would pull in the under-thirties. Or even the under-fifties.'

'So, the allegations came at a very convenient time for you?'

'Well, that is a *little* harsh, but yes, I suppose it's true.'

'When did you last see Rick Kelsall?'

There was another hesitation.

'Actually, it was just the week before he died. We met up in Soho for a few drinks and a bite to eat.' A pause. 'It was in a way a farewell celebration. Just the two of us. Obviously, I couldn't do anything more formal – we could hardly have a jolly leaving bash in the office – but it seemed a bit heartless just to send him on his way after all those years. He'd seen the company through some difficult times. There were periods when his show kept us afloat.'

They'd definitely had a fling.

'How did he seem?'

'Surprisingly buoyant,' Baker said. 'And I don't think it was all bravado. He said he had other fish to fry. He was moving in a new direction. We drank too much champagne, then I staggered home and hadn't heard from him since. It was a shock to see his face all over social media yesterday.'

'He didn't give any details of his new ventures?'

'No,' Baker said. 'It was all very mysterious. But then there was nothing Rick liked better than a good mystery.'

Holly's research into Rick Kelsall's agent had pulled up her website. Cecilia Bertrand ran an agency representing clients who worked mostly in the news media. There was one photograph, showing a tiny, elderly and very elegant woman. Everything about her was beautifully styled and understated. She was sitting in a wood-panelled office, behind a large desk, with a long window behind her. References from other sources described her as 'the queen of broadcasting' and 'deliciously ruthless'.

Cecilia was obviously expecting Holly's Zoom call and she answered immediately. Her voice was beautifully modulated, almost regal, but as the conversation went on Holly discovered that she could swear like a Newcastle United fan on match night.

'How can I help you, Constable? Of course, I'll give you everything you need. Such a fucking tragedy, just as Rick was about to embark on his exciting new project.'

'What exactly was that?'

'He'd turned his hand to writing. A thriller. Of course, every bugger in the media is doing it at the moment, but it seems he was really rather good. Not my field, but my co-agent got him a very good deal with a major publisher on the strength of a synopsis and some early chapters. He promised me he was writing like a demon and he'd have the first draft finished by the end of the year.'

'Had you seen what he'd written so far?'

'I'm afraid not. He was most secretive about the whole thing.'

'So would that have replaced his television income?' This was a completely new world and Holly was struggling to work out the implication of the information.

'Well, he made more from personal appearances and lectures than he did from his salary. These days the Beeb is notoriously mean-spirited when it comes to presenters. But Rick Kelsall was no pauper, Constable. He had a good lifestyle, despite paying off two wives and supporting his kids. And yes, he got a very nice advance from publishers here and in the US. He was using incidents from his personal experience to kickstart the story, and there's nothing the media likes more than revelation about a celebrity's past.'

'Can you give me any detail about the content of the novel? It could be useful in our inquiries.'

'I'm afraid I can't. As I said, he submitted a short synopsis, but that was rather vague. Sketchy even.' A pause then an admission. 'Hardly more than a paragraph, actually.'

Holly wondered how the woman could make any judgement about the quality of Kelsall's writing on the strength of a brief synopsis. And how a publisher might be persuaded to part with an advance. Perhaps celebrity would be enough.

Cecilia seemed to read Holly's mind. 'If Rick was struggling a bit with the *structure* of the writing, the daily grind so to speak, the thought was that a good editor would be able to help.'

Or even write the thing for him . . . 'You must have some idea about the plot.'

'Well of course! It started with a killing on a small island. He was absolutely fired up by the idea, though he's been hugely secretive ever since.' She stopped suddenly. 'Shit, that's all rather prescient, isn't it? As if he were predicting his own death.'

'Could I see what he'd written?'

'Of course! I'll email it across.' Cecilia Bertrand paused for a moment. 'If you find any material on his computer, of course, we'd love to see it. It would be ours under contract. He might even have nearly finished that first draft. My God, the publisher would wet themselves if we could deliver something they can use. They might be able to find some big name willing to complete it. Can you imagine the publicity? It would be a worldwide sensation.'

She closed her eyes, dreaming, it seemed, of posthumous fame and fortune for Rick Kelsall. And fortune for her. All pretended sadness at her client's death had disappeared.

Holly ended the meeting and sat for a moment at her desk. She thought that Vera would be delighted at the information she'd gained. The advances from publishers, which Cecilia had negotiated on her client's behalf, meant that Kelsall's decision to leave a proportion of his estate to Annie Laidler and Charlotte Thomas was even more relevant as a motive. And the fact that his thriller was about a death on an island brought Isobel Hall's car crash back into focus. She was about to call Vera to pass on the information, when her own phone rang. It was the boss, asking if Holly was ready yet to interview Charlotte Thomas. And with a request of her own.

Chapter Twenty-Seven

KATHERINE WILLMORE STILL WASN'T ANSWERING HER phone. The schoolboy secretary told Vera that the Police and Crime Commissioner had given instructions that she wasn't to be disturbed. Vera had left messages asking the woman to call her back urgently, but so far, there'd been no response.

When she returned to Kimmerston from Rede's Tower, it was earlier than Vera had expected. The conversation with Eliza had left her excited. Suddenly she'd been given a new perspective on the case, and her brain was jumping with possibilities. Eliza's exaggeration of her problems as an intern at last provided a concrete motive for Kelsall's death. Katherine Willmore would be vilified by the press if it came to light that her daughter had made a false allegation of rape. Throughout her career, Katherine had insisted that women should be listened to. Her position as PCC would be untenable. And Vera couldn't see why the information *wouldn't* have come to light. Kelsall was hardly a shrinking violet and he would surely have loved the chance to be vindicated, to prove to the world that he'd been forced to resign without reason. Vera wondered why the man hadn't gone public before. Perhaps he was waiting for the optimum time, financially, or perhaps there were other motives for the delay which might explain his murder.

Vera decided that it was time to refocus the investigation. She found it hard to believe that Watkins could be right in any situation, but perhaps she had been wasting time by digging into the past. It was much more likely that this crime was rooted in the present. Perhaps she *did* allow herself to become distracted by history, by the need to understand.

She didn't feel ready to return to the police station, and parked the Land Rover in the town, next to the river. There was a group of children in the play park on the other side of the water. The wind seemed to be making them flighty, unable to settle. They raced and chased and their screams of laughter, and the mothers' chatter, provided a background to her thoughts.

Vera turned her attention to the other possible motive that had come to light during the day: Kelsall's will and the money left to Annie Laidler and Charlotte Thomas. She'd asked Holly to interview the life coach about the legacy, but now she regretted the decision. Charlotte, after all, was at the centre of the investigation, and Vera wanted to be in on the discussion. It wasn't that she didn't trust Hol to do a good job, but she was a control freak. She'd always found it hard to delegate to the team.

'Have you visited the glamorous Charlotte yet, Hol?'

'Sorry, boss, I've been trying to get more of a handle on the state of her business before doing the interview. I've just had two fascinating conversations with Kelsall's agent and his former employer, and that took up a load of time too.'

'Okay, great. You can pass on all *those* details when we meet up.' But Vera's focus was on Rick's ex-wife now. 'What have you got on Charlotte's finances? Any indication, for example, that Gerald or Robbie Thomas invested in her company?'

It was a long shot, because the men were so elderly, but Vera was thinking that a smart yoga studio in Kimmerston might be a good vehicle for the family to launder any profit from organized crime.

'Not yet. I think that's beyond me and we'd need forensic accountants to check on it. But you were right. Charlotte's business is in a pretty ropy state. The inheritance from Kelsall might just keep it afloat. And after the discussion I've just had with his agent, it seems that he had even more to leave than we supposed.'

'How would you feel if I joined you for the chat with Charlotte Thomas? You can carry on being her best buddy and I can ask the awkward questions.'

There was a silence. 'Sure.' Because what else could Holly say after such a request from her boss? Vera couldn't tell whether the younger woman was resentful that her inspector was muscling in, or relieved that she wouldn't have to take full responsibility for the encounter. 'Of course.'

'I've had a most interesting conversation with Eliza and I'll fill everyone in at this evening's briefing. But let's track down Miss Thomas and see what she has to say for herself.'

Holly joined her on the bench looking out over the river. Vera had bought them takeaway coffees. She'd bought sticky buns too but she'd eaten them before Holly had arrived. The wind caught at their hair and their clothes, and snatched away the words as they spoke. The play park on the opposite bank of the river was quiet now.

'What's the deal with Charlotte's business then?' Vera wiped away cappuccino froth from her upper lip.

'She took over a building near here a couple of years ago. It had been a pub, but she had it stripped out and turned into a space for yoga, meditation, Pilates, and somewhere her fitness coaches could do their personal training. All very flash. There are photos on her website.' Holly paused. 'The bar had once belonged to her father, Gerald. He'd let it run down. It must have been losing money over the years, so I suspect he was glad to get shot of it. Although she didn't have to pay for the building, Charlotte still needed a loan for all the work on converting it, and of course it takes time to build a clientele. My guess is she over-extended herself.'

So, Charlotte had *benefited indirectly from the family's criminal activity.* Vera couldn't see, though, how that might be a factor in Kelsall's death.

'Her father and uncle couldn't help her out with the development?'

'I don't think the financial crash was very kind to their businesses either. It's a long time since they were real players. They moved into hospitality when they were too old for organized crime. And they're very elderly now. One's in a care home with dementia and the other's living with his other daughter in Fenham. They're pretty well back where they started, financially and geographically.'

'The big question is whether Rick Kelsall told Charlotte she was a beneficiary in his will when he stayed with her the night before he headed for the island.' Vera got to her feet. 'I imagine that's a bit of information he'd have wanted to pass on in person.' She lobbed her empty coffee cup into the nearest bin. 'Let's go and find out.'

The house was a three-storey Georgian end of terrace in a quiet road set back from the bars and cafes of the town's main street. It ran from the market square to the river.

'She could sell this to prop up the business.' Vera wouldn't fancy living here, surrounded by neighbours, but she thought that lots of people would.

'It's been re-mortgaged,' Holly said. 'Besides, I suppose it suits the image. Her whole business is about helping people to be successful and fulfil their ambitions. It would be hard to convince people to trust her if she were working out of a scuzzy ex-council house on the edge of town.'

'I suppose.'

They'd reached the front door. Vera knocked. No answer.

'Perhaps she's working,' Holly said. 'If she's on a call with a client she probably wouldn't break off to open the door.'

Vera looked through the window and saw a formal dining room. A polished table and six chairs. A sideboard with gleaming glassware. But this was the shop window. It would be interesting to know what was going on further into the house. 'Let's see if there's a way in at the back.' This was what Vera missed, now she had to spend so long at her desk. The prying and nebbing into other folk's business.

There was a narrow road at the side of the house, leading to an alley running behind the terrace. A high brick wall marked the boundary of the houses. Some had garage doors leading into the backyards, but the entrance to Charlotte's was through an arched door. It wasn't bolted and Vera pushed her way in. The yard would be a sun trap in mid-summer. There were terracotta pots with flowering plants and bushes, a set of garden furniture. Nothing fancy, but pleasant. Charlotte wouldn't be ashamed to have her friends here for drinks. A French window led into the house. Vera peered through and saw a comfortable living room, everything well used and a bit shabby. A smaller window to the right looked into the kitchen. No sign of Charlotte. Vera tried to open the French window but it was locked.

'She must have an office upstairs,' Holly said.

'Aye, but she'd have seen us, wouldn't she? Heard us banging around, at least? Surely she'd come down and let us in.' Vera looked up to the windows on the first floor, but the angle was too steep for her to see anything.

'Perhaps we should phone when we get back to the station and make an appointment.'

'Aye, I suppose so.' Vera knew she sounded churlish, and Holly was right. They should have phoned in advance. It wasn't Charlotte Thomas's fault that she wasn't there when they just landed on her doorstep. All the same, Vera couldn't help feeling a sharp, illogical frustration that made her want to blame someone. 'Where's this yoga studio of hers?'

'Not far. At the other end of the street.'

'Let's just check that out then, shall we? While we're here.'

The studio was on a corner site, not very far from the busy main street. There was nothing now of the pub it had once been. Vera could remember it, a dark, cavernous place, with too many television screens showing football or snooker. Slot machines that competed in sound with thudding background music. As Kimmerston had gone upmarket, the place's customer base had shrunk. The people in the new estates went to the sleek wine bars or artisan pubs where earnest bar staff sold craft ale. Not to this place. She tried to recall its name.

'The Greyhound!' Triumphant because it had come to her.

'Sorry?'

'That's what it was called. There used to be fights every Friday night.'

The front had been painted primrose yellow. *Only Connect* was written in grey cursive script along the fascia. There were blinds at the windows, a deeper yellow, all pulled down. Vera supposed you wouldn't want passers-by gawping when you were doing a downward dog or standing on your head. She'd tried yoga once when her doctor told her she should give it a go, that it might help her to relax. She'd found it boring and faintly ridiculous, and she'd been intimidated by the wiry old women who could do things with their bodies that she'd never have thought possible. She'd soon given it up.

There was a bell by the door, a little sign. *Please ring and wait.* Vera pushed it and heard it ring inside. But she didn't wait. Instead, she tried the door. It opened.

She was aware of Holly following, but she gave her full attention to the large open space. The interior of the old pub was transformed. The place was still cavernous, but this was a cathedral to healthy bodies, with white walls, a ballet barre and mirrors along one side. It must have cost a fortune to refurbish. Light filtered through the thin blinds. A lithe and Lycra-clad Charlotte was lying on a yoga mat in the centre of the floor, eyes shut. The high priestess of fitness. An open laptop was on a tall stand, facing her.

'She must use that to record her sessions.' Holly was whispering, assuming that the woman was in deep meditation. 'You can access them for a price through her website if you can't make it here to the studio.'

But Vera had never known anyone lose themselves in a meditation that was this deep. Meditation had caused *her* mind to race and her body to fidget. And her mind was racing now.

She moved quickly towards Charlotte. There was no movement as she approached.

'Boss?' Holly finally suspected that something was wrong.

Vera didn't answer. She was already stooping over Charlotte, feeling for a pulse. She saw the burst blood vessels in the eyes, and at the same time noticed a foam cushion lying on the floor close to the woman's head. It would be used to support the head during some of the more demanding yoga poses. But the killer had found another use for it.

Vera stood up and now she did look back at Holly. 'She was smothered,' she said. 'Just like Rick Kelsall. Can you phone Doc Keating and Billy Cartwright? Let's get the carnival on the road.' A pause. 'You okay to stay here as first officer on the scene?'

Holly nodded.

'I'll go back to the station and let the rest of the team know that we're now working on a double murder. Then I'll go and notify her father of her death. He might be a crooked bastard, but he shouldn't hear from the press.' Vera didn't move towards the door though. She pulled on a pair of gloves. 'I'll do a quick search before I go. Just to see there's no one lurking in the back there somewhere. We could have frightened them off as we came in.' *And to have a bit of a nose, before the crime scene team come and chase me away.*

A door at the back of the studio led to a series of treatment rooms, with couches, sinks and an array of oils and creams on identical yellow shelves. It seemed to Vera again that this must have been a very pricey venture. No wonder the woman had had to re-mortgage her house. Charlotte's optimism that her former glory would bring in the punters had been misplaced. Beyond the treatment rooms, a corridor led to

Charlotte's office – all pale wood and more signature primrose paint. The computer was still switched on. Presumably she'd been working here before recording the yoga class. Vera wondered if there was a facility for the yoga to be live streamed. If so, the session must have been finished before Charlotte had been killed. Otherwise, a group of wealthy, middle-class women, stretching and breathing in their living rooms, would have witnessed a murder, and though Vera had a very low opinion of that particular group, she thought one of them would surely have had the gumption to phone 999.

She was tempted to look at the material on the computer, but the cyber team would find out and she'd have to explain why she was nebbing. There'd be a timer on the laptop which had been filming her yoga session, so it should be possible to pinpoint death with some accuracy. It would be between the last videoed class and Vera and Holly's arrival.

Vera walked back to the main hall. Holly was on her phone, talking, it seemed, to Paul Keating.

'No sign of anyone there,' Vera said. 'No break-in. They must have used the same door as us. Someone in the street might have noticed. Let's get a team out canvassing.'

As she made her way out, Vera looked down at Charlotte Thomas, a woman who'd spent her whole life striving to look young. All that effort, Vera thought. And what good had it done her in the end?

Chapter Twenty-Eight

VERA WALKED FROM THE CRIME SCENE in Kimmerston to the place where she'd left the Land Rover, glad of the few minutes' exercise, the breeze on her face. From there, she drove straight to a Newcastle suburb and the house where Gerald Thomas now lived with his younger daughter. In the spring it would be a leafy street of substantial Victorian terraced houses. Now the trees were bare, but the place was still attractive, welcoming. They weren't far from the Town Moor, the large open space in the city where cattle grazed, and the wide street felt airy, open to the sky. Holly had been wrong; Thomas hadn't quite slipped back to the poverty into which he'd been born.

Vera had expected to hit rush hour traffic, but she'd sailed through the city centre without any hold-up. She squeezed into a parking space just big enough for the Land Rover, and sat for a moment. It was never pleasant to inform a relative of an unexpected death, especially the death of a son or daughter, and she needed some time to prepare herself for the ordeal. Even if the recipient of the news was a man who should be serving a prison sentence.

She rang the bell and heard it resonate inside, then came the sound of footsteps. The door opened to reveal a young woman. A student perhaps. Jeans, sweater and specs. Air pods. She must have been expecting someone else because she looked surprised. She took out the headphones. 'Yes?' Faintly hostile, but then Vera did look like someone collecting for Christian Aid.

'Who are you, pet?' Vera thought it was always best to know who she was dealing with.

'Ellie. Ellie Thomas.'

'I'm looking for Gerald.' Vera hadn't been sure until then that she'd got the right place. The floor in the hall had been stripped and sanded. A bike was leaning against the wall. This could be a shared student house.

'Why do you want Grandad?' Ellie was still wary. Perhaps she'd grown up with strangers looking for her grandfather.

'It's personal, pet. I've got some bad news for him.' A pause. 'For you all.'

'Everyone's in the kitchen. We're just about to eat.'

'I'll come through then, shall I? Is it this way?'

Before Ellie could object, Vera had marched on to the end of the hall, and through another door into a large kitchen. The two rooms at the back of the house must have been knocked through at some point. One of the walls was painted a deep, warm red, on the other, a noticeboard held photos, newspaper cuttings. There was a long table, set for a meal. This felt like a real, multi-generational family home.

An older woman – Charlotte's sister and this young woman's mother perhaps – stood by a stove. She seemed just about to dish up, and turned, a large serving spoon in her hand. At one end of the table sat a very elderly man. At the other end, another man, in late middle age, probably the cook's partner. In the middle a third, in his twenties, her son. The Thomas clan glared at Vera. Gerald stared at her through rheumy eyes and thick glasses but still he recognized her, even after all these years.

'Inspector Stanhope.' The voice was wheezy. It took a lot of effort for him to speak. 'I'm guessing that you are still an inspector? I never thought you'd climb the greasy pole much beyond that rank.'

'Never wanted to, Gerald.' Vera took an empty seat next to him.

'What's this about? Bursting in here without warning. Just as we're about to eat.' His daughter, the woman at the stove, interrupted. Vera could tell that she was spoiling for a fight. She must have been a good bit younger than Charlotte, but she hadn't worn so well, or perhaps she hadn't bothered to have the surgery.

'It's about Charlotte.'

'What about her?' The woman set down the spoon on the kitchen bench. She'd obviously decided that the meal would have to wait.

Vera ignored the question. 'And you are?'

'Amanda. Charlotte's sister.'

'Maybe you'd best sit down, Amanda. I've got some bad news.'

Amanda looked at her father, who gave a little nod, and then she too took her seat at the table.

'Charlotte's dead.' Vera had always thought it best to be blunt when she was giving bad news, so there was nothing to distract the listener, nothing to suggest false hope.

'How?' Gerald almost coughed out the question. She thought

that he'd been expecting it, or something similar. He'd known as soon as she'd appeared at the kitchen door that it would be bad news. Why else would she be there, on her own? Without the support of another officer. The others looked blank, numb.

'It's still down as a suspicious death at the moment,' Vera said, 'but your daughter was murdered. We found her in her yoga studio. The old Greyhound. You'll know the place, Gerald. You used to own it.'

He gave another almost imperceptible nod and Vera continued. 'I'm as sure as I can be that she was smothered.'

'Who killed her?' Gerald demanded, his eyes bright, feverish.

'Eh, pet, we've not reached that stage yet.'

'But you'll have some idea. Her ex was murdered two days ago.' The man was as sharp as he'd always been. 'You're not telling me that was coincidence.' The rest of the family were watching the exchange in silence. Gerald Thomas might be old but he was still very much in charge.

'I've come straight from the crime scene,' Vera said. 'I thought you'd want to know. I've not had time to gather my thoughts yet, never mind form any sort of theory.' She paused. 'When did you last see your daughter?'

He looked at Amanda. 'When was it? In the summer? July?'

'Aye,' Amanda said. 'She deigned us with her presence for an afternoon.'

Vera looked at her. 'So, you didn't see very much of her?'

'No. Not since Dad's business went tits up and he couldn't bail her out anymore.'

'That's not fair!' But Gerald's voice was uncertain.

'She's always been ashamed of us,' Amanda said. 'Even when we were living in Kimmerston and she was at the Grammar, how often did she bring her friends home? You spoiled her like a bloody princess and she treated you like shite.' Years of sibling resentment seemed to be fermenting inside the woman's head and spewing out through her mouth. Maybe, Vera thought, the woman had been waiting for a time when she could say these things to her big sister. She'd planned how to confront her with the injustice, and now she realized that the opportunity had been lost forever.

'Mandy!' Her father seemed on the verge of tears. 'That's enough.'

But it seemed that the woman couldn't stop. 'She didn't even want us at her wedding! They were going to slope off and do it without telling us. Until Rick made her see sense.'

'You got on all right with Rick, then?' Vera thought it was time to stop the outburst. The woman would regret it later, and Vera had to be back in Kimmerston soon, to talk to the team and catch up with the latest information.

'Yes,' Amanda said. 'Rick was okay. He could mix with anyone. No airs and graces with him, when she did allow him the occasional visit. He always took an interest in us all; he was full of questions even as a lad. I wasn't surprised when he turned out to be a journalist.'

'Have you seen *him* recently?'

Amanda shook her head. 'Not for years. Only on the telly. And he's not been on there for a while.'

'Charlotte met Rick while they were both at school,' Vera said. 'They were together at a weekend team-building course on Holy Island. Rick Kelsall was killed when he was attending a reunion of old school friends there. Any reason, do you think, why Charlotte didn't ever join them?'

'She just didn't fancy it,' Gerald said. 'She didn't like it the first time round. It was a cold, miserable place. Shared bathrooms and everyone having to muck in with the cooking and washing-up. She was used to better.'

'You do remember her going then?'

'Yeah,' the man said. 'She phoned me halfway through the first day, asking if I'd pick her up and take her home. It was bloody inconvenient. I had a box booked at St James' Park for the football. I'd invited people I needed to impress.'

'But you went all the same?'

'Of course he did.' Amanda spat out the words. 'She was his golden girl, his little princess.'

'She was miserable.' Gerald glared at her. 'I'd have done the same for you.'

'Like hell you would.'

'Can you think of anyone who might have wished Charlotte harm?' Vera directed the question to the whole table.

In the end, it was Amanda who spoke for them all. 'Nah, she could be a stuck-up bitch, but I can't think of any reason why anyone would want to hurt her.' Round tears, as big and smooth as pearls, had started rolling down her cheeks. The student daughter got to her feet and put her arms around her. 'Not now,' Amanda went on. 'She was a nobody now. A sad, lonely cow. No man in her life and she hardly ever saw her kids.' She looked at Vera, a sudden moment of realization. 'You know what? I felt sorry for her. What harm could she possibly do to anyone?'

When Vera let herself out, nobody seemed to notice.

Chapter Twenty-Nine

VERA GOT BACK TO KIMMERSTON HALF an hour before the evening briefing. When she arrived in the big room, the whole team was waiting for her, sitting in rows. As she stamped to the front, she could feel their eyes on her, waiting for answers. As if she was part matriarch, part guru. Suddenly she felt the weight of responsibility, because at this point, she had nothing definitive to tell them.

Billy Cartwright was there to update them with information from the scene. Paul Keating had already been in touch to confirm the cause of death: 'No chance of finding fibres in her nostrils this time. The pillow was used for yoga. Plastic-covered. But you were right, Vera. As you usually are. She was smothered.' The Belfast voice was dry. 'There's a chance that we'll find some stray DNA, but don't hold your breath.'

It was dark outside. They spoke under the stark light of the neon strip lamps. A summer's haul of dead flies was trapped in the plastic casing. Vera had gone straight to see Watkins on her return from informing the Thomas family of Charlotte's death. It had been a fractious meeting. At first, he'd seemed frozen by panic, incapable of taking in the information that there'd been another murder on his patch. He was aware of his own lack of experience, but didn't have the confidence to trust his team. Vera had spent thirty minutes massaging his ego and reassuring him that all would be resolved. Neither sat well with her, but she was learning some pragmatism as she got older. There was no point, she'd learned, in raging against the inevitable, and incompetent bosses seemed to be as inevitable as death.

Now though, she was still scratchy after the encounter. The superintendent's tension was contagious. She stood at the front of the room, looking at them.

'So,' she said. 'We've got two high-profile victims on our patch and we need a result fast.' A pause. 'Rick Kelsall was murdered on Holy Island and three days later his ex-wife Charlotte Thomas was killed in her fancy yoga studio only half a mile from here. Both were smothered to death, so I think we can safely assume that these incidents are linked, though they were divorced more than twenty years ago. The pair met on Thursday night before Kelsall headed out to the island on Friday.' She paused and turned to the whiteboard behind her.

'At first, we focused on the people staying with Kelsall in the Pilgrims' House: Ken and Louisa Hampton, Philip Robson and Annie Laidler. Annie lives in Kimmerston and works in Jax's deli, so she's only a couple of minutes' walk away from the latest crime scene. I want to know if any of the remaining individuals were in Kimmerston this afternoon. That's a priority for tomorrow. More recently, we've been widening our pool of potential suspects, and that brought us to Daniel Rede and Katherine Willmore. You'll all have heard of Willmore.'

There were nods and muttered murmurs of recognition.

'Her daughter Eliza made allegations of sexual harassment, which led to Kelsall losing his job. Eliza had since admitted that the allegations were false. That might have given Eliza, or perhaps even Willmore, a motive for murder. Neither of them would want the lass portrayed as a malicious liar. So, this is sensitive, but we will of course investigate without fear or favour.'

She paused for a moment, and saw that most of them had recognized the reference, and noticed the sly little grins, before continuing. Investigating without fear or favour had become a mantra for the commissioner. She trotted it out at every possible occasion.

Vera went on. 'Holly, you've been talking to the TV company. Can you tell us a bit more about that?'

Holly stood for a moment without speaking. She was always cautious, always determined to use the right words. Vera felt herself becoming impatient, but she held her tongue.

'Sally Baker was Rick's boss,' Holly said at last. 'She was surprised when Eliza made the allegations against him. According to Baker, Rick didn't usually go for innocent young interns. But the management team felt they had to support her. In this climate, they couldn't be seen not to take the allegations seriously.' There was a pause. 'Baker came across as pretty hard-nosed to me. She wasn't bothered about what had really happened, and I don't think she felt any real sympathy for Eliza. It was all about the image of the company, and they weren't too sorry to lose Kelsall, whose ratings were dropping.'

'So, the company had got what it wanted.' Vera looked out over the group. 'I chatted to Eliza this morning. Informally. Kelsall was an insensitive boor, but it doesn't sound as if he'd done anything that might lead to a criminal charge. Eliza got duped by a journo, and that's how the story got splashed all over the tabloids. Honestly, I can't see any reason why she'd want to kill the man – she was mortified by the fact that she'd got him sacked – and she had no motive at all for Charlotte, but let's keep an eye on her.' She turned back to Holly. 'What else have you got from your phone calls to London?'

Holly described her conversation with Cecilia Bertrand.

'Kelsall was writing a novel, a thriller set on an island where a murder takes place. Using his own experience.' Holly paused. 'There wasn't a murder on Holy Island though, was there? Not until *he* died. It all feels a bit weird, a bit creepy. As if Rick Kelsall was predicting his own death in a novel. Or using another, earlier death as a jumping-off point for his story.'

'Would that be a kind of revenge, do we think?' That was Joe getting immediately to the point. He looked over at her. 'It could be a way of getting back at someone who was never charged with a crime.'

'But who Kelsall thought was guilty all the same?' she said. 'Could be.' Then she remembered the words of her neighbour Joanna and repeated them as if she knew exactly what she was talking about. 'But all writers are parasites. They use the information that comes their way to make the story. Perhaps it was a kind of laziness. Perhaps Kelsall used something that had really happened to save him making stuff up. It wasn't necessarily revenge.'

And if that stirred things up, caused trouble for other people, Rick Kelsall wouldn't be the sort to be too concerned. And if he was challenged, he'd say it was all fiction.

'Of course, there *was* an earlier death,' Holly said. 'Isobel

Hall drove her car off the causeway at the Only Connect first reunion. And we're already looking into the circumstances surrounding that incident.'

'Do you think Kelsall was suggesting in his book that Isobel's death was murder rather than an accident?' Joe said.

'We won't know, will we, until we read the thing.' Vera glared, not angry at him, but that the process of getting hold of the novel was going so slowly.

'His agent has only read a sketchy synopsis,' Holly said. 'She's sending that over to me. There's no evidence that very much else exists, though Kelsall had already been paid an advance.'

Vera was thinking she'd need to talk to Joanna about how this publishing business worked. 'That doesn't sound as if that'll tell us much. But there was a laptop in his room. Perhaps his book will be saved on that. I assume the machine will still be with the digital team.'

'Yes,' Holly said, 'but I think they'll be concentrating on communication and social media, rather than saved documents.'

'Give them a ring, Hol. See if they can track it down and email it across to you.'

'Will do.'

Vera turned to Billy Cartwright, the crime scene manager, who was sitting at the back. 'Have you got anything for us? On either locus?'

'Nothing beyond the obvious. Both victims were killed where they were found according to Doc Keating.' He paused for a moment and was uncharacteristically serious. 'We're stretched, Vera. The scene on Holy Island is a bugger to get to and now we've got another right on our doorstep. We can't use the same team on both because of cross contamination. So, don't expect the impossible. Okay?'

Vera nodded to show she understood. She didn't have to like it though. With bloody Watkins breathing down her neck, she needed a quick result.

At home in her cottage in the hills, she was about to put the kettle on, when it occurred to her that Joanna would be back from her bookish weekend away. She pulled on her wellies and walked down the track to the farm. The clouds had cleared and there was light enough from the moon to see where she was going. She tapped on the door of the house and walked into the kitchen without waiting for an answer.

Joanna was standing by the range, stirring a pot of something savoury, which made Vera realize that it was a long time since she'd eaten. The sticky bun by the river was a distant memory. Joanna was tall, stately, with long dark hair, recently streaked with a little grey.

'How did it go?' Vera was genuinely curious.

'Okay. I was a bit nervous. My first time in front of such a big audience. Some of the other writers were okay but there were a couple of pretentious pricks. You didn't miss much.' She turned to face Vera. 'I was just about to open a bottle of wine. Fancy a glass?'

'Eh, pet. I'd love one.'

'I saw on the news about the murder on Holy Island. I assume that's where you've been all weekend?'

'There's been another. Not on the island.' Vera knew it would be all over the late evening's news – there'd been press and cameras outside the studio before she'd left – so no harm in telling her neighbour. 'Just down the road from the police

225

station.' A pause. 'I found the body. Charlotte Thomas. I don't suppose you knew her?'

'The model? My brothers had her posters all over their walls when they were growing up. I suspect she provided their first sexual experience.' Joanna was wielding a corkscrew with the ease of someone for whom it was a daily ritual. 'Supper's a bit late tonight. Jack's been wrestling with the tractor again. Do you want to stay? I don't suppose you've had time to eat. It's nothing special. Mutton stew. And I called into the farm shop for some Northumberland cheese this afternoon.'

'Are you sure?'

Joanna smiled. 'You know me, Vee. No polite gestures. I wouldn't ask if I didn't want you here.' She poured a glass of red and handed it to Vera, who settled herself into the rocker next to the range, a dog at her feet.

She must have been snoozing, because the next thing she knew, Jack was washing his hands at the kitchen sink and the table was laid. A loaf of home-baked bread on the board and bowls for the stew. There was still wine in her glass.

'How's it going, Vee?' Jack was a Scouser. Joanna called him, with love and respect, her bit of rough. He'd been a scally when he was younger, had had his brushes with the police. It still astonished him that there was an officer he could like and welcome into his home.

'She's working on a double murder.' Joanna was ladling stew into the bowls. 'So probably a bit knackered.'

'No more than usual.' Vera thought this was the best meal she'd ever eaten. She turned to Joanna. 'I could use some inside info on the publishing business. Apparently, Kelsall was writing a thriller, and basing it on a death which happened years ago. He could do that?'

'Sure. Lots of writers have used true crimes as a jumping-off point for their novels.'

'That's the point though. There wasn't a crime. Not officially. At the time, it was put down as an accident.'

There was a moment of silence. 'I'm not any sort of expert,' Joanna said, 'but I'd have thought it would be very risky to make an allegation of murder, if the setting or the event were recognizable. Even if it was in a novel, and especially if any of the people involved were still alive.'

Vera nodded. *But the one thing we know about Rick Kelsall is that he did love taking a risk. And he did love making mischief.*

Joanna cleared the bowls and brought out plates and cheese. She poured more wine.

Vera hadn't been sure about this couple when they'd first moved in. Now, she wasn't sure what she'd do without them.

Chapter Thirty

WHEN VERA GOT INTO HER OFFICE early on Tuesday morning there was a voicemail message from Katherine Willmore. Very sharp. Very stern.

'I'm surprised that you thought it necessary to speak to my daughter without having the courtesy to talk to me first. I understand that you'd like to speak to me now. I'm tied up for most of the day, working from home. You can see me here at ten o'clock if it's something so urgent that it can't be done on the phone.'

Well, Vera thought, that's me told. Ma'am.

She was tempted to send Holly and Joe to interview the woman, to put her in her place and show her that she wasn't worth the attentions of a senior officer, but they'd both be too over-awed to ask the hard questions. So she set off up north again, out to the coast.

There was no Range Rover parked outside the house, and no face looking down from an upstairs window. Katherine Willmore let Vera in, and led her, without a word, not to the large sunlit room looking out over the bay, but to an office shaded by trees. This time, she wasn't to be treated as a guest, but as an unwelcome intruder.

Vera thought it was best to go on the attack from the start. 'I came to speak to *you* yesterday. I didn't even know that your daughter was here. You didn't mention that you had a daughter when I was here to see your partner on Sunday, or that she was the complainant in a sexual assault allegation against a murder victim.'

'In a case like that, she has a right to anonymity.'

'But not in *this* case, not in a murder inquiry. And not to an investigating officer. Anyway, from what Eliza told me there was no real case against Rick Kelsall. She made a false allegation, spurred on by an unscrupulous journalist and the company chiefs.'

Silence. Then: 'Not entirely false. It's clear that Kelsall was a bully.'

'Rick Kelsall was here on Friday morning, before he went onto the island. It didn't occur to you to tell me that?' Vera paused. 'Besides anything else, you must have realized that we'd find out. It was foolish. Someone would have seen him! We'll be able to trace his movements from the satnav in his car or his phone.'

'I must admit that my judgement was a little clouded.' The defiance of the voicemail was completely gone now. The woman was pale and scared. 'But Eliza's my only daughter. I was trying to protect her. She's got her life ahead of her. The last thing she needed was some sort of scandal, Rick Kelsall accusing her of lying.'

'Is that what he was threatening? To go public with what had actually happened?'

'No! No, he was actually very decent about it. We'd worked

out a statement, which we could give to the press, saying that Eliza and Rick had both been victims of a hostile tabloid press and a television company who wanted rid of an older presenter for their own ends. We'd agreed to release it at the end of this week. Now of course, the press will still be poking their grubby little fingers into his affairs, sniffing into the reasons that he left his job, trying to make some spurious link between the allegations and his murder.'

Vera wondered about the timing of that. Could it be significant that Kelsall had been killed before the statement had been made public? She didn't see why it should be.

Willmore looked up at her. 'So you see, Inspector, the last thing we wanted was Rick Kelsall dead. A bland statement, leaving Eliza's name out of the copy but giving her side of the story, would have diffused the situation. Rick would have gone in front of the media as a wronged man, saying he completely understood how a young woman had been manipulated by unscrupulous individuals, and the whole affair would have been over. Now, it's likely to linger on.'

'How did Eliza come to be working for him in the first place?'

'Well, that was why the whole thing was so awkward. Kelsall was doing us a favour. Daniel asked him if Eliza could do some work experience there. She's always been fascinated by the news. Not because she wanted to be a politician; she's a shy little thing. But rather presenting it, making it clear for the ordinary reader, listener or viewer, and it's almost impossible to get an internship in the media if you don't have contacts.'

'You didn't have contacts in the field?' Vera sounded deliberately sceptical.

'Well of course, but I couldn't be seen to be lobbying on behalf of my daughter.'

'But you could ask your boyfriend to do it for you?'

Willmore had the grace to blush. She didn't reply.

'Daniel and Rick were still friends?' Vera said. 'That wasn't the impression Daniel gave when we talked.'

'Not friends exactly. But they were acquaintances, and Daniel was willing to ask Rick. For Eliza's sake.'

'Oh no, for your sake, surely.' Because Daniel is besotted, Vera thought. Even I could tell that. 'And Rick agreed?'

'He did. I can show you the email. "Anything to help my old friends in the North. Let's catch up when you're visiting Eliza. I need to pick your brains about a project of my own." Daniel was surprised. I don't think he was expecting such a positive response.'

'Did they meet up?' Vera thought this contradicted everything Daniel had told her about his relationship with the people who'd spent the weekend at the Pilgrims' House. He'd given the impression that they'd had nothing in common, even as teenagers.

'Yes! Rick's company helped Eliza find a room in a shared house in London with some other employees and Daniel drove her down. I was caught up with work here, or I'd have taken her. Daniel booked himself into a hotel and he and Kelsall went out for a meal and a few drinks.'

So, Daniel lied to me. All to protect his lover's daughter.

'What was the project that Rick wanted to discuss?'

Katherine Willmore shrugged. 'Oh, I don't know. I don't think Daniel ever told me. Maybe Rick wanted to move north again. Lots of people seem to be deserting the city at the moment.'

'Maybe.' But Vera thought this might have had more to do with Kelsall's novel. That seemed to have been preoccupying him in the weeks before his death. 'Is Daniel around? I can ask him myself.'

'No,' Katherine said. 'He's out on the road, scouting another development opportunity. We can't fit in more accommodation here at the tower without it feeling overcrowded, so he wants to find new sites. We think the climate emergency will generate a move to holiday at home. Who knows, global warming might even make Northumberland the perfect place for a staycation.'

'Could you ask him to give me a ring. I'd like to speak to him.'

'Of course.' The woman had regained her confidence, her poise.

'Where's Eliza?'

'We sent her to stay with her father. He's a professor in Durham. He's not her favourite person – she took my side in the divorce – but we thought she could do with a change of scene.'

'Where the police couldn't find her?'

Katherine smiled. She'd decided to take Vera's comment as a joke. 'Something like that!' She shifted in her seat and looked at her watch. A sign that she thought the interview was over.

'Did you ever meet Charlotte Thomas? Rick Kelsall's ex-wife.'

There was a brief hesitation. 'Not in person. I'd heard of her, of course. The famous model turned actress. Though I was just too young to be aware of her when she was at the height of her career. I have friends who've become her clients.' A pause. 'I believe that Daniel had some business dealings with her. She was hoping to open a studio here at Rede's Tower. Yoga. Pilates. It might have gone down well with our customers, but I don't think he could get the figures to add up.'

'You were never tempted to consult her?'

'I think I've become sufficiently successful without the help of a life coach, don't you, Inspector?'

Vera nodded to concede the point. 'Mr Kelsall was staying with Charlotte the night before he came here to discuss plans for dealing with the harassment allegations.'

'Was he? I don't think I knew that. Daniel made the arrangements for the meeting.' Willmore gave the impression of being not the least bit interested. 'Is that important? And I'd have thought you'd do better speaking to Charlotte than keeping me from important business.'

'Oh, I would have spoken to her,' Vera said. 'In fact, I tried to speak to her yesterday. But by the time I got to her yoga studio she was dead. Murdered. Smothered like Rick Kelsall.'

Willmore stared at the detective. The colour drained from her face. She seemed incapable of speech. A breeze blew a branch onto the window. The sound as it scratched the glass startled them both.

'You really didn't know?' Vera found that hard to believe. Even if the PCC hadn't heard the news reports, Watkins would have told her. It was her role to know, to keep on top of anything happening in her patch.

'Honestly, Inspector, I didn't. I've had my work phone switched off. There were dozens of messages and I haven't checked them all. I needed some time to think about Kelsall's death, to decide what to do for the best.'

'You got back to me.'

'So I did.' Katherine gave a little smile, but offered no other information.

Vera continued: 'Where were you, ma'am, yesterday? We don't have a precise time of death yet, so I need your movements for the whole day. And it would be helpful if you could confirm where Daniel was, as he's not here to tell me himself. Neither of your cars were here when I was talking to Eliza.'

'I don't know about Daniel. He was out all day. I think there was a meeting in Kimmerston with the council planning officer in the morning. Again, that would be about his ideas for expanding the business, looking at options for further development.'

'And in the afternoon?'

'I'm not Daniel's keeper, Inspector.' Anxiety was making Katherine shrill. 'You could talk to Mel on reception. She keeps his diary.'

Vera nodded. 'Thanks, that's very helpful. I'll talk to her on the way out.' A pause. 'And where were you, ma'am?'

'You're asking me to provide an alibi?' The voice was even tighter, higher.

'A matter of procedure. Following the rules without fear or favour. I'm sure you understand.' Repeating the commissioner's catchphrase.

Katherine took a deep breath and seemed to bring herself back under control. 'Of course, Inspector. You must excuse me. This has all been rather a shock and I haven't been thinking clearly. I was in Kimmerston but only in the morning. I had a meeting with Superintendent Watkins. I'm sure that will be alibi enough.'

'I'm sure it will. And the afternoon? We believe that was when Charlotte Thomas was killed.'

'I was on Holy Island. Nothing to do with work. I had plenty of time owing and I wanted to clear my head. Your turning up on Sunday afternoon with news of Rick Kelsall's death had thrown me rather. I knew I should have told you about Eliza's involvement and I suppose I wanted to work out a game plan. I always think better when I'm walking. It was an impulse.'

'You were on your own?'

'Yes. And I didn't go anywhere near the Pilgrims' House. There was no attempt at all to interfere with the investigation. But I suppose the island was in my head, because of the news.'

'Did anyone see you while you were there?' Vera was keeping an open mind. Walking helped her to think too, though she wasn't sure she'd have gone back to the site of a murder as a civilian, if murder was the subject of her work.

'I had tea in the Old Hall hotel!' The woman sounded relieved. 'It wasn't terribly busy. Half-term was over and the weather wasn't as good as it was over the weekend, so there was a gaggle of journos, but very few tourists. The staff might remember me.'

'How did you pay for your afternoon tea?'

'I'm not sure. With my debit card probably. Don't we all pay with our cards these days? Cash seems almost obsolete.'

'Then we'll be able to check,' Vera said. She smiled and got to her feet. She hoped that they'd hear less of the 'keeping to the rules without fear or favour' mantra, and that Katherine Willmore might be a little less inflexible in the future. 'Please tell Daniel to get in touch with me. We do need to speak to him.'

She drove again past the pool, stopped for a moment and wound down the window to listen to the calls of the waterfowl. In the distance, a woodpecker was drumming.

The same receptionist was at the desk in the tower. She recognized Vera. 'I'm sorry, but Mr Rede is out. I think Katherine is at the house.'

'I know. I saw her. She said you might be able to help me. I need to know where Daniel was yesterday afternoon. Katherine said that you keep his diary.'

'I do.' The woman clicked on her computer. 'He was in Kimmerston from late morning. A planning meeting.'

Vera nodded. That confirmed what Katherine had said. 'And the afternoon?'

'I've got nothing marked in, so I presume he was working here, either on site or in his office at home.'

'Did you see him yesterday at all?' Vera kept her voice conversational, but Mel was a good employee, and was non-committal.

'Honestly? I can't remember. I'm pretty sure he was around later on, but I can't be sure.' Which was no help at all.

Chapter Thirty-One

BACK IN THE POLICE STATION, VERA shouted Joe and Holly into her cramped office to sort out the detailed plans for the day. She'd made coffee for them. *That* didn't happen very often. Outside, it was market day and she could hear the traders shouting jokes to the passing shoppers. Everything seemed vibrant and alive. There was something joyous about the activity, the bustle.

It hit her suddenly that apart from Eliza, all the suspects in this case were ageing. Death was a reality to them in a way that it wasn't for younger people, including Joe, for example, who sat across the desk from her now and was wittering about planning a holiday with his family. She supposed that older people made fewer plans. They had less time to fill, no endless possibilities stretching into the future. Could this be important for the way this case worked out? If so, as an older woman herself, she had no excuse for getting it wrong.

'Chase up the digital team again,' she said. 'I want whatever was on Rick Kelsall's laptop. Most especially a novel about a murder on Holy Island.'

'I've already asked them,' Holly said. 'They say all his files had been deleted. They're struggling to recover them. They'll be able to do it, but possibly not by end of play today.'

'Are they saying the killer could have deleted everything on his laptop?' This was new information. She was about to rage against Holly for not telling her sooner, then realized that would be unfair. She'd only just returned to the station from her jaunt to talk to Willmore.

'I think it's a possibility.'

'Wouldn't they need a passcode?' Vera was getting better at tech, but she was still unsure. 'If they were going in to delete all his files?'

'Perhaps,' Holly said. 'Unless Kelsall was using his laptop when he was killed. Or he'd closed it without turning it off. In that case, you'd just need to click to sign in again.'

'We need to talk again to that group from the Pilgrims' House.' Vera leaned forward across the desk to make her point. 'If Charlotte Thomas's murder isn't some sort of coincidence – and I really can't believe that it is – then we have to consider all those individuals as suspects in the second killing too.'

'You really think one of those people came into Charlotte's yoga studio and smothered her?' Joe obviously found the idea impossible. Did he think all elderly people were benign, harmless? Vera smiled at the notion. Hector, her father, had been cruel into his eighties. And even with the dementia of alcoholism, he'd raged against death, fought it as if he were one of his beloved peregrines ripping into a pigeon with talon and beak. Hector had died just as he'd lived: angry at the world which had deprived him of Vera's mother, the only person he'd ever loved.

'I don't think we can dismiss them,' Vera said. 'It might seem improbable, but surely not as improbable as two random killers targeting victims who knew each other, who'd been to school together and had recently met up.' She paused. 'The killer must have known where Charlotte would be. So, a client perhaps?'

'Judith Marshall had used her yoga classes,' Joe said. 'She described Charlotte as empathetic.'

'The teacher? She'll be worth talking to then. Another link.'

Outside, a busker started singing. Something sweet and lyrical about teenage love.

'Joe, you've already built a relationship with Louisa and Ken Hampton,' Vera went on. 'Go and see them. Louisa's a smart woman and she might be more prepared to talk about the others if you can get them on their own. It was her sister who died at the first reunion, after all. I know the focus has shifted to Eliza Willmore and the harassment allegations, but I still have a feeling that Isobel Hall's death wasn't a straightforward accident. Rick Kelsall's novel makes it more significant, doesn't it?'

'I suppose that makes sense.'

'Find out where they were yesterday afternoon.' Vera paused. 'I can't see Ken having a clue where he'd find Charlotte's yoga studio, let alone knowing how to kill her, but Louisa strikes me as ruthless, organized. We know there was no love lost between her and her sister. I wonder if Isobel's accident was some sort of prank that went wrong. Could Louisa have given her the wrong tide times in the hope that she'd be stranded, embarrassed? She wouldn't want that to come out after all this time.' She grinned. 'Besides, a trip to Cumbria will do you good. It might widen your horizons.'

'Yeah, yeah.'

'I'll have a chat to Annie Laidler. It seems to me that she was closer to Rick Kelsall than anyone.'

'Now that Charlotte's dead,' Holly said, 'will Annie inherit all the money from the sale of the Kelsall house in Kimmerston?'

Vera didn't answer immediately. The busker changed tunes. This was louder, angrier. Some sort of protest song.

'Good point, Hol. I'll have to check with the lawyer.' But Vera couldn't see profit as a motive for Annie. She'd cared for Rick since they'd been teenagers together. Perhaps she'd even been in love with him all that time, despite his decades of chasing other women.

'What about Philip Robson?'

'Ah, the God-bothering Phil, who's still in a holiday cottage on Holy Island. Let me think about him. Perhaps you're right, Hol, and I've dismissed him too easily.'

When Vera got to the deli, she filled a basket with goodies. It was about time she contributed something when she next went to visit Jack and Joanna. The smell in the shop almost made her faint with desire. When she reached the till, Vera asked Jax for Annie. 'Is she on her break?'

'Nah,' Jax said. 'She phoned in sick this morning. Hardly surprising, the shock that she had at the weekend. I wasn't really expecting her in yesterday.'

'But she came into work?'

'Yeah, she wasn't really herself, but she was here.' Jax paused. 'Her ex came to see her, took her out for coffee. To offer his support, he claimed. A bit late for that, I'd have said.'

'What do you mean?'

'It's not really my story to tell. They lost a baby and she still hasn't got over it, even after all these years. I suspect he could have been a tad more sympathetic at the time.' Jax raised her eyebrows, an expression of disapproval. 'No, that's being kind. He could have been a *lot* more sympathetic.'

In the queue behind Vera, the customers were starting to get restive.

'Look,' Jax said. 'Like I said, not my story. You'll need to ask Annie for the details. If you think it's important. But it happened years ago!'

Vera thought that everything important to this case had happened years ago. She asked Jax to remind her of Annie's address, paid for her shopping and left.

Annie lived in a narrow, terraced house. The street had been built on a slope, and there were communal gardens across a paved path, where a mother was playing with a toddler, a little girl pushing a toy pram. Because of the slope, steps led up to the front door. There was a cat sitting on the windowsill in the autumn sunshine. Annie didn't seem surprised to see Vera, had perhaps been waiting for her.

'Jax told you I was on my way?' Because that was what any friend would do.

'She did.' Annie looked as if she hadn't slept for days. 'Come in.' The cat slid in with Vera.

Annie had knocked through the whole of the ground floor into one space, so the sunlight flooded into what must once have been a very dark house. There was art on the walls and shelves full of books.

'Well, this is lovely.' Vera couldn't imagine putting this much effort into somewhere to live. She'd never really bothered about her immediate surroundings, though she'd always needed outside space. A long horizon. A place to breathe.

'It was all rather gloomy when I moved in.' Annie seemed pleased with the response. 'Coffee?'

'No thanks, pet, I'm awash with the stuff. I've just got a few more questions.' She sat on the sofa. There was a small wood burner, lit, giving out enough heat to make the room cosy.

'You'll have heard that Charlotte Thomas was killed yesterday.'

Annie nodded. She sat on the floor close to the stove, with her back to an easy chair. Her normal position in the room.

'Only it seems a coincidence,' Vera said. 'Two Kimmerston Grammar former pupils, murdered within a week of each other. You do understand why I need to speak to you?'

'I suppose so.'

'Give me a clue.' Vera had to make an effort to stay sharp. She liked Annie, and in this comfortable room she felt more like a friend than a police officer. Relaxed, easy. 'Tell me a story which would make sense of it all.'

'I can't!' Annie said. 'Honestly, I've been awake all night, thinking about it.'

'Is there anything to link Charlotte Thomas's death with Rick Kelsall's? Apart from the fact that they were once married. Why would anyone want them both dead now?'

'Really,' Annie said. 'I don't have any idea.'

'Money's always a very potent motive.' Vera shot a glance at Annie, who just looked confused. 'Has Mr Kelsall's solicitor been in touch with you?'

She shook her head.

'Rick left you money in his will. A half share in the proceeds from the sale of his parents' house. The other half was to go to Charlotte. Now that she's dead, I'm presuming you cop for the lot.'

'You really think I'd kill for money?' Annie shook her head in apparent disbelief.

'What will you do with it? Retire?'

'God no! What would I do all day? Jax has dreams for the business. She'd love to open a restaurant. Something relaxed and unpretentious but with brilliant food. Maybe I can make that happen.' The idea seemed to cheer her.

'Did you know that your ex is shacked up with our Police and Crime Commissioner?'

'I'd heard.'

Of course you had. People would have been rushing to tell you.

'Her daughter is the lass Rick was supposed to have abused.'

'He wouldn't have done that.' Her voice was stubborn, immovable.

'Did you know she was the apparent victim? Her name's Eliza. A bonny little thing. Daniel dotes on her apparently.'

A shadow of pain flashed across Annie's face. Vera thought that had been cruel. The woman had lost a daughter.

'No, I didn't know. Rick could be discreet about some things.'

'Rick was at Daniel's place on Friday morning before he went over to the island. Though both Katherine and Daniel lied about that when I first asked about Kelsall. According to the girl's mother, they were putting together a statement to the press, which would have made them both come out of this smelling of roses.' A pause. 'I can't see that happening now.'

'So now everyone will remember Rick as a sexist bully! Because the girl lied to the media.'

Vera supposed that was true. It wasn't much of a legacy. 'Yes, he died before he could put his name to the statement which would have implied both he and Eliza had been victims of the press. It's almost as if someone didn't want him cleared . . .'

She allowed her voice to tail off, hoping that Annie might suggest a possible answer, but the woman remained silent.

'Where were you on Monday?' Vera made no attempt to hide the reason behind the question.

'I was at work.'

'All day?'

'I started at eight and finished at four.'

'We're still trying to trace Charlotte's movements, but we're pretty sure she was killed after four. She was in her yoga studio. It's hardly any distance from the deli.'

'I came straight home after my shift.'

'Can anyone confirm that?'

'No! I live alone. How could they?'

'These are tight little houses. Someone might have heard the cistern fill while you were running a bath, been aware of you moving about.'

'There's a deaf old man on one side and a single mother with a teething baby on the other, so they're hardly likely to have noticed!' Annie was starting to get rattled.

Vera didn't mind that. The woman might lose control and let things slip out.

'Jax said Daniel came to see you yesterday. I visited him on the way back from the island on Sunday. Very flash place he's got at the tower.'

'I wouldn't know.' Annie was spitting out the words now. 'I've never been in the new house. When I lived there, we were in a shitty caravan.'

'But he did come to see you in Kimmerston yesterday. You

and Daniel must still be friendly, if he came all the way from Rede's Tower to offer his support.'

'I doubt if that was the only reason for him turning up in town.'

'Ah yes, he had a planning meeting apparently. We're checking that out too. Did he say where he was going, once he'd left you?'

Annie shook her head. 'We weren't together very long. Just went out for a coffee. It was kind of him, I suppose.'

'No hard feelings then, about the divorce?'

'We married too early,' Annie said. 'That was all. I was infatuated. I adored him. He wasn't quite as smitten. We both worked to make a go at it, but we grew up in different ways.'

'Why the rush to get married?' Vera was interested. That curiosity again, making her pry. 'I know there was a bairn, but even that long ago, marriage wasn't compulsory if you found yourself pregnant.'

'Really, we'd been a couple since school. Settled, I thought. Marriage seemed a logical step.' A pause. 'I thought we'd be together forever.'

'What happened to the baby?'

'You've been speaking to Jax. I'm sure she'll have told you.' The bitterness was back in her voice.

'Nah, pet. She said it was your story to tell.'

'She was called Freya. She died at four months. An unexplained death they called it. Your people came in, not accusing me of murder. Not in so many words. But implying it. Perhaps that's why I understand what Rick was going through. I know what it's like: people talking about you behind your back, believing the rumours. Not that I cared then. I didn't care about anything except losing my baby. And the guilt. I knew I didn't mean to kill her, but I must have done something wrong, mustn't I? Because babies don't just die, do they? You don't just wake up in the morning and find them dead. It had to be my fault.'

'Sometimes.' Vera's voice was gentle, like a whisper. 'Sometimes folk do just die. That's why we call the deaths unexplained. And that's the worst experience ever for the people left behind.'

'They did find a cause. Infant meningitis. Everyone thought that should make me feel better about myself. Honestly, though, it didn't help. Because I should have noticed she was ill. I should have done something. But it was our wedding night. A party. I'd drunk champagne. My mother had offered to take her for the night, but I wanted her to stay with us. If I hadn't done that, she might be alive. She'd be middle-aged. With children of her own. Even grandbairns if she'd been like me and got started early.'

'You know, pet, you can't live like that. The guilt will ruin you.'

'I know,' Annie said. 'It already has.'

There was a moment of silence. Annie opened the stove, using a glove on the hearth so her hand wouldn't burn and she threw in a log.

'Daniel didn't feel the same way?'

'Daniel just thought we should go ahead and have another child. As soon as possible. He never said, but I could tell he thought I was morbid. Self-indulgent. He found my grief boring. He did say that he wanted a life.'

'You never had another baby?'

Annie shook her head. 'I couldn't face it. What if we lost her or him too? Besides, it would have seemed as if we didn't care about Freya. As if a replacement would do just as well.'

Vera thought she could understand Daniel's desire to move on. Annie was still haunted by guilt after more than forty years. She couldn't have been an easy woman to live with. Katherine Willmore, with her ambition and her principles, would have seemed uncomplicated in comparison.

'He knew how close you were to Rick,' Vera said. 'He understood how another apparently unexplained death would affect you. That showed some sensitivity.'

'I know!' Now Annie just seemed exhausted, as if all the emotion had drained away from her. 'He was never insensitive. Not really. He was just able to move on more quickly than I could and I resented it. I was jealous, I think, that he seemed to find it easier to do.'

'He was there at the first reunion, the weekend that Isobel died in the car crash?'

'Yeah, the one and only time!' Annie gave a little smile. 'It was okay though. He really made the effort to get on with people.'

'Has he kept in touch with any of that group? Perhaps some of them were friends in their own right, not just through you?'

Annie shook her head. 'He was always different from the rest of us. Sporty. Practical. More into football than talking.'

'Yet he talked Rick Kelsall into giving his woman's daughter a job.'

'I don't know anything about that. Perhaps he wanted to impress Katherine Willmore that he had friends in high places too.' Annie's voice was hard, bitter.

Vera paused for a moment. After all, perhaps she'd have to trawl back through past relationships, past events. 'How did Daniel end up at the Pilgrims' House in the first place, if it wasn't his thing? That Only Connect weekend was voluntary, wasn't it?'

Annie turned away. Vera thought her cheeks were flushed and not because of the heat. The woman was blushing!

'Because of you! It was his chance of getting off with you!'

'Aye.' Annie turned back, shyly. 'Something like that.'

'Did you know Rick was writing a novel?'

The change in tone seemed to shock Annie and she stared at Vera. 'No.'

'But he was talking about it, that night in the Pilgrims' House. Not long before he died.'

'He was talking a lot,' Annie said. 'He always did when he was drunk. I must have zoned out.'

'He was very excited about it apparently. It's set in Holy Island. Based on real events. I wondered if that could give us some kind of motive for his death. He might be planning to wake dogs that the killer wanted to let lie.'

'I'm sorry.' Annie gave a little shake of her head. 'I don't know what you're talking about.'

Vera couldn't quite accept that Rick wouldn't have confided in Annie about his book. Even if she hadn't listened when he'd talked about it in general terms to the group, he would have discussed it with her. Probably in more detail. Annie had been his admirer and his support since he was a boy. His validation. Surely he'd have wanted to share his excitement with her. But Vera could tell this wasn't the time to push it. Reluctantly, she got up from the comfortable sofa, and stood for a moment in the pleasant sunlit room.

She reached into her bag and took out the photograph of the group taken at the first Only Connect weekend. 'I thought you'd like this back. Thanks for lending it to us.'

Annie took it. 'It seems such a very long time ago.'

'If you think of anything that might help, do get in touch with me. Okay?'

Annie scooped the cat into her arms, cradled it and nodded.

Outside, the toddler was still playing. Vera checked her phone. There was a message from Ashworth to tell her he'd made an appointment to see Louisa and Ken and was heading out now. And giving the Holy Island crossing times for the following day if she wanted to talk to Phil Robson, so she wouldn't have to check for herself. Vera gave a self-satisfied smile as she walked back to the car. She'd trained her boy well.

Chapter Thirty-Two

ANNIE LAIDLER STOOD AT THE BAY window and watched Vera walk away down the alley. There was something comforting about the woman, her bulk and her determination. When the detective reached the road, Annie turned back into the room.

She thought about Rick leaving her all that money, suddenly moved almost to tears. It wasn't the money itself that was so important, though it would certainly take away some of the stress of everyday living. To go to the supermarket without checking the price of every item before buying! To put on the heating in the bedroom before ice started to coat the inside of the window! To think that when she got very old and frail she might afford proper sheltered accommodation, somewhere pleasant with a view and no smell of piss! All that would be wonderful of course. And to help turn Jax's dreams into reality would pay back some of her friend's kindness.

More emotional was the idea that Rick had been thinking about her. Properly considering her needs and comfort. Leaving her money hadn't been one of his fleeting notions or grand gestures. He'd taken time to go to his solicitor and write it into his will. He hadn't even boasted to her and the others what he was doing. It hadn't been about the gratitude and applause. It was almost as if Rick had known that he'd die before her, and had wanted to see her properly provided for.

Annie went to the bedroom and changed for work. After all, she couldn't sit brooding here all day. She and Jax had plans to make.

Chapter Thirty-Three

IT STARTED RAINING AS SOON AS Joe Ashworth hit the Cumbrian border and that fed into all his prejudices. He saw Cumbria as a place of floods, of wild westerlies, of chaos and ignorance. Only the Lake District had a semblance of civilization but that was overrun by tourists from the South, and he distrusted the South even more than the West.

Louisa and Ken lived in a smart new-build on the edge of a village outside Carlisle. It was detached, stone-built, with views to the hills, but an easily managed garden. A sensible place for a couple of retirees. Joe thought of Louisa as a sensible woman.

'You will have heard about Charlotte Thomas's death.' They were sitting in an uncluttered living room, all pastel shades and soft furnishing. Ken's attention came and went. When he'd come into the room, the dog at his heels, Joe had thought he'd been recognized by the man. Now, he wasn't so sure. The rain beat against the window. In the field beyond the garden half a dozen soggy sheep were sheltering behind a drystone wall.

'Yes.' Louisa was dressed as if she were at work, Joe thought.

A skirt and soft wool jersey. Shoes, not slippers. She was carefully made-up. Perhaps she considered this interview as work, at least that she had a role to play, a position to maintain. 'We saw it on the news this morning.'

'Charlotte was the same age as your sister Isobel?'

'Yes, they were in the same year at school as Ken, Phil, Daniel, Annie and Rick.'

'It must have been a terrible shock when Isobel died.'

'Of course. Unthinkable.' Louisa stared out at the rain. 'My parents were never quite the same again. It was as if the sun stopped shining.'

'And you?'

It took Louisa a long time to answer, and when she did speak, there was nothing glib in her words. They were considered. Shockingly honest. 'It was a horrible time. As the second child, I'd rather resented Isobel. She was brighter than me, certainly prettier. Much more confident. She'd gone to a good university and I'd only made it to teacher training college. I'd envied the attention she'd got. When she died, of course, I was stricken with guilt. It was almost as if I'd wished her to die. As if I'd caused it.' She turned to Joe. 'And she was still the centre of attention. She became saintly in my parents' eyes. Even at her funeral, I knew that I'd never be able to live up to her. It's easy to be perfect if you're not still around to make mistakes.'

Joe Ashworth said nothing. He'd learned the power of silence from Vera, and he sensed that Louisa had more to say.

'But of course, she wasn't saintly. None of us are. She was demanding and petulant if she couldn't get her own way. She was more sly than me. She told my parents she was revising at a friend's house when she was in the pub or out with a boy.

I couldn't see the point of lying. Perhaps I should have culti-vated the knack.'

'Were there lots of boys in her life?'

'Oh yes, she was a terrible flirt. She thrived on admiration. And she was very good-looking.'

'I've seen a photo of you all at that first reunion,' Joe said. 'You were stunning, just as pretty as her.'

'Perhaps I was,' Louisa said. 'Though I didn't see it at the time. And perhaps that's why she couldn't quite like me.'

Joe thought how clear-eyed the woman was. There was no sentimentality in her vision of the past.

'Why are you asking all these questions, Sergeant? Why the obsession with the not-so-good old days?'

'Rick Kelsall was planning a novel,' Joe said. 'Set in the past. A thriller set around a death on Holy Island, and based, appar-ently, on real events.' A pause. 'It was as if he was predicting his own murder. Or digging up buried secrets. That's why we're interested again in Isobel's death. I'm sorry if it seems callous, insensitive, to take you back to those times.' He paused. 'Did you have any idea why Isobel was in such a rush to get off the island that day?'

Louisa looked at him. 'It was the sort of woman she was. Impulsive. If she wasn't happy, she would leave. Nothing would stop her. Only of course the tide did. Not even Isobel could stop the water as it flooded the causeway.'

Ken got to his feet and began to wander up and down. Louisa seemed glad of the interruption. She stood up too and took his hand.

'Are you bored, love? Why don't I find you a programme to watch?'

She led him into another room. The dog lumbered after

them. Joe heard the theme music of a popular daytime soap, then a door shutting, as Louisa came back to join him.

'I'm sorry, Sergeant. Ken can get restless.'

'Did you know that Rick was writing a novel? I was thinking he might have consulted you if he intended to use Isobel's death as a jumping-off point.'

She seemed genuinely amused. 'That wasn't Rick's way of working! It would never have occurred to him that it might upset me if he turned Isobel's death into some sort of entertainment. Which would also make him a profit.'

'Would it have upset you?'

There was a silence. The rain seemed to be easing a little. 'Probably not! Not after all this time.'

'Do you know a woman called Katherine Willmore?'

Louisa frowned. 'The name's familiar.'

'She's the Police and Crime Commissioner for Northumberland.'

'Of course. I've heard her talking on the radio.'

'It was her daughter Eliza who'd made the complaints against Rick Kelsall.'

'And lost him his job? I can see that the TV company would have been reluctant to take on Willmore's daughter in a legal wrangle.' Louisa gave a little smile. 'Poor Rick. He'd tried it on with the wrong woman this time.'

Joe didn't want to explain that the case was more nuanced than it appeared. Now everyone would assume Kelsall was guilty, just as Louisa had done. He moved on.

'How well did you know Charlotte?'

'Not well at all. She and Isobel were close friends though. Two of a kind. She was very upset when Isobel died.'

'Charlotte wasn't on the island that day?' Joe still couldn't

ANN CLEEVES

see how Isobel's accident on Holy Island could have anything
to do with the recent murders, but Vera would want to know
all the details.

'No, I think she'd moved on, made much more exciting
friends in those early days. Rick was always loyal to us and
rearranged his affairs so he could be there. Charlotte was very
different. A weekend with us, certainly with me, wouldn't have
appealed.'

Joe thought that sounded as if there was some sort of personal
animosity between the women.

'You didn't get on with Charlotte?'

Louisa shrugged. 'We just didn't have very much in common.
Her life was full of glamour and excitement. I started teaching
and got married to Ken. Worked hard, and later took a degree
in education. We had children of our own. We must have seemed
very conventional to her. I suspect we would have bored her.'

'So you haven't seen her since you were at school together?'

'We kept in touch for a while.' Louisa still seemed reluctant
to give a direct answer. 'I suppose because of our shared
connection through Isobel. She and Charlotte really were the
very best of friends. Some years it was only Christmas cards.
I watched her career from a distance, with, I must admit, a
little envy. She must have heard about Ken's illness on the
grapevine, because she sent me a note, saying she was thinking
about me. That was kind.'

'What about the others at Pilgrims' House this weekend?
Philip and Annie. Were you closer to them?'

There was a moment of silence while Louisa chose her
words carefully. 'Philip has changed since I knew him as a
teenager. He was more challenging in those days. He made
me think. I suppose he's happier now, but not so interesting.'

'He never married? Never had a permanent relationship?'

She shook her head. 'Not so far as I know.'

'Not even in those early days, while you were all at school?'

'No. He was always rather a loner.'

'What about you? You were very young when you met Ken.'

She looked up at him, amused. 'What are you asking, Sergeant? If I had an affair?'

Joe thought she might not have been to university, but she was highly intelligent. Before he could answer, she went on:

'Rick was always suggesting a fling. It had become rather a boring standing joke. Now, with Ken as he is, I might have agreed. I miss physical contact, intimacy.'

Joe was shocked, embarrassed, which was probably what she'd intended.

'Can we go back to Charlotte? When did you last see her?'

'I'm not being awkward or obstructive, Sergeant, because I can't be certain that it *was* her. It seems such a strange coincidence.'

'Tell me.' He realized that was classic Vera. After a few drinks, she could get quite lyrical about prising info from suspects. *Witnesses all have stories to share. Give them time and space and they'll tell them. They might not be true stories, but they can still give us a glimpse of the truth.*

'I thought I saw her on Holy Island.'

'She was there, of course,' Joe said. 'We called her on Saturday after Rick Kelsall's body was found.' He remembered the woman, turning up in her ridiculous little car, wearing her smart clothes, confident and polished.

'No, it was the evening before that. The Friday. I went for a walk just before chapel. Philip had already arrived and they said he'd keep an eye on Ken. You see, he's very kind. I don't like to leave Ken on his own now, especially in strange places. He gets confused very easily. It was a treat to go out on my own. I've missed that the most since his illness has progressed: the peace of being alone. It was a beautifully clear afternoon, and I got the last of the sun. I only walked into the village and back. There were lots of people around. Families, enjoying the weather. And I saw Charlotte. At least I thought it was her. She really hasn't changed so much over the years. From a distance at least. She glanced up the street and then disappeared into one of the cottages.'

'You didn't knock?'

Louisa shook her head. 'No, how embarrassing if it had been a complete stranger! And even more embarrassing if it had been Charlotte. What would I say? As I've explained, we were never close friends. We'd both have found the encounter extremely awkward.'

'You say she looked up the street before going into the cottage. Didn't she see *you*?'

'She saw me, Sergeant, but she didn't recognize me. Unlike Charlotte, I've aged considerably since we last met. To her, I would have been just another older woman in anorak and walking boots. The island is full of them.'

'Was she on her own?' Joe thought that this might be some sort of breakthrough. He imagined Vera's pleasure, the excited glint in her eye, when he passed on the information.

'She was when I saw her. But I had the sense that someone had let her in to the cottage. That she'd knocked and then the door had opened, but I didn't see anyone inside.' Louisa paused. 'I must admit that I was rather curious. I walked past and glanced in through the window. But the room next to the street was empty.'

'Can you show me exactly where the cottage was on Google Maps?'

'Oh, I think so. On street view. It had a pale green door.'

Joe started fiddling with his phone, but she had the image on the screen of her iPad before he'd even found the app.

'Here, this is the one.' Joe saw a pretty cottage in the main street. 'If you give me your email address, I'll send it across to you.'

'I have to ask where you were yesterday afternoon.'

'That was when Charlotte died?'

He nodded.

'I was here,' she said. 'I'm always here unless I can get some respite care for Ken, and that's become much more difficult as his condition has progressed. It's a very pleasant prison, but it feels like a prison all the same.'

'Lou!' It was Ken, calling her from the other room. 'Lou, where are you?' It sounded like panic. 'Where are you?'

Chapter Thirty-Four

THE CONVERSATION WITH ANNIE LAIDLER WAS still haunting Vera. She hated the idea of the woman grieving for the baby who'd died more than forty years before. Not just grieving, but blaming herself for it. Rick's murder seemed to have made the sadness more intense, more immediate. It was as if Annie had kept her guilt locked up for all this time, but now the memories were out of the cage.

Her phone rang. Joe. 'Yes? I hope you've got some good news for me, because there's bugger all to smile about here.'

There was a moment's pause. Even mild swearing shocked him. Especially when it came from a middle-aged woman.

'Louisa Hampton thinks she saw Charlotte Thomas on Holy Island the evening Rick Kelsall was killed.'

'And she didn't think to tell us! The victim's ex-wife was wandering round the place on the evening of his death, but she didn't think it was important until after the woman died.'

'She wasn't certain. After all, she'd not seen her for years.' A pause. 'I know the house she went into. Louisa picked it out on Google Maps. She thinks somebody else was inside.'

'Well, that's something, I suppose.' Vera knew she sounded grudging. 'Katherine Willmore claims to have been on the island when Charlotte was killed. She's used afternoon tea in the Old Hall as her alibi. What is it with the place? It's as if the island's some sort of magnet, sucking people in. Some bloody black hole. It has to be the centre of the investigation.' Her mind was chasing through the options. 'Someone will have to go and check. They can talk to Philip Robson at the same time.'

'I can't do it.' Joe's voice was so firm that Vera could tell this was probably non-negotiable. 'It's Sal's birthday, and to get all that done, I'd have to stay over. She's planned a special evening.'

'Eh, pet, I wouldn't want to be the cause of marital disharmony. I'll get Hol up there.' She paused for a moment, because sometimes the thought of Holly stealing his thunder made Joe change his mind. Not today though.

There was a moment's hesitation, and the background sound of a truck rumbling past, before he asked: 'Did you get anything useful from Annie Laidler?'

'I'm not sure. Probably not. I'll fill you in on the details when you get back. I take it you *will* be back for the briefing. You're not sloping home straightaway. We're not paying you for part-time work.'

Joe didn't say anything. Vera suspected he *had* been hoping for a sneaky end-of-shift getaway. 'We'll make it an afternoon meeting,' she said brightly, 'so Holly can be there at least at the beginning and still get onto the island while there's some daylight. You'll be home in plenty of time for the candle-lit supper. I'll make sure to speed it through.'

'Thanks.'

Vera could tell he was still grumpy, but she was the boss, and, really, she didn't care.

They were at the briefing in front of the whiteboard, all crammed in to the room. Gurgling radiators and peeling paint providing the backdrop to their deliberations. Billy Cartwright had managed to sit himself next to the prettiest lass in the room, and she seemed to be laughing at his jokes. Vera could never work out how Billy did it. He was no oil painting and weedy with it. Maybe there was something of the Rick Kelsall about him. He had that persistence that came across to younger women as old-fashioned charm. Or flattering adoration.

'So, we've got two murders, connected in the present and the past. The victims, Rick Kelsall and Charlotte Thomas. Formerly school friends, lovers and husband and wife. And Kelsall must still have felt something for the woman, or felt that he owed her, because he'd left her a heap of money in his will. You'll all be aware now of the details surrounding the murders. Two high-profile people, which is seriously giving Mr Watkins the jitters, and because of that, we're under pressure to clear it up quickly. The other complication, of course, is that our respected Police and Crime Commissioner Katherine Willmore . . .'

Someone chortled in the back row, but Vera continued without appearing to notice.

'. . . is also very much involved in the case; her daughter Eliza was Rick Kelsall's intern and ostensibly made allegations of sexual harassment against him, and was the cause of him losing his job. Though according to Katherine, there was no assault, it was all a misunderstanding, and Rick had agreed to put out a statement blaming the press and the TV company for fake news.'

Joe stuck up his hand. It seemed he was still managing to focus on the investigation, despite his plans for a romantic evening with Sal. 'Does that statement exist anywhere? Surely, if Kelsall and Willmore had a meeting they'd have put something in writing?'

'Good point, Joe. We need to know if they *did* cobble together the statement and it's not a fantasy dreamed up after the man died. I'm assuming it'd be child's play for a journo and a lawyer to write something bland to shift the blame from both Kelsall and Eliza. Willmore didn't volunteer it, but then I wasn't bright enough to ask.'

'It might be on Kelsall's laptop,' Holly said.

'So it might. Along with his bloody novel, and that hasn't appeared yet either.' She looked out at the room. 'Before you disappear to wherever you're going, Billy, put a rocket up the bums of your digital team. Tell them they're slowing down the course of this investigation big style.'

Billy looked hurt in a theatrical way and turned to the young PC beside him for support, but Vera saw him tapping away on his iPhone, presumably passing on the gist of her comments.

'I'd really love to know what Charlotte was doing on the island on the Friday night.' Vera was talking to herself now, rather than the team. 'I can't think that it was to meet Kelsall. He'd stayed the night with her on Thursday, so there was no need for another secret assignation. Was there someone else in the group she'd agreed to meet? Another man? A potential lover? It wouldn't be Ken, surely. Or is Philip the vicar hiding something from us?'

There was no reply and Vera continued. 'But why didn't the

woman tell us she'd been on the island when we interviewed her on Saturday afternoon? And if she was there for social reasons, to catch up with a friend, why the secrecy? Why not just bowl up to the Pilgrims' House with a bottle of wine and join in the party? Surely she wouldn't have been there just for a night away on her own, for the peace and the solitude. She could get that at home.'

Vera paused and ran the evening of Kelsall's death in her mind. They'd all been drinking, that was clear, but surely if any individual had slipped out of the house for a meeting with Charlotte, the rest would have noticed the absence. But perhaps not. You could make a plausible excuse. Need for fresh air, to look at the stars, to take the elderly dog for a walk. 'We'll have to talk to them again,' she said. 'Find out if they remember anyone going AWOL at all.' It seemed to her once more that the answer to both murders lay back on the island.

Joe stuck up his hand again. Tentative this time. 'Something did occur to me while I was talking to the couple in Cumbria. We dismiss Ken, because of his dementia, but he wasn't ill that time when they were young, on the island for the first reunion. Nothing to have stopped him then being the cause of Isobel's accident. And Louisa is protective of him. Not exactly affectionate, but I can see her fighting for him. For the reputation he had as a head teacher. A good man. And I'd say she's cold enough to be a killer.'

Vera nodded her agreement. 'We keep an open mind then. We can't rule any of them out.' She turned to Holly. 'So, you're our shining hope for a breakthrough. We need you to find out what Charlotte Thomas was doing on Holy Island, and to check Katherine Willmore's alibi for Monday afternoon.'

She smiled out at her team, but it was all show. The progress on the case felt frustratingly slow. There were times at this point in a case, when it felt as if she was wading through treacle.

Holly was about to answer when her phone buzzed. 'Sorry, boss, it's Kelsall's mobile provider. I've been waiting for them to get back to me.' She listened for a moment, ended the call and looked out at the room. 'Kelsall had a call very early on Saturday morning – just after midnight. I asked them to track down the caller and let me know.'

'And?'

'It came from Judith Sinclair. Whose maiden name was Judith Marshall.'

'The teacher who brought them all together in the first place?'

Holly grinned and nodded.

'That's for me then,' Vera said. 'I'll head out there this evening when I've done here.'

When everyone had left, she went back to her desk and her computer. There was always a backlog of work that had more to do with the management of the team than the work in progress. She was about to leave, when she saw that Rick Kelsall's agent had finally sent through the short synopsis she'd used to entice publishers. Vera looked at it briefly, but couldn't focus and decided that it could wait for tomorrow. It was more important now to talk to Judith Sinclair.

Chapter Thirty-Five

HOLLY FOUND HOLY ISLAND DIFFERENT, QUIETER. The children were back at school and there were always fewer people staying during the week. The place was left to the locals and to older people, who'd retired with proper pensions and who had the freedom to holiday when they liked. The weather had changed. A sea fret had blown in from the east, blocking out the sun.

Holly booked into the Seahorse. She was given the same room as she'd had before. Number five. A double bed squeezed into a single room, with a shower room attached. Black mould crawling up the plastic shower curtain. No sea view. An ill-fitting sash window looked out over the empty street. She wondered about asking if there was anything else available, but she doubted if another room would be much better. Besides, this was cheap and the police service budget was always tight.

Di, the landlady, recognized her, peered at her through her thick spectacles. 'Oh, I thought you'd finished your investigation here on the island.'

'Not quite.' Holly smiled across the reception desk. 'I don't suppose you've had any more thoughts about the single woman who stayed here on Friday night?' It would be another loose end to tie up. Something else to make Vera happy. At least for a moment.

'Yes! I spoke to my staff. One of our barmaids reckons she recognized her as a regular. She'll be working later.'

'Thanks.'

'Would you like dinner?' Di had turned back to hostess mode. 'The kitchen's open until nine.'

'No, not this evening.' The Seahorse served traditional pub food, mostly carbs and all of it fried. Vera's idea of heaven, but not Holly's. She'd brought a picnic to eat in her room.

Before that, she headed out onto the island. She wanted to check out the cottage Charlotte had visited before it was too late for a polite enquiry. The mist was thicker now, and though it wasn't yet dark, everything was shadowy and very still. There were people in the public bar, but from the street she could only hear the buzz of quiet conversation. Occasionally, people emerged from the gloom. A couple of teenagers, very young, shyly holding hands, not expecting anyone to see them. An elderly man with a stick, who used it to push his way into the Seahorse bar. There was a sudden shaft of light on the pavement before the door swung closed behind him.

Holly got out her phone and checked the photo of the cottage, which Joe had sent through. She found it easily enough. A green door leading straight from the pavement. Small, white-washed, in the middle of a terrace. It was quite dark now and the curtains had been drawn. Somebody was in, because there was a chink of light where the curtains didn't quite meet, but the gap was tiny and she couldn't see through it. In the distance she could hear the mewling of a foghorn.

She knocked on the door. Close to the house now, she could tell that there was music playing inside, so indistinct that she could only make out the beat, an accompaniment to the foghorn on the shore. There were footsteps and the door opened. A large man stood inside, silhouetted against the light behind him. It took her a moment to make out who it was and he spoke first.

'Oh, hello.' The man seemed surprised to see her, but not shocked. 'I'm sorry, I don't remember your name. We met at the Pilgrims' House on that terrible day when Rick's body was found.' His voice was rich, welcoming, and it was that which identified him for her. 'Everything about that day is such a blur. Do come in!'

'Mr Robson.' *Should it have been Reverend Robson?* Holly wasn't sure. She introduced herself.

'Philip, please.'

He stepped aside and she walked straight into a warm and comfortable room, with an open fire and a couple of armchairs facing it. On the windowsill a pair of binoculars and an RSPB field guide. The music was unfamiliar. Jazz, coming from a radio. Philip Robson switched it off.

'I'm guessing you have more questions for me about Rick Kelsall. Please do sit down.' He pointed to a chair next to the one where he'd obviously been sitting. There was a book on the arm, opened, page down. Mick Herron's *Slow Horses*. One of Vera's favourites. She'd given a copy to Holly, who'd enjoyed it too.

'How can I help you? It must be urgent for you to have come all this way. Can I get you something? Coffee? Tea?'

Holly shook her head. There was an air of concentration in the small room, a focus she didn't want to break.

'Have you heard that Charlotte Thomas is dead?'

'No!' Philip seemed genuinely astonished. 'I'm still treating the week as a kind of retreat and I've been trying to avoid the news. I have no computer here, no television.' There was a pause as he tried to process the information. 'Poor Charlotte, what a dreadful thing.' He looked at Holly. 'What exactly happened? How did she die?'

'She was murdered. Just like Mr Kelsall.'

A moment of silence.

'None of your friends contacted you?' Holly couldn't quite believe that Annie or Louisa hadn't been in touch with the news. Another violent death within the group. Wouldn't that trigger a frisson of excitement or even of fear? Surely, they'd be wondering if one of them would be the next victim.

'I have no phone reception here, Constable. I thought that was why you turned up unannounced on my doorstep.'

'Have you been here on the island since you left the Pilgrims' House?'

'I have. I've had some wonderful walks. It's been very peaceful. Just what I needed after a busy year. Most of the trippers left on Sunday, so I've almost had the place to myself.' Robson gave a little laugh. 'There's been no more skinny-dipping though.'

Holly ignored the comment. 'You haven't been tempted to go further afield – to catch up with family or friends on the mainland?'

'What is this about, Constable? Are you asking me to provide an alibi? If so, I'll need to know where and when poor Charlotte was killed.'

'She died in her yoga studio in Kimmerston,' Holly said. 'It's impossible to pinpoint a precise time of death, but it was yesterday. Late afternoon or early evening.'

'I haven't driven at all, since I moved my car from outside the Pilgrims' House to the alley at the back of the cottage here, but of course I have no way of proving that.' He paused. 'I have been going to the chapel every evening for six o'clock prayers. Some of the islanders might have noticed the candlelight.'

'Charlotte Thomas was seen coming into this cottage on the Friday night when Rick died,' Holly said. 'That's why I'm here. I hadn't realized it was where you were staying.' *Though I should have checked. That was stupid.*

'She was in this house?'

'Yes. Our witness thinks someone else was already in the cottage to let her in.' Holly looked over at him. 'You weren't here, before chapel on Friday, to check the place out?'

'No! I knew it wouldn't be mine until the Sunday lunchtime. I assumed there'd be other holidaymakers here over the weekend.'

'Wouldn't Charlotte have told you all she was here and come to see you in the Pilgrims' House?' Holly paused. 'You were old friends after all.'

'Charlotte wasn't really one of us.' For the first time Philip seemed uncomfortable. 'She didn't even stay for the first weekend of Only Connect. She got her father to come and get her in his very smart car on the first day.'

'And she wasn't here for your first reunion.' A statement not a question.

'That's right. She said she had better things to do. I think she regretted not being here after Isobel died. They really were very good friends, and it would have been a chance to see her for the last time.'

The fire cracked, sending up sparks. Holly thought this wasn't helping very much. The man seemed to have no knowledge of Charlotte's stay, and hadn't much of an alibi for the day before. Perhaps the owner would be able to tell her more. She'd check that in the morning.

'Can you let me have the contact details for your landlord?'

'Landlady,' Philip said. 'Here's her card.'

Holly took it and glanced at it. Gull Cottage, Holy Island. Then the owner's name.

'Judith Sinclair. She's the teacher who set up Only Connect?'

'Yes.' Philip glanced up at Holly. 'I've kept in touch with her, and we've become quite close over the years. She and her husband belonged to a church in Kimmerston. Judy still does. Her husband inherited some money when his grandparents died and they bought this place. A kind of bolthole, when teaching got a bit stressful. Now she lets it out to supplement her pension.'

'Was Judith here over the weekend?'

'No, at least I don't think so; she would have told me if she was.' The response was easy, just like the rest of the conversation, but Holly sensed a moment of hesitation. 'And I really think she'd have let me know if Charlotte was going to be on the island too.'

'Who let you in to the cottage on Sunday?'

'Nobody! I knew where the keys would be: in an old privy in the backyard.'

'Had the cottage been cleaned since the last tenants?' This was important, Holly thought, though if Charlotte had been here, there would surely be some sign of her presence, a stray fingerprint, whether it had been cleaned or not.

'Oh yes.' Philip was relaxed again. 'Someone had definitely been in to clean. The grate had been swept, the pots and pans in the kitchen all put away. Clean sheets on the bed.'

'When do you leave?' Holly asked.

'Friday. I'm back on duty on Sunday. It's a long drive and there'll be a sermon to prepare.'

She stood up then. She couldn't get through the barrier of his warmth and his politeness. Charlotte had been here – it would be too much of a coincidence otherwise – but Holly was no clearer why or how Philip Robson fitted in to the investigation.

In the Seahorse, the landlady had been looking out for Holly and scurried from the bar to catch her before she headed up to her room. 'If you want to chat to Linz, the barmaid who remembers that single woman who paid by cash, she's on shift now.' Desperate to help, to be able to tell her friends she'd been part of a major police investigation.

Holly had been looking forward to some time to reflect on the conversation in Gull Cottage, before sending a report across to Vera, but if they could dismiss the mystery guest, she could let Vera know about that too.

Linz was waiting in the lounge bar, so Holly found herself sitting on a stool there.

'What's your tipple?' The landlady hovered beside her.

'Well, G&T, but really, I don't need anything yet.'

'Nonsense.' The landlady nodded to Linz and a large gin appeared on the bar. 'It's on the house. Only glad to help.'

Holly insisted on paying, and explained it would be against the rules to accept it for free.

Linz was skinny with sharp features and black hair. She had something of the Goth about her. Panda eyes and a long black skirt. She told Holly that she'd grown up in Ashington, but she loved it here. 'I like it best in the winter,' she said. 'Then it's mostly locals and regulars in the bar – some real characters – and you can have the island to yourself. It's not so good for business though. Di makes most of her money over the summer, when the trippers come.' She nodded towards the landlady, who was standing at the other end of the bar, pretending not to listen.

'So, you recognized the single woman, who paid cash at the last minute?'

'Yep. She's a regular. Joanne Haswell. Her name was in the booking, but Di didn't recognize it. I did as soon as she asked. She works at the Ministry at Benton. She quite often turns up on the offchance, when she knows there'll be time to get off the island if we don't have space. If you're a civil servant, I guess the work's pretty boring and sometimes you want to be impulsive, take a bit of a risk.'

Holly nodded. She finished her drink and was about to head back upstairs, when Linz started talking again.

'I'll tell you who else was here on Friday night.' Linz spoke quickly and her accent – pure Pitmatic – was so thick that Holly struggled to follow. 'Cathy, who works in the kitchen, pointed her out to me. Apparently, she was famous at one time. A bit of a celebrity. I wouldn't have known her of course. Before my time.'

'Who was that?'

'The woman who was murdered in Kimmerston yesterday!' Linz looked across the bar, her black-rimmed eyes almost mischievous. She understood the impression she was making. 'I only just saw it on Facebook before coming down to work. Charlotte Thomas. She was here in the bar sitting over in the window.' She nodded towards a padded bench seat with a table in front of it.

ANN CLEEVES

'She wasn't on her own?' Because even now, women didn't go into a bar on their own. Certainly not older women, unless they were waiting for someone and even then, they'd feel uncomfortable.

'Nah, she was with another woman and a guy.'

'Can you describe them?'

Linz screwed up her face to show she was thinking. 'The woman looked even older. But she was bonny with it, like. Good cheekbones. You knaa.'

Holly nodded. Could that be Judith Sinclair? It seemed possible. But the description could also apply to Annie Laidler or Louisa Hampton. 'And the man?'

Linz shook her head. 'Sorry, I didn't really see him at all. He had his back to me all the time and the pub was crazy busy all night. I only had glimpses of the women through the crowded tables and they weren't here for very long.'

'He didn't buy the drinks?' Because that was still usually how it worked, especially for older people. It was the man who went to the bar, even if a woman had slipped him the cash to pay.

'It's all table service,' Linz said. 'Di's trying to take the place upmarket. I didn't take their orders, so I wouldn't know.' A pause. 'I didn't see them leave either. I googled the woman when I took five minutes to go to the loo, and when I got back another group had taken their place.'

'Do you know what time they were here?'

'Mid-evening? Seven? Seven-thirty? Sorry, like I said, the pub was really busy.'

Holly went up to her room, switched on the kettle and made a mug of herbal tea. She never travelled without teabags these days. Orange and cranberry, her favourite flavour. She sent an email to the boss and to Joe, describing her conversation with Robson and the barmaid's description of the people in the Seahorse. She ate the salad she'd made, and then, guiltily, the packet of biscuits that was on the tray next to the kettle.

When she'd finished, it occurred to her that it would be reassuring to have someone else to email or to text. Someone special. She hadn't really had a boyfriend since she'd moved north. Work had always come first. She felt a sudden stab of loneliness, like a physical pain, and thought she couldn't carry on like this.

She checked her emails once more and saw that Cecilia Bertrand had sent through the synopsis of Kelsall's novel. There were still no further details from the digital investigations team. There was hardly more than a paragraph but, perhaps because she was so tired, the words seemed to make little sense. She couldn't see how the story hung together. She forwarded it to Vera and decided she'd look again in the morning. She cleaned her teeth and got into bed, and fell asleep listening to the mournful wail of the foghorn.

Chapter Thirty-Six

HOLLY'S EMAIL ARRIVED, JUST BEFORE VERA set out to see Judith Sinclair. It was another reason to talk to the former teacher. She'd already phoned in advance, playing the role of slightly disorganized older woman.

'You don't mind, do you, pet? I know you've already had a chat with my officers, but I just want to check a couple of their details. It wasn't quite clear from their notes.'

Judith lived in a village just out of the town. It was surrounded by established housing developments, and had become hardly more, these days, than a suburb of Kimmerston. She and her husband had probably bought their home from new, Vera thought. It felt to her as if Judith was rooted in the community. When Vera arrived, she was still in the small front garden, raking leaves from the lawn. It was almost dark and in the other houses lights were being switched on. Vera thought it was a strange kind of obsession to be working at this time of the evening. A need for order, or for activity. She moved easily. This woman was fit. She'd have no difficulty holding a cushion over Rick Kelsall's head. Or even, Vera thought, hoisting him into a makeshift noose.

Charlotte might be more difficult to overpower, but if Holly's information was right, the women knew each other. Judith would be able to approach her without causing suspicion.

'Come in, Inspector. I waited until you arrived before I stopped for tea.'

The kitchen looked out on a garden, which was longer, backing onto a field of sheep, very white in the dusk. Here, there was still a sense of space, of the village it had once been. Judith put on the kettle and made tea in a pot.

'Have you been here long?'

'Since we were first married. When we retired, we thought we might move further out into the country, but we never quite got round to it, and then when Martin died, I was glad to be here, among people I knew well.'

'After all, you had your bolthole in Holy Island if you needed an escape.' Vera heaved herself onto a stool at the breakfast bar. She thought Judith had probably planned to take her into an immaculate lounge, but this seemed less formal. The woman would like to be in control of situations. This might throw her a little.

'Oh, are you comfortable there, Inspector? We could go into the other room.' Frowning. Not answering the question implied in Vera's comment.

'This is perfect.' She sipped the tea. 'How often do you get up to the cottage?'

'Oh, not as often as I did when Martin was alive. Now it's more useful as an alternative form of income. I suppose I could sell this house and downsize, but I'm happy here. All my memories are in the place. It's good to have the space when my children visit with *their* families.' She smiled. 'I love to travel. The holiday home supports my wanderlust.'

'When were you last at the cottage?'

There was a pause. Vera thought this was a woman who'd feel awkward about lying. Was she trying to find a form of words which would be true, but would also manage to imply that she hadn't been close to the place where a man she'd taught had died? In the end, Judith decided that truth was the best option.

'I was there on Friday. I needed to clean the place for a new tenant. There's a woman who usually cleans for me, but she's away on holiday, so I went up and made a night of it.'

'But you didn't go to the Pilgrims' House? You must have realized all your former students were there.'

'No!' The answer was quick and firm. No need to think about this one, to twist words to form a story, a half-truth. 'I knew they were there of course. I'm friendly with Philip. But no, I didn't meet any of the Pilgrims' House group. Not even him. I left very early on Saturday morning. It was a very swift stay.'

'You were in the pub though, the Seahorse, with a couple. Who were they?'

A silence. A white face. Anger. 'Has somebody been spying on me, Inspector?'

Vera smiled at the thought. 'Of course not! But a man was killed there. We're detectives. Of course we make inquiries.' A pause. 'The barmaid thought that the woman with you was Charlotte Thomas.' Another longer pause. 'You've probably heard that she's dead now too. Of course, it's probably a coincidence, but you were seen within a mile of one victim on the night of his death, and you were with the other just a couple of days before she was killed. You do see that you have questions to answer.'

'You can't possibly suspect me of being a murderer.' Her voice was imperious. It would have quelled the noise in any classroom. 'That's ridiculous. What reason would I have?'

'Why did you meet Charlotte Thomas on Friday evening?' Vera had stood up to plenty of teachers in her time.

'She phoned me before I left here on Friday morning. On my landline. I very nearly didn't answer, because nobody ever uses that these days. Only scammers and cold callers. I suppose I was still in the directory. She said she wanted to catch up, or rather to ask my advice. I told her I was just setting off for the island – hoping to put her off – but she said she'd meet me there.'

'What did she want to discuss with you?'

'I'm afraid I can't tell you, Inspector. It was a confidential conversation.'

'She's dead!' Vera couldn't believe what she was hearing. 'This might help me catch her killer.'

'She might be dead, Inspector, but she has living children. Sometimes a reputation is all that the dead have left to them, and I intend to honour that. We had a drink in the Seahorse. One drink because she was driving back to Kimmerston that night. We talked about old times. She asked for my advice and I gave it. I can't see at all how our conversation might relate to her death.'

'You lied to my officers when they asked you if you'd seen any of your students recently.'

'I did,' Judith said. 'I regretted that. I'm not by nature a liar. But I knew there would be more questions and it was Charlotte's secret to keep and not mine to share.'

'Who was the man with you in the pub?'

'Some local birdwatcher.' Judith was dismissive. 'If you talk to your spies in the pub, they'll tell you he was there when we arrived. We asked if we could share his table. The place was busy. One of the reasons we only had one drink was that we couldn't talk without being overheard. Charlotte had wanted a glass of wine and I had nothing in the cottage to give her, but we didn't stay long.'

The women stared at each other over the granite counter. Vera had the power to intimidate when she needed it, but Judith was steely, unmoved. Vera couldn't help admiring her courage. She gave it one last shot. 'What is this really about? You're either lying to me or to yourself. There's more going on here than a need to preserve a dead woman's reputation. Charlotte Thomas revelled in notoriety. She wouldn't mind the gossip. She'd have enjoyed any press she could get, even after her death.'

Judith shook her head. 'I won't be drawn, Inspector. Would you like another cup of tea? You're very welcome. If not, I think perhaps you'd better leave. I'm sure that you've had a very busy day.'

Vera didn't move. 'Why did you phone Rick Kelsall late on Friday night?'

There was a silence.

'I don't know what on earth you're talking about.'

'We checked the calls made to Mr Kelsall's mobile. The last call he received came from you. Not from your landline, but from your mobile phone.'

Judy Sinclair sat, motionless. 'You must be mistaken.'

'Are you telling me that you didn't make that call?'

Still there was no reply. At last, the woman spoke. Vera couldn't help admiring her poise. 'Are you charging me, Inspector? If so, we should probably complete this conversation somewhere more formal. If not, I believe I'm not obliged to answer your questions.'

'Perhaps somebody else made that call using your phone.'

Judith Sinclair stared at Vera. 'Perhaps they did, Inspector, but I've already explained that this conversation is at an end.'

Vera slid off the stool. Without a word, Judith walked her to the door and saw her into the garden.

Chapter Thirty-Seven

THE NEXT DAY, VERA WOKE EARLY, before it was quite light. On impulse, she decided on a walk before heading for the office. The movement of walking sometimes helped to shuffle facts into place, and made her see things more clearly. She pulled on her boots and the old waxed jacket that had hung behind the door when she was a teenager, and set off. The rising sun shone on the dying bracken on the hill behind the cottage, turning it to bronze. The whole hillside seemed to glow. She'd not go far. Just to the crags, where the peregrines bred most years, and she'd seen her first ring ouzel. She'd been seven or eight and she'd run back down the hill, full of it.

'A male, Dad. I got the white crescent at the throat.'

He'd hardly looked up from the table where he'd been working on a dead badger, stuffing it for a farmer who hated animals and wanted it as a kind of trophy.

'Oh aye,' he'd said. 'I get the eggs every year for my collection.' She'd not known collecting eggs was illegal then, but she'd known it was wrong, and whenever she'd seen anything special after that, she'd kept the information to herself.

At the top of the hill, she stopped, her back to the rocks and, squinting against the sun, looked east towards the sea. A line of light on the horizon, glimpsed through the gleaming silver blades of the wind turbines in the mid-distance. She didn't mind them, thought they had a beauty of their own. From here, they looked like dandelion clocks, as if a strong enough gust would blow them away. Joanna was a bit of a green activist, and when people moaned about the turbines, she'd come out with the same response. 'Which would you rather? A wind farm or a nuclear power station? Or no heat in the winter?' Vera had started using the same line.

She realized she was dodging the problem of the murders, pushing them to the back of her mind, letting in stray memories, odd encounters. Hector was always there, bullying her from the grave. She couldn't judge Annie for her inability to let go of the past when she allowed Hector to rule her life. She pulled herself to her feet and started down the hill. The sun had risen. This was a new day. Perhaps today, she'd make sense of these murders.

When she arrived at the police station, Vera phoned Holly. There was no reception on her mobile, so Vera tried the landline of the pub. The landlady answered. 'Ooh yes, Inspector, I'll see if I can find her.'

They carried out their conversation with the noise of a hoover in the background.

'I've never met a witness before who just refused to talk,' Vera said. 'I don't mean the scallies who "no comment" in the interview room, but respectable people. Even if they have things to hide, they usually make up some sort of story. They need to justify their actions if only to themselves. But I got nothing out of the woman. No excuses even. She didn't deny making that call to Kelsall, but she simply refused to discuss it.'

'You sound impressed, boss.'

'Aye well, Judith's a worthy opponent. But she'll end up talking. They all do in the end. In the meantime, I want you to check her story. Let's see if you can track down the mysterious birder who was sitting at the women's table in the Seahorse. I'm still not convinced he's the stranger Judith makes him out to be.'

'I've found no evidence that they were together. He didn't buy their drinks. I've checked. Judith bought hers and Charlotte's on her card.'

'That doesn't mean anything. Two independent women, nothing to stop them buying their own drinks.' But Vera was wavering. She could see what Holly was getting at. 'See if you can track him down. He might even be staying at the pub. Did you get any sort of description?'

'No. It was busy and he had his back to the bar.'

'Someone must have seen him!' Vera wished she was there, asking the questions. She was tempted just to drive up and take over.

'I'll ask.' Holly was clearly resentful now. She didn't need Vera's interference, the implication that she couldn't do her own job. 'I'm just on my way to the Old Hall to check Katherine Willmore's alibi for Monday afternoon. I'll come back to the pub at lunchtime when there are more people around.'

'Yeah.' Vera thought that she should apologize, but couldn't quite find the words. 'Just let me know as soon as you get anything.'

'Of course, boss. Of course.'

Vera ranged around the open-plan office looking for Joe

and Charlie, but they weren't there. She phoned the digital investigators, pushing for action on Kelsall's laptop. A grumpy young woman said that all major files in Kelsall's computer had been deleted and would take time to access, but they'd found some notes, which he'd sent as an email to himself and which seemed to relate to the novel. Would Vera like to see it?

'What do you think?' The response sounded too loud and too angry even to her. 'Sorry, pet. Yeah, just send it over.'

The forwarded email came through almost immediately. It was, as the investigator said, just a series of notes. There were clumps of scene-setting and snatches of dialogue. She thought it was like Kelsall's brain. She had the impression of an over-active imagination, a lack of focus. What did they call it in kids? Attention deficit disorder? Kelsall seemed to be jumping from one character to another, without a single storyline. She couldn't see how it could mean anything even to the writer.

One short paragraph made more sense than the others:

Outside. Tide coming in. R tries to tell I that this has to end. He's being responsible for once. It really isn't a good idea. But she refuses to listen. Tells him it's her decision. This is the jumping-off point for the whole plot.

Vera tried to make sense of this. R and I were obviously Rick and Isobel. Annie had said that Rick and Isobel had been rowing before Isobel stormed off in her car. Annie had assumed that they'd had a fling while Charlotte was elsewhere, or that Rick had been flirting and Isobel had rejected his advances. But this read as if something different had been going on. If Rick was ending an affair, it wouldn't be Isobel's decision, as the snippet of text implied. She couldn't force him to stay with her.

She got on the phone to Paul Keating, her impatience growing while his assistant went to find him.

'If there was a car crash, an accident, no suspicious circumstances at the time, would there be a PM? We're talking forty years ago. And would it be able to tell if the woman was pregnant?'

She listened to the answer and switched off her phone.

Chapter Thirty-Eight

THE OLD HALL WAS THE MOST expensive hotel on the island. It was small, beautifully restored to its Elizabethan glory, surrounded by a high stone wall to stop curious tourists from peering inside. The restaurant was much lauded for its traditional British cuisine. Holly thought the place was certainly more Katherine Willmore's style than the Seahorse. She decided that she'd come here for a night when or if she ever got promotion, then wondered who she might invite to celebrate with her. She experienced the same sense of loneliness, of emptiness, as she had the night before, because she couldn't come up with even one name.

There was a small courtyard garden and Holly walked across that and then into the building through an arched door, which looked as if it might be original. Inside, she was met by a smooth young man in a suit, who asked if he might help.

She introduced herself and showed her warrant card. 'Just routine inquiries.'

'About the murder on the island last weekend?' There

was that same salacious curiosity as had been shown by the landlady in the Seahorse. They wanted the killer caught of course, because murder might be bad for business, but it also generated excitement, a vicarious sense of danger. Besides, killers became famous, the stuff of headlines and social media, and these days, everyone wanted to be close to celebrity.

'Among other things.' Holly tried to sound boring. 'Could I look at your guest list for Friday night?' The mysterious birdwatcher seen by Linz and then mentioned by Vera might have been staying at the Old Hall. If they could get contact details, he could be dismissed from the inquiry.

'Of course!' He went behind a desk and opened his computer, clicked on the keyboard. 'I'll print it out for you.'

'Could you email it to me too?' She'd send it on to Joe and the rest of the team. Let them do some of the leg work. She put her card on the desk beside the computer, saw a framed photo there of him with a woman and a baby. He looked too young to have a family and again she had the sense of time slipping by, of middle age approaching, of time leaving her stranded and alone.

'Of course,' he said again. On a shelf below the desk, a printer whirred and he pulled out a copy of the registration page.

'Could you talk me through them? I'm interested in a man on his own. Possibly a birdwatcher.'

'Sure. We have a lot of return guests. Our clients are *very* satisfied by the service we provide.' He was becoming corporate once more. 'Look, the lounge is empty now. Why don't I order us both some coffee and I can talk you through the list there?'

Holly suspected the coffee here would be very good. 'Why not?'

The coffee came in a silver pot with home-made shortbread biscuits. He introduced himself as Jason, one of the assistant managers, and chatted about the hotel until the waitress left them alone. Then he put the sheet of paper on the low table in front of them and talked her through it.

'These three are families. One from Hampshire and two from Manchester. They've never stayed with us before. They booked together. Friends from uni, I think.'

'Could you describe the men?' Holly made neat notes on the paper.

'In their thirties. Obviously minted. I heard them talking over dinner. I think they all work in IT.'

'They had dinner with you on Friday?'

'They ate with us every night, so they could keep checking on their children, who were sleeping in their rooms. We gave the kids afternoon tea.'

Unlikely then, that one of them would have met two older women in the Seahorse.

Jason worked down the list. Most of the guests were elderly: two widows who were friends and came every year, several couples in their seventies, a group of retired academics, who'd first met when they were undergraduates on a field trip on the island.

They aroused Holly's interest briefly. One of them might be the birdwatcher in the pub. 'Did you notice if any of them went out on Friday evening?'

He shook his head. 'They'd hired a room for private dining and we laid on a special dinner. Man, could they drink! I'm sure that none of them left. By the end of the night, they could hardly stagger up to bed.'

Holly finished her coffee and allowed Jason to pour her another cup. She'd get the team in Kimmerston to follow up the details, but it seemed unlikely that the person sitting with Judith and Charlotte in the Seahorse had stayed in the Old Hall. 'I'm also interested in Monday. Not a resident this time but a woman who said she had afternoon tea here.'

'Ah,' he said. 'I wouldn't necessarily have details for those. Most people book, of course. We do get very busy. But we allow walk-ins especially mid-week.'

'This woman says she's a regular. Her name's Katherine Willmore.' Holly realized he might jump to the conclusion that the PCC was some sort of suspect. 'Of course, again this is routine. We have to check even people on the periphery of a case. To follow the rules without fear or favour.'

Jason smiled to show that he understood. 'Of course. She and Daniel are regulars. He runs Rede Tower, so there's a business connection too. We work very closely on promotion.'

'Could you check if Katherine was here on Monday afternoon?' There was, after all, only so much coffee a woman could drink, and Holly wanted to get back to the mainland.

'I wasn't on duty, but I can talk to a colleague who was.'

'If she was here, could you check if she paid by card? That might confirm her account of events and give us a definite timeline to work on.' Holly smiled. 'And I know I can be assured of your discretion. Rumours can start very easily and you wouldn't want a respected public figure to be the subject of gossip or false news.'

'Oh, of course! Katherine and Daniel are valued guests. I

can check the card details first then there'll be no need to include anyone else in the conversation.'

Holly thought of the woman and child in the photograph on his desk. He was smart, this man of theirs. He had the knack of making himself indispensable. He'd go far.

Jason returned very quickly with another printout. 'Yes, Katherine was definitely here on Monday afternoon and she did pay for afternoon tea by card. A Visa debit.'

Holly looked at the receipt and thought that the cost of afternoon tea for one was more than she'd expect to pay for a decent dinner for two. The payment had been made at twelve minutes past four. It was highly unlikely, therefore, that Katherine had made it to Kimmerston in time to smother Charlotte Thomas before she and Vera had found her body in the studio. Not quite impossible, but very unlikely.

She was about to leave, when she had another thought. 'Charlotte Thomas,' she said. 'The woman who was killed in town on Monday. Was she a regular here too?'

Jason got to his feet. 'Not recently,' he said. 'When I first started here, she was in the place all the time. Often with famous friends. But no, I haven't seen her for ages.'

Out in the courtyard, Holly realized that the mist had rolled in again. Perhaps it was something to do with the tide or the time of year. She could hardly make out the wall on the other side of the garden, and the foghorn had started its haunting call once again. Holly had a sudden image of drowning sailors crying for help. And that made her think of Isobel Hall, who'd been younger than she was, in a car tipping off the causeway into the water. It wasn't cold, but she found that she was shivering.

She made her way back to the Seahorse to prepare for

leaving. She still had several hours before the tide would cut off the island from the mainland, but she thought she'd done nearly all she could here. She wanted to talk again to Di and Linz about the man who'd been sitting at the window table in the lounge bar with Charlotte and Judith. Judith had told Vera that he was a stranger, a visiting birdwatcher, and Holly wanted to confirm that it might have been true. Linz was the better witness of the two but she hadn't been serving breakfast. Di had said she'd start her shift at lunchtime so she should be there now.

The dining room was quiet, and Linz was leaning on the public side of the bar, waiting to show guests to their tables. She greeted Holly as an old friend.

'Hiya! You here for lunch?'

'Why not?' She could have something light. A sandwich. She wouldn't have a chance once she got back to the station, and by the time she got home, she wouldn't feel like eating much.

Linz showed her to the table in the window and gave her a laminated menu, freshly wiped with a grubby cloth. 'The crab's good. Local.'

'I'll have that then. A crab sandwich. With a side salad.'

'Good choice.' Linz was just about to walk away, but Holly called her back. 'Last Friday night when the three people were sitting here, are you sure the guy was part of the group? We've spoken to the older woman and she reckons he was nothing to do with them, that he was some visiting birdwatcher, who was just sharing the table with them.'

Linz shrugged. 'I dunno. He could have been, I suppose.'

'You didn't recognize him as a regular?'

'Sorry, as I said, he was just a back, a jacket and grey hair.

I only got a glimpse of those. There were other tables between him and the bar.'

Holly was disappointed. She'd have loved something more to take back to Vera.

Linz spoke again.

'If he's a regular birder, one of the locals would know. A few of them moved here once they retired. They're all friends. I can ask around for you. See if any of them were in Friday night and recognized him.'

'Thanks,' Holly said. 'That'd be great. You've got my number.'

Linz was about to go into the kitchen with the order, when she stopped and turned back. 'I did see that woman again though.'

'Charlotte Thomas? The woman who died?'

'No, not her. The older one with the white hair.'

'When did you see her?' Holly wasn't quite sure how important that would be. They knew already that Judith Sinclair had spent the night in Gull Cottage.

'Later that Friday night. After my shift I went out on the island.' She paused, suddenly a little awkward. 'I've got a bloke who lives here. One of the fishermen. Most nights I stay with him unless I'm on early breakfasts.'

'How late?'

'Eleven? Something like that. We're quite strict about closing the bar at ten-thirty, and then there was a bit of tidying up. It certainly wouldn't have been later than eleven-thirty.'

'Where did you see her?'

'Out to the east of the island.'

So not close to Gull Cottage. 'Could she have been coming back from the Pilgrims' House?'

Linz looked at her, aware of the implications of the question. 'Yeah, she could.'

293

Holly went outside to phone Vera. She passed on the information. 'I was going to come back to Kimmerston now, but what do you think?'

'Stay,' Vera said. 'You've got a while before the tide. See if anyone else saw Judith Sinclair wandering around the island at night. And if your barmaid can get a fix on that birdwatcher.'

Holly went back inside to finish her lunch.

Chapter Thirty-Nine

PHILIP SLEPT POORLY AFTER THE VISIT from the young detective. He wished he'd gone straight back to London after the reunion weekend. He felt that his orderly world was falling apart. He couldn't see how Charlotte's death could fit into any sort of pattern. He'd understood why Rick had married her – she'd been a trophy, a validation for a small man with an inflated ego – but Philip had assumed that she'd been out of Rick's life for years. Now, it was the chaos that most disturbed him, the unexpected. Rick had lived his life on the edge and really his death had come as no surprise. Rick was never going to leave this world easily, peacefully, without drama. He wouldn't have wanted to. Charlotte's murder, however, had shocked Philip profoundly.

In the early hours, it occurred to him that he could go now. The tide was out so he could pack up the car and he could drive away. Who could stop him? Not Vera Stanhope and her team. Back in the suburban rectory there would be nothing to remind him of his old life, the guilt and the anger. People would be pleased to welcome him home a little earlier than expected. They'd have seen the news and be sympathetic.

Then he remembered that Judith had planned to come to the cottage. She'd phoned while he was still at the Pilgrims' House, asking if she could visit for a night. She'd sounded distressed, but also eager to see him. He'd been flattered by the request and was looking forward to the woman's company. He admired her and she'd been in his mind recently.

Once the decision to stay had been made, Philip fell into an uneasy sleep. He woke to an image, part memory, part dream. They were young, all in the basement of the Halls' house in Kimmerston. Ken was bent over his guitar, and he was singing: James Taylor's 'You've Got A Friend'. Ken had always been musical and in middle age, he'd joined a choir, amateur but celebrated. Philip had gone to watch a performance in Carlisle. Now, he supposed, all that was lost to the man. It had been so much a part of his life and now it was gone.

He must have drifted back to sleep, because when he woke again it was day and a milky light was coming through the window. Philip got up and saw that the light was filtered through mist. There was a loud knocking on the front door. He pulled a sweater over his pyjamas and went to answer.

Judith stood there, looking very small, very anxious. 'Oh,' she said. 'I've woken you after all. I came on early, before the tide, but I've been waiting in the car for a reasonable hour.' She walked into the house. 'Oh Philip, I've been so very foolish.'

She seemed close to tears. He gathered her into his arms and held her tight.

Chapter Forty

JOE WOKE UP THE MORNING AFTER Sal's birthday feeling old. He'd never had a hangover when he was younger. He and Sal must have polished off a bottle of fizzy wine each to celebrate, because there were two empties in the recycling bin in the kitchen. He didn't drink much these days, especially on a school night, and now it showed. Sal seemed okay. She was singing along to Radio Two and getting the kids ready for school, eating toast thick with marmalade, and emptying the washing machine all at the same time. Crumbs had sprayed all over her top. She realized and wiped them off with a cloth, then folded the clothes ready for the line. Multitasking. Something he'd never quite got the hang of. He made himself tea and didn't bother with the toast she'd left for him.

Vera was already in the office, though he'd got in early. She called him into her room. The radiator had decided to work again, and it was as steamy as a sauna in there. Outside it had started to drizzle again and she'd hung her damp coat on the back of a chair.

'Sal enjoy her birthday?' Vera's voice was bright. 'Good night?'

'Yeah!' As he said it, he knew it was true. He'd got all that he'd ever wanted with Sal and the kids, a kind of contentment, and it *had* been a good night. He was about to explain about the cake that Jess had made for her mam, and the presents Sal had got, but Vera had already shifted her attention back to work. Whenever she asked about the family, it was just going through the motions. She had no real interest. But then, he thought, he wasn't much interested in other people's kids either.

'I want you to do a bit of digging around Annie Laidler and Daniel Rede,' Vera said. 'Their baby died when it was just a few months old. Cot death, they thought at first, but the parents came under suspicion too. Poor Annie's still haunted by it. They were living in a caravan up at Rede's Tower when the bairn died and it must have seemed a bit of an unconventional lifestyle at the time. They were very young. Our lot were involved anyway, stomping in with their big boots, just at the time when everything was most raw. The death was viewed as unexplained until it turned out in the end that the poor little scrap had been suffering from infantile meningitis. But it happened around the time there was that second death. Louisa's sister Isobel driving off the Holy Island causeway in a temper, too close to the tide. That was unexplained too. Both incidents would have happened forty-five years ago, but there's a bloke who was a young officer then who's still alive and up for a bit of a chat about the olden days.' A pause. 'I remember him from my cadet days. Not a cheery soul, but a good policeman. Solid.'

'There'll be files.' Joe thought an in-person interview was a lot of effort for two accidental deaths.

'Of course there'll be files. They might even have been computerized and easy to access, though I very much doubt it. But files don't tell us what was really going on in a cop's head when they were interviewing the witnesses. And I've never yet met a cop who hasn't got a long memory.' Vera stopped up sharp. 'There'd have been post-mortems in both cases. And those records *would* be more detailed. It occurred to me that Isobel might have been pregnant and Doc Keating says you'd be able to tell, even if she was only a few weeks. She looked up at Joe. 'I'll follow that up later. I'm seeing Judith Sinclair first, to find out why she's pissing us about. I want you to chat to the police officer who was involved in the Isobel Hall accident. Make him very happy by asking his advice. Buy him a pint at lunchtime. Or a pie. Or both. Let's find out what was going on all those years ago.'

Joe nodded. When the boss had a bee in her bonnet, it was best to humour her.

'He lives on the coast. Before you meet him, call in at Rede's Tower and see if our friend Daniel is there. Hol's tracking down Katherine's alibi on Holy Island, but we still don't know where her bloke was on Monday afternoon. I've left messages for him but he's not called me back. I'd like to know what's going on with him. Everyone says he's a very busy chap, but it's starting to look suspicious to me. And if not that, then bloody rude.'

Joe was glad of an excuse to go back to Rede's Tower. It was a trip into nostalgia. As he'd explained to Holly, he'd spent weeks of his childhood summers there. His grandfather had owned an old caravan, very close to the shore. There'd been no fancy facilities in those days. No facilities at all, except one outside tap for drinking water and a concrete block with two stinking toilets and a shower that rarely worked. But to Joe, it had been paradise. Freedom. In his memory the days had been endlessly sunny. He'd gone crabbing with his grandad and disappeared for hours with the other feral lads on the site, playing on the beach or in the scrubby piece of woodland just inland.

There *had* been rain but only at night. He remembered the sound of rain on the metal roof of the caravan, the sense that this was his den, safe, warm, protective. Now, he had a shed at the bottom of the garden and when it was raining, he went there to bring the memory back. Sal thought he was doing useful tasks – sharpening tools or tidying the shelves – but very little got done because he sat on a broken garden chair, his eyes shut, remembering the past as the rain rattled the corrugated iron roof.

When the kids had come along, he'd wanted to get a caravan at Rede's. 'It'd be great for weekends away. They'd love it!' But Sal had put her foot down. The nearest she was prepared to get to camping was a lodge at Center Parcs.

There was a lay-by just before the turn-off to the holiday park, and Joe stopped there, to allow a few more minutes of childhood memory, but nothing was at all as he recalled it. A mist had rolled in from the shore and made everything shadowy, shifting. Occasionally it cleared and Joe saw the shape of wooden cabins where once his grandfather's caravan had stood with a few others, forming a circle, like a wagon train in an old-fashioned Western.

Now, in the spinney, they'd built an elaborate children's adventure playground. One of the structures rose above the layer of mist, and reminded Joe of a scaffold with its gibbet. His imagination was running wild. It was drinking too much the night before and not enough sleep, or a weird kind of prejudice. Because it wasn't as he'd remembered, he was deter-mined to dislike the place.

The pele tower itself had been derelict when they'd stayed on the site, and now the stone had been cleaned and repointed and the slate roof replaced. Proper windows put in. He thought he might persuade Sal to consider a weekend here now, but he wouldn't suggest it. It wouldn't be the same.

He drove on and pulled in to the visitors' car park. He sat for a moment to get a sense of the place. There was a new stone building attached to the tower, glass fronted. A cafe and restaurant. All very tasteful. Joe got out of the car and made his way to find Daniel Rede.

Once she realized that Joe wasn't a guest checking in, the receptionist thought he must be a salesman and tried to put him off. 'I don't think Mr Rede is on site today. I'm sure I can find someone else to help you.'

He showed her his warrant card. 'I won't take up a lot of his time, but it is rather urgent.'

'As I said . . .' But before she could insist that Daniel wasn't there, a man walked in through a door behind her.

'Don't worry, Jan. I'm back on site. I'm very happy to help the officer.'

Joe wasn't sure what he'd been expecting. Some kind of businessman perhaps, but not this. Daniel Rede was wearing a checked shirt and jeans and looked more like a retired farmer than the head of a multimillion leisure company. 'I know Inspector Stanhope has been trying to get hold of me. I'm sorry. We seem to keep missing each other. It's been a busy week. How can I help you?'

'Just a few more questions,' Joe said. 'You'll have seen there's been another death.'

'Of course! Charlotte. Kelsall's first wife. Another dreadful tragedy. And quite unnerving actually. Do you mind if we walk while we talk? There's been a complaint about the hot tub attached to one of our superior lodges. The filtration system wasn't working properly. The customers are regulars and I want to check it's properly fixed.'

'Fine.' Joe followed him out of the building. 'You're still very hands-on then?'

'It's the only way, a place like this.' He turned to Joe, gave a quick grin. 'We charge a fortune – you wouldn't believe what people will pay for a sea view, fresh air straight from Scandinavia with a bit of luxury thrown in. But the punters are demanding. They expect personal service. I like to keep on top of the detail, and as your boss is aware, I've not been on site much in the last few days.'

Joe thought there was more to Rede's focus on the everyday detail of the operation than a desire to give good customer service. The man seemed restless, unsettled. He was probably one of those practical men who were better at making and mending than sitting and staring at a screen. And perhaps he was jittery because murder was bad for business. 'I stayed here as a kid,' Joe said. It seemed a way in to break the ice. 'It's a bit different now.'

'I started working here as soon as I left school,' Daniel said. 'My grandfather ran the place then and it was mostly people from the region who came to stay. Newcastle families wanting to escape the smoke and soot of the city. Pitmen needing a bit of fresh air in their lungs. But everything changed. People wanted more from a holiday. We were having to compete with package tours to Spain. We couldn't give them guaranteed sun, but we could provide the other things they got abroad: a bar, entertainment in the evening, play spaces for the kids. Then staycations got a bit more fashionable and we decided to move upmarket. Now we get regulars who come from London for a couple of short breaks a year.'

'I can see that makes business sense . . .'

'But you miss the old days?'

'Aye.' Joe laughed. 'Maybe.'

'Sometimes,' Daniel said, 'I do too.'

They'd arrived at the row of wooden lodges closest to the water. These were as different from Joe's grandfather's caravan as it was possible to be.

'Each site is different.' Rede seemed to have forgotten his nostalgia for the past. Now, he could have been selling the place to a potential visitor. 'And each has its own outdoor space. If you live in the city, you don't want to be overlooked by your neighbour. We planted the hedges. Sea buckthorn. Authentic. We know they'll want outdoor facilities so we've added a firepit, a covered balcony in case the weather's bad, like today.' He sounded as proud as the new father he'd once been. 'The hot tubs are all wood burners. With all this managed woodland, we're not short of logs, and we make sure they're properly dried before we hand them over. Let me just check this has been properly fixed by the maintenance guy, then I'm all yours.'

Joe walked on a few yards to the bank of pebbles that separated the beach from the development. He looked back at the lodge, which could have accommodated a family of eight in comfort. His father would have made a comment about the injustice of it: these palaces for the rich to holiday while the poor lived in modern slums or were homeless. The mist cleared for a moment and he could see the shadow of Holy Island on the horizon, suddenly very large, very close.

Daniel Rede joined him, looking out over the water. 'All

sorted,' he said. 'I knew it would be – we've got a great team – but I still feel the need to check. Katherine says I should delegate more, but in the end, I'm responsible. It's my name on the place.'

'You're not tempted to sell up, retire?'

'Nah! What would I do all day? My life would seem point-less.'

Joe thought of the other people who'd been at the Pilgrims' House on the night of Rick Kelsall's death. Annie was still working, but perhaps she needed the income. Louisa and Ken had retired and Philip was talking about giving up the priest-hood soon. They all seemed content. But he wasn't here to discuss the possibility of ageing well.

'We're just checking people's movements for Monday after-noon. That was when Charlotte Thomas died.' Joe paused. 'We know you were in Kimmerston in the morning.'

Daniel didn't seem to resent the question. 'That's right. A planning meeting first thing, then I called in on Annie. She and Rick had always been close. I don't think there was ever anything romantic between them, but they were very good friends. I just wanted to check that she was okay.'

'And later?'

'I was out recceing potential sites along the coast. As I said, we want to expand the business.' He paused. 'I didn't meet anyone until early evening. That was when I called in on a farmer near Amble, but I didn't think we'd get planning permis-sion for a development of the scale that we'd need to be viable, so we didn't chat for very long. I can give you his details. In the afternoon, I was looking at a caravan site near Whitley Bay. Whitley's going up in the world these days. All artisan bakers and indie shops. It might suit us very well. But that was a

covert operation. I didn't want the owner to know I was interested.' He stopped. 'I know you have to ask, but really I didn't
know Charlotte very well. I certainly had no reason to want
her dead.'

'You were at school with her though?'

'Even then, we didn't really know each other. I didn't start
at the Grammar until I was thirteen and we didn't come from
the same sort of background. Like I said, my grandad ran this
place then, and you'll know what it was like. Run-down. A bit
of a shambles. There was no money in it until I took it on.
The other Grammar school lads treated me like some sort of
gypsy.'

'You haven't seen Charlotte more recently?'

'Once or twice.' A pause. 'She wanted to set up a well-being
centre here on site. A kind of glorified spa. We had a couple
of meetings.'

'You didn't take her up on the suggestion?'

'Nah. It was a bit awkward because Katherine liked her, but
I couldn't see it making us much profit once she'd taken a cut.
She wanted us to fund the initial set-up. I thought we'd be
better keeping it in-house. It sounds harsh, but Charlotte
Thomas wouldn't have been the draw she might once have
been. Our target demographic is people in their thirties and
early forties. They would never have heard of her.'

Later, Joe found himself sitting in a pub in an ex-mining
community by the coast, buying a pint for a former sergeant,
who'd been based in Northumberland for the whole of his
career. The man was called Pete Allen, and as Vera had said,
he had a memory that went back years. By the time Joe got
there, it was lunchtime and the place was empty apart from

a few other men of Allen's generation. Regulars, who nodded gravely to each new customer as they walked through the door. They were coming together for company, and to help the day slide on.

Allen had a grey moustache, which dipped into the beer, grey hair, grey eyes. A sadness, which he wore like his grey overcoat. His missus had left him years before. He'd told Joe that even before they'd met. When Joe had phoned to make the appointment, he'd asked Allen if he'd be free for a pie and a pint or if he'd need to be home for his midday meal. 'I'm always free.' Allen's voice had been flat, uncomplaining.

Joe got more details in the pub. The wife had run away with an insurance broker from Bellingham, apparently. She'd claimed it was Pete's fault, the shifts, never knowing when he'd be home. 'But it wasn't that,' Allen said. 'I bored her. She was a lively thing. I knew from the start that it wouldn't last.'

That gave Joe a jolt. Sometimes Sal said *he* was boring, staid, old before his time. It always came across as a joke, but there was a moment of fear. Might she be attracted by someone more exciting, more reckless?

Gentle, misty rain ran down the dirty windows, which wouldn't have let in much light, even on a sunny day. Everything in the place was covered with a sticky, brown varnish, the colour of toffee: the wood panels on the walls, the bar, the settles where the old men sat sharing a desultory conversation.

'Aye,' Allen said. 'I remember that year. Two deaths within months of each other and the same people involved. It would stick in your mind.' He looked up. 'What's your interest then?' For the first time showing a spark of curiosity

'Two more deaths with the same people involved.' Joe paused. 'But this time murder.'

'That man from the telly on Holy Island? And the woman who'd been some sort of model and actress in the seventies and eighties?'

Joe nodded.

'They'd be the sort who'd end up fighting their way out of the jungle on a reality show. I can't abide folk who think they're celebrities.' There was a long silence. 'But I suppose we can't go round killing them.' Another pause. 'More's the pity.' For the first time, he gave a little smile.

'It's the same group of people,' Joe said. 'The same witnesses and suspects, as the deaths you were looking into of the bairn and the young student. My boss thinks it's a weird coincidence.'

'I suppose it is.'

'Tell me what you remember,' Joe said. 'While you're sorting things out in your head, I'll get you another pint.'

'Eh, bonny lad, I've not finished this one yet.'

'All the same, I won't want to interrupt once you get started.'

Allen nodded to show that made sense, and watched Joe go up to the bar.

'The baby dying,' Allen said, once Joe had settled down again, his orange juice untouched on the table in front of him, 'that was just sad. But we had to investigate. A young couple, living as they did, in a caravan up at Rede's Tower. Suspicion was that the poor little lass might have been shaken to death by one of the parents. They were all cramped into such a small space and they might have been desperate. I've never had a bairn, but you could see how you might be driven to it, if it was the sort that cried all night. And you had a bit of a temper.'

'Did Rede have a temper?'

'We asked around but found no evidence of that. A nice enough chap, everyone said. Laid-back. Supportive of his woman. I'm not sure he ever wanted the child – a young man, it'd surely cramp his style and Daniel Rede was ambitious for his business even then – but he went along with it for her sake.' Allen paused. 'I don't think he grieved the loss in the way that the lass did, but that didn't mean he'd commit murder to get his freedom back.'

Joe nodded to show he understood what Allen was saying. He sipped his orange juice, thought that this liquid had never been anywhere near an orange, and he waited for the man to continue.

'I was pleased when the doctors said it was meningitis. Natural causes. Without that, the pair would have been under a cloud all their lives. Rumours that they were child-killers. People don't forget.'

'I'm sure there were still rumours,' Joe said. 'Sometimes folk prefer the drama to the fact.'

'That's true too.'

They sat for a moment, the silence broken by a sudden heavier shower of rain clattering against the window and the muted conversation of the men on the other side of the room.

'Then there they were,' Allen said, 'three months later, on Holy Island and another death. A car crashing off the causeway into the sea and a young woman drowned. I knew them at once. You wouldn't miss them. Annie Rede she still was then, and such a pretty thing even though she was so skinny. She'd lost weight. I suppose it was the grief.'

Joe could hear the sympathy in his voice and thought the man had had a bit of a crush on Annie Laidler. Perhaps that was why the facts of these cases were so strong in Allen's mind. 'That was put down as an accident,' Joe said. 'Is that how you saw it?'

Pete Allen took a while to answer. 'It was an odd one,' he said at last. 'It's not unusual for cars to get stranded on the causeway. Trippers misread the tide tables at each end of the road, or think they've got a car that's big enough and fast enough to outrun the tide. Each year people get caught out. But they don't die. There are towers along the road. You see that you're not going to make it and you leave the car and climb the tower until the water goes down again. You get a bit wet and the car is ruined, but you're okay. Even if it's a high spring tide and in bad weather.' He paused. 'And the water was well up by the time Isobel Hall left the island. Anyone with any sense would see that they wouldn't make it across. It was pure recklessness.'

'You pushed for a post-mortem?'

'Aye, the boss did. We just wanted to be sure, you know, because something jarred. No real suspicion of foul play, but we wanted an explanation.'

'Had she been drinking?'

'Well, that was our thought too. There was a bit of alcohol in her blood, but that could have been left over from the night before. They'd all been boozing then, apparently. Not enough to cloud her judgement though. Not according to the doc.' Allen paused. 'I did wonder about suicide.'

'You think she drove into the water deliberately? Not a nice way to go.'

'She wouldn't know that though, would she?' Allen looked up from his beer and stared at Joe with his sad, grey eyes. 'She was young. Hardly more than a bairn herself.'

'The same age as Annie Laidler. I suppose they were friends?' Joe didn't let on about Only Connect, the fact that they were there for its five-year anniversary.

'There was a group of them, all staying in the Pilgrims' House.' Allen looked up sharply. 'That was where the TV journalist was found dead.'

Joe nodded.

'Unlucky sort of place then,' Allen went on. 'A strange coincidence. Maybe that's the reason they're planning to close the retreat.'

'It's being closed for the season?'

'Not for the season. Forever. I saw it in the local paper. The nuns are selling it off. I suppose they'll turn it into some sort of private self-catering or guest house. It'd need someone with money to take it on. Places on Holy Island sell for a fortune.'

Joe wondered if that was significant, but couldn't see how it might be. He'd pass on the information to Vera and let her decide. 'What conclusion did you come to in the end about Isobel Hall's death?'

Allen shrugged. 'It went down as accidental, but it didn't sit quite right with me. To be honest, it's one of those ones that stick with you. The cases that you wake up wondering about.'

'You'd have checked the car?'

'Yes, nothing wrong with the vehicle. Nothing they could find, at least, after hours in the water, being battered by the current.' He looked at Joe over his beer. 'You're thinking one of them might have tampered with it?'

'It must have occurred to you too.'

'Something was going on there. They came across as bright young things with their lives ahead of them. But they were a weird bunch. Arrogant. Secretive. I couldn't take to them. Except Annie Laidler. She was different.'

Oh yes, Joe thought. You definitely took to her.

'You say they did a post-mortem on the lass in the car,' Joe said. 'My boss wondered if she might have been pregnant.'

'Is that what she told her boyfriend? Wanting to hang on to him?'

Joe shook his head. 'We don't know anything for certain. Just a line of inquiry.' Then he had a thought. 'Did she have a boyfriend? One of the group staying at the Pilgrims' House? Rick Kelsall playing away while his woman was at work in London?'

'It seems she was the kind to play those sorts of games.' Allen drained the last of the beer from his second pint. 'But they all closed ranks and if she was having a fling, nobody admitted it. And no, she wasn't pregnant. I'd have remembered that. Two babies, it'd have stuck in my mind. Another coincidence. Besides, like I said, this case is not one I've ever forgotten.'

Outside on the pavement, after the gloom of the pub, it was a shock to see how light it was, to realize that it was still early afternoon. Joe had parked by the scruffy little harbour and sat there to phone Vera.

'So, Isobel wasn't pregnant,' she said. 'Another fine theory out of the water. I've heard back from Hol. Katherine Willmore's alibi for Monday checks out. Did you manage to get hold of Daniel Rede?'

'Aye.' Joe replayed the conversation. 'He had no concrete alibi between seeing Annie Laidler late morning and meeting a farmer in Amble early evening. It would have been tight but he could have killed her. We could look at CCTV in Whitley to rule him out.'

'I'll get Charlie onto it.' Vera sounded preoccupied. 'Get back here, Joe. This case is doing my head in. All these respectable elderly people making out that they're innocent. I need a younger mind to make some sense of it.'

Chapter Forty-One

IN HER OFFICE, VERA WAS WAITING impatiently for Joe to return. Restless and needing something to focus on, she looked again at the synopsis Kelsall's agent had sent through. She'd skimmed it when Holly had first shared it, and had thought it was too vague to be important. Having read Kelsall's notes now she thought it might be more relevant.

The novel was titled 'Stranded'. She'd expected something with a little more detail, but the piece was scarcely more than a few lines long. It read more like a blurb on the back of a jacket, something to tease the readers and hook them in. Perhaps Kelsall's name and notoriety had been enough to sell the project to a publisher. Perhaps it was a giant scam to get a huge advance and he'd never have got round to completing it.

The man could write though, she'd give him that. The synopsis certainly made her want to find out more. And not just because she thought the finished work might contain a clue to the double murder.

A group of twenty-somethings find themselves stranded on Holy Island, in North Northumberland. The place carries with it an atmosphere of spirituality, almost of the supernatural. After all, this is where Christianity first arrived in England, and the centuries of worship and prayer seem trapped in the landscape itself. There's been a tension between the friends throughout the weekend. They've obviously known each other for years and are very close, but something has happened to fracture the friendships. As the story progresses, the reader discovers that secrets of the past have come back to haunt them. An autumn fog blurs the boundary between the land and the sea, and in this strange marginal world there's a tragedy. A young woman dies. It seems, at first, that this was an accident, but an accident would surely be too convenient . . .

The theme of the novel is hypocrisy, and it explores the lengths some people will take to hide the sins of the past.

The last sentence struck a chord. Surely this was the theme of the investigation too. These respectable older people – a priest and a couple of teachers – might all have their own reasons for hiding the sins of the past. The others on the periphery of the case were pillars of the community too: the Police and Crime Commissioner, a prominent businessman and an elderly churchgoer famous for her good works. Even Annie had a certain position within the town. The least respect-able members of the group – Rick Kelsall and Charlotte Thomas – were already dead.

Her phone rang. It was Holly with news that Judith Sinclair had been seen wandering round the island, on the evening of Kelsall's death. Through her open door, Vera saw that Charlie was back in the office. She stood up and shouted him in.

'I need all you can get on Judith Sinclair. Seems there's a chance she was close to the Pilgrims' House after all on the night Kelsall died. Despite her denying any contact. And she was part of the group from the beginning. She started the whole thing off.'

Charlie nodded. Vera knew he was the best person in the team to get what they needed. He knew this town. Elderly women and young tearaways both confided in him. He could listen. There was something unthreatening and sympathetic about him. He was a universal favourite uncle.

He'd slid out of her office before she realized he was gone.

Still restless, she got her coat and car keys. Judith Sinclair had been pissing her about with her moral high-handedness and refusal to speak. Now it was time for her to talk. She drove out to the tidy street where Judith had lived since she'd first been married. This time it was a neighbour in his garden, pruning back shrubs before the winter. He straightened when he heard the latch on Judith's gate.

'You won't find Mrs Sinclair in,' he said. He had a pleasant voice. Vera wondered briefly if he and Judith had been more than friends, then saw a wife peering through immaculately white nets. *How bored she must be!* Vera thought. *If she's got nothing better to do than vicarious gardening.*

'Any idea how long she'll be?' Because he would know. Nothing would be hidden in this suburban paradise. Except, perhaps, murder.

'There's a friend staying in her cottage on Holy Island. She's gone to see him. She must have left canny early. Her car was gone when I woke up.'

Vera swore in her head, but smiled at the neighbour. This wasn't his fault. 'Of course. Thanks.'

When she got back to the station, Joe had returned and was at his desk.

'Any news from Hol?'

He shook his head.

'Judith Sinclair is there, apparently. On Holy Island. She's staying the night with Philip Robson in Gull Cottage.'

Joe seemed not to think this important. 'Yeah, she told us that she was going to see them at some point during their stay.'

'She was out on the island the night Kelsall was murdered.'

'You can't really think she's our killer?' Joe looked at Vera as if she was crazy.

'I think she knows more than she's letting on.' Vera hit the buttons on her phone. 'No response from Holly.' Reception on the island was notoriously patchy, but Vera felt irrationally resentful at the lack of an answer. She left a message. 'Holly, just to let you know Judith Sinclair's up on the island. Call me back as soon as you get this!'

It was still only late afternoon, but the whole police station was dark. No sun and no light. Vera padded through the main office, unable to settle. Joe was trying to feed back his interviews with Daniel Rede and Pete Allen but she was finding it almost impossible to focus.

'Who has most to gain from these people's deaths?' The words came out as a cry, stopping Joe in mid-flow.

'Annie Laidler if we're talking about money,' Joe said. He was always down to earth. Always prosaic. Vera knew he kept her grounded. 'Eliza Bond if we're talking reputation, and by extension Katherine and Daniel who might want to protect her. We've only got their word that Rick Kelsall was prepared to be gracious about the false accusations she'd made against him. He might have been planning something dramatic as an act of revenge on the lass for losing him his job. Katherine would hate that, wouldn't she? Her daughter being one of those women she claims don't exist. The women who cry rape.'

'I don't think this is about money.' Again, Vera found it impossible to keep still. She was pacing once more, knowing it was irritating Joe as well as ratchetting up the tension in the room, but not being able to help herself. She remembered the paragraph Kelsall had put together to sell his book to a publisher. 'This is about hiding the sins of the past.' She punched Holly's number into her phone. Again, it rang through to voicemail.

'She's probably driving back.'

'She'd answer though, wouldn't she?' Vera snapped. 'She's got hands free. What's she playing at?'

Charlie came in, so quietly and unobtrusively, that for a moment neither of them registered his presence.

'What have you got for me, Charlie?' Vera came finally to rest in front of his desk.

'I've been chatting to one of Judith's former colleagues. He started teaching in the Grammar at the same time as her. Apparently, she was quite wild in her early days. Not above fraternizing with the students. Drinking. Going to their parties.' A pause. 'There was talk of relationships.'

'You mean sex, Charlie? Is that what you're saying?'

'There were rumours.'

'She'd be scared, wouldn't she, if that came out in Kelsall's book? A respectable woman of God with a history of debauching young lads.'

'More likely the other way round,' Charlie muttered. 'From what I could gather.'

Vera ignored the comment. 'Was Kelsall one of her conquests?'

'According to the chap I spoke to. But again, he stressed they were staffroom rumours. Apparently, one of the senior teachers had a word with her. Told her to be more careful.'

Which was why, Vera thought, Judith didn't take up the young people's invitation to join them at the first reunion.

'Then she got religion,' Charlie said, 'and she went the other way. Strait-laced and upright. Spiritual.'

'We're going to the island!' She thought she'd been bubbling up to this all day, like a pan simmering on the hob, and finally coming to the boil. Now the action seemed inevitable. 'I don't like the fact that Holly's not communicating with us, we know that at least two of our suspects are there, with others not far away. That's where it started and that's where it'll end.' She was aware that the dramatic voice, the impulsive decision, didn't suit her. Her colleagues were staring as if they hardly recognized her.

'H'away then,' she said, changing tone. 'Get your coats. Charlie, take your own car. Joe, you're with me.' A pause. 'You'd better tell Sal it's likely to be an all-nighter. If we get a move on, we'll just get there before the tide, but there's no way we'll get back.'

Chapter Forty-Two

HOLLY HAD PACKED HER BAG AND put it in her car, ready to head off back to the mainland when the text came through. A number she didn't recognize. She'd given her contact details to Linz, in fact to everyone she'd met on the island since her arrival, so that didn't provide any information about who might be ringing.

Understand you're looking for the birder who was in the Seahorse on Friday night. Might be able to help. Just heading out to do a migration census in the area around the lough. Could see you there in half an hour? Phone reception impossible there so will have to meet in person.

There was nothing to identify the sender. Was the assumption that Holly had been told to expect the communication? Perhaps Linz had put the word out on the island, had asked anyone who might be able to help to get in touch with Holly direct. The text didn't give a clue as to gender, but Holly assumed it was a man. She tried to phone the number, but it didn't even go to voicemail, just cut off. Crappy reception, she supposed. She checked the time. The lough was just beyond the Pilgrims' House, so she should be able to drive most of the way and park there. There was still more than an hour before she'd need to leave for the mainland. She went back into the Seahorse and paid her bill. Di was there, behind the desk in reception.

'All done then?' Curiosity oozing out of every pore.

'For now.'

Holly got into her car and drove not towards the causeway, but down the main street of the village and into the centre of the island. The fog had lifted during the middle of the day, but was thicker again now. She almost missed the narrow turning towards the Pilgrims' House. When she pulled up outside, there was another vehicle parked there. She wondered if this belonged to the birdwatcher who was offering information. She sat in her car for a moment and tried to phone Vera to let her know what was happening, but she couldn't get through.

Outside the air was damp and chill. She couldn't imagine how anyone would be able to see a bird in these conditions. This felt like a pointless game of hide and seek and she had the same tension as she'd felt when she'd been a child, searching for hidden classmates, anxious that they might suddenly jump out to frighten her.

She climbed a stile and walked east towards the lough. She could hear the calls of wading birds, and then heard voices. She didn't see the group until she almost stumbled on them. Four people of indeterminate gender, dressed in wax jackets and wellingtons, crouched over a ditch. A fine net had been placed across it, only visible because of the drops of moisture caught on the mesh. They seemed to be extricating a bird from it. She waited, watching, before speaking. It seemed a delicate

THE RISING TIDE

operation, and the bird was so frail that she was anxious an interruption might damage it.

'I'm DC Clarke. Did one of you ask to speak to me?'

They looked blank.

'The message said you were doing a migration census and asked me to meet you here.'

'This isn't a census.' The youngest of the group straightened and gave a joyous laugh. 'This is a bloody rarity. A paddyfield warbler. A new bird for me. A lifer.'

'What are you going to do with it?' She was distracted momentarily by his enthusiasm.

'We're going to ring it, take a few photos to convince the world that it is what we claim it to be, and then we'll release it.'

'Were any of you in the Seahorse on Friday night?'

'No, when we're on the island we use the Anchor.' An older man who could have been the young speaker's father. 'But we weren't here on Friday. It gets busy at weekends and it was clear. You need a bit of cloud and murk for a good fall of migrants.'

Holly thought this was ridiculous. Could the presence of these men be a coincidence, with the person she was supposed to meet waiting for her somewhere closer to the lough? She looked at her phone. Still no reception. But she did see the time. If she didn't get to the mainland soon, she'd miss the tide and be stuck here for another night. She couldn't bear the thought of returning to the Seahorse, to the noisy bar and the depressing room. She turned and followed the path back to the stile and the road.

All the way back to the lane she had the same sense that she was in the middle of an elaborate game of hide and seek.

ANN CLEEVES

This time though, she thought, she was the hider. Somewhere in the gloom, the seeker was following. She caught the sound of long grass moving and once, she believed she heard the squelch of a boot in wet mud. But when she stopped to listen, there was nothing. Her imagination and the fog playing tricks with her. The noises could be anything: cattle in an adjoining field, the birdwatchers bringing their trophy bird to be ringed. The text message could have been a hoax, sent by a local who enjoyed taunting the police. Or from a genuine member of the public who was still waiting for her in the marsh. Well, she thought, let them wait. As soon as she got back to Kimmerston, she'd trace the number and speak to them.

When she was on the lane and she could see the grey silhouette of the Pilgrims' House, her heart rate slowed. She pictured herself at home in her clean, white flat, running a bath, pouring herself a glass of wine. There'd be the evening briefing first, but she had plenty to report back. She didn't imagine that Joe would have discovered as much.

She'd reached the car, when she saw there was a light in the chapel. The flicker of candlelight. It wasn't dusk, just the gloom of late afternoon, but perhaps it was Robson, observing the ritual of peace and prayer. She was about to drive off, but curiosity got the better of her. Curiosity and the possibility of another snippet of information to pass on to Vera. Again, she wondered why Vera's approval was so important to her, why she felt this need to please.

Holly pushed open the chapel door. Inside, everything was quiet. Nobody was sitting on the pews in silent meditation. It occurred to her that she should blow out the candles, because they might be a fire risk. Then there was a footstep behind her. She heard that, and then there was nothing.

322

Chapter Forty-Three

THEY JUST CROSSED THE CAUSEWAY BEFORE the tide came in. Everything was grey and shadowy in the sea fret, so it felt like a drive into the unknown. The unfamiliar. Nothing looked quite the same. Charlie had gone ahead of them in his faster car. Vera had sent him first, knowing that the more robust Land Rover would fare better than his old vehicle. All the same, seawater tugged at their wheels as they drove along the road towards the island.

They'd still heard nothing from Holly and Vera was scared for her. She felt as if she was drowning, that she couldn't breathe, couldn't think. It was anxiety filling her mind, but also, mostly, it was guilt. For having sent Holly to the island alone; for all the barbed comments and criticisms during the course of the young woman's career. For the sins of omission, the times when Holly had done brilliant work and Vera had refused to recognize it.

She'd told Charlie to go to the Seahorse, to book their rooms and find out when Holly had left. It was possible that she'd still be there; she might even be interviewing a suspect in the lounge, having left them a message at the police station. But Vera didn't believe that. Holly was punctilious and she'd have made every effort to be back for the briefing. Or at least to have contacted Vera and Joe direct.

They parked outside Gull Cottage. Vera recognized Judith Sinclair's car, a small and sensible hatchback, pulled tight into the pavement. She was out of the Land Rover and banging on the door before Joe could join her. Philip Robson opened it.

'Inspector, come in.'

The fire was lit and the warmth of the room hit her and made her feel slightly giddy. Joe followed her into the room. Judith Sinclair sat by the fire, shocked it seemed by the violence of the knocking. She was drinking tea. Robson's hair looked slightly damp, and he was using the wide wooden windowsill as a seat. He had the air of someone who has just come in from the cold, red-faced. The news was on the radio. Something gloomy to match the weather.

'Have you seen DC Clarke? Holly.'

'I saw her yesterday.' Philip reached out and switched off the radio. 'I answered all her questions then.'

'And *you* spoke to me yesterday, Inspector.' Judith Sinclair's voice was precise. Disapproving. 'I have nothing to add.'

'Well, I have something to add to you.' A pause. 'Are you willing to talk in front of your friend? Or would you prefer to speak somewhere a little more private?'

There was a hesitation. Judith would have liked to say that she didn't have anything to hide, but perhaps she wasn't sure that was true. Philip saved her from further awkwardness. He stood up and gathered the empty cups. 'You stay in here. I should be making a start on supper anyway.'

Vera took a seat, leaving the windowsill to Joe. 'You haven't seen my colleague?'

'I haven't. I arrived early this morning and I've been here ever since.'

'And your friend?'

'Philip was out a while ago. He said he needed a walk. Fresh air. He's not long come back.'

'We've been talking to some of your former colleagues,' Vera said. 'Apparently you were quite wild when you started teaching. You went to students' parties, drinking. There were rumours of relationships.'

'I was young, Inspector. And things were very different in those days. It wasn't unknown for teachers to have relationships with their students. Not quite such a crime. Though most of the wayward teachers were male. Of course.' A pause. 'I should have explained when you came to my house this morning.'

'Why the sudden change in attitude?' Vera was always suspicious when a witness suddenly became reasonable.

'Philip reminded me that these things seldom stay hidden, and he seemed to think you would be discreet.'

'Only if what you have to say has nothing to do with murder.'

'I went to the Pilgrims' House on Friday night.' Judith paused. 'As I told you yesterday I was here to change the sheets and clean before Philip moved in on Sunday. I have a standing invitation to the reunions and I thought it would be fun to turn up and surprise everyone.'

'Did you drive?' Nobody had heard a car.

'No. I decided to walk. It was a beautiful evening, cold but very clear. There was a moon. I didn't even need a torch.'

'You didn't go in?'

'No, when I got there, I felt a little nervous and hesitated a while before I opened the door. I was standing just outside the common room window and I could hear Rick Kelsall talking. Boasting. Recounting his exploits.' There was another hesitation. 'He was never a brilliant actor, but he always had a voice which would carry. "I once slept with Miss Marshall." Those were the words I heard. And the laughter. And the others egging him on to tell the rest of the story. I didn't know what to do. It was a ridiculous situation. There I was, eavesdropping, carrying a couple of bottles of prosecco to share with the group, but I couldn't go and join them.'

'Had you slept with him?'

There was a little nod. 'Once. At a student party. I'm sure you can understand how I felt. My past coming back to haunt me in such a cruel way.'

Vera thought she could. 'Embarrassing. What did you do then?'

'I walked back here.'

'You didn't wait until they'd all gone to bed, go into his room and confront Rick Kelsall?'

'No! That would have been shameful. How could I face him after those things he'd said?'

'Perhaps you waited until he was asleep. Easy enough then to hold a cushion over his face until he stopped breathing. The only way to ensure your reputation. To be certain he didn't write that scene into his book. The general reader wouldn't recognize you, but your former students and colleagues would.'

'No!' Her face was white, drained of all colour. 'I swear I didn't kill him. I couldn't commit murder.'

'But you did phone him? We have a record of the call.'

'Yes, I phoned him. I had to know if he planned to use the incident in his novel. That was what he was talking about in the common room. How he was writing a thriller, which would expose everyone's secrets.' She paused. 'He answered the phone, but he didn't even seem to know who I was and what I was talking about. He was drunk, barely conscious.'

'Where does Charlotte Thomas come into the tale?'

'I'm sorry?'

'She was seen coming into your cottage earlier that day. Late afternoon, and then you were together in the Seahorse in the evening. You've already admitted that.' Vera paused. She wanted to shake the woman. To force the information from her. 'You've told me this much. I need the rest.'

'Charlotte had met Rick on Thursday night. I'd done yoga classes with her, so we were acquaintances, and she called me at home on Friday morning. She'd been upset by something Rick had told her, she said. She needed my advice. Could she come and see me? I was just about to set out for Holy Island and the cottage. I told her if the matter was that important, she could come and meet me here.'

'Was it that urgent?' Vera was growing increasingly impatient. There was still no news of Holly and this was wasting time.

'It was Rick's book again.' In the kitchen there was the sound of pans, of a table being laid. 'I assume that you've researched Charlotte's background. I hadn't realized that her family had such an unsavoury past.'

'A criminal past,' Vera said.

'That would feature in Rick Kelsall's novel too, apparently. Charlotte was distraught. She'd been a wealthy young woman. Her children hadn't realized how much of her wealth had come from the proceeds of crime. She didn't want them to know. She wondered if there was a way we could get together – all of us who'd been in the Pilgrims' House for Only Connect

– and persuade him to let the past go. To write real fiction, not a kind of sensationalized reality. All of us had secrets of a kind. Kelsall seemed to be using them to mock us all. Making mischief.'

Vera remembered the conversation with the Thomas family in Fenham. Charlotte had clearly been trying to keep her distance for decades. The last thing she'd want, as she was trying to establish her shiny new business, would be for their past to be rehashed. 'What reason would Kelsall have for mischief making?'

Judith didn't answer immediately. 'I think he was bored, Inspector. As a teenager, he couldn't bear to be bored. Recently, he'd been attracting less attention. Perhaps he wanted to feel powerful again, alive, even if that meant being the object of people's fear and hostility.'

'An odd way to go about feeling alive.' But, Vera thought, perhaps that was why Hector had been so irascible, had drunk so much when he got older. In his belligerent moods and bad temper, at least he got a reaction. It was a kind of living. 'What advice did you give to Charlotte?'

'I agreed that the two of us, at least, could make a joint approach to Rick. Charlotte gave me his mobile number, in case I wanted to talk to him, and we planned to meet up later this week to plan tactics. But then, of course, he died.'

He was killed, which is rather different. Someone taking matters into their own hands perhaps. Someone not prepared to wait.

'Who was the man in the pub with you?'

'Really, it was nobody we knew. As I told you, it was just a random birdwatcher. The place was busy and we shared our table with him. There was no more to it than that.'

This time Vera felt inclined to believe her.

Chapter Forty-Four

THEY FOUND CHARLIE IN THE SEAHORSE, talking to the landlady and a barmaid with a white face and black eyes. The bar was open but quiet. They were sitting in the lounge around the table where Vera had eaten breakfast with Holly and Joe only three days before.

'Your colleague definitely checked out,' Di said. 'I took the payment myself. And her car's not there.'

'She was here for lunch.' That was the Goth. 'She was asking about a birdwatcher, a guy who was in the bar on Friday night, with Charlotte Thomas and an older woman. I'd thought the three of them were part of the same group, and she was asking if I could have been wrong. He might just have been sharing their table.' She looked up at them. Vera could tell that she wanted to help. 'I'm sorry. I didn't see him. Not properly. Only his back.'

'But you do table service,' Joe said. He was being very stiff, very formal, trying to hide his fears and control his panic. Vera had seen him act that way before when he was scared of losing it. He and Holly had grown closer during the case. This wasn't just about a colleague in danger. It was personal. 'You must have seen him while you were taking the order.'

Linz looked between the detectives and her boss. 'But it's only table service for food and that group weren't eating.' A pause. She seemed almost close to tears. 'I wish I could help, but honestly, I can't remember anything about him.'

'That's okay, pet. Not your fault at all.' Vera could see how everyone had assumed that the strange man sitting with Judith and Charlotte had been known to them. It seemed even more likely now that Judith had been telling the truth.

'I told Holly I'd put the word out. Ask if any of the regulars or the locals knew who he might be.' The barmaid's voice was eager now. 'And I did!'

'Did any of them get back to you?'

'No, but then they wouldn't. I gave them Holly's mobile number and told them to contact her direct.'

'Could you ask again?' Vera said. 'See if anyone has been in contact with her. She's missing and we're starting to get anxious.'

'Sure.' Linz was on her phone already. 'Sure.'

'Holly was in the Old Hall this morning.' Di, the landlady, leaned across the table. 'I saw her go in at around coffee time.'

Vera nodded. She knew about that visit. Holly had been there to ask about Katherine Willmore's alibi and it had checked out. If the DC had picked up anything else that was useful there, surely she'd have passed on that information to Vera too. But perhaps something had come to Holly later. A little niggle. An itch. It happened to Vera sometimes during the course of an investigation. And perhaps Holly had gone back to scratch. It was what *she* would have done and she'd trained all her staff well.

'I'll just wander along to the hotel,' she said, 'just in case something occurred to her and she went back.' Not believing that it would help, but needing to move again. Not bearing just to sit here, doing nothing. 'Joe, you wait here in case she comes back or we get more information. Charlie, you drive around the island. Everywhere. Farm tracks and lanes, private drives. We're looking for Holly's car.' She hesitated, felt in her pocket and held out her keys. 'Take the Land Rover. That'll get you down some of the rougher paths.'

Charlie stared at her, astonished by the honour. Nobody was allowed to drive the boss's vehicle. But he said nothing and he took the keys.

Out in the road, the light had seeped away to nothing. The mist held in the orange glow of the street lamps. Vera had been to the Old Hall once before. She'd been invited to dinner by her smart relative, Harriet, as a thank you for finding a killer. She hadn't really wanted to go, but had accepted the invitation, only because she'd known that Harriet had been hoping she'd refuse. Let the old woman pay for a decent meal and endure her company for one evening! Harriet had booked to stay the night there. Vera had driven home. One way of making sure she wouldn't drink too much. She hadn't wanted Harriet thinking she was like Hector, and besides, drink made her argumentative.

She'd decided that there was no point in arguing with an old woman who was seeing her world change and become almost unrecognizable. In the end, it had been a pleasant enough occasion. Harriet was used to being courteous to her tenants, and had treated Vera as if she were a farm worker, competent and necessary but not socially her equal. Vera had held her tongue and, when she got home, she'd poured herself a large whisky. She'd drunk a grateful toast to Hector for escaping his family and for making his own way in the world. It was one of the few times she'd ever felt grateful to him.

The Old Hall was busier than she'd been expecting. The lobby opened into the bar, where couples were taking pre-dinner drinks. Everybody was dressed up, very smart in a glitzy, celebratory way, and she was out of place, in her grubby jacket, her mud-spattered boots. She had, in the past, been mistaken for a bag lady. And more recently at Rede's Tower as a cleaner. A young man in a suit approached her, all smiles. Perhaps he thought she was a rich, eccentric, potential guest.

'Can I help you, madam?'

Discreetly, she showed him her warrant card. People were already staring, and she didn't need any more of an audience.

'Please, come into the office.'

He led her away from public view.

'My colleague was here this morning.'

'Ah yes, I was on duty and I spoke to her myself. She asked about one of our regulars.'

'Katherine Willmore?'

'Yes, I was able to tell her that Ms Willmore was here. I found a copy of her credit card receipt.' He smiled. Someone else, Vera thought, needing to be praised just for doing his job.

'You haven't seen DC Clarke since then?'

'No, and I've been at the front desk for most of the day.' The smile crawled over his face again. 'She asked about another potential guest. A single man. A birdwatcher. I'm afraid I wasn't able to help with that inquiry.'

'We're a little anxious about my officer,' Vera said. 'We've lost contact with her. Probably nothing. Signal problems or a mislaid phone. There's nothing else you can tell me?'

She sensed a moment of hesitation, but when she looked at his face, the smile was back in place.

'I'm sorry, Inspector, I wish I could help. It's a horrible evening for anyone to get lost.'

She nodded and went outside. In the car park, she took out her torch, and checked all the vehicles, but Holly's car wasn't there and she didn't recognize any of the other registration plates as belonging to witnesses in the case. She made her way back to the Seahorse. But now, she had her own itch, her own need to explore it, to scratch.

In the Seahorse, the lounge was filling up and Linz, Joe and Di had moved to the landlady's private sitting room on the first floor. It looked out over a courtyard at the back, where empty bottles and kegs were stacked. Inside, heavy red velvet curtains had been drawn against the gloom. A Calor gas heater had just been lit. It gave off little heat as yet, but a considerable smell of fumes. The room had been furnished with cast-off furniture from the bar and one low sofa, with a red velvet throw tucked over it. The effect was that of a junk shop crossed with a traditional curry house and Victorian brothel. Vera found it very comforting.

When Vera was shown in by another member of staff, Linz was talking on the phone. She seemed excited and was talking very fast. Then she listened. 'When was that? Did you see where she went?' She switched off her phone and faced the room. 'That was Tom Cadwallender, one of the local ringers. Nobody he knows had contacted your mate, but they did see her earlier. There was a rarity in a ditch by the lough and they were trying to catch it.'

Vera nodded. 'In a small mist net?'

'Yeah!' Linz eyed the inspector with increased respect. 'She seemed to think one of them had asked her to meet him. She'd had a text apparently saying he'd be there, but it hadn't come from one of them.'

'No name, I suppose?'

Linz shook her head.

Of course not. It would be a trap. Like the mist net catching the bird.

'Did they see anyone else?'

'Nah,' Linz said. 'One of them thought they heard someone, banging around in the fog, but it could have been anything.'

'The nearest place to park for the lough is the Pilgrims' House.'

'Charlie phoned earlier, boss.' Joe, still at his most formal, still anxious. 'He checked for Holly's car there. No sign of it.'

'We'll check ourselves, shall we? Let's walk, so we don't miss anything. Holly's car might not be there, but we might find Holly.'

Chapter Forty-Five

Joe hated this. Being out in the dark and no street lights at all once they got beyond the boundary of the village. Worrying about Holly, because Holly didn't get herself into dangerous situations. She was sensible and followed the rules, not like the boss. And although she was younger and fitter than the boss, he sensed that she wasn't so resilient, so cunning or so brave.

They walked in silence. Vera seemed to be thinking. He hoped she'd pull some solution out of the bag at the last minute, like some overweight female magician. She often did. But Joe thought this scenario was unlikely to be so easily resolved. It didn't feel like any sort of magical illusion, and anyway, occasionally tricks went wrong; surely people could drown in tanks of water or get sawn in half or stabbed when knives were thrown.

They walked at the same pace, one each side of the road. There were no other cars out tonight. It was late now, and sensible people were eating their supper or watching television. The tide must be nearing its height because in the distance he could hear the scrape and suck of shingle on the shore. Every so often, there came the howl of the foghorn. Each time, the sound shocked him.

They shone their torches into the side of the road and into the rough grazing beyond the hedges and the stone walls. Nothing but motionless sheep, blurred by the mist, staring back with yellow eyes, dazed by torchlight. Once, he was startled by a wispy figure, standing quite still in a field. It was a scarecrow, wearing a coat like Vera's.

When they got to the Pilgrims' House, there were no cars parked outside. There was still a strip of blue and white tape strung across the width of the building, telling everyone to keep out. Vera was crouching, looking at tyre marks.

'More than one car has been parked here, but they could have belonged to those birding friends of Linz's.' She ducked under the tape and tried the front door. It was locked and she walked on until she was standing next to the window, right at the end of the house. 'Get in there, Joe. It leads to Rick Kelsall's room. If the killer opened it, you should be able to manage it.' A pause. 'And if he was smothered by someone already in the house, this is your chance to show me how clever you are. Otherwise, just break it.'

At first, he thought he would have to break the glass, but the original sash window was only just held by the catch inside and when he jiggled it, he could lift the pane. He climbed into the room, where once Kelsall's body had been hanging from a beam. 'No lights,' Vera said. 'We don't want the world knowing we're here. Just open the door and let me in.'

The place was silent, and already felt damp, colder than it had been outside. He let Vera through the front door and they went round all the rooms, shining light into every corner.

'No sign that anyone's been here since the forensic team left,' she said. There was fingerprint dust everywhere, congealing in the damp air.

He went back into Kelsall's room, shut the window and slid the catch across again, and they went outside, pulling the door behind them to lock it.

He thought they'd head back then, to the warm red room above the bar in the Seahorse, but Vera was already on her way to the chapel. This door opened immediately. She stood on the threshold and shone her torch ahead of her.

'Someone's been in here. Mucky footwear prints on the floor.'

'That could have been from days ago. Philip Robson using it for his dusk meditation.'

'Aye, maybe.' She didn't sound convinced. 'There's that smell of candlewax too. Strong. I'd say the candles have been lit very recently.'

They walked in, avoiding the footprints. Vera walked up to the altar and shone a light on the candlesticks. 'Look, they've been left to burn right down. Philip strikes me as a careful man. He'd have blown them out.'

'So, you think Holly lit them for some reason?'

'Nah!' Vera was dismissive. 'This was another trap. They were lit to lure her in. She met the birders on the marsh and then she'd have come back to her car to drive off the island. But if there was candlelight in the chapel, she'd have gone inside, wouldn't she? She'd want to investigate.'

She walked back towards the door, shining her torch under each of the pews. Nothing. The place was as bare and austere as it had always been. Then she stopped so suddenly that Joe, following behind her, always a few steps in her wake, the Prince

Consort to her Queen, almost bumped into her. She crouched again, moving easily in spite of the weight she carried. He saw a stain on the flagstone.

'Blood,' she said.

'It could be anything.'

She didn't answer, but continued outside, leaving him to follow.

Back at the Seahorse, they saw the Land Rover parked outside and found Charlie in Di's sitting room, drinking tea. It was much warmer now, the heater giving a steady glow. Linz was serving in the bar downstairs, but the landlady was in the room too. There was the smell of bacon frying. 'I thought you might be hungry.'

'She was there.' For once, Vera didn't seem distracted by the thought of food, though Joe saw that she ate the sandwich in a couple of bites when it was presented. 'In the Pilgrims' House chapel. No sign of her car, Charlie?'

'Honestly, boss, I've been all over the island. Up to the castle and along the track as far north as I could go. I looked in the Herring House courtyard. The hotel car parks. That house on the Snook. Everywhere I can think of.'

'Still, it must be somewhere.' Anxiety was making Vera snappy and irrational. 'It can't have disappeared into thin air.'

Joe tried to focus on practicalities. The thought of Holly, being held somewhere against her will, made his brain turn to water and that would help nobody. He remembered their drive over the causeway, the water splashing against the Land Rover as Vera drove too fast ahead of the tide. 'They couldn't have taken her off the island? Just before we came on or just after?'

'After would be a stretch,' Vera said, 'especially in Holly's car. You'd get so far, but I doubt you'd make it all the way across.'

'Isn't that what happened to Isobel Hall?'

Vera looked at him, held his eyes. 'You're thinking history repeating itself?'

'I don't know. Just thinking aloud.'

'This fog,' she went on, 'nobody would see to call the alarm. If she was unconscious, you'd just leave her in her car, halfway across and wait for the tide to take her. The authorities might put that down as an accident. Any head wound could be a result of the car being swept away.'

By the time she'd finished speaking, they had their coats back on and they were halfway down the narrow stairs. Joe was praying to the God of his grandfather that he was wrong, that they'd find Holly's car hidden in the acres of dune near the causeway, that his imagination was running wild. All three of them crammed into the Land Rover's bench seat. They drove past the Lindisfarne Hotel, where a solitary smoker stood in the doorway, his back to the light, and the row of bungalows. It seemed to Joe that there was a bit of a breeze and that the mist was lifting a little. But that could be wishful thinking, or his imagination playing tricks again.

Vera drove too fast and almost slid where driven sand had made the road slippery. She only came to a stop when the water was lapping the wheels.

'It must be high water,' she said. 'Soon it'll be on its way out.' She was out of the vehicle, shining her torch into the darkness, but all it hit was a grey bank of fog. 'We need the lifeboat!' She was panicking now and Vera never panicked. 'Charlie, get on to them.'

'No evidence she's out there, boss.'

'And no evidence that she's not. Do it!'

Charlie was on his phone, muttering a message they couldn't hear because he was still in the Land Rover. He raised his voice. 'The nearest lifeboat is Seahouses. They're shouting them now.'

'Surely some bugger on this island has a boat!'

'I'm talking to the coastguard.'

Joe was standing beside his boss, peering into the gloom. Vera was right about the tide. The water was sliding away from them. Again, he thought he felt a breeze on his face. Looking up, there was one star, which disappeared almost as soon as he glimpsed it. The mist might be clearing above them, but over the water it seemed to be as thick as ever. The light of their torches bounced back at them. Vera got back into the Land Rover and put the headlights on full beam. And that was when he saw it. The fog thinned briefly and the image was sharp and clear, held for only seconds in the beam. A car, a hundred yards away from them and no longer on the causeway. It had rolled onto its side, so swamped with water that only a few inches of the door panel and the wing mirror showed. If Holly had been in there, she'd had no chance of survival.

He'd shouted to Vera, but she'd already seen it. 'Charlie, tell the coastguard that we need that boat now! And an ambulance on standby at the mainland end of the causeway.'

Joe marvelled at his boss's ability to act. He was frozen in grief. There was nothing he could do. Even if he swam to the car, it would be too late to save Holly, and besides, his boots seemed rooted to the concrete. He was overcome with a dreadful lethargy and his only thought was that Holly wouldn't have responded like this. She wouldn't have been as pathetic as him if *he* were in trouble. Holly would have known the right thing to do. He climbed in beside Vera, opened the window.

She switched on the Land Rover engine and backed up a little. Joe had no idea what plan she might have in mind. They were in no danger now the tide was on its way out. But there was a dip in the road and by reversing a few yards, the front of the vehicle was tilting up slightly. Again, Joe felt wind on his face. Definitely not his imagination this time and looking up there was a scattering of stars. With her headlights still on full beam, Vera turned the steering wheel a touch to the right. The beam moved above the water, until it hit what she was looking for. Still shadowy, a wooden tower, with a ladder to reach it. One of the refuges for trapped drivers and walkers. The closest tower to the island.

'There's something there.' Vera was talking very quietly to herself.

Joe could see it too, but thought it wasn't Holly. This was a pile of rubbish, seaweed and discarded plastic left by an abnormally high tide. The water was ebbing away from them quickly now.

'Any news on the lifeboat, Charlie?' The boss, calm. Icy.

'They've launched. On their way from Seahouses. But the locals are scrambling too.'

'That might be too long. I'll drive in as far as I can get with the Land Rover. Then it's down to you, Joe.'

'You think that's her?'

'I'm willing to take a chance on it.' A moment's pause. 'Are you?'

'Of course.' Though he wasn't sure. The fog had thickened again and the water would be freezing. He wasn't a strong swimmer and had nightmares about drowning. About cold saltwater covering his head and the tide pulling him under. But he knew that Holly would do the same for him, and really there was no question.

Vera drove the Land Rover forward at walking speed until the sea reached the top of the wheel arch. 'I'll have to stop now, or you'll not get the door open.'

'Where's the tower?' Panic was overwhelming him, just like the water of his dreams.

'Ahead and to your left. Look, I could go.'

'No!' That would be shameful. This was a fool's errand. But he couldn't let Vera show him up. He'd be ridiculed for the rest of his career. He thought Charlie had had more sense than to volunteer, but the man turned to him, apologetic.

'I'm sorry. I can't swim.' The words a cry. He would rather be out in the water, than sitting here, helpless.

Joe put a hand on Charlie's arm, then he pushed the door open and slid out. He stumbled immediately on the uneven surface beneath his feet, and tripped forwards so the water reached his chest. The cold seeped through his clothes and took his breath away. He pushed against the weight of it, staying on the causeway, following the beam of the headlight. It shone a path through the mist.

He only saw the refuge when Vera shifted the car slightly so the light pointed to the left and he could see the base of the tower again. Steps leading up, like the structure in the Rede's Tower adventure playground. It looked close enough to touch, but when he moved towards it, suddenly, he was out of his depth, weighed down by his jacket and boots. He'd stepped off the causeway without realizing. The water covered his face and he panicked. This would be the end then. No glory, no saving of a colleague, but another officer's life wasted.

Then his thoughts cleared like the fog and he lunged forward and grabbed on to one of the underwater rungs of the ladder, and pulled himself clear of the tide. He stood there for a moment, spluttering, gripping the slippery wood, his life depending on holding tight. Then he began to climb, every step an effort because of the weight of his waterlogged clothing.

As he reached the platform, he was above the level of the headlights' beam, but the mist was definitely clearing and the darkness wasn't quite so dense. He felt for the shape they'd seen from the shore. Wet cloth. Nothing moving. He heaved himself onto the platform and took his torch from his jacket pocket. It was still working. The first thing he saw was Holly's face. White. No sign of life. He wrapped himself around her. He was cold, but not as cold as she was and if she was close to death, he didn't want her dying alone, with no human contact.

Then suddenly he heard the call of wading birds, frightened from their roost by the sound of an engine and more lights, and the fat inflatable rib circling the tower and a man in a yellow oilskin climbing the ladder as easily as if it were an obstacle in a kids' playground. His own voice demanding to know if his friend was alive.

Chapter Forty-Six

VERA WATCHED THE SCENE FROM THE vehicle, wishing she was there, sitting with Holly at the top of the tower, holding her, trying to breathe some warmth and some life back into her body. Holly had saved Vera's life once. Vera wondered briefly if that was why she was feeling so wretched. Because, above anything she hated a sense of obligation, of a kindness done that might have to be repaid. Or perhaps, it was a kind of arrogance. If anyone could keep Holly alive, it was Joe, but she'd never really trusted her team to do the important things without her. It was about time she learned that lesson and gave her team some freedom to act alone.

The mist was shifting now, patchy, so her view of the tower was dream-like, unreliable. There was no communication with Joe. She didn't know what he'd found there. Perhaps she'd imagined the shape as a body, and she'd set off this whole drama with no cause. Then the coastguard's inflatable arrived, scaring the roosting birds with its noise and capturing the tower with flashlights, so the platform looked like a stage, a scene in a bit of performance art. Joanna had taken her once to a place in Newcastle, an avant-garde theatre, hoping to broaden her mind, but Vera had just been confused. Her thoughts now were swirling like the mist, unfocused. Charlie was still beside her, muttering under his breath, his own kind of prayer or incantation. It could have been an odd musical accompaniment to the unfolding performance. Then the boat was off again, heading to the mainland, and the platform was empty.

By now, the tide was ebbing fast. It was impossible to judge the depth of the water on the causeway in the dark, but Vera was willing to take a chance. Anything was better than this ignorance. She drove on slowly, heading for the opposite shore and the flashing lights of the waiting ambulance. Then the water level dropped and she could move more quickly. The crew in their thigh waders had already lifted Holly ashore and she was in the ambulance. The door was open and a paramedic was leaning over her. Joe was standing on dry land, wrapped in a foil blanket, shivering. Vera jumped from the Land Rover. With surprise she noticed that there were no creaking joints, no pain in her knees. She supposed that adrenaline would do that to you. Fear would take you away from the mundane trials of the present.

'Well?' The question directed to Joe and to the boat crew. 'Is she alive?'

'Just,' he said.

'You should come too, mate!' The paramedic. 'Get checked over.'

'No.' He looked at Vera. 'I've got work to do.'

'Where are you taking her?' Vera was at her most imperious.

'The emergency and trauma hospital just outside Kimmerston.' He looked at her. 'They won't let you question her tonight.'

'I'll have one of my team there, keeping an eye on her. Let them know.' Vera stared at him. 'Tell them this was an assault dressed up as an accident. Attempted murder. Not some daft young woman taking a chance with the tide.' For some reason it mattered to her that the medical team shouldn't think that of Holly. There was nothing irresponsible about her officer.

He nodded.

She saw that Charlie was already back on his phone arranging for someone to be waiting at the hospital for Holly.

The ambulance was off then, blue lights flashing. They heard the siren when it hit the main road. Vera thanked the coastguard crew, but they were awkward. They didn't need her kind words and just wanted to get home and warm. The three detectives were left standing there.

'We need to get you out of those wet clothes,' she said to Joe. 'Or you'll catch your death. And I need a drink.'

She turned the Land Rover round and they drove back to the Seahorse. There were still stragglers in the bar but Di was waiting for them in her snug red lounge. She found clothes for Joe. 'I'll stick yours in the washer and put them to dry. They'll be ready for you in the morning. My Trev died three years ago, but I can't quite bear to give away his things.' Trev had been considerably larger than Joe, and the sergeant sat in an enormous tracksuit, his feet in a pair of sheepskin slippers. Vera allowed herself a brief grin, but made no comment.

Di disappeared for a moment and returned with a bottle of whisky and three glasses. She was still curious, but sensed their anxiety and understood that they needed to be alone. 'I'm off to my bed. My turn to do the early breakfasts. Just shut the door behind you when you head off yourselves.'

Vera could have kissed her. 'Thanks. You're a life-saver.'

She poured the whisky and they sat for a moment in silence.

'All being well, we'll talk to Hol in the morning.' Vera was holding her glass with two hands. 'No guarantee she knew who knocked her out though. I'd guess she was hit from behind in the chapel, and she only gained consciousness briefly when the water got into the car. Most people wouldn't have been able to get out and find the refuge. It was a mixture of luck and courage.'

Charlie's phone rang. There was a brief conversation, unenlightening to Vera and Joe.

'That was the guy at the hospital. They're giving her a brain scan and keeping her sedated until they know the results. She was hypothermic. Any later and the cold would certainly have killed her.'

'She'll be all right though? She will pull through?'

Charlie shrugged. 'You know what doctors are like. They've not really told him anything.' A pause. 'Still critical they say. Life-threatening injuries.'

A silence. Vera couldn't allow herself to think about that. Holly was tough, a fighter. 'Let's make plans then. We'll get a bit of sleep then head off before the next tide.'

'You don't think the killer's still here?'

Vera shook her head. 'I don't think so. They'll have left just before the water took Holly's car off the causeway, and headed away to set up an alibi for themselves. No evidence of contact then. They knew we were here and wouldn't want to be on the island when we heard about the *accident*.' She waved her fingers in the air to indicate quotation marks.

'What about the vicar?'

Vera reconsidered. It was too easy to dismiss Philip. He might seem settled and content, but he had a reputation to lose too. His identity was bound up with the notion that he was a *good* man.

'You're right of course. The killer could have come back to the island to hide in plain sight, instead of making a run for the mainland. Charlie, you stay here, go and talk to him.' She thought Philip would underestimate Charlie. They'd think he was plodding, unimaginative. 'Check the tread on his car tyres. See if there's sand there and if it matches the marks we found outside the Pilgrims' House.'

'You have an idea who it is, don't you?' The question came from Joe, who knew her too well.

'Nothing certain.' She shot him a quick grin. 'And I've often been wrong.' But an idea was starting to form, like shapes emerging in a landscape when the fog starts to clear. Vera remembered the notion that had come to her walking away from the Old Hall Hotel earlier, the itch that had to be scratched. 'We should know by the end of tomorrow, though.' She looked at the clock on the mantelpiece. 'By the end of today.'

She was waiting outside Bread and Olives when it opened. Jax and Annie were inside, deep in conversation, and Jax didn't see her until she unlocked the door.

'I was hoping for a word with Annie.' Vera was hit as usual by the distinctive, delicious smell of the place.

'Okay.' Jax sounded a little dubious. Wary on behalf of her colleague. 'She's not been well. This business has really upset her.'

'Of course,' Vera said. 'It would.'

'Go into the garden. We won't get busy for an hour.'

They'd turned the yard behind the shop into an outside

social space. It was hardly a garden, though they'd planted up a few pots. There was an assortment of tables and chairs: wrought iron, plastic, wood. They still served breakfast and lunch here at weekends. Annie looked tired, almost frail. Vera tried to imagine her hitting Holly hard enough to cause possible brain damage. She'd have had to be desperate.

Jax made them coffee and served it in large mugs, hot milk in a jug on the side, then retreated into the shop. Vera could see her watching them from inside, tense and anxious. She nodded towards the window. 'She's a good friend.'

'She is,' Annie said. 'The best.'

'First off, where were you yesterday evening?'

'At home.'

'On your own?'

'I'm usually on my own, Inspector.' There were dark rings around her eyes.

'Do you get lonely?' Vera wondered where the question had come from.

There was a silence. 'When Daniel and I first separated I loved the time to myself. As I've got older, I've found it more difficult. People surrounded by families. Children and grand-children.' A pause. 'I get very jealous. I have friends of course.'

Vera nodded. She had Joanna. And her colleagues at work. Joe and Charlie. Holly. Who was still sedated, still unconscious. Still a weight on Vera's conscience.

'You have Jax,' Vera said. 'You had Rick Kelsall.'

Annie looked up at her. 'He was my best friend. I miss him so much.'

'I want to take you back forty-five years.' They were sitting on the wrought-iron garden chairs, a table between them. 'The day Isobel Hall died. You said there was a row between her and Rick just before she set off too close to the tide. It would help me to know exactly what it was about. You must have been curious. You must have asked him.'

Annie shut her eyes. Vera thought the woman was back there, outside the Pilgrims' House, still in pain because her baby had died only months before. It seemed cruel to make her relive that weekend, but Vera had to know.

'I did ask him,' Annie said. 'After she'd driven off in such a hurry, but before we heard her car had crashed. "What is it with you two?" He said Isobel was a flirt and a tease. Impossible. He was trying to laugh it off, but I could tell he was angry, irritated.'

'You assumed something had gone on between them over the weekend? Even though he was already engaged to Charlotte? And then Isobel had wanted more? Some sort of commitment?'

'Maybe, though that wasn't really her style either. But he had that sort of charisma that led to his women making demands.'

'You never made demands on him.' It wasn't a question.

Annie smiled. 'That's why we got on so well.'

There was a moment of silence. A murmur of conversation in the shop behind them.

'One of my officers was attacked on Holy Island last night,' Vera said. 'If there's anything else you can tell me, even if it's just a suspicion, a little niggle, it might help us find out who killed Rick.'

And Charlotte, though you've never cared for her.

For a minute Vera expected Annie to speak, that there might be a revelation, even some sort of confession, but she just shook her head. 'I should go back to work. It's getting busy.' Vera followed her into the shop and then out into the street.

Outside on the pavement, there was a queue of people waiting to go into the deli. Vera heard Annie shout in the next customer. She sounded friendly and professional, but Vera thought she could hear a shake in her voice, which was almost like the start of a sob, and that was a kind of confession in itself.

Vera had left her car at the police station and started the walk back. She knew she should arrange a meeting with Watkins, feed back the latest information on Holly, ask permission for the next move. But the thought of crawling to Watkins and begging him to let her take the next step horrified her. She knew now. No proof, but she knew. The killer was panicking – the attack on Holly had been planned at the last minute and irrational. People under pressure didn't think straight and Vera was good at getting suspects to make mistakes.

She was walking away when Charlie phoned. 'I checked out Gull Cottage.'

'Yes?' She'd almost forgotten he was going to see Philip Robson.

'They've gone. Him and Judith. Cleared out. When they didn't answer the door, I found the key where you said it would be, in the old outside lav. All their stuff has gone, their cars too.' He paused. 'It might not mean anything.'

'No,' she said. 'It might not.'

There's only one way to find out.

Instead of going into the station and to her stuffy office, she climbed into her Land Rover. She'd have to do this solo. The others had too much to lose. She fumbled for her phone, which was at the bottom of her bag, and made a phone call. No answer, but she wasn't expecting one. Katherine Willmore was a busy woman, who always let her secretary take her calls, and it was too early for him to be in the office yet. Vera left a message. 'This is urgent. Please make sure Miss Willmore gets it immediately, wherever she is.' She looked at her watch, then she made one more call and drove north.

Chapter Forty-Seven

IT WAS CLEAR AND SUNNY, MUCH as it had been when she'd first arrived at the Pilgrims' House five days before. Dead leaves underfoot. Quiet and still. Because the door was shut, she wasn't sure whether the man had done as she'd asked and come to meet her. As she approached there was the familiar smell of creosote. All bird hides smelled the same and it was the scent of her childhood, trailing after Hector, being told to sit still, while he recced the sites of nests he could rob. She opened the door and saw that the place was empty, except for one figure, back on. The flap overlooking the lake was open and sunlight flooded in from the east. You'd see practically nothing on the lake with the sun in your eyes, but that wasn't why he was here in the Rede's Tower nature reserve. He wasn't birdwatching today.

'Daniel,' she said. 'Good of you to meet me.'

'Why here?' He turned towards her. 'We could have talked in the house if you needed to see me. It'd be more comfortable there. I'd even make you a coffee.'

'Ah,' she said. 'Neutral territory. I wasn't sure whether Eliza would be back. We wouldn't want her earwigging.' A pause. 'Or Katherine.'

Because Katherine's the unknown quantity here. Who knows how she'll react? And what Watkins will make of it.

Vera squinted into the sun, saw the silhouettes of mallard and tufted duck on the water. 'We don't want to involve her unless we have to. Besides, I'm at home in a place like this. My father was a birdwatcher. Of a kind.'

'How can I help you, Inspector?'

'I spoke to Annie this morning. I caught her at the deli, just as it was opening.'

'Oh? How's she doing?'

'She's sad. Maybe a bit lonely. She's lost a good friend.'

'I'm sorry,' he said. 'I'm still very fond of her.'

'But Katherine? She's the love of your life these days?'

'You know, I might sound like a soppy git, but really, she's the best thing that ever happened to me. I adore her.' He turned towards Vera and gave her an open smile, wide and lovely. She could see how Katherine might have fallen for him.

'Is that what all this is about? Are you protecting Katherine here?'

'I don't know what you mean.'

'Then let me explain. Tell you the story that Rick Kelsall was going to tell in his novel. Though I don't think it was so much a novel as a piece of mischief. I'm not even sure that he'd written much more than a synopsis and a few notes. Planning it was enough, a way of bringing the past back to life. Making the man feel alive and young again. Replacing the attention that he had when he was on the telly every week. Stirring things up.'

'Aye well,' Daniel said. 'He was always good at doing that. Not so good at putting things back together again.'

'He had a row with Isobel Hall just before she drove off the causeway and died. Everyone blamed him for that. There was always a lingering sense that he'd caused the accident, by treating her badly. He didn't enjoy being cast as the villain in the piece.' Vera leaned forward, her elbows on the shelf where the birders rested their telescopes, the smell of stagnant water and rich vegetation seeping into the hide. 'He wanted to set matters straight and tell his own side of the tale after all this time.'

'I wouldn't know,' Daniel said.

Vera ignored that and continued. 'It was a terrible time for you, that first reunion on the island. You were only there for Annie. You'd lost your baby a few months earlier and Annie was severely depressed, wrapped up in her grief.'

'Aye.' Daniel spoke slowly, reliving the pain. 'She couldn't let it go. Every thought was a torment, about what we might have done, what we should have done. The possibilities going round and round in her head like a whirlpool, but knowing that nothing would change the outcome. It was as if she was drowning in the guilt.'

Oh, Vera thought, I know exactly how that feels.

Rede was still talking. 'It was a kind of madness.' He looked up at Vera. 'I think she's a bit mad now, after all this time, though she hides it very well.'

'You're still very fond of her.'

'Of course.'

'Still protective?'

He turned his attention back to the pond. 'I don't know where you're going with this.'

'I'm exploring all the possibilities. I like Annie, but liking someone doesn't stop me thinking they might have done something criminal.' A pause. 'Wicked.'

'Now you're being crazy! Annie wouldn't hurt a fly. She certainly wouldn't kill Rick Kelsall.'

'Maybe not, but humour me, will you? Let's go back to that weekend. The first reunion. The end of a long, hot summer, apparently. Even here in the North. You'd lost your baby. Everyone's nerves would be frayed. You were all just in your twenties by then, but not quite ready to be adults. Not quite grown up. Except for Annie, who'd had to grow up very quickly.'

He stared out at the water in silence. A pair of mallard flew off, all noise and splash.

'You must have felt trapped,' Vera went on. 'You didn't want to be there with the people you didn't have much in common with. You'd only agreed to come along to support Annie, to stop her doing something silly.' A pause. 'She'd talked about suicide? Maybe made a few tentative tries at it.'

Daniel nodded. She could just see his profile. 'I saw marks on her wrists. She wouldn't talk to me! I think she'd had a sort of breakdown. But she refused to see a doctor. She kept saying that she was okay. That it was normal to be sad when you've lost a baby.'

'But this was more than sadness, wasn't it, pet? This was depression. Deep and dangerous. And you were young too. It was a stressful time for you. We didn't understand mental illness then. Not as we do now. Maybe you saw the weekend as some sort of escape. A way of sharing the burden at least. There'd be other people around to help look after her.'

'Yes!' He was grateful that she understood.

'You were hoping for a breakthrough in her mood, but some time to yourself too. Company. Even a bit of fun.'

'That makes me sound heartless.' Daniel shot her a glance. 'But you're right. I loved Annie, but she was dragging me down with her. I tried to help her, but it seemed there was nothing I could do.'

'Eh, pet, I'm not judging. Sometimes we do what we have to, just to survive.'

'Aye well. That was what it felt like. Like I was swamped by responsibility, that if I didn't get a break, I'd go mad myself.'

'And then along swanned Isobel,' Vera said. 'Full of light and energy. Just graduated and full of confidence. She'd always fancied you. Her mam told my sergeant, there was someone special in her life, but that he was already taken. I think that was you. So, there she was. Flirting and giving you the sort of attention you'd not had since the baby died. Seeming sympathetic, but really hoping to get her man at last. The man of her dreams. Who could resist that?' Vera paused. 'I'm guessing that you two had a bit of a fling that weekend. Sex in the sand dunes? Sneaking off together while Annie was still grieving and guilty.'

He smiled sadly. 'Something like that. It seems a bit pathetic now, but at the time it felt . . .' He struggled to find the words. '. . . just what I needed.'

'A kind of tonic?'

'Like you said: an escape. And Isobel made me laugh. We both knew it wasn't serious.'

'Well, not serious for you perhaps. Serious enough for Isobel, who'd always needed what she couldn't have.' Vera looked across at him again, but he was still staring out of the slit window of the hide. 'Did Annie work out what you were up to? All the sudden disappearances? Never being there for her?'

'No!' he said. 'She was still lost in that world of her own.'

Vera nodded. 'You're saying she was too depressed to notice you carrying on under her nose? Too depressed to see the betrayal, to want some sort of revenge?'

'Yes!' His voice was loud now. 'And we were discreet. Honestly, we didn't want to hurt her. She couldn't have known.'

'Not that discreet,' Vera shot back. 'While Annie might just have been too wrapped up in her own memories to realize what you were doing, the others noticed.'

'No,' Daniel said. 'You've got this all wrong.'

'Or perhaps not all the others.' Vera continued speaking as if there'd been no interruption. 'Just Rick Kelsall, who was Annie's special friend. Who loved her like a brother and understood her better than anyone in the world.'

Silence.

'Rick didn't blame you,' Vera went on. 'He knew what you'd gone through. He blamed Isobel. Arrogant, entitled Isobel, who'd decided to seduce you, to get the man she'd always wanted. That was what the row was about.' A pause. 'Did Annie hear them arguing?'

'I think she must have done,' Daniel said at last. 'She'd been to the village and appeared in the middle of it.'

'So, she *did* know that you and Isobel had had a fling?'

'Maybe. At that point she might have guessed from the words flying between Isobel and Kelsall. But she never mentioned it.'

'It was something else that festered between you for the rest of your marriage. Something else for her to chase round and round in her head when she was lying awake at night.'

Now he did turn to her. 'I did try to make a go of that marriage, you know. I wasn't some kind of unfeeling monster. I did my best to mend it. We went to counselling and I was as kind as I could be. I stayed as long as I could. But in the end, the only sane thing was to walk away.'

'To focus on your work.' *That's always been my answer.*

He nodded again. 'Yes, until Katherine came along and I fell for her. Head over heels. Then work didn't seem quite so important.'

'Was it Annie, who sent Isobel off to her death? Is that what you've all been hiding all these years?'

He took a moment to respond. 'She might have said something. Some recrimination or challenge. But I never saw it as Annie's fault. It was Isobel's decision to rush away like that. It was an accident.'

'Aye,' Vera said, 'and it was in Isobel's nature to make the grand gesture. Maybe she imagined herself stranded on one of the refuge towers waiting to be rescued. By a knight in shining armour. *Her* knight.'

'Maybe.'

'Do you think Annie killed Rick Kelsall? Because he was planning to bring the whole thing out in the open after all these years? To bring back all those dreadful memories.' Now, Vera thought, they were getting to the heart of the matter.

'The way he's always behaved, he had no right to make any kind of fuss.'

This, Vera thought, was no kind of answer.

'But he was Annie's friend,' she said. 'He thought the world of her. I'm not sure he'd have done anything now to hurt her.'

'Rick Kelsall was a selfish man.' Daniel turned towards Vera in his effort to make her understand. 'He was totally absorbed

359

in his own desires. He'd sacrifice anyone, even Annie, to pull himself back into the limelight.'

'But he wasn't planning to sacrifice Annie.' Vera kept her voice very low. 'Was he, pet? He had someone very different in mind as villain of his piece.'

'I don't know what you mean.' With these words, Daniel seemed to lose the veneer of sophistication he'd developed during his life with Katherine. He turned back into a churlish teenager. The secondary modern kid, who'd scraped a place in the Grammar at the last chance. Still the chippy outsider, who'd never quite fitted in.

'Oh, I think you do. In his book, Rick never intended to blame Annie for Isobel's death. It was a much more interesting target. Rich businessman married to the Police and Crime Commissioner, famous for her moral stance on all issues.' A pause. 'Annie would never have killed Rick Kelsall.'

'What are you saying?' The words came out as a growl.

'Let me explain, if you don't quite understand.' Now Vera could have been Judith Sinclair, a teacher standing in front of her classroom. 'Though I think you know perfectly well what I'm saying. We'll go back a few months. Back to the early summer. People were listening to a young Swedish lass and deciding it wasn't cool to be flying to exotic places. They'd holiday in Britain instead. You'd long divorced from Annie, and taken up with Katherine. You'd built this business up into the success it is now, and people were flocking to the seaside for a change of scene. Everything rosy. Perfect. No longer any reason for you to prove yourself. You could finally believe you were as good as the rest of the world.'

Vera paused for a moment and shot a glance at Daniel. He was staring out at the reserve. Still and silent and as hard as granite.

'There were obviously no hard feelings between you and Kelsall,' Vera went on, 'because he took on your stepdaughter as an intern. Only then Eliza made some foolish allegations, exaggerating his behaviour, and he lost his job. And he felt the need to fight back. To re-establish himself in the eyes of his public. And to get his own back for his misfortune, like some pathetic schoolboy scrapping in the playground, after someone's called him a rude name. That's how we come to be here, exploring the past and the reasons for two people's deaths.'

'It wasn't my fault Kelsall lost his job.' Daniel spat out the words. 'That was down to him. His responsibility. His inappropriate behaviour. And he had the nerve to preach to me about something that happened forty-five years ago.'

'Yes,' Vera said, staying almost calm. 'I can see that must have rankled. None of us likes a hypocrite.' She took a breath. 'When did Kelsall come to see you to let you know what he was planning? To tell you he was writing a fictionalized version of an event that happened all that time ago. Something sufficiently close to the truth that the people involved and their friends and family would understand, and not look at you in quite the same way again. Something that might sour your relationship with the love of your life.'

'He came here to the house to talk to Katherine about the statement they'd make jointly about Eliza's allegations. The way she'd been manipulated by the press.'

'You saw him then? Is that when he threatened to expose you?'

'He tracked me down after that meeting. I was here on site. He called into reception on his way out, and they pointed him in my direction. It was one of those glorious days that we had last week. We walked on the beach. *He* talked. Kelsall always very much liked the sound of his own voice. He was playing with me. Mocking the business in that sarky way that some people do. Calling it a holiday camp, as if it was fucking Butlins. He said he wasn't entirely sure he would agree to the statement about Eliza, and whatever happened things wouldn't be the same for us. Not once his book came out. People might not be so keen to stay in our *holiday camp* once they knew the sort of man I was. A man who'd driven one young woman to consider suicide and another to her death. He might have the reputation of being a bastard to women, but he'd never had that effect on them. He'd never driven them to kill themselves.' Daniel paused for breath. 'His tone was jokey but it was a very real threat.'

'You had a lot to lose,' Vera said. 'Katherine. This place. Your perfect life.'

'Everything I've worked for!' It came out as a scream. His control was unravelling at last. Vera could see now that she'd get a confession from him.

'So, that night you drove onto Holy Island.'

He stared at her, with his mouth clamped shut.

'And you killed Rick Kelsall.'

Still, he didn't answer.

'You can tell me!' Vera forced herself to smile. 'We're on our own here and I'm not recording the conversation. I wouldn't know how. I just want to understand for my own satisfaction.' A beat. 'And besides, I think you want to tell me. You want someone to know the truth. You're not some kind of monster.'

Daniel was still staring over the water. The sun had shifted a bit, had moved behind a clump of trees, so the view was clearer; he wasn't looking into the light. 'I didn't go there to kill him. I wanted to talk to him, just to sort things out between us. To persuade him.'

'But you *did* kill him, didn't you, Daniel?'

'I had a key to the Pilgrims' House,' Daniel said. 'I'm planning to buy it. I've told you we wanted to expand the business and I already have interests on the island.'

'The Old Hall Hotel.' Vera didn't want to stop his flow, but that was part of the story too. 'You hold a share in that.'

He nodded.

'I knew where Kelsall slept.' His voice was bitter. 'Always the best room in the place. I went in and he was asleep. Looking so pathetic. His mouth open, stinking of booze. Snoring.'

'So, you held a cushion on his face and you killed him. Then you strung him up to make it look like suicide.'

'Lying there. So weak. It was as if he was inviting me to do it.' Daniel paused. 'I was home before Katherine woke up. It's not very far around the bay.' He turned to face Vera. 'She knew nothing about this. I did it for her. Think of the embarrassment if the whole thing came out. If Kelsall backed down on his agreement to tell the truth about Eliza's allegations.'

'And the fact that you had a sexual romp with a young woman just weeks after your baby had died. In front of your wife.'

'I didn't do it for me!' He sounded as if he almost believed it. 'It was for Katherine and Eliza. And for everyone who works here.'

'What about Charlotte?' Vera asked. 'How does she fit into all this?'

'That was bad luck. She'd been on the island that afternoon.'

'She was there with Judith Sinclair. They had a drink together in the Seahorse.' Vera looked up at him. 'Were you there with them?'

'No!' He seemed genuinely confused.

So, that had been a stray birder just as Judith had claimed, but he'd played his part in the story all the same. He'd had a walk-on part in the drama.

'So, tell me, Daniel, why did Charlotte have to die?'

'She was driving off the island as I was driving on that Friday night. The night Kelsall died. She recognized me. Waved.'

'And later, she tried her hand at a bit of blackmail.'

We know she was hard-up and she'd been brought up to make the most out of any situation. Her family had been in the business of extortion too.

'Yes, by then the whole thing was running out of control. I didn't know how to stop it.' He was close to tears. Vera could almost feel sorry for him. If it weren't for two people dead. And Holly lying barely alive in the hospital in Kimmerston.

'And my officer?' Her voice sharp now. Icy. 'What happened there? I know that was no accident. She wasn't a woman to take risks.'

'She was in the Old Hall, asking questions about me and Katherine.'

'Not about you. About a single birdwatcher. The man sitting in the pub. Some stranger we thought might be involved.'

'I thought she was looking for me. I always carry binoculars when I'm out and about. A habit. I don't feel dressed without them.'

Vera nodded. Hector had been just the same. He was never without them, even on a trip to the shop in Kirkhill, even drinking tea on the bench outside the cottage.

'And Jason at the hotel phoned you to tell you the police were making enquiries.'

'He thought I'd want to know. He's a good lad. I told you

I have a stake in the hotel. I've been grooming him to be manager.'

'So, you set a trap for her. The barmaid at the Seahorse was asking people to contact the officer if they were the person she was looking for. You'll know all the locals if you've got interests in the island and you'll have heard about the request on the grapevine. You sent her a text, asking her to meet you.'

Daniel said nothing, so Vera continued. 'You followed her from the lough back to her car. You'd lit the candles in the chapel hoping that she'd go in to investigate, and of course she did. She wouldn't miss something like that. She's one of my best officers. Then you hit her. So hard that she was unconscious, that she's still in hospital with possible brain damage. You put her in her own car and drove her off the island. Halfway across the causeway, just as the tide was coming in, you got out and lifted her into the driver's seat. You left her there. The fog was so thick that nobody saw the car. You waded back to the island. I suspect that you had your grand four-by-four waiting, hidden in the dunes. You must have driven off to the mainland just before the island was cut off by the sea.'

'I saw your Land Rover arriving,' Daniel said. 'Just before I put her car on the causeway.'

So, if we'd been half an hour later, we might have seen Holly's car. We could have rescued her, saved her the cold wait on the tower before she lapsed back into unconsciousness.'

Vera felt like weeping, but this wasn't a time for self-pity. 'Then you went home. Another alibi established. I presume it was Isobel's death that gave you the idea. It was like rewriting history.'

'You have no evidence,' he said. His mood had changed

again. Now he was the ruthless businessman, crushing his rivals, fighting for his empire. 'No proof at all.'

He turned towards her and for the first time in the encounter, Vera felt real fear. After all, Rede had been prepared to throw suspicion on Annie Laidler, a woman he'd once cared for. He'd tried to kill Holly Clarke. What arrogance had led Vera to believe that she could persuade the man to confess, to be led quietly away to the police station? If any of her officers had been so foolish, she'd have thought them unfit for the job.

'People know where I am,' she said.

But she could tell that he wasn't listening. Daniel Rede was beyond reason and logic. He believed he'd achieved the perfect life as he approached old age – a beautiful, intelligent woman, a daughter to replace the one he'd lost, wealth and position to give him the confidence he'd lacked as a teenager – and now he saw it all slipping away from him. She could see now that he would fight to protect it, even if the fight was irrational and pointless.

He moved slowly and deliberately. She supposed she could run, but although he was older, he was fitter than she was. He'd catch her. And even now, as he took the binoculars from his neck, and leaned across to put the strap around hers, she thought there was something undignified in running. There were worse places to die than here, with the smell of warm creosote and vegetation, to the soundtrack of bird calls. He pulled the leather tight. She tried to get her fingers underneath it to pull the strap away, but everything seemed to be in slow motion and she was too late. The breath was being squeezed from her and she was light-headed, dreamy. There was no pain now. Out of the hide window, she saw a buzzard, sailing high over the trees and she was there with it, looking down on the woodland and the lake and the sea beyond. At a landscape that was as close to home as it was possible to be. In the distance, from her vantage point in the sky, she fancied she could glimpse the hills, the wind turbines like dandelion clocks, the crags where she'd seen her first ring ouzel.

There was a sudden noise, which shattered the peace and fractured the dream. It was a human voice, screaming, horrified. It seemed to come from a long way off, but it got closer, more discordant. Vera found herself back on earth, in the hide, in pain, struggling to breathe.

'Let her go!' A woman was shouting. The tone was shrill and unpleasant to the ear, but it was effective. The strap loosened. Daniel's face was still so close to Vera's that she could smell him. Aftershave, attractive and rather heady. His breath with a hint of coffee. The woman's voice again, each syllable given equal weight. 'Let her go!'

This time, Rede did as he was ordered. Vera felt the drag of the binoculars on her neck, as he released the tension on the strap. The skin hurt where the leather had cut into it. She breathed deeply, felt her lungs fill.

The door was pushed open and Daniel was gone. He barrelled past Katherine Willmore and they heard his running footsteps on the boardwalk, disappearing further into the reserve. Katherine came further into the hide. She lifted the binoculars from Vera's neck and set them on the wooden shelf. Vera raised her head and saw that the PCC was crying. She was dressed for a meeting, and the tears ran through her mascara and made black trails down her face. Vera wanted to warn her of the mess on her face, because surely the press would soon get wind of the story and the woman wouldn't want to be seen like that. But she could hardly speak. There was just a croak like a raven.

'I very nearly didn't come.' Katherine collapsed onto the bench, her back to the window, her legs facing the door. 'My secretary passed on your message, but I thought it was ridiculous.'

'Did you . . . ?' That was all Vera could manage.

'I listened,' Katherine said. 'Just as you told me to. I heard it all.' The tears hadn't stopped. They rolled down her cheeks. Vera found herself fascinated and tried to remember the last time *she'd* cried. Hector's funeral? Nah, she hadn't thought him worth her tears. Unless it was for a sad life, wasted.

'I'll contact Superintendent Watkins.' Katherine took a spotless handkerchief from the pocket of her jacket, wiped her face. 'Tell him we need Daniel to be found, arrested.'

'Did you suspect?' Vera had found her voice at last.

There was no reply.

Vera had wanted to drive straight back to Kimmerston to coordinate the search for Rede, but Katherine wouldn't hear of it, of her driving alone, so they were sitting together in the perfect house with its view of the sea, drinking perfect coffee. Distant. Civilized. Vera had refused the ambulance, the doctor.

'Eh, pet, some people would pay for that kind of experience. What do they call it? Auto-erotic.' Knowing it was the last sort of thing the PCC would want to hear, but feeling sorry for the woman, needing awkwardly to lighten the mood.

Was it shame that had driven Daniel to kill to maintain the illusion of perfection? Or a genuine desire to protect Katherine and her daughter from hurt? Vera could have forgiven him that, could have forgiven him even the deaths of Rick Kelsall and Charlotte Thomas, but not the attack on Holly. *Her* officer. That was unforgivable.

Katherine got to her feet and walked to her office. She left the door open and Vera could hear her talking on the phone, maintaining the professional voice even while she continued to weep, silently. Vera wondered if that was a genuine reaction to the fact that her man was a killer, or because her own professional standing had been compromised. Certainly, she'd take a huge hit in the press. Any good work she'd done in the past would be ridiculed. She'd be forced to resign. Was that the cause of her tears? Perhaps, Vera thought, she was getting cynical in her old age. It was possible that Katherine would support Daniel through the trial and visit him in prison, bring him back here and look after him when he was released as a very elderly man. But she couldn't really see it.

She dozed. It was the warmth of the sun shining through the glass and the shock. Hardly sleeping the night before. The satisfaction of a case brought successfully to a conclusion.

She woke when Katherine came back into the room. She was no longer crying but her face was drawn, serious.

'They've found him?'

'Yes. He was in his car in a lay-by on the A1. He just seemed to be waiting for them to get him. He didn't put up any sort of fight.'

Vera nodded. It was a bit of an anticlimax maybe. Rick Kelsall would have injected a bit more drama if he'd been telling the story. But it was a satisfactory conclusion.

'Your team has been trying to get in touch with you.'

'Oh aye? Wondering why I've gone AWOL?' *Why I didn't take them into my confidence.*

'It's your DC. Holly Clarke.'

Vera brightened. 'She's come round? They've started to question her?'

A silence. 'Her head wound was too severe,' Katherine said. Her voice was very gentle. 'Nobody can understand how she had the strength to swim out of the car and drag herself onto the tower.' A pause. 'She died in the night.'

That was when everything went silent and the light seemed to leave the room.

Chapter Forty-Eight

HOLLY'S FUNERAL WAS IN KIMMERSTON, in the church where Joe and Charlie had first talked to Judith Sinclair. Vera had expected her parents to take their daughter's body home, but they'd said Holly would want to be remembered here, where she'd been so happy, so satisfied at work.

'She was always rather a restless child,' Raymond Clarke said. 'A little apart. Rather driven. Other people never quite lived up to her expectations. She found her true home in the police service.' He was a thin, quiet man, with Holly's face and Holly's reticence. The mother was larger, more outgoing. She hugged Vera when they first met, then immediately apologized, for being so forward.

'I'm so sorry, Inspector. I don't know what came over me. But my daughter admired you so much.'

Vera had been expecting anger from the parents, a desire for vengeance, directed not perhaps at Daniel Rede, but at the Kimmerston team and Vera in particular. It would have been much easier to accept than their forgiveness. They were Christians and had made, Vera could tell, a conscious decision to forgive her, to be kind. Somehow, their strength and understanding made her own guilt harder to bear.

The couple were staying in Holly's flat, but they came first to the police station and that was where the meeting had taken place. They'd wanted, they said, to see where Holly had worked, where she'd been so content. Vera could hardly say that contentment hadn't been the most obvious trait in their daughter's character.

The mother, Joan, sat in Holly's chair in the open-plan office. 'It isn't quite as I imagined,' she said. 'I was expecting more noise, more bustle.'

Vera didn't know how to say that usually it would have been busier, but that the team were grieving. 'We're all feeling very quiet,' she said in the end. 'Very sad.'

Joan looked up and apparently on impulse, she invited Vera for supper. 'Come to the flat tomorrow.' It would be the evening before the funeral. Vera could hardly refuse. She felt she was responsible for their daughter's death and she would have given them anything they asked.

'Could I bring my sergeant? Joe Ashworth. Holly worked most closely with him.' Vera didn't think she could survive an evening alone with this gentle couple, who were struggling so hard to be generous in their grief. Rage against the injustice of a daughter lost would have been very much easier to bear.

'Oh, of course, Holly spoke of him all the time.'

In the end, they survived the occasion better than Vera could have imagined. She wished she'd met Holly's parents earlier. It might have helped her understand her officer better. They were earnest and principled. Holly had inherited that from them, but rebelled against their gentleness in her ambition and her desire for justice at any cost. And for success. Hers had been a black and white world. Theirs was a muted shade of grey.

The four of them sat round the pale wood table, eating a simple meal. There was wine, a good red, of which Joanna would have approved. Vera and Joe said very little. They listened to the parents remembering their daughter. By the end they were all weeping quietly but without embarrassment. Vera was weeping because now she understood the woman better than she had done when she was alive. She blamed herself for that. Her stubbornness. Her hard certainties.

The funeral service was quiet. Most of the people in the pews were colleagues. Philip Robson must have driven back from London to be there. He was sitting with Judith Sinclair, and Annie joined them just before the service started. Some of the Clarkes' relatives had travelled up for the occasion. Katherine Willmore was in a pew at the back. Unobtrusive and alone. Vera thought that had taken courage. The county knew now that the Police and Crime Commissioner's partner was a killer. The police officers in the church would recognize her. The hymns were traditional. Everything was very civilized, very polite, very reasonable.

Outside it had started to rain, a November drizzle, boring like the service. Vera suddenly wanted to shout out loud, to howl at the grey, overcast sky, to let the world know that Holly Clarke had *not* gone gentle into that dark night. She'd been fierce and strong and brave and she'd fought to the end.

But in the end, she had no right to express her opinion. Not here and now, though she might when she got drunk later with Joe. So, she went up to Raymond and Joan, hugged them first, and thanked them again. She offered them all the support the service could give. Then she got into her Land Rover and drove back to her cottage in the hills to grieve in her own way. There, she could howl to her heart's content.

Detective Matthew Venn returns in

THE HERON'S CRY

North Devon is enjoying a rare hot summer with
tourists flocking to its coast-line. Detective Matthew Venn
is called out to a rural crime scene at the home of
a group of artists. What he finds is an elaborately
staged murder.

Then another body is found – killed in a similar
way. Matthew finds himself treading carefully through
the lies that fester at the heart of his community and a
case that is dangerously close to home . . .

Turn the page for an extract.

Chapter One

JEN HAD DRUNK TOO MUCH. They were in Cynthia Prior's garden, lounging on the grass, and it was just getting dark. The party had moved outside, become quieter and less frenetic. Jen could smell cut grass and honeysuckle, the scent intense, heady and oversweet. She found herself mesmerized by the rhythm of the flashing fairy lights that Cynthia had strung along the high brick wall and woven between the ivy and climbing roses.

Cynthia's place was the kind of gaff to have a wall around it: a large detached house looking out over Rock Park, only a few hundred yards from Jen's narrow terraced home, but a million miles in terms of class. Jen was a Liverpudlian and carried the idea of class with her like a badge of honour. Her dad had been a docker and her mother still stacked shelves in a supermarket.

Although it was dark, the air remained hot and the fire in the pit was there for effect, and to toast marshmallows, not because it was needed. They'd had an early heatwave. It was only the end of June but already there were calls for water rationing, talk of standpipes if the weather didn't break soon. In North Devon, they weren't usually short of rain.

Earlier, inside the house, there'd been loud music and, despite the warmth, dancing; Jen loved a good dance and could move like a demon. Her husband had disapproved, but she no longer had to care what he thought. Now they'd all drifted outside and Wes, one of Cynthia's arty mates, was playing guitar, something moody and slow. Nobody could do moody like Wes. Jen had fancied him like crazy when she'd first met him, but then she fancied most of the single men she bumped into. She was a tad desperate. Wes was brooding, dark-haired and fit, the stuff of Jen's dreams. Later she'd decided that a weed-smoking musician, who lived with a bunch of hippies in the hills, and supplemented his income by making weird furniture from driftwood, wasn't the best fit for a woman with sole responsibility for two teenage kids. Who was also a cop.

Next to the wall a table had been set up and covered with a cloth. The cloth was Cynthia all over, and showed how classy she was. With the general exodus, Cynthia had brought out all the bottles and put them there, proving to the world that she was still organized and in control, though she must have had just as much to drink as Jen. Jen poured herself another glass of red and sat on the grass too. She told herself, and everyone else within earshot, that it had been years since she'd been to such a great party. Bloody years.

Later, only a small group was left close to the fire. Jen found herself talking to a middle-aged man, one of Cynthia's neighbours. She'd seen him inside earlier, before they'd turned up the music, working the room, chatting politely to the other guests. He was small and sturdy, built like a troll from a fairy story, with a square head and short legs, and a wide smile that just prevented him from being ugly. Jen didn't fancy him in the slightest, but everyone else seemed to have paired off, and she hated that sense of being the only single person in the group. Since her divorce the world seemed made up of happy couples. She even envied the ones who weren't so happy. This man wore a checked shirt and walkers' trousers, lightweight, easily dried. Jen could imagine him a member of a ramblers' club. She thought he might be an accountant or a lawyer. Cynthia was a magistrate, sitting in the lower court, passing judgement on the petty criminals, the misfits and saddos, whom Jen was trying to convict, and she knew lots of lawyers. She and Jen had first met in court. Despite their different roles, they'd always got on. Cynthia's husband was something important in the local hospital trust and she didn't need a paid job.

Now, Jen was at that stage when she knew she'd had enough to drink, but she couldn't quite stop. Her ex-husband had always said she had an addictive personality, the words spoken with a sneer and an edge of pity, just before giving her a good slap, and then blaming her for provoking him.

She thought Nigel had been holding the same glass of dry white for most of the evening.

'So, Nigel. What do you do for a living?' He'd already told her his name, slightly apologetically, as if it wasn't a name to be proud of.

Nigel. Nigel Yeo. Yeo being a local name means he's obviously from the West Country. Nigel ages him though. Who calls their kid Nigel these days?

Now she smiled, her best flirty smile. He might be older than she usually liked her men and was probably a boring sod, but chatting to him was better than sitting here on her own like a Billy No-Mates. Although Cynthia always said she shouldn't try so hard and that the right man would come along eventually, Jen couldn't bear the idea of being lonely for the rest of her life. Soon the kids would be flying the nest and she imagined her little house, as silent and cold as a grave, when she got in from work.

'I work in the health sector.' His knees were bent and she could see his shoes. Good quality, recently polished.

'Oh, a medic?' That made him more interesting. Jen might never want to think of herself as a snob, but she liked the idea of hanging out with a doctor.

'Not any more.' He smiled too, as if he knew what she was thinking, and again, there was something lovely about the smile, something that made up for the troll-like stature. 'You could say I'm in the same line of business as you. Sort of. Though I'm more of a private investigator at the moment. In fact, there was something I wanted to discuss, but I'm not sure this is the right place after all.' He seemed distracted for a moment. 'Actually, it's probably time for me to head home, I think.' Nigel got to his feet, the movement smooth and easy, and wiped a few grass clippings from his bum. It was rather a nice bum too.

He hesitated when he was on his feet. 'Is it okay if I get your number from Cynthia and call you?'

'Yeah,' Jen said. 'Sure.' She thought he might be suggesting a date and was flattered, almost excited, but it seemed he had something more formal in mind.

'Work contact details will be fine if you don't want to give me your personal number.'

She watched him walk away to say a polite goodbye to Cynthia. She felt ridiculously bereft, and that she'd missed an important opportunity for friendship.

The evening went downhill from there. She sat alone for a while with a beer, staring into the flames. When she saw Wes dancing slowly to music that he was humming and nobody else could hear, his arms round a woman young enough to be her daughter, she stumbled to her feet and walked home.

THE RAGING STORM

**Detective Matthew Venn of *The Heron's Cry* returns
in the next captivating novel in the Two Rivers series
from Ann Cleeves, the number one bestselling
author and creator of Vera and Shetland.**

When Jem Rosco – sailor, adventurer and local legend –
blows into town in the middle of an autumn gale, the
residents of Greystone, Devon, are delighted to have
a celebrity in their midst.

The residents think nothing of it when Rosco disappears
again; that's the sort of man he is. Until the lifeboat is
launched to a hoax call-out during a raging storm and his
body is found in a dinghy, anchored off Scully Cove,
a place with legends of its own.

This is an uncomfortable case for DI Matthew Venn.
He came to the remote village as a child, its community
populated by the Barum Brethren that he parted ways
with, so when superstition and rumour mix and another
body is found in the cove, Matthew soon finds his
judgement clouded.

As the stormy winds howl and the village is cut
off, Venn and his team start their investigation, little
realizing their own lives might be in danger . . .

Publishing Autumn 2023

THE TWO RIVERS SERIES

Discover Ann's latest lead character
Detective Matthew Venn

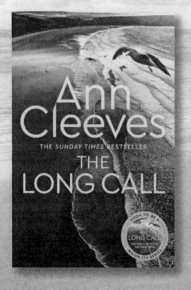

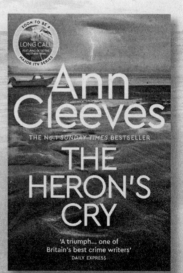

THE COMPLETE DCI VERA STANHOPE COLLECTION

'Nobody does unsettling undercurrents
better than Ann Cleeves'

Val McDermid